PASSIONS

Isaac Bashevis Singer

FAWCETT CREST • NEW YORK

PASSIONS

THIS BOOK CONTAINS THE COMPLETE TEXT OF THE
ORIGINAL HARDCOVER EDITION.

Published by Fawcett Crest Books, a unit of CBS Publications, the
Consumer Publishing Division of CBS Inc., by arrangement with
Farrar, Straus & Giroux, Inc.

ISBN: 0-449-24067-3

Selection of the Literary Guild, February 1976

Printed in the United States of America

10 9 8 7 6 5

Contents

Author's Note

As the reader can see, many of these stories were translated by me in collaboration with those whose names are given at the end of each story. I have worked on these translations with my editors, Rachel MacKenzie, Robert Giroux, and lately also William Maxwell, to all of whom I am grateful.

While obscurity in content and style may now be the fashion, clarity remains the ambition of this writer. This is especially important since I deal with unique characters in unique circumstances, a group of people who are still a riddle to the world and often to themselves—the Jews of Eastern Europe, specifically the Yiddish-speaking Jews who perished in Poland and those who emigrated to the U.S.A. The longer I live with them and write about them, the more I am baffled by the richness of their individuality and (since I am one of them) by my own whims and passions. While I hope and pray for the redemption and the resurrection, I dare to say that, for me, these people are all living right now. In literature, as in our dreams, death does not exist.

Isaac Bashevis Singer

Hanka

This trip made little sense from the start. First, it didn't pay financially to leave New York and my work for two and a half months to go to Argentina for a lecture tour; second, I should have taken an airplane instead of wasting my time on a ship for eighteen days. But I had signed the contract and accepted a first-class round-trip ticket on *La Plata* from my impresario, Chazkel Poliva. That summer, the heat lasted into October. On the day I embarked, the thermometer registered ninety degrees. I was always assailed by premonitions and phobias before a trip: I would get sick; the ship would sink; some other calamity would occur. An inner voice warned me, Don't go! However, if I had made a practice of acting on these premonitions, I would not have come to America but would have perished in Nazi-occupied Poland.

As it happened, I was provided with all possible comforts. My cabin looked like a salon, with two square windows, a sofa, a desk, and pictures on the walls. The bathroom had both a tub and a shower stall. The number of passengers was small, mostly Latin Americans, and the service staff was large. In the dining room I had a special wine steward who promptly filled my glass each time I took a sip of wine. A band of five musicians played at lunch and dinner. Every second day the captain gave a cocktail party. But for some reason I could not make any acquaintances on this ship. The few passengers who spoke English kept to themselves. The men, all young six-foot giants, played shuffleboard and cavorted in the swimming pool. The women were too tall and too athletic for my taste. In the evening, they all danced or sat at the bar, drinking and smoking. I made up my mind that I would remain isolated, and it seemed that others sensed my decision. No one spoke a word to me. I began to wonder if by some magic I had become one who sees and is not seen. After a while I stopped attending the cocktail parties and I asked that my meals be served in my cabin. In Trinidad and in Brazil, where the ship stopped for a day, I walked around alone. I had taken little to read with me, because I was sure that the ship would have a library. But it consisted of a single glass-doored bookcase with some fifty or so volumes in Spanish and perhaps a dozen in English—all moldy travel books printed a hundred years ago. This bookcase was kept locked, and each time I wanted to exchange a book there was a commotion about who had the key; I would be sent from one member of the staff to the other. Eventually an officer with epaulets would write down my name, the number of my stateroom, the titles and authors of my books. This took him at least fifteen minutes.

When the ship approached the equator, I stopped going out on deck in the daytime. The sun burned like a flame. The days had shortened and night came swiftly. One moment it was light, the next it was dark. The sun did not set but fell into the water like a meteor. Late in the evening, when I went out briefly, a hot wind slapped my face. From the ocean came a roar of passions that seemed to have broken through all barriers: "We must procreate and multiply! We must exhaust all the powers of lust!" The waves glowed like lava, and I imagined I could see multitudes of living beings—algae, whales, sea monsters—reveling in an orgy, from the surface to the bottom of the sea. Immortality was the law here. The whole planet raged with animation. At times, I heard my name in the clamor: the spirit of the abyss calling me to join them in their nocturnal dance.

In Buenos Aires I was met by Chazkel Poliva—a short, round person—and a young woman who introduced herself as my relative. Her name was Hanka and she was, she said, a great-granddaughter of my Aunt Yentel from her first husband. Actually, Hanka was not my relative, because my Uncle Aaron was Yentel's third husband. Hanka was petite, lean, and had a head of pitch-black hair, full lips, and eyes as black as onyx. She wore a dark dress and a black, broad-brimmed hat. She could have been thirty or thirty-five. Hanka immediately told me that in Warsaw someone had hidden her on the Aryan side—the way she was saved from the Nazis. She was a dancer, she said, but even before she told me I saw it in the muscles of her calves. I asked her where she danced and she replied, "At Jewish affairs and at my own troubles."

Chazkel Poliva took us in his car to the Hotel Cosmopolitan on Junín Street, which was once famous as the main street of the red-light district. Poliva said that the neighborhood had been cleaned up and all the literati now stayed in this hotel. The three of us ate supper in a restaurant on Corrientes Avenue, and Chazkel Poliva handed me a schedule covering my four weeks in Argentina. I was to lecture in Buenos Aires at the Théâtre Soleil and at the Jewish Community Center, and also I was to go to Rosario, Mar del Plata, and to the Jewish colonies in Moisés Ville and in Entre Ríos. The Warsaw Society, the Yiddish section of the P.E.N. Club, the journalists of the newspaper that published my articles, and a number of Yiddish schools were all preparing receptions.

When Poliva was alone with me for a moment, he asked, "Who is this woman? She says that she dances at Jewish affairs, but I've never seen her anywhere. While we were waiting for you, I suggested that she give me her address and telephone number in case I needed to get in touch with her, but she refused. Who is she?"

"I really don't know."

Chazkel Poliva had another engagement that evening and left us after dinner. I wanted to pay the bill—why should he pay for a woman who was supposed to be my relative?—but he would not permit it. I noticed that Hanka ate nothing—she had only a glass of wine. She accompanied me back to the hotel. It was not long after Perón had been ousted, and Argentina was in the midst of a political and perhaps economic crisis. Buenos Aires, it seemed, was short of electricity. The streets were dimly lit. Here and there a gendarme patrolled, carrying a machine gun. Hanka took my arm and we walked through Corrientes Avenue. I couldn't see any physical resemblance in her to my Aunt Yentel, but she had her style of talking: she jumped from one subject to another, confused names, places, dates. She asked me, "Is this your first visit to Argentina? Here the climate is crazy and so are the people. In Warsaw there was spring fever; here one fevers all year round. When it's hot, you melt from the heat. When the rains begin, the cold eats into your bones. It is actually one big jungle. The cities are oases in the pampas. For years, the pimps and whores controlled the Jewish immigrants. Later, they were excommunicated and had to build a synagogue and acquire a cemetery of their own. The Jews who came here after the Holocaust are lost creatures. How is it that they don't translate you into Spanish? When did you last see my great-grandmother Yentel? I didn't know her, but she left me as an inheritance a chain with a locket that was perhaps two hundred years old. I sold it for bread. Here is your hotel. If you're not tired, I'll go up with you for a while."

We took the elevator to the sixth floor. From childhood

I have had a liking for balconies; there was one outside
my room and we went there directly. There were few
high constructions in Buenos Aires, so we could see a part
of the city. I brought out two chairs and we sat down.
Hanka was saying, "You must wonder why I came to
meet you. As long as I had near relatives—a father, a
mother, a brother, a sister—I did not appreciate them.
Now that they are all ashes, I am yearning for relatives,
no matter how distant. I read the Yiddish press. You
often mention your Aunt Yentel in your stories. Did she
really tell you all those weird tales? You probably make
them up. In my own life, things happened that cannot
possibly be told. I am alone, completely alone."

"A young woman does not have to be alone."

"Just words. There are circumstances when you are
torn away like a leaf from a tree and no power can
attach you again. The wind carries you from your roots.
There's a name for it in Hebrew, but I've forgotten."

"*Na-v'nad*—a fugitive and a wanderer."

"That's it."

I expected that I would have a short affair with Hanka.
But when I tried to embrace her she seemed to shrink in
my arms. I kissed her and her lips were cold. She said,
"I can understand you—you are a man. You will find
plenty of women here if you look for them. You will find
them even if you don't look. But you are a normal person,
not a necrophile. I belong to an exterminated tribe and
we are not material for sex."

My lecture at the Théâtre Soleil having been postponed for some days, Hanka promised to return the next
evening. I asked for her telephone number and she said
that her telephone was out of order. In Buenos Aires,
when something is broken, you can wait months until it
is repaired. Before she left, Hanka told me almost casually that while she was looking for relatives in Buenos
Aires she had found a second cousin of mine—Jechiel,
who had changed his name to Julio. Jechiel was the son
of my granduncle Avigdor. I had met Jechiel twice—

once in the village of Tishewitz, and the second time in
Warsaw, where he came for medical treatment. Jechiel
was about ten years older than I—tall, darkish, and
emaciated. I remembered that he suffered from tubercu-
losis and that Uncle Avigdor had brought him to Warsaw
to see a lung specialist. I had felt sure that Jechiel did not
survive the Holocaust, and now I heard that he was alive
and in Argentina. Hanka gave me some details. He came
to Argentina with a wife and a daughter, but he divorced
his wife and married a Frampol girl whom he met in a
concentration camp. He became a peddler—a knocker,
as they were called in Buenos Aires. His new wife was
illiterate and was afraid to go out of the house by herself.
She hadn't learned a word of Spanish. When she needed to
go to the grocery for a loaf of bread or for potatoes, Jechiel had to accompany her. Lately, Jechiel had been
suffering from asthma and had to give up his peddling.
He was living on a pension—what kind of a pension
Hanka did not know: perhaps from the city or from some
charitable society.

I was tired after the long day, and the moment Hanka
left I fell onto the bed in my clothes and slept. After a
few hours, I awoke and went out onto the balcony. It
was strange to be in a country thousands of miles from my
present home. In America fall was approaching; in Argentina it was spring. It had rained while I slept and
Junín Street glistened. Old houses lined the street; its
stalls were shuttered with iron bars. I could see the rooftops and parts of the brick walls of buildings in adjoining
streets. Here and there a reddish light glimmered in a
window. Was someone sick? Had someone died? In Warsaw, when I was a boy, I often heard gruesome tales
about Buenos Aires: a pimp would carry a poor girl, an
orphan, away to this wicked city and try to seduce her
with baubles and promises, and, if she did not give in,
with blows, tearing her hair and sticking pins into her
fingers. Our neighbor Basha used to talk about this with
my sister Hinda. Basha would say, "What could the girl
do? They took her away on a ship and kept her in chains.

She had already lost her innocence. She was sold into a brothel and she had to do what she was told. Sooner or later she got a little worm in her blood, and with this she could not live long. After seven years of disgrace, her hair and teeth fell out, her nose rotted away, and the play was over. Since she was defiled, they buried her behind the fence." I remember my sister's asking, "Alive?"

Now Warsaw was destroyed and I found myself in Buenos Aires, in the neighborhood where misfortunes like this were supposed to have taken place. Basha and my sister Hinda were both dead, and I was not a small boy but a middle-aged writer who had come to Argentina to spread culture.

It rained all the next day. Perhaps for the same reason that there was a shortage of electricity, the telephones didn't work properly—a man would be speaking to me in Yiddish when suddenly I was listening to a female laughing and screaming in Spanish. In the evening Hanka came. We could not go out into the street, so I ordered supper from room service. I asked Hanka what she wanted to eat and she said, "Nothing."

"What do you mean by nothing?"

"A glass of tea."

I didn't listen to her and I ordered a meat supper for her and a vegetarian platter for myself. I ate everything; Hanka barely touched the food on her plate. Like Aunt Yentel, she spewed forth stories.

"They knew in the whole house that he was hiding a Jewish girl. The tenants certainly knew. The Aryan side teemed with *szmalcownicy*—this is what they were called —who extorted the last penny from Jews to protect them and then denounced them to the Nazis. My Gentile— Andrzej was his name—had no money. Any minute someone could have notified the Gestapo and we would have all been shot—I, Andrzej, Stasiek, his son, and Maria, his wife. What am I saying? Shooting was considered light punishment. We would have been tortured. All the tenants would have paid with their lives for that crime. I often told him, 'Andrzej, my dear, you have

done enough. I don't want to bring disaster on all of you.'
But he said, 'Don't go, don't go. I cannot send you away
to your death. Perhaps there is a God after all.' I was
hidden in an alcove without a window, and they put a
clothes closet at the door to conceal the entrance. They
removed a board from the back of the closet and through
it they passed my food and, forgive me, they took out the
chamber pot. When I extinguished the little lamp I had,
it became dark like in a grave. He came to me, and both of
them knew about it—his wife and their son. Maria had a
female sickness. Their son was sick, too. When he was a
child he developed scrofula or some glandular illness
and he did not need a woman. I don't think he even grew
a beard. He had one passion—reading newspapers. He
read all the Warsaw papers, including the advertisements.
Did Andrzej satisfy me? I did not look for satisfaction.
I was glad that he was relieved. From too much reading,
my eyesight dimmed. I became so constipated that only
castor oil would help me. Yes, I lay in my grave. But if you
lie in a grave long enough, you get accustomed to it and
you don't want to part from it. He had given me a pill
of cyanide. He and his wife and their son also carried such
pills. We all lived with death, and I want you to know
that one can fall in love with death. Whoever has loved
death cannot love anything else any more. When the
liberation came and they told me to leave, I didn't want to
go. I clung to the threshold like an ox being dragged to the
slaughter.

"How I came to Argentina and what happened between
me and José is a story for another time. I did not deceive
him. I told him, 'José, if your wife is not lively enough,
what do you need a corpse for?' But men do not believe
me. When they see a woman who is young, not ugly, and
can dance besides, how can she be dead? Also, I had no
strength to go to work in a factory with the Spanish
women. He bought me a house and this became my
second grave—a fancy grave, with flowerpots, bric-a-brac,
a piano. He told me to dance and I danced. In what way
is it worse than to knit sweaters or to sew on buttons?

All day long I sat alone and waited for him. In the evening he came, drunk and angry. One day he spoke to me
and told me stories; the next day he would be mute. I
knew that sooner or later he would stop talking to me
altogether. When it happened I was not surprised, and
I didn't try to make him talk, because I knew it was
fated. He maintained his silence for over a year. Finally
I told him, 'José, go.' He kissed my forehead and he left.
I never saw him again."

The plans for my lecture tour began to go awry. The
engagement in Rosario was called off because the president of the organization suffered a heart attack. The
board of directors of the Jewish Community Center in
Buenos Aires had a falling out over political differences,
and the subsidy that they were to give to the colonies for
my lectures there was withheld. In Mar del Plata, the
hall I was to speak in suddenly became unavailable. In
addition to the problems of the tour, the weather in Buenos Aires worsened from day to day. There was light-
ning, thunder, and from the provinces came news of
windstorms and floods. The mail system didn't seem to
be functioning. Proofs of a new book were supposed to
come by airmail from New York, but they did not arrive
and I worried that the book might be published without
my final corrections. Once I was stuck in an elevator
between the fourth and fifth floors and it took almost two
hours before I got free. In New York I had been assured
that I would not have hay fever in Buenos Aires, because
it was spring there. But I suffered from attacks of sneez-
ing, my eyes watered, my throat constricted—and I didn't
even have my antihistamines with me. Chazkel Poliva
stopped calling, and I suspected that he was about to
cancel the whole tour. I was ready to return to New
York—but how could I get information about a ship
when the telephone did not work and I didn't know a
word of Spanish?

Hanka came to my room every evening, always at the
same time—I even imagined at the same minute. She

entered noiselessly. I looked up and there she was, standing in the dusk—an image surrounded by shadows. I
ordered dinner and Hanka would begin her soliloquy in
the quiet monotone that reminded me of my Aunt Yentel.
One night Hanka spoke about her childhood in Warsaw.
They lived on Hoźa Street in a Gentile neighborhood.
Her father, a manufacturer, was always in debt—on the
edge of bankruptcy. Her mother bought her dresses in
Paris. In the summer they vacationed in Zoppot, in the
winter in Zakopane. Hanka's brother Zdzislaw studied in
a private high school. Her older sister, Edzia, loved to
dance, but their mother insisted it was Hanka who must
become another Pavlova or Isadora Duncan. The dance
teacher was a sadist. Even though she was ugly and a
cripple herself, she demanded perfection from her pupils.
She had the eyes of a hawk, she hissed like a snake. She
taunted Hanka about her Jewishness. Hanka was saying,
"My parents had one remedy for all our troubles—as-
similation. We had to be one-hundred-per-cent Poles. But
what kind of Poles could we be when my grandfather Asher,
your Aunt Yentel's son, could not even speak Polish?
Whenever he visited us, we almost died from shame. My
maternal grandfather, Yudel, spoke a broken Polish. He
once told me that we were descended from Spanish Jews.
They had been driven from Spain in the fifteenth century,
and our ancestors wandered first to Germany and then,
in the Hundred Years' War, to Poland. I felt the Jewishness in my blood. Edzia and Zdzislaw were both blond
and had blue eyes, but I was dark. I began at an early
age to ponder the eternal questions: Why is one born?
Why must one die? What does God want? Why so much
suffering? My mother insisted that I read the Polish and
French popular novels, but I stealthily looked into the
Bible. In the Book of Proverbs I read the words 'Charm
is deceitful, and beauty is vain,' and I fell in love with
that book. Perhaps because I was forced to make an idol
of my body, I developed a hatred for the flesh. My mother
and my sister were fascinated by the beauty of movie
actresses. In the dancing school the talk was always of

hips, thighs, legs, breasts. When a girl gained as much
as a quarter of a pound, the teacher created a scene.
All this seemed petty and vulgar to me. From too much
dancing, we developed bunions and bulging muscles. I
was often complimented for my dancing, but I was possessed by the dybbuk of an old Talmudist, one of those
whitebeards who used to come to us to ask for alms and
were chased away by our maid. My dybbuk would ask,
'For whom are you going to dance—for the Nazis?'
Shortly before the war, when Polish students chased the
Jews through the Saxony Gardens and my brother
Zdzislaw had to stand up at the lectures in the university
because he refused to sit on the ghetto benches, he became a Zionist. But I realized that the worldly Jews in
Palestine were also eager to imitate the Gentiles. My
brother played football. He belonged to the Maccabee
sports club. He lifted weights to develop his muscles.
How tragic that all my family who loved life so much had
to die in the concentration camps, while fate brought me
to Argentina.

"I learned Spanish quickly—the words seemed to flow
back into me. I tried to dance at Jewish affairs, but everything here is rootless. Here they believe that the Jewish
State will end our misfortunes once and forever. This is
sheer optimism. We are surrounded there by hordes of
enemies whose aim is the same as Hitler's—to extermi-
nate us. Ten times they may not succeed—but the
eleventh, catastrophe. I see the Jews being driven into the
sea. I hear the wailing of the women and the children.
Why is suicide considered such a sin? My own feeling is
that the greatest virtue would be to abandon the body
and all its iniquities."

That night, when Hanka left, I did not ask her when
she would return. My lecture in the Théâtre Soleil had
been advertised for the next day, and I expected her to
attend. I had slept little the night before, and I went to
bed and fell asleep immediately. I wakened with a feeling
that someone was whispering in my ear. I tried to light
the lamp by my bed, but it did not go on. I groped for the

wall switch, but I could not locate it. I had hung my
jacket containing my passport and traveler's checks on a
chair; the chair was gone. Had I been robbed? I felt my
way around the room like a blind man, tripping and
bruising my knee. After a while, I stumbled into the chair.
No one had taken my passport or my traveler's checks.
But my gloom did not lessen. I knew that I'd had a bad
dream, and I stood in the dark trying to recollect it. The
second I closed my eyes, I was with the dead. They did
things words cannot express. They spoke madness. "I
will not let her into my room again," I murmured. "This
Hanka is my angel of death."

I sat down on the edge of the bed, draped the covers
over my shoulders, and took calculation of my soul. This
trip had stirred up all my anxieties. I had not prepared
any notes for my lecture, "Literature and the Supernatural," and I was apprehensive that I might suddenly
become speechless; I foresaw a bloody revolution in
Argentina, an atomic war between the United States and
Russia; I would become desperately sick. Wild absurdi-
ties invaded my mind: What would happen if I got into
bed and found a crocodile there? What would happen if
the earth were to split into two parts and my part were to
fly off to another constellation? What if my going to
Argentina had actually been a departure into the next
world? I had an uncanny feeling of Hanka's presence. In
the left corner of the room I saw a silhouette, a dense
whorl that stood apart from the surrounding darkness and
took on the shadowy form of a body—shoulders, head,
hair. Though I could not make out its face, I sensed in the
lurking phantom the mocking of my cowardices. God in
heaven, this trip was waking all the fears of my cheder
days, when I dared not sleep alone because monsters
slithered around my bed, tore at my sidelocks, screeching
at me with terrifying voices. In my fright, I began to pray
to God to keep me from falling into the hands of the Evil
Ones. It seems that my prayer was heard, for suddenly
the lamp went on. I saw my face in the mirror—white as

after a sickness. I went to the door to make sure it was locked. Then I limped back to the bed.

The next day I spoke in the Théâtre Soleil. The hall was filled with people in spite of the heavy rain outside. I saw so many familiar faces in the audience that I could scarcely believe my eyes. True, I did not remember their names, but they reminded me of friends and acquaintances from Bilgoray, Lublin, Warsaw. Was it possible that so many had been saved from the Nazis and come to my lecture? As a rule, when I spoke about the supernatural, there were interruptions from the audience— even protest. But here, when I concluded, there was ominous silence. I wanted to go down into the audience and greet these resurrected images of my past; instead, Chazkel Poliva led me behind the stage, and by the time I made my way to the auditorium the overhead lights were extinguished and the seats empty. I said, "Shall I speak now to the spirits?"

As if he were reading my mind, Poliva asked, "Where is your so-called cousin? I didn't see her in the hall."

"No, she did not come."

"I don't want to mix into your private affairs, but do me a favor and get rid of her. It's not good for you that she should trail after you."

"No. But why do you say this?"

Chazkel Poliva hesitated. "She frightens me. She will bring you bad luck."

"Do you believe in such things?"

"When you have been an impresario for thirty years, you have to believe in them."

I had dozed off and evening had fallen. Was it the day after my lecture or a few days later? I opened my eyes and Hanka stood at my bedside. I saw embarrassment in her eyes, as if she knew my plight and felt guilty. She said, "We are supposed to go to your cousin Julio this evening."

I had prepared myself to say to her, "I cannot see you again," but I asked, "Where does Julio live?"

"It's not too far. You said that you like to walk."

Ordinarily I would have invited her to dinner, but I had no intention of dallying with her late into the night. Perhaps Julio would offer us something to eat. Half asleep, I got up and we walked out onto Corrientes. Only an occasional street light was lit, and armed soldiers were patrolling the streets. All the stores were closed. There was an air of curfew and Black Sabbath. We walked in silence, like a pair who have quarreled yet must still go visiting together. Corrientes is one of the longest boulevards in the world. We walked for an hour. Each time I asked if we were nearing our destination Hanka replied that we had some distance to go yet. After a while we turned off Corrientes. It seemed that Julio lived in a suburb. We passed factories with smokeless chimneys and barred windows, dark garages, warehouses with their windows sealed, empty lots overgrown with weeds. The few private homes we saw looked old, their patios enclosed by fences. I was tense and glanced sideways at Hanka. I could not distinguish her face—just two dark eyes. Unseen dogs were barking; unseen cats mewed and yowled. I was not hungry but unsavory fluids filled my mouth. Suspicions fell on me like locusts: Is this my final walk? Is she leading me into a cave of murderers? Perhaps she is a she-devil and will soon reveal her goose feet and pig's snout?

As if Hanka grasped that her silence made me uneasy, she became talkative. We were passing a sprawling house, with no windows, the remnants of a fence, and a lone cactus tree in front. Hanka began, "This is where the old Spanish Gentiles live. There is no heat in these houses—the ovens are for cooking, not for heating. When the rains come, they freeze. They have a drink that they call maté. They cover themselves with ragged clothes, sip maté, and lay out cards. They are Catholics, but the churches here are half empty even on Sunday. The men don't go, only the women. They are witches who pray to the devil, not to God. Time has stopped for them—they are a throwback to the era of Queen Isabella and Torquemada. José left me many books, and since I stopped dancing and have no friends I keep reading. I know Argentina. Sometimes I think I have lived here in a former incarnation. The men still dream of inquisitions and autos-da-fé. The women mutter incantations and cast spells on their enemies. At forty they are wrinkled and wilted. The husbands find mistresses, who immediately begin to spawn children, and after a few years they are as jealous, bitter, and shabby as the wives. They may not know it, but many of them descend from the Marranos. Somewhere in the faraway provinces there are sects that light candles Friday evening and keep a few other Jewish customs. Here we are."

We entered an alley that was under construction. There was no pavement, no sidewalk. We made our way between piles of boards and heaps of bricks and cement. A few unfinished houses stood without roofs, without panes in the windows. The house where Julio lived was narrow and low. Hanka knocked, but no one answered. She pushed the door open, and we went through a tiny foyer into a dimly lit room furnished only with two chairs and a chest. On one chair sat Jechiel. I recognized him only because I knew that it was he. He looked ancient, but from behind his aged face, as if from behind a mask, the Jechiel of former times showed. His skull was bald, with a few wisps of side hair that were neither gray nor black but colorless. He had sunken cheeks, a pointed chin, the throat of a plucked rooster, and the pimpled nose of an alcoholic. Half of his forehead and one cheek were stained with a red rash. Jechiel did not lift his eyelids when we entered. I never saw his eyes that evening. On the other chair sat a squat, wide-girthed woman with ash-colored, disheveled hair; she was wearing a shabby housecoat. Her face was round and pasty, her eyes blank and watery, like the eyes one sees in asylums for the mentally sick. It was hard to determine whether she was forty or sixty. She did not budge. She reminded me of a stuffed doll.

From the way Hanka had spoken, I presumed that she was well acquainted with them and that she had told them of me. But she seemed to be meeting them for the first time.

I said, "Jechiel, I am your cousin Isaac, the son of

Bathsheba. We met once in Tishewitz and later in Warsaw.

"*Sí.*"

"Do you recognize me?"

"*Sí.*"

"You have forgotten Yiddish?" I asked.

"No."

No, he had not forgotten Yiddish, but it seemed that he had forgotten how to speak. He dozed and yawned. I had to drag conversation from him. To all my questions he answered either "*Sí,*" "*No,*" or "*Bueno.*" Neither he nor his wife made an effort to bring something for us to sit on or a glass of tea. Even though I am not tall, my head almost touched the ceiling. Hanka leaned against the wall in silence. Her face had lost all expression. I walked over to Jechiel's wife and asked, "Do you have someone left in Frampol?"

For what seemed a very long time there came no answer; then she said, "Nobody."

"What was your father's name?"

She pondered as if she had to remind herself. "Avram Itcha."

"What did he do?"

Again a long pause. "A shoemaker."

After a half hour, I wearied of drawing answers from this numb couple. There was an air of fatigue about them that baffled me. Each time I addressed Jechiel, he started as if I had wakened him.

"If you have any interest in me, you can call the Hotel Cosmopolitan," I said at last.

"*Sí.*"

Jechiel's wife did not utter a sound when I said good night to her. Jechiel mumbled something I could not understand and collapsed into his chair. I thought I heard him snore. Outside, I said to Hanka, "If this is possible, anything is possible."

"We shouldn't have visited them at night," Hanka said. "They're both sick. He suffers from asthma and she has

a bad heart. I told you, they became acquainted in Ausch-
witz. Didn't you notice the numbers on their arms?"

"No."

"Those who stood at the threshold of death remain
dead."

I had heard these words from Hanka and from other
refugees before, but in this dark alley they made me shudder. I said, "Whatever you are, be so good as to get me a
taxi."

"*Si.*"

Hanka embraced me. She leaned against me and clung
to me. I did not stir. We stood silent in the alley, and a
needle-like rain began to fall on us. Someone extinguished
the light in Julio's house and it became as dark around us
as in Tishewitz.

The sun was shining, the sky had cleared, it shone blue
and summery. The air smelled of the sea, of mango and
orange trees. Blossoms fell from their branches. The
breezes reminded me of the Vistula and of Warsaw. Like
the weather, my lecture tour had also cleared up. All kinds
of institutions invited me to speak and gave banquets for
me. Schoolchildren honored me with dancing and songs. It
was bewildering that such a fuss should be made about a
writer, but Argentina is isolated and when they get a guest
they receive him with exaggerated friendliness.

Chazkel Poliva said, "It's all because you freed yourself of Hanka."

I had not freed myself. I was searching for her. Since
the night we visited Julio, Hanka had not come to see me.
And there was no way I could get in touch with her. I
did not know where she lived; I didn't even know her sur-
name. I had asked for her address more than once, but she
had always avoided answering. Neither did I hear from
Julio. No matter how I tried to describe his little alley,
no one could identify it for me. I looked in the telephone
book—Julio's name was not listed.

I went up to my room late. Going onto the balcony at
night had become a habit with me. A cool wind was blow-

ing, bringing me greetings from the Antarctic and the South Pole. I raised my eyes and saw different stars, different constellations. Some groups of stars reminded me of consonants, vowels, and the musical notations I had studied in cheder—an *aleph*, a *hai*, a *shuruk*, a *segul*, a *tsairai*, a *chain*. The sickle of the moon seemed to hang reversed, ready to harvest the heavenly fields backward. Over the roofs of Junín Street, the southern sky stretched, strangely near and divinely distant, a cosmic illumination of a volume without a beginning and without an end—to be read and judged by the Author himself. I was calling to Hanka, "Why did you run away? Wherever you are, come back. There can be no world without you. You are an eternal letter in God's scroll."

In Mar del Plata, the hall had become available, and I went there with Chazkel Poliva. On the train he said to me, "You may think it crazy, but here in Argentina Communism is a game for the rich. A poor man cannot become a member of the Communist Party. Don't ask me any questions. So it is. The rich Jews who have villas in Mar del Plata and will come tonight to your lecture are all leftists. Do me a favor and don't speak about mysticism to them. They don't believe in it. They babble constantly about the social revolution, although when the revolution comes they will be its first victims."

"This in itself is a mystery."

"Yes. But we want your lecture to be a success."

I did what Poliva told me to do. I didn't mention the hidden powers. After the lecture, I read a humorous sketch. When I finished and the question-and-answer period began, an old man rose and asked me about my inclination toward the supernatural. Soon questions on this subject came from all sides. That night the rich Jews in Mar del Plata showed great interest in telepathy, clairvoyance, dybbuks, premonitions, reincarnation: "If there is life after death, why don't the slaughtered Jews take revenge on the Nazis?" "If there is telepathy, why do we need the telephone?" "If it is possible that thought influences inanimate objects, how does it come that the bank in the casino makes high profits just because it has one chance more than its clients?" I answered that if the existence of God, the soul, the hereafter, special providence, and everything that has to do with metaphysics were scientifically proven, man would lose the highest gift bestowed upon him—free choice.

The chairman announced that the next question would be the last one, and a young man got up and asked, "Have you had personal experience of that sort? Have you ever seen a spirit?"

I answered, "All my experiences have been ambiguous. None of them could serve for evidence. Just the same, my belief in spirits becomes ever stronger."

There was applause. As I bowed and thanked them, I saw Hanka. She was sitting in the audience, clapping her hands. She wore the same black hat and black dress she had worn at all our meetings. She smiled at me and winked. I was stunned. Had she traveled after me to Mar del Plata? I looked again and she had vanished. No, it had been a hallucination. It lasted only one instant. But I will brood about this instant for the rest of my life.

Translated by the author and Blanche and Joseph Nevel

Old Love

Harry Bendiner awoke at five with the feeling that as far as he was concerned the night was finished and he wouldn't get any more sleep. Actually, he woke up a dozen times every night. He had undergone an operation for his prostate years before, but this hadn't relieved the constant pressure on his bladder. He would sleep an hour or less, then wake up with the need to void. Even his dreams centered around this urge. He got out of bed and padded to the bathroom on shaky legs. On the way back he stepped out onto the balcony of his eleventh-story condominium. To the left he could see the skyscrapers of Miami, to the right the rumbling sea. The air had turned a bit cooler during the night, but it was still tropically tepid. It smelled of dead fish, oil, and perhaps of oranges as well. Harry stood there for a long while enjoying the breeze from the ocean on his moist forehead. Even though Miami Beach had become a big city, he imagined that he could feel the nearness of the Everglades, the smells and

26

vapors of its vegetation and swamps. Sometimes a seagull
would awake in the night, screeching. It happened that the
waves threw onto the beach the carcass of a barracuda or
even that of a baby whale. Harry Bendiner looked off in
the direction of Hollywood. How long was it since the
whole area had been undeveloped? Within a few years a
wasteland had been transformed into a settlement crowded
with hotels, condominiums, restaurants, supermarkets, and
banks. The street lights and neon signs dimmed the stars
in the sky. Cars raced along even in the middle of the
night. Where were all these people hurrying to before
dawn? Didn't they ever sleep? What kind of force drove
them on? "Well, it's no longer my world. Once you pass
eighty, you're as good as a corpse."

He leaned his hand on the railing and tried to recon-
struct the dream he had been having. He recalled only
that all those who had appeared in the dream were now
dead—the men and the women both. Dreams obviously
didn't acknowledge death. In his dreams, his three wives
were still alive, and so was his son, Bill, and his daughter,
Sylvia. New York, his hometown in Poland, and Miami
Beach merged into one. He, Harry or Hershel, was both
an adult and a cheder boy.

He closed his eyes for a moment. Why was it impossible
to remember dreams? He could recall every detail of events
that had happened seventy and even seventy-five years ago,
but tonight's dreams dissolved like foam. Some force made
sure that not a trace of them remained. A third of a person's life died before he went to his grave.

After a while Harry sat down on the plastic chaise that
stood on the balcony. He looked toward the sea, to the
east, where day would soon be dawning. There was a time
when he went swimming the first thing in the morning,
particularly during the summer months, but he no longer
had the desire to do such things. The newspapers occasionally printed accounts of sharks attacking swimmers,
and there were other sea creatures whose bites caused
serious complications. For him it now sufficed to take a
warm bath.

His thoughts turned to matters of business. He knew full well that money couldn't help him; still, one couldn't constantly brood about the fact that everything was vanity of vanities. It was easier to think about practical matters. Stocks and bonds rose or fell. Dividends and other earnings had to be deposited in the bank and marked down in an account book for tax purposes. Telephone and electric bills and the maintenance of the apartment had to be paid. One day a week a woman came to do his cleaning and press his shirts and underwear. Occasionally he had to have a suit dry-cleaned and shoes repaired. He received letters that he had to answer. He wasn't involved with a synagogue all year, but on Rosh Hashanah and Yom Kippur he had to have a place to worship, and because of this he received appeals to help Israel, yeshivas, Talmud Torahs, old-age homes, and hospitals. Each day he got a pile of "junk mail," and before he discarded it, he had to open and glance at it, at least.

Since he had resolved to live out his years without a wife or even a housekeeper, he had to arrange for his meals, and every other day he went shopping at the local supermarket. Pushing his cart through the aisles, he selected such items as milk, cottage cheese, fruit, canned vegetables, chopped meat, occasionally some mushrooms, a jar of borscht or gefilte fish. He certainly could have permitted himself the luxury of a maid, but some of the maids were thieves. And what would he do with himself if other people waited on him? He remembered a saying from the Gemara that slothfulness led to madness. Fussing over the electric stove in the kitchen, going to the bank, reading the newspaper—particularly the financial section—and spending an hour or two at the office of Merrill Lynch watching the quotations from the New York Exchange flash by on the board lifted his spirits. Recently he had had a television set installed, but he rarely watched it.

His neighbors in the condominium often inquired maliciously why he did things himself that others could do for him. It was known that he was rich. They offered him advice and asked him questions: Why didn't he settle in Israel? Why didn't he go to a hotel in the mountains during the summer? Why didn't he get married? Why didn't he hire a secretary? He had acquired the reputation of a miser. They constantly reminded him that "you can't take it with you"—as if this were some startling revelation. For this reason he stopped attending the tenants' meetings and their parties. Everyone tried in one way or another to get something out of him, but no one would have given him a penny if he needed it. A few years ago, he boarded a bus from Miami Beach to Miami and found he was two cents short of the fare. All he had with him was twenty-dollar bills. No one volunteered either to give him the two cents or to change one of his bank notes, and the driver made him get off.

The truth was, in no hotel could he feel as comfortable as he did in his own home. The meals served in hotels were too plentiful for him and not of the kind that he needed. He alone could see to it that his diet excluded salt, cholesterol, spices. Besides, plane and train rides were too taxing for a man of his delicate health. Nor did it make any sense to remarry at his age. Younger women demanded sex, and he hadn't the slightest interest in an old woman. Being what he was, he was condemned to live alone and to die alone.

A reddish glow had begun to tinge the eastern sky, and Harry went to the bathroom. He stood for a moment studying his image in the mirror—sunken cheeks, a bare skull with a few tufts of white hair, a pointed Adam's apple, a nose whose tip turned down like a parrot's beak. The pale-blue eyes were set somewhat off-center, one higher than the other, and expressed both weariness and traces of youthful ardor. He had once been a virile man. He had had wives and love affairs. He had a stack of love letters and photographs lying about somewhere.

Harry Bendiner hadn't come to America penniless and uneducated like the other immigrants. He had attended the study house in his hometown until the age of nineteen; he knew Hebrew and had secretly read newspapers and worldly books. He had taken lessons in Russian, Polish, and even German. Here in America he had attended Cooper Union for two years in the hope of becoming an engineer, but he had fallen in love with an American girl, Rosalie Stein, and married her, and her father, Sam Stein, had taken him into the construction business. Rosalie died of cancer at the age of thirty, leaving him with two small children. Even as the money came in to him so did death take from him. His son, Bill, a surgeon, died at forty-six, of a heart attack, leaving two children, neither of whom wanted to be Jewish. Their mother, a Christian, lived somewhere in Canada with another man. Harry's daughter, Sylvia, got the very same type of cancer as her mother, and at exactly the same age. Sylvia left no children. Harry refused to sire any more generations, even though his second wife, Edna, pleaded that he have a child or two with her.

Yes, the Angel of Death had taken everything from him. At first his grandchildren had called him occasionally from Canada and sent him a card for the New Year. But now he never heard from them, and he had cut them out of his will.

Harry shaved and hummed a melody—where it had come from he didn't know. Was it something he had heard on television, or a tune from Poland revived in his memory? He had no ear for music and sang everything off-key, but he had retained the habit of singing in the bathroom. His toilet took a long time. For years the pills he took to relieve constipation had had no effect, and every other day he gave himself an enema—a long and arduous process for a man in his eighties. He tried to do calisthenics in the bathtub, raising his skinny legs and splashing his hands in the water as if they were paddles. These were all measures to lengthen life, but even as Harry performed them he asked himself, "Why go on living?" What flavor did his existence possess? No, his life made no sense whatsoever—but did that of his neighbors make more sense? The condominium was full of old people, all well

off, many rich. Some of the men couldn't walk, or dragged
their feet; some of the women leaned on crutches. A number suffered from arthritis and Parkinson's disease. This
wasn't a building but a hospital. People died, and he didn't
find out about it until weeks or months afterward.
Although he had been among the first tenants in the condominium, he seldom recognized anybody. He didn't go
to the pool and he didn't play cards. Men and women
greeted him in the elevator and at the supermarket, but
he didn't know who any of them were. From time to time
someone asked him, "How are you, Mr. Bendiner?" And
he usually replied, "How *can* you be at my age? Each day
is a gift."

This summer day began like all the others. Harry prepared his breakfast in the kitchen—Rice Krispies with
skimmed milk and Sanka sweetened with saccharin. At
about nine-thirty he took the elevator down to get the mail.
A day didn't go by that he didn't receive a number of
checks, but this day brought a bounty. The stocks had
fallen, but the companies kept paying the dividends as
usual. Harry got money from buildings on which he held
mortgages, from rents, bonds, and all kinds of business
ventures that he barely remembered. An insurance company paid him an annuity. For years he had been getting
a monthly check from Social Security. This morning's yield
came to over eleven thousand dollars. True, he would have
to withhold a great part of this for taxes, but it still left
him with some five thousand dollars for himself. While he
totaled up the figures, he deliberated: Should he go to the
office of Merrill Lynch and see what was happening on
the Exchange? No, there was no point to it. Even if the
stocks rose early in the morning, the day would end in
losses. "The market is completely crazy," he mumbled to
himself. He had considered it an iron rule that inflation
always went along with a bullish market, not with a bear-
ish market. But now both the dollar *and* the stocks were
collapsing. Well, you could never be sure about anything
except death.

Around eleven o'clock he went down to deposit the

checks. The bank was a small one; all the employees knew
him and said good morning. He had a safe-deposit box
there, where he kept his valuables and jewelry. It so happened that all three of his wives had left him everything;
none of them had made out a will. He didn't know himself
exactly how much he was worth, but it couldn't be less
than five million dollars. Still, he walked down the street
in a shirt and trousers that any pauper could afford and a
cap and shoes he had worn for years. He poked with his
cane and took tiny steps. Once in a while he cast a glance
backward. Maybe someone was following him. Maybe
some crook had found out how rich he was and was
scheming to kidnap him. Although the day was bright and
the street full of people, no one would interfere if he was
grabbed, forced into a car, and dragged off to some ruin
or cave. No one would pay ransom for him.

After he had concluded his business at the bank, he
turned back toward home. The sun was high in the sky
and poured down a blazing fire. Women stood in the shade
of canopies looking at dresses, shoes, stockings, brassieres,
and bathing suits in the store windows. Their faces expressed indecision—to buy or not to buy? Harry glanced
at the windows. What could he buy there? There wasn't
anything he could desire. From now until five, when he
would prepare his dinner, he needed absolutely nothing.
He knew precisely what he would do when he got home—
take a nap on the sofa.

Thank God, no one had kidnapped him, no one had
held him up, no one had broken into his apartment. The
air conditioner was working, and so was the plumbing in
the bathroom. He took off his shoes and stretched out on
the sofa.

Strange, he still daydreamed; he fantasized about unex-
pected successes, restored powers, masculine adventures.
The brain wouldn't accept old age. It teemed with the same
passions it had in his youth. Harry often said to his brain,
"Don't be stupid. It's too late for everything. You have
nothing to hope for any more." But the brain was so con-

stituted that it went on hoping nonetheless. Who was it who said, A man takes his hopes into the grave?

He had dozed off and was awakened by a jangling at the door. He became alarmed. No one ever came to see him. "It must be the exterminator," he decided. He opened the door the length of the chain and saw a small woman with reddish cheeks, yellow eyes, and a high pompadour of blond hair the color of straw. She wore a white blouse.

Harry opened the door, and the woman said in a foreign-accented English, "I hope I haven't wakened you. I'm your new neighbor on the left. I wanted to introduce myself to you. My name is Mrs. Ethel Brokeles. A funny name, eh? That was my late husband's name. My maiden name is Goldman."

Harry gazed at her in astonishment. His neighbor on the left had been an old woman living alone. He remembered her name—Mrs. Halpert. Hs asked, "What happened to Mrs. Halpert?"

"The same as happens to everybody," the woman replied smugly.

"When did it happen? I didn't know anything about it."

"It's more than five months already."

"Come in, come in. People die and you don't even know," Harry said. "She was a nice woman . . . kept herself at a distance."

"I didn't know her. I bought the apartment from her daughter."

"Please have a seat. I don't even have anything to offer you. I have a bottle of liqueur somewhere, but—"

"I don't need any refreshments and I don't drink liqueur. Not in the middle of the day. May I smoke?"

"Certainly, certainly."

The woman sat down on the sofa. She snapped a fancy lighter expertly and lit her cigarette. She wore red nail polish and Harry noticed a huge diamond on one of her fingers.

The woman asked, "You live here alone?"

"Yes, alone."

"I'm alone, too. What can you do? I lived with my husband twenty-five years, and we didn't have a bad day. Our life together was all sunshine without a single cloud. Suddenly he passed away and left me alone and miserable. The New York climate is unhealthy for me. I suffer from rheumatism. I'll have to live out my years here."

"Did you buy the apartment furnished?" Harry asked in businesslike fashion.

"Everything. The daughter wanted nothing for herself besides the dresses and linen. She turned it all over to me for a song. I wouldn't have had the patience to go out and buy furniture and dishes. Have you lived here a long time already?"

The woman posed one question after another, and Harry answered them willingly. She looked comparatively young —no more than fifty or possibly even younger. He brought her an ashtray and put a glass of lemonade and a plate of cookies on the coffee table before her. Two hours went by, but he hardly noticed. Ethel Brokeles crossed her legs, and Harry cast glances at her round knees. She had switched to a Polish-accented Yiddish. She exuded the intimate air of a relative. Something within Harry exulted. It could be nothing else but that heaven had acceded to his secret desires. Only now, as he listened to her, did he realize how lonely he had been all these years, how oppressed by the fact that he seldom exchanged a word with anyone. Even having her for a neighbor was better than nothing. He grew youthful in her presence, and loquacious. He told her about his three wives, the tragedies that had befallen his children. He even mentioned that, following the death of his first wife, he had had a sweetheart.

The woman said, "You don't have to make excuses. A man is a man."

"I've grown old."

"A man is never old. I had an uncle in Wloclawek who was eighty when he married a twenty-year-old girl, and she bore him three children."

"Wloclawek? That's near Kowal, my hometown."

"I know. I've been to Kowal. I had an aunt there."

The woman glanced at her wristwatch. "It's one o'clock. Where are you having lunch?"

"Nowhere. I only eat breakfast and dinner."

"Are you on a diet?"

"No, but at my age—"

"Stop talking about your age!" the woman scolded him. "You know what? Come over to my place and we'll have lunch together. I don't like to eat by myself. For me, eating alone is even worse than sleeping alone."

"Really, I don't know what to say. What did I do to deserve this?"

"Come, come; don't talk nonsense. This is America, not Poland. My refrigerator is stuffed with goodies. I throw out more than I eat, may I be forgiven."

The woman used Yiddish expressions that Harry hadn't heard in at least sixty years. She took his arm and led him to the door. He didn't have to go more than a few steps. By the time he had locked his door she had opened hers. The apartment he went into was larger than his and brighter. There were pictures on the walls, fancy lamps, bric-a-brac. The windows looked out directly at the ocean. On the table stood a vase of flowers. The air in Harry's apartment smelled of dust, but here the air was fresh. "She wants something; she has some ulterior motive," Harry told himself. He recalled what he had read in the newspapers about female cheats who swindled fortunes out of men and out of other women, too. The main thing was to promise nothing, to sign nothing, not to hand over even a single penny.

She seated him at a table, and from the kitchen soon issued the bubbling sound of a percolator and the smell of fresh rolls, fruit, cheese, and coffee. For the first time in years Harry felt an appetite in the middle of the day. After a while they both sat down to lunch.

Between one bite and the next, the woman took a drag from a cigarette. She complained, "Men run after me, but when it comes down to brass tacks they're all interested only in how much money I have. As soon as they start talking about money I break up with them. I'm not poor;

I'm even—knock wood—wealthy. But I don't want anyone to take me for my money."

"Thank God I don't need anyone's money," Harry said.
"I've got enough even if I live a thousand years."

"That's good."

Gradually they began to discuss their finances, and the
woman enumerated her possessions. She owned buildings
in Brooklyn and on Staten Island; she had stocks and
bonds. Based on what she said and the names she mentioned, Harry decided that she was telling the truth. She
had, here in Miami, a checking account and a safe-deposit
box in the very same bank as Harry. Harry estimated that
she was worth at least a million or maybe more. She
served him food with the devotion of a daughter or wife.
She talked of what he should and shouldn't eat. Such
miracles had occurred to him in his younger years. Women
had met him, grown instantly intimate, and stuck with
him, never to leave again. But that such a thing should
happen to him at his age seemed like a dream. He asked
abruptly, "Do you have children?"

"I have a daughter, Sylvia. She lives all alone in a tent
in British Columbia."

"Why in a tent? My daughter's name was Sylvia, too.
You yourself could be my daughter," he added, not knowing why he had said such a thing.

"Nonsense. What are years? I always liked a man to be
a lot older than me. My husband, may he rest in peace,
was twenty years older, and the life we had together I
would wish for every Jewish daughter."

"I've surely got forty years on you," Harry said.

The woman put down her spoon. "How old do you take
me for?"

"Around forty-five," Harry said, knowing she was older.

"Add another twelve years and you've got it."

"You don't look it."

"I had a good life with my husband. I could get anything out of him—the moon, the stars, nothing was too
good for his Ethel. That's why after he died I became
melancholy. Also, my daughter was making me sick. I

spent a fortune on psychiatrists, but they couldn't help me.
Just as you see me now, I stayed seven months in an institution, a clinic for nervous disorders. I had a breakdown
and I didn't want to live any more. They had to watch me
day and night. He was calling me from his grave. I want
to tell you something, but don't misunderstand me."

"What is it?"

"You remind me of my husband. That's why—"

"I'm eighty-two," Harry said and instantly regretted it.
He could have easily subtracted five years. He waited a
moment, then added, "If I were ten years younger, I'd
make you a proposition."

Again he regretted his words. They had issued from his
mouth as if of their own volition. He was still bothered by
the fear of falling into the hands of a gold digger.

The woman looked at him inquisitively and cocked an
eyebrow. "Since I decided to live, I'll take you just as you
are."

"How is this possible? How can it be?" Harry asked
himself again and again. They spoke of getting married
and of breaking through the wall that divided their two
apartments to make them into one. His bedroom was next
to hers. She revealed the details of her financial situation
to him. She was worth about a million and a half. Harry
had already told her how much he had. He asked, "What
will we do with so much money?"

"I wouldn't know what to do with money myself," the
woman replied, "but together, we'll take a trip around the
world. We'll buy an apartment in Tel Aviv or Tiberias.
The hot springs there are good for rheumatism. With me
beside you, you'll live a long time. I guarantee you a hundred years, if not more."

"It's all in God's hands," Harry said, amazed at his own
words. He wasn't religious. His doubts about God and
His providence had intensified over the years. He often
said that, after what had happened to the Jews in Europe,
one had to be a fool to believe in God.

Ethel stood up and so did he. They hugged and kissed.

He pressed her close and youthful urges came throbbing back within him.

She said, "Wait till we've stood under the wedding canopy."

It struck Harry that he had heard these words before, spoken in the same voice. But when? And from whom? All three of his wives had been American-born and wouldn't have used this expression. Had he dreamed it? Could a person foresee the future in a dream? He bowed his head and pondered. When he looked up he was astounded. Within those few seconds the woman's appearance had undergone a startling transformation. She had moved away from him and he hadn't noticed it. Her face had grown pale, shrunken, and aged. Her hair seemed to him to have become suddenly disheveled. She gazed at him sidelong with a dull, sad, even stern expression. Did I insult her or what? he wondered. He heard himself ask, "Is something wrong? Don't you feel well?"

"No, but you'd better go back to your own place now," she said in a voice which seemed alien, harsh, and impatient. He wanted to ask her the reason for the sudden change that had come over her, but a long-forgotten (or a never-forgotten) pride asserted itself. With women, you never knew where you stood anyhow. Still, he asked, "When will we see each other?"

"Not today any more. Maybe tomorrow," she said after some hesitation.

"Goodbye. Thanks for the lunch."

She didn't even bother to escort him to the door. Inside his own apartment again, he thought, Well, she changed her mind. He was overcome with a feeling of shame—for himself and for her, too. Had she been playing a game with him? Had malicious neighbors arranged to make a fool of him? His apartment struck him as half empty. I won't eat dinner, he decided. He felt a pressure in his stomach. "At my age one shouldn't make a fool of oneself," he murmured. He lay down on the sofa and dozed off, and when he opened his eyes again it was dark outside. Maybe she'll ring my doorbell again. Maybe I should

call her? She had given him her phone number. Though
he had slept, he woke up exhausted. He had letters to answer, but he put it off until morning. He went out onto
the balcony. One side of his balcony faced a part of hers.
They could see each other here and even converse, if she
should still be interested in him. The sea splashed and
foamed. There was a freighter far in the distance. A jet
roared in the sky. A single star that no street lights or
neon signs could dim appeared above. It's a good thing
one can see at least one star. Otherwise one might forget
that the sky exists altogether.

He sat on the balcony waiting for her to possibly show
up. What could she be thinking? Why had her mood
changed so abruptly? One minute she was as tender and
talkative as a bride in love; a moment later she was a
stranger.

Harry dozed off again, and when he awoke it was late
in the evening. He wasn't sleepy, and he wanted to go
downstairs for the evening edition of the morning paper,
with the reports of the New York Exchange; instead he
went to lie down on his bed. He had drunk a glass of
tomato juice before and swallowed a pill. Only a thin wall
separated him from Ethel, but walls possessed a power of
their own. Perhaps this is the reason some people prefer
to live in a tent, he thought. He assumed that his broodings
would keep him from sleeping, but he quickly nodded
off. He awoke with pressure on his chest. What time was
it? The luminous dial on his wristwatch showed that he
had slept two hours and a quarter. He had dreamed, but
he couldn't remember what. He retained only the impres-
sion of nocturnal horrors. He raised his head. Was she
asleep or awake? He couldn't hear even a rustle from her
apartment.

He slept again and was awakened this time by the
sound of many people talking, doors slamming, footsteps
in the corridor, and running. He had always been afraid
of a fire. He read newspaper accounts of old people burning to death in old-age homes, hospitals, hotels. He got
out of bed, put on his slippers and robe, and opened the

door to the hall. There was no one there. Had he imagined it? He closed the door and went out onto the balcony.
No, not a trace of firemen below. Only people coming
home late, going out to nightclubs, making drunken noise.
Some of the condominium tenants sublet their apartments
in the summer to South Americans. Harry went back to
bed. It was quiet for a few minutes; then he again heard
a din in the corridor and the sound of men's and women's
voices. Something had happened, but what? He had an
urge to get up and take another look, but he didn't. He
lay there tense. Suddenly he heard a buzzing from the
house phone in the kitchen. When he lifted the receiver, a
man's voice said, "Wrong number." Harry had turned on
the fluorescent light in the kitchen and the glare dazzled
him. He opened the refrigerator, took out a jug of sweetened tea, and poured himself half a glass, not knowing
whether he did this because he was thirsty or to buoy his
spirits. Soon afterward he had to urinate, and he went to
the bathroom.

At that moment, his doorbell rang, and the sound cur-
tailed his urge. Maybe robbers had broken into the building? The night watchman was an old man and hardly a
match for intruders. Harry couldn't decide whether to go
to the door or not. He stood over the toilet bowl trembling.
These might be my final moments on earth flashed through
his mind. "God Almighty, take pity on me," he murmured.
Only now did he remember that he had a peephole in the
door through which he could see the hall outside. How
could I have forgotten about it? he wondered. I must be
getting senile.

He walked silently to the door, raised the cover of the
peephole, and looked out. He saw a white-haired woman
in a robe. He recognized her; it was his neighbor on the
right. In a second everything became clear to him. She
had a paralyzed husband and something had happened to
him. He opened the door. The old woman held out an
unstamped envelope.

"Excuse me, Mr. Bendiner, the woman next door left
this envelope by your door. Your name is on it."

"What woman?"

"On the left. She committed suicide."

Harry Bendiner felt his guts constrict, and within seconds his belly grew as tight as a drum.

"The blond woman?"

"Yes."

"What did she do?"

"Threw herself out the window."

Harry held out his hand and the old woman gave him the envelope.

"Where is she?" he asked.

"They took her away."

"Dead?"

"Yes, dead."

"My God!"

"It's already the third such incident here. People lose their minds in America."

Harry's hand shook, and the envelope fluttered as if caught in a wind. He thanked the woman and closed the door. He went to look for his glasses, which he had put on his night table. "I dare not fall," he cautioned himself. "All I need now is a broken hip." He staggered over to his bed and lit the night lamp. Yes, the eyeglasses were lying where he had left them. He felt dizzy. The walls, the curtains, the dresser, the envelope all jerked and whirled like a blurry image on television. Am I going blind or what? he wondered. He sat and waited for the dizziness to pass. He barely had the strength to open the envelope. The note was written in pencil, the lines were crooked, and the Yiddish words badly spelled. It read:

Dear Harry, forgive me. I must go where my husband is. If it's not too much trouble, say Kaddish for me. I'll intercede for you where I'm going.

ETHEL

He put the sheet of paper and his glasses down on the night table and switched off the lamp. He lay belching and hiccuping. His body twitched, and the bedsprings

vibrated. Well, from now on I won't hope for anything, he
decided with the solemnity of a man taking an oath. He
felt cold, and he covered himself with the blanket.

It was ten past eight in the morning when he came out
of his daze. A dream? No, the letter lay on the table. That
day Harry Bendiner did not go down for his mail. He did
not prepare breakfast for himself, nor did he bother to
bathe and dress. He kept on dozing on the plastic chaise
on the balcony and thinking about that other Sylvia—
Ethel's daughter—who was living in a tent in British
Columbia. Why had she run away so far? he asked himself. Did her father's death drive her into despair? Could
she not stand her mother? Or did she already at her age
realize the futility of all human efforts and decide to become a hermit? Is she endeavoring to discover herself, or
God? An adventurous idea came into the old man's mind:
to fly to British Columbia, find the young woman in the
wilderness, comfort her, be a father to her, and perhaps
try to meditate together with her on why a man is born
and why he must die.

Translated by Joseph Singer

Errors

The talk turned to errors, and Zalman the glazier said, "These days, you can make the worst mistake and no one even says an unkind word about it. That's why so many mistakes are being made. In olden times an error wasn't treated so lightly. The Pentateuch says that if a person chops wood and the head of the ax slips from the helve and slays someone, that person has to flee to a distant city or else the victim's relatives may take revenge on him. In Radoszyce, there was a Squire Zablocki—not a bad man, but if he was crossed he flew into a wild rage, his mustache bristled like a tomcat's, he began to wave his riding crop, and whoever was close by got it. One time he ordered a pair of boots from a cobbler, and when they came they were too tight. He had a fire built and he burned them. It's not so easy to burn leather. It smokes and it stinks to high heaven. He ordered the cobbler, Shmerl, to drop his pants and he beat him bloody. He tore a fur coat to shreds because the furrier sewed a hook too

low. It finally got to the point where the cobblers and
tailors refused to do work for him. Zablocki was always
befuddled, and he made a good many mistakes of his own.
One day he wanted to go to Żelechów, but he told the
coachman to take him to Węgrów. After going miles, he
suddenly realized that the road was unfamiliar. The coachman later told people that the squire was so angry he
punched himself in the nose.

"He had tormented his wife to death. It was already
after the emancipation, but he used to flog his peasants.
He would shout, 'On my estate, *I* am the law.' The
peasants trembled before him. He even terrified his dogs.
He had a pack of hounds the size of wolves and each one
had a name. If he called one dog to the table and another
came instead, he locked the offending dog in a dark room
for three days and nights.

"The squire was constantly involved in lawsuits—he
squandered his entire fortune on them. He always lost, he
never won. He would appeal to Lublin and to Warsaw,
but he lost there, too. Once, the squire received a lawyer
in his drawing room and the lawyer asked, 'Your excel-
lency, may I smoke a cigar?'

"The squire said, 'You may.'

"The lawyer took out a cigarette and lit it. Cigarettes
were still a novelty at the time. The squire had a cane
that was twisted like a horn and had a silver knob. He
grabbed the cane and began to beat the lawyer. The lawyer
cried, 'What have I done?'

" 'I gave you permission to smoke a cigar, not a cigarette,' the squire said. 'This is a newfangled fad picked up
from the French, and no one is going to bring any damned
foreign customs into my house!' That was Zablocki for
you.

"He had a daughter, Zofia, and he loved her like his
very life, but she had to do everything he told her. If he
told her to braid a blue ribbon into her hair and she
braided in a green one, he slapped her in front of whatever
guests might be there.

"Because of his reputation, the daughter couldn't get a

husband. Who would want to be the son-in-law of such a
wild man?

"I don't have to tell you that with females fashions keep
changing. Among the gentry it was the custom for a lady
to give a dress she had worn once or twice to some poor
relative. But Zablocki's daughter had to wear dresses from
King Sobieski's time. The nobles laughed at her and she
wasn't invited to their balls. She was ashamed to be seen
in the streets.

"Now listen to this: One time, the czar's uncle or
brother—I forget which—came to Poland and he had to
spend the night in Radoszyce. I think he had been hunting
in the forests nearby. But where could such a dignitary
stay? The authorities called on the squire and told him
that he had to put the prince up at his palace. Zablocki
squirmed like a snake, but Poland had lost all the wars,
and among the Gentiles might makes right. He was forced
to give in. His marshal or steward wanted to fix up the
quarters the prince would have, but Zablocki threatened
that if so much as a straw was picked up there heads would
roll.

"When the prince finally arrived, all the town officials
and the priests and nobles came out to greet him, including
Zablocki. The Jews, I recall, brought bread and salt on a
silver tray. An official presented Zablocki and told the
prince that he would be his host. The prince began to
mouth compliments, as is the custom among the gentry,
but as he did so he made an error and mispronounced the
name of Zablocki—he called it Zaprocki.

"When the squire heard his name mispronounced, he
cried out, 'I am Zablocki, not Zaprocki!' He was holding
a document he was supposed to read to the prince and he
flung it to the ground and stormed away. You can imagine
the commotion! For such an offense a whole city could
be leveled. The top official—the *nachalnik*—fell to his
knees and the priests apologized to the prince by telling
him that Zablocki wasn't in his right mind. The Jews became frightened, too, since it's the rule among the strong
to vent their rage on the weak. The Cossacks took off

after the squire. If they had caught him, they would have finished him on the spot. But he hid in the forest until the prince and his retinue left. He came home tattered, half raw from mosquitoes and thorns, and wasted as if from consumption.

"When the authorities heard that he was back, they sent the police to drag him to prison in chains, but Zablocki armed his peasants and ordered them to keep the Russians out of the courtyard. He himself loaded a rifle and went to an attic room, and when the Russians came near the gate he began to shoot at them from the window. Radoszyce had only a few policemen, and they didn't want to risk their lives. The *nachalnik* sent a courier to the governor asking for troops. The governor said he would telegraph Petersburg. He let the courier wait a week, then told him that Zablocki was a madman on whose account it didn't pay to shed blood. Apparently those in command didn't want to bring about a confrontation.

"The squire didn't live long after that. He got an infection in his lungs. Squires from far away came to the funeral, music was played, and Zablocki was praised for saving the Polish honor—and all this just because the Russian prince had made an error in pronouncing his name."

"An error is no trifle," said Levi Yitzchok. "Because Kamtsa was invited to a banquet and Bar-Kamtsa came instead, Jerusalem was destroyed. If a scribe makes a single error in the Torah, one is forbidden to read from that copy. A hundred years ago or maybe earlier, there lived a scribe in Szczebrzeszyn called Reb Meshulam. This Meshulam was well known. They said that each time before he wrote the Holy Name on a scroll he immersed himself in the ritual bath. For all his fine qualities, he charged exorbitant prices. He could ask five guldens or more for a couple of phylacteries. Poor people couldn't afford it, but the rich traveled to him from Bilgoray, Zamość, Janów, and Hrubieszów. He had a handwriting like pearls. He used ink and parchment that he imported from Leipzig. He elaborated every letter. On the Sabbaths

and holidays young men gathered at his home and he
preached to them. My grandfather was one of them.
Usually a scribe is an impractical man, but Reb Meshulam
had a head on his shoulders and he was called to other
towns as an arbitrator when there was a conflict among
the community elders. It seems that he had no children—
at least, I never heard of any.

"In Szczebrzeszyn, there lived in those days a wealthy
man named Reb Mottele Wolbromer. He owned a house
in the marketplace, and he dealt in grain and lumber.
Talk started in town that something had turned Reb
Mottele's luck sour. First he got sick, then his wife got
sick, and then the children. He had a granary full of
grain—suddenly it caught fire and burned down. Reb
Mottele sent rafts of lumber down the rivers San and Bug
—the storm winds scattered and crushed them and he had
great losses. It is said that when a person is assailed by
misfortunes he must ponder his deeds. Reb Mottele was
a pious man, and he probed his conscience. He found
many defects in his conduct, and he began to observe
frequent fasts. He rose earlier to study a portion of the
Talmud before morning prayers. He gave more to charity.
The old-time magnates weren't like those of today. But
nothing helped.

"As if he didn't have enough trouble, an evil spirit
invaded his house. In the middle of the night footsteps
could be heard and wanton female laughter. Doors opened
by themselves. When Reb Mottele went to bed, some invisible being dragged the bed across the floor. When things
like this happen, a person tries to keep it secret. It doesn't
do his business any good and it's certainly no asset for
arranging matches for his daughters. Besides, one thinks
maybe it's all just self-deception. But how long can you
keep the truth hidden—especially in a small town?

"There was a maid in the household and she ran away.
A spirit had pulled her hair and, if you'll forgive me,
soiled her with filth. Things got worse from day to day.
The Dark Ones were busy in the attic. All night long they
rolled barrels there.

"One Thursday Reb Mottele's eldest daughter kneaded some dough, covered the slab with a pillow so that it would rise, and went to sleep. She woke up in the middle of the night to find the dough beside her in bed. She screamed for help and roused the family. My grandmother—may she rest in peace—was their neighbor and she found out all about it. She told me everything. The demons had turned over the pots, defiled the food in the pantry, poured out the preserves, and even thrown the Passover dishes down from the attic.

"One evening a demon or an imp rapped on the window with such force that half the town came running. The secret was public. They recited, 'And let there be contentment,' but the Evil Ones would not leave. It was known that Reb Meshulam the scribe had amulets that came from ancient saints. Reb Mottele's family went to him and paid the high price he demanded. They hung the amulets in every corner, but this only excited the spirits and they smashed more utensils. A stone fell just at Reb Mottele's feet. If it had struck him in the head, it would have crushed his skull. The stone had fallen from the beam and it was as hot as if it had just come out of the fire.

"When trouble comes, all kinds of strange things enter the mind, but it's hard to arrive at any clear conclusions. It just so happened that it was Thursday when the beggars come calling from door to door. A wanderer opened the door, saw the commotion, and asked, 'What's going on?'

"The wife or one of the girls told him the story and the stranger asked, 'Have the mezuzahs been examined?'

"Reb Mottele was washing his hands in the kitchen and he said, 'Perhaps he is right.'

"But his wife argued, 'Reb Meshulam's mezuzahs don't need to be examined.'

'Still, the thought stuck with Reb Mottele. He ordered all the mezuzahs taken down and he read them. His mezuzahs had carved sheaths. He took a single glance at the first mezuzah and cried out bitterly. The letter *daleth* in the word '*Echod*'—'One'—looked like the letter *reish*, which made the sentence blasphemous. Reb Mottele examined the other mezuzahs and they were all the same. It is possible for a letter to peel or fade, but the ink on these was fresh. The town erupted in an uproar. Why drag it out? Whoever had one of Reb Meshulam's mezuzahs found the same error. While they were at it, the people checked Meshulam's phylactery inscriptions as well and found that they were all blemished, too. It became clear that Meshulam was a secret follower of Sabbatai Zevi. Members of this sect believed that the Messiah would come either when all was pure or all corruption. They caused Jews to sin. They defaced holy books. They threw the bone of a corpse into the house of a man of priestly descent to make him impure. In former times the Council of Four Lands had excommunicated the sect by blowing the ram's horn and lighting black candles, and it was assumed later that only a handful was left, because many had converted. Nevertheless, some were still active, and Meshulam was one of them.

"I forgot to mention that in some of his phylacteries he had written the names of demons as well as the name of the false Messiah, Sabbatai Zevi—may it be blotted out. If Meshulam had been in town at that time, he would have been torn to pieces. But he had gone to Lublin for an arbitration. His wife was a simple woman who didn't know her left hand from her right. A mob gathered and broke all her windows. They even tried to tear down her walls, but the rabbi stopped them. How was she guilty, poor soul?

"It turned out that Reb Meshulam wasn't the only one of the sect in town. There was a whole gang of them, and when they saw that their scandalous deeds had been uncovered they sent a rider to Lublin to warn Meshulam to flee. They also fled, deserting their wives."

"What happened to them?" asked Zalman the glazier.

"They all converted."

"Were their wives allowed to remarry?"

"A convert's wife is considered a married woman. I think one of them got divorce papers from her husband."

"Is a convert allowed to divorce?"

"According to law, he remains a Jew."

Meyer Eunuch closed one eye and with the other he stared at the window. He said, "That a prince makes an error in pronouncing a name is little wonder. Perhaps the one who was the czar's uncle considered it beneath his dignity to call some Polish squireling by his right name. The Sabbatai Zevi sect, on the other hand, did what they did out of spite. Those weren't errors but acts of malice. But I know a story of a true error. There is a town, Betchów, that's the size of a dot in a small prayer book, and there was a rabbi there called Reb Berish, a famous scholar. He had a yeshiva of ten students—no more and no less. Rabbi Berish could have had hundreds of students, but he had decided that ten were enough. When one of the youths became engaged and was about to leave Betchów, there were already many candidates waiting to take his place and they fought like the dickens to get into Rabbi Berish's yeshiva. Rich men from all over Poland came to Betchów to snatch up the students for their daughters. When I was a boy, Rabbi Berish's best student was an orphan named Gabriel Makover. This Gabriel came to love Rabbi Berish and his method of learning with such ardor that he wouldn't accept an outside match and so have to leave Betchów. Betchów is a poor village. There was just one rich man there—Reb Hayim Pinchever, who was himself a scholar. They said that he had his books bound in silk. He, too, had once been a student of Rabbi Berish. He had an only daughter. None of the rabbi's children had lived to maturity, and he was without an heir. To make it short, Gabriel became engaged to Reb Hayim Pinchever's daughter, and all Betchów danced at their wedding. It became clear to everyone that a hundred years hence Gabriel would become the rabbi's successor.

"Rabbi Berish had written commentaries throughout the years, but he didn't want to have a book published. He would say, 'There is enough food for the moths already without my scribblings.' Since he was in his sixties, his admirers insisted that he publish at least one book. After lengthy discussions the rabbi consented to publish those commentaries he thought most highly of. It took several years for him to decide what was worthy. Well, but there wasn't a printing shop in Betchów or the vicinity, and Rabbi Berish lived in terrible fear of errors and misprints. By then his eyesight was almost ruined and he studied from what he knew by heart. Gabriel helped him in every way and rewrote what needed rewriting. Finally the work was finished. The only printing shop in that part of Poland happened to be in Warsaw, and after many warnings Rabbi Berish handed over the manuscript to Gabriel to give to the printer and ordered him to oversee every stage of the job so that—God forbid—no error should occur. Gabriel promised his rabbi that he would read the proofs ten times.

"There is a saying: 'An author doesn't die of typhus but of typos.' His father-in-law gave Gabriel carfare and he went to Warsaw with the manuscript. Today you can take a train, but in those times a trip to Warsaw was almost like a journey to the Land of Israel. On the way, Gabriel never let the manuscript out of his hands.

"In Warsaw a former student of Rabbi Berish's offered Gabriel a room, and he stayed there for months. He stopped studying altogether and spent whole days and half the nights at the printer's. When a page was set, he counted each letter and word as if they were ducats. A printer doesn't like it when an author or his proxy sits on his head too much, and he grumbled and played tricks on Gabriel. But Gabriel took it all without complaint. Even after the book was printed he read it again, word by word. He couldn't find a single error, and he went back to Betchów proudly.

"When he arrived in Betchów and handed the book to Rabbi Berish, the rabbi weighed it in his hand. He liked to joke. He said, 'Oh, a heavy volume. There'll be something to heat the oven with when the Messiah comes.'

"During the time that Gabriel had been in Warsaw,

Rabbi Berish's students had presented their rabbi with a powerful magnifying glass, and he began to leaf through the pages, read a line here and there, mumbling, 'What is he babbling about, this author? What does he want? Why is he scribbling such nonsense?'

"Suddenly he became silent and grew white. He raised his brows toward Gabriel. 'So you want to be a rabbi? A shoemaker you should be!' He had found an error in the book—a dreadful error.

"After a while Rabbi Berish felt sorry. People were standing around. He had shamed the young man publicly. He began to beg Gabriel's pardon and told him that it didn't matter—little children didn't die from such errors. But Gabriel was crushed. At first he was speechless. Afterward, though, the master and his pupil spoke together, and before Gabriel left, the rabbi kissed him on the forehead. Gabriel promised the rabbi that he wouldn't take the matter to heart and that he would come to the yeshiva the next day.

"Gabriel had gone to the rabbi before coming home to his wife, and his father-in-law and mother-in-law were incensed. How could he leave a young wife alone for so long? She was overcome with longing. And now that he had returned he should have come home first. They would have heaped recriminations on him, but when he walked into the house they became alarmed. In the half hour at the rabbi's he had grown wax yellow, like a dying man. The family and other people quickly found out what had happened, and the town buzzed with gossip. Still, Gabriel came back to his old self, and it seemed that the incident would blow over. After all, he hadn't killed anybody.

"But the next morning when the family got up Gabriel was missing. He had left in the middle of the night with only his prayer shawl and phylacteries. A Gentile had seen him at dawn, crossing the bridge that led out of town.

"Well, what happened in Betchów that day and on the days that followed you can figure out for yourself. Messengers were hired to look for Gabriel, but he couldn't be found. Letters were sent to relatives. The young man had vanished like a stone in water. Rabbi Berish was so distressed that he told his students to go back home, and the yeshiva closed down. Rabbi Berish had never believed in fasting, but following this incident he began to fast every Monday and Thursday.

"A year went by. As a rule, when a wife is forsaken she grows depressed and neglects herself, but Gabriel's wife continued to help her father in his business and her mother at home, and her spirits stayed cheerful. There were rumors in town that she knew something but was sworn to keep a secret. And that's how it really was. One day Gabriel showed up in Betchów dressed like a common laborer and carrying a sack on his shoulders. This time he went straight to his father-in-law's house. The mother-in-law opened the door, and when she saw her son-in-law all dusty and with a sack on his shoulders she started to cry so loud that the neighbors became alarmed. Gabriel said, 'The rabbi told me to become a shoemaker and that's what I did.'

"The sack was full of lasts and tools. On the night before he went away, he had told his wife what he was going to do and had sworn her to secrecy; otherwise, he couldn't have managed the act of penance. He went to a faraway town and learned shoemaking there. I forgot the main things: he had left his wife pregnant, and during the time he had been away she had borne him a son.

"Rabbi Berish came to Reb Hayim Pinchever's house and asked Gabriel, 'How is it possible that you could do such a thing?'

"And Gabriel replied, 'Rabbi, your word is holy to me. When you told me to become a shoemaker, I had to become one.'

"Rabbi Berish hadn't lost his tartness and he said, 'It's a miracle I didn't tell you to become a wet nurse.'

"Gabriel rented a shop and sat down to cut and hammer shoes. No words or arguments could dissuade him. Reb Hayim Pinchever wanted to arrange a divorce, but his daughter warned that if he did she would drown herself

in the well. The fondness between the rabbi and pupil
didn't diminish but grew even stronger. Gabriel worked by
day, but after the evening services he went to Rabbi
Berish. They debated learned subjects, and Gabriel wrote
down his teacher's opinion. It turned out that during the
year Gabriel had been learning his trade he had also
devoted himself to the Talmud and the Commentaries.
If you want to, you find time for everything.

"Rabbi Berish grew so enthusiastic over Gabriel's in-
tellect that he compared him to the ancient Jochanan the
shoemaker. People said that Betchów had never had
such a shoemaker as Gabriel. He took measurements not
once but three times. He used the finest leather. Even
the Gentile landowners ordered boots and gaiters from
him. Rabbi Berish suffered from bad feet in his old age,
and Gabriel made him a pair of slippers that fit him like
a glove. Yes, the yeshiva was reestablished.

"Rabbi Berish lived nine more years. In the last few
years, he became completely blind and Gabriel took
over, answering those questions of religious law that
required sight. The housewives and the butchers came to
his workshop and abided by his decisions. After Rabbi
Berish's death, the town elders came to Gabriel's shop
and declared him the rabbi. He took over the yeshiva,
too, and ordered the students to learn a trade. They say
that he made shoes till the end of his life, for those close
to him as well as for the paupers in the poorhouse."

"That means that some good came out of this error,"
Zalman the glazier observed.

Meyer Eunuch began to rub his hands. "There are no
such things as errors. How can there be errors if everything comes from divine sources? There are spheres
where all errors are transformed into truth."

Translated by Joseph Singer

The Admirer

First she wrote me a long letter full of praise. Among other things, she said that my books had helped her "find" herself. Then she called and arranged a meeting. Soon afterward she called again, since it turned out she already had an engagement that day, and she proposed another. Two days later a long telegram came. It seemed that she would be visiting a paralyzed aunt on the new meeting day. I had never received such a long telegram, with such fancy English words. A call followed, and we settled on a new date. During an earlier telephone conversation I had mentioned that I admired Thomas Hardy. In a few days a messenger brought a luxuriously bound set of Thomas Hardy's works. My admirer's name was Elizabeth Abigail de Sollar—a remarkable name for a woman whose mother, she told me, came from the Polish town of Klendev, the daughter of the local rabbi.

On the day of the visit I cleaned my apartment and

put all my manuscripts and unanswered letters in the laundry hamper. My guest was due at eleven. At twenty-five past eleven the phone rang and Elizabeth Abigail de Sollar shrieked, "You gave me a phony address! There is no such building!"

It seemed she had mistaken East Side for West. I now told her precisely how to find me. Once she got to my street on the West Side, she should enter a gate bearing the number she had. The gate opened onto a courtyard. There she would find an entrance with a different number, which I gave her, and I explained that I lived on the eleventh floor. The passenger elevator happened not to be working and she would have to use the service elevator. Elizabeth Abigail de Sollar repeated all my directions and tried to find a pencil and a notebook in her handbag to write them down, but at that moment the operator demanded a nickel. Elizabeth Abigail de Sollar didn't have a nickel, and breathlessly she uttered the number of the phone booth from which she was calling. I called her at once, but no one answered. I must have dialed the wrong number. I picked up a book and began to read from where I opened it in the middle. Since she had my address and phone number, she would show up sooner or later. I hadn't managed to get to the end of the paragraph when the telephone rang. I picked up the receiver and heard a man cough, stammer, and clear his throat. After a while he regained his voice and said, "My name is Oliver Leslie de Sollar. May I speak to my wife?"

"Your wife made a mistake and went to a wrong address. She should be here soon."

"Excuse me for disturbing you, but our child has suddenly got sick. She started coughing violently and choking, and I don't know what to do. She suffers from asthma, Elizabeth has drops for these emergencies, but I can't find them. I'm distraught."

"Call a doctor! Call an ambulance!" I shouted into the mouthpiece.

"Our doctor isn't in his office. One second, excuse me . . ."

I waited a few minutes, but Oliver Leslie de Sollar didn't come back and I hung up the receiver. "That's what happens when you deal with people—right away complications arise," I said to myself. "The deed itself is a sin," I mentally quoted an Indian sacred book—but which one? Was it the Bhagavad Gita or the Dhammapada? If the child choked to death, God forbid, I would be indirectly responsible.

My doorbell rang in a long and insistent summons. I hurried to open it and saw a young woman with blond hair falling to her shoulders, a straw hat, with flowers and cherries, of the kind worn when I was still a cheder boy, a white blouse with lace at the neckline and sleeves, a black embroidered skirt, and buttoned shoes. Although it was sunny outside, she carried an umbrella with ribbons and bows—all in all, a photograph come to life from an album. Before she could even close the door behind her, I said, "Your husband just called. I don't wish to alarm you, but your child is having an attack of asthma and your husband can't get a doctor. He wants to know where the drops are."

I was sure my visitor would dash to the telephone, which stood on a table in the hall, but instead she measured me with her eyes from head to toe, then back again, while a sweet smile spread across her face. "Yes, it's you!" She held out a hand in a white glove reaching to the elbow and presented me with a package wrapped in shiny black paper and tied in a red ribbon. "Don't be concerned," she said. "He does this every time I go somewhere. He can't stand my leaving the house. It's pure hysteria."

"What about the child?"

"Bibi is as stubborn as her father. She doesn't want to let me out of the house, either. She's his child from a former wife."

"Please come in. Thank you for the present."

"Oh, you filled a gap in my life. I've always been a

stranger to myself. By chance I discovered one of your novels in a bookstore and from then on I've read everything you've written. I believe I've told you that I'm the Klendev rabbi's grandchild. That's on my mother's side. On my father's side I stem from adventurers."

She followed me into the living room. She was short and slim, with a smooth white skin seldom seen in adults. Her eyes were pale blue tinged with yellow, and somewhat squinty. Her nose was narrow and on the long side, her lips thin, her chin receding and pointed. She had on no cosmetics. Usually I form a concept of a person from the face he presents, but I couldn't form a clear one of this young woman. Not healthy, I thought: sensitive, aristocratic. Her English seemed to me not American but foreign. As I chatted with her and asked her to have a seat on the sofa, I unwrapped the package and took out a Ouija board with a planchette, obviously handmade, of costly wood and edged in bone.

She said, "I gather from your stories that you're interested in the occult, and I hope this is a fitting gift."

"Oh, you give me too many gifts."

"You've earned them all."

I asked her questions, and she responded willingly. Her father was a retired lawyer. He was separated from Elizabeth's mother and was living with another woman in Switzerland. The mother suffered from rheumatism and had moved to Arizona. She had a friend there, an old man of eighty. Elizabeth Abigail had met her husband in college. He had been her philosophy professor. He was also an amateur astronomer and used to sit up with her half the night at the observatory studying the stars. A Jew? No, Oliver Leslie was a Christian, born in England but descended from Basques. Two years after she married him he became sick, fell into a chronic depression, quit his job, and settled in a house a few miles from Croton-on-Hudson. He had isolated himself completely from people. He was writing a book on astrology and numerology. Elizabeth Abigail smiled the smile of those who have long since discovered the vanity of all

human endeavors. At times her eyes grew melancholy
and even frightened.

I asked her what she did in that house in Croton-on-
Hudson and she replied, "I go crazy. Leslie doesn't
speak for days or weeks at a time except to Bibi. He
tutors her—she doesn't go to school. We do not live as
man and wife. For me, books have become the essence
of my being. When I find a book that speaks to me, this
is a great event in my life. That's why—"

"Who takes care of the household?"

"No one, really. We have a neighbor, an ex-farmer
who left his family, and he brings us food from the
supermarket. At times he cooks for us, too. A simple
man, but in his own fashion a philosopher. He is also our
chauffeur. Leslie can't drive the car any more. Our
house stands on a hill that's awfully slippery, not only in
winter, but whenever it rains."

My visitor grew silent. I was already accustomed to
the fact that many of those who wrote me or came to see
me were eccentrics—odd, lost souls. Elizabeth Abigail
happened to resemble my sister slightly. Since she came
from Klendev and was a rabbi's grandchild, she might
have been my relative. Klendev isn't far from the towns
where generations of my ancestors lived.

I asked, "How is it that Bibi is with her father, not her
mother?"

Elizabeth replied, "The mother committed suicide."

The telephone rang and I heard the same stammering
and throat clearing I had heard earlier. I immediately
called Elizabeth, who approached slowly and with the
reluctance of one who knows what's coming. I heard her
tell her husband where the drops were and order him
sharply not to annoy her again. He spoke at length and
she responded with an occasional brief phrase. "What?
Well, no." Finally she said, "That I don't know," in a
tone of impatience. She came back into the room and
resumed her seat on the sofa.

"It's become a system with them—the moment I go
somewhere, Bibi gets these chest spasms and her father

calls to alarm me. He can never find the drops, which
don't help in any case, because her asthma is deliberately
brought on by him. This time I didn't even tell him
where I was going, but he eavesdrops on me. I wanted
to ask you a number of questions, but he has driven them
from my mind. Yes, where in heaven's name is this
Klendev? I couldn't find it on any map."

"It's a village in the Lublin area."

"Were you ever there?"

"It just so happens that I was. I had left home and
someone recommended me for a teaching position there.
I gave a single lesson, and the school authorities and I
agreed at once that I am no teacher. The very next day I
left."

"When was this?"

"In the twenties."

"Oh, my grandfather was no longer living then. He
died in 1913."

Although what my visitor had to say held no special
interest for me, I listened closely. It was hard for me to
believe that only one generation separated her and the
Klendev rabbi, his milieu, and his way of life. Her face
had in a mysterious fashion molded itself to that of the
Anglo-Saxons whose culture she had absorbed. I de-
tected within her traces of other lands, other climates.
Could it be that Lysenko was right after all?

The clock showed twelve-thirty and I invited my guest
to go downstairs with me for lunch. She said that she
didn't eat lunch. The most she might have was some tea,
but if I wanted to have lunch, she'd go along with me.
After a while we went into the kitchen and I brewed tea.
I put cookies on a plate for her and for myself fixed
bread with cottage cheese. We sat at a card table, facing
each other like a married couple. A cockroach crawled
across the table, but neither Elizabeth nor I made any
effort to disturb it. The cockroaches in my apartment
apparently knew that I was a vegetarian and that I felt
no hatred for their species, which is a few hundred million years older than man and which will survive him.

Elizabeth had strong tea, with milk, and I had mine weak, with lemon. When I drank, I held a cube of sugar between my teeth as had been the custom in Bilgoray and Klendev. She didn't touch the cookies, and gradually I finished them off. There had evolved between us a familiarity that requires no preliminaries.

I heard myself ask, "How long is it since you've stopped sleeping with him?"

Elizabeth began to blush, but when the blood had colored half her face it receded. "I'll tell you something, though you won't believe it."

"I'll believe anything you say."

"I'm physically a virgin." She blurted out the words and seemed astonished to have said them.

To show that she had not shocked me, I said casually, "I thought this was an extinct breed already."

"There is always a Last Mohican."

"You never asked a doctor about the situation?"

"Never."

"What about psychoanalysis?"

"Neither Leslie nor I believe in it."

"Don't you need a man?" I asked, bewildered by my daring.

She raised her glass and took a sip of tea. "Very much so, but I've never met a man I wanted to be with. That's how it was before I met Leslie and that's how it's been since. When I first knew him, I figured that Leslie would be a man to me, but he said that he wanted to wait for marriage. This seemed foolish to me, but we waited. When we were married we made several attempts, but they didn't work out. At times I imagined that the Klendev rabbi wouldn't let it happen because Leslie was a Gentile. After a while we both developed a revulsion toward the whole thing."

"You are both ascetics," I said.

"Eh? I don't know. I indulge in passionate affairs in my daydreams. I've read Freud, Jung, Stekel, but I'm convinced that they cannot help me. I'm amazed at my frankness with you. I've never written to an author be-

fore. I generally don't write letters. It's even hard for me
to write to my father. Suddenly I write you and phone
you. It's as if one of your dybbuks had entered me. Now
that you seem to have opened, so to say, a sealed source
within me, I'll tell you something else. Since I've started
reading you, you've become the lover in my fantasies—
you have driven off all the others."

Elizabeth took another sip of tea. She smiled and
added, "Don't get scared. This isn't the purpose of my
visit."

I felt a dryness in my throat and had to strain to make
my voice emerge clearly. "Tell me about your fantasies."

"Oh, I spend time with you. We take trips together.
You take me along to Poland and we visit all the villages
you describe. Strange, but in my imagination your voice
is the same as your voice is now and I can't conceive
how this can be. Even your accent is as I imagined it.
This is something really irrational."

"Every love is irrational," I said, embarrassed by my
own assumption.

Elizabeth bowed her head and gave this some thought.

"At times I go to sleep with these fantasies and they
are transformed into dreams. I see towns full of movement. I hear Yiddish spoken, and although I don't know
the language, I understand everything in the dream. If I
didn't know that these places have been destroyed, I
would go there to see if everything matches my
dreams."

"Nothing matches any more."

"My mother always spoke to me of her father, the
rabbi. She came to America with her mother—my
grandmother—when she was eight. My grandfather was
married for the second time when he was seventy-five to
a girl of eighteen, and my mother was the result of this
marriage. Six years later, my grandfather died. He left
many exegeses. The whole family perished under the
Nazis, and all his manuscripts were burned. My grandmother brought along a small Hebrew book he had pub-

lished and I have it in my purse in the foyer. Would you
like to see it?"

"Absolutely."

"Let me wash the dishes. You wait here. I'll get
Grandfather's book and you can look it over in the time
I do them."

I remained at the table and Elizabeth brought me a
slim book entitled *The Outcry of Mordechai.* On the title
page the author listed his genealogy, and as I studied it I
saw that my visitor and I were actually related by a connection many centuries back. We were both descended
from Rabbi Moses Isserles and also from the author of
The Revealer of Profundities. The book by the Klendev
rabbi was a pamphlet against the Radzyń rabbi, Reb
Gershon Henoch, who believed that he had found in the
Mediterranean Sea the murex whose secretion was used
in ancient Israel to dye the ritual fringes blue, although
it was traditionally accepted that the murex had been
concealed after the destruction of the Temple and would
be found again only when the Messiah came. Reb
Gershon Henoch hadn't reckoned on the storm of protest
from the other rabbis, and he directed his followers to
wear the blue fringes. This aroused great controversy in
the rabbinical world. Elizabeth's grandfather called Reb
Gershon Henoch "betrayer of Israel, apostate, messenger of Satan, Lilith, Asmodeus, and their evil host." He
warned that the sin of wearing these sham fringes could
bring dire punishment from heaven. The pages of *The
Outcry of Mordechai* had grown yellow and so dry that
pieces flicked off the margins when I leafed through
them.

Elizabeth washed the plates and our glasses in the sink
with a sponge. "What's written there?" she asked me.

It wasn't easy to explain to Elizabeth de Sollar the
dispute between the Radzyń rabbi and the other rabbis
and Talmudic scholars of his generation, but I somehow
found the words. Her eyes sparkled as she listened. "Fas-
cinating!"

The telephone rang and I left Elizabeth to answer it.

It was Oliver Leslie de Sollar again. I told him that I would fetch his wife, but he said, "Wait. May I have a few words with you?"

"Yes, of course."

Oliver Leslie began to cough and clear his throat. "My daughter, Bibi, nearly died from her attack today. We barely saved her. We have a neighbor here, a Mr. Porter, who is a friend, and he found some medicine that another doctor had once prescribed. She's asleep now. I want you to know that my wife is a sick woman, both physically and spiritually. She has tried to commit suicide twice. The second time she took so many sleeping pills she had to be kept three days in an iron lung. She has an enormously high opinion of you and is in love with you in her own fashion, but I want to warn you not to encourage her. Our marriage is extremely unhappy, but I'm like a father to her because her own father deserted her and her mother when Elizabeth was only a child. Her father's indifference instilled in her a puritanism that has made our existence a nightmare. Don't promise her anything, because she lives entirely in a world of illusions. She needs psychiatric care, but she refuses it. I'm sure that you understand and that you will act like a responsible person."

"You may be completely sure."

"She exists on tranquillizers. I used to be a philosophy professor, but after we married I could no longer hold my position. Fortunately, I have wealthy parents, who help us. I've suffered so much from her that my own health has deteriorated. This is the type of woman who robs a man of his potency. If, heaven forbid, you became involved with her, your talent would be the first casualty. If she lived in the sixteenth century, she would have been surely burned at the stake as a witch. In the years I've known her, I've come to believe in black magic—as a psychological phenomenon, naturally."

"I hear you're writing a book on astrology."

"Is that what she told you? Nonsense! I'm doing work on Newton's last thirty years and his religious convictions.

You undoubtedly know that Newton considered gravity a divine force—the purest expression of godly will. The greatest scientist of all times was also a great mystic. Since gravity controls the universe, it follows that the celestial bodies influence the organic and spiritual world in every manner and form. This is aeons removed from the usual astrology with its horoscopes and other folderol."

"Shall I get your wife?"

"No. Don't tell her I called. She is capable of causing me terrible scandals. She once attacked me with a knife . . ."

During the time Oliver Leslie had been talking to me, Elizabeth didn't appear. I wondered why it was taking her so long to dry two plates and glasses, but I assumed that she hadn't wanted to disturb my conversation. The moment I hung up I went into the kitchen, but Elizabeth wasn't there. I guessed what had happened. A narrow passage led from the kitchen to my bedroom, where an extension telephone stood on a night table. I opened the door to the passage and Elizabeth was standing on the threshold.

She said, "I had to go to the bathroom."

From the manner in which she said this—quickly, guiltily, in a defensive tone—I knew that she was lying. She might have been on the way to the bathroom (although how could she know that this door led to it?) and spied the extension phone. Her eyes reflected a blend of anger and mockery. So that's the kind of baggage you are, I thought. Every trace of restraint I might have felt toward her vanished. I put my hands on her shoulders. She trembled, and her face assumed the mischievous expression of a little girl caught stealing or dressing up in her mother's clothes.

"For a virgin, you're a shrewd piece," I said.

"Yes, I heard everything, and I'll never go back to him," she said in a voice grown firmer and younger as well. It was as if she had thrown off a mask she had worn a long time and in that split second become someone else—someone youthful and frolicsome. She pursed her

lips as if about to kiss me. I was overcome with desire
for her, but I remembered Oliver Leslie's warning. I bent
toward her and our eyes came so close I saw only a blue-
ness like that within a grotto. Our lips touched but didn't
kiss. My knees pressed against hers and she began to move
backward. While I pushed her slightly and playfully, a
solemn voice admonished me: "Beware! You're falling
into a trap!"

At that moment the phone rang again. I lurched with
such force that I nearly knocked her over. A ringing telephone evokes a reaction of wild expectations in me—I
often compare myself to Pavlov's dogs. For a moment I
wavered between hurrying forward into the bedroom or
back to the hall; then I ran to the hall with Elizabeth at
my heels. I took up the receiver and she tried to wrest
it from me, obviously convinced that her husband was
calling again. I thought so myself, but I heard a firm,
middle-aged female voice ask, "Is Elizabeth de Sollar
with you? I'm her mother."

At first I didn't grasp the meaning of the words—in
my confusion I had forgotten my visitor's name. But soon
I recovered. "Yes, she is here."

"My name is Mrs. Harvey Lemkin. I just received a
call from my son-in-law, Dr. Leslie de Sollar, telling me
that my daughter is paying you a visit and that she left
her sick little stepdaughter and all the rest of it. I want
to warn you that my daughter is an emotionally ill and
irresponsible person. My son-in-law, Professor de Sollar,
and I have spent a fortune to help her—with negative
results, I am sorry to say. At thirty-three she is still a
child, although she is highly intelligent and writes poems
that in my opinion are remarkable. You are a man and
I can well understand that when a pretty and greatly
gifted young woman demonstrates her admiration you
should be intrigued, but don't let yourself become involved
with her. You'll fall into a mess from which you'll never
escape. Because of her, I've left New York, a city I love
with all my heart and soul, and I've buried myself away
out here in Arizona. My daughter spoke so much of you

and praised you so highly that I began to read what you write in English and in Yiddish too. I am the Klendev rabbi's daughter and my Yiddish is pretty good. I could tell you a lot and I would be more than glad to meet you in New York—I come there from time to time—but I beseech you by all that's holy: Leave my daughter alone!"

The whole time her mother was speaking, Elizabeth stood apart and looked at me sidelong, inquisitively, half frightened and half ashamed. She made a gesture as if to come closer, but I motioned her away with my left hand. She made me think of a schoolgirl listening to a teacher or principal accuse her in front of her parents and unable to restrain herself from denying the charges. Her mother's voice was so loud she must have heard every word. Just when I was about to make some reply, Elizabeth jumped forward, tore the receiver from my hand, and exclaimed in a wailing voice, "Mother, I'll never forgive you! Never! Never! You're no longer my mother and I'm no longer your child! You sold me to a psychopath, a capon . . . I don't need your money and I don't need *you!* Whenever I might snatch a moment's happiness you spoil it all for me. You're my worst enemy. I'll kill you! I'll leave you a corpse for what you're doing to me . . . Bitch! Whore! Thief! Criminal! You sleep with an eighty-year-old gangster for money! I spit on you! I spit, spit, spit, spit!"

I stood there and watched foam bubble from her mouth. She bent over and writhed in pain. She clutched at the wall. I reached out to help her, but at that moment she fell with a crash, dragging the telephone down with her. She lay cramped and tossing, while one hand beat rapidly against the floor as if she were trying to signal the tenant below. Her mouth twisted and I heard a gasping growl. I knew what was happening—Elizabeth had suffered an epileptic fit. I lifted the phone and yelled into the mouthpiece, "Mrs. Lemkin, your daughter is having a seizure!" But the connection was broken. Should I call an ambulance? How did one go about doing that? My telephone had apparently stopped working. I wanted to open the window and call for help, but in the clamor and clang of Broadway no one would hear me from the eleventh floor. Instead, I ran into the kitchen, filled a glass with water, and poured it on Elizabeth's face. This caused her to bellow weirdly, and saliva sprayed my forehead. I rushed out into the corridor and began to pound on my neighbor's door, but no one answered. Only now did I notice that a stack of magazines and envelopes lay on his threshold. I turned to go back to my apartment and to my consternation saw that I had let the door slam shut. I didn't have the key on me. I pushed the door with all my might, but I'm not one of those bruisers who can break down a door.

In all my desperation I remembered that a duplicate key to my apartment hung in the office in the courtyard. I could also ask there that an ambulance be called. I realized full well what charges Elizabeth's husband and mother could bring against me in the event she died in my apartment. They might even accuse me of murder . . . I pressed the button for the service elevator and the pointer showed that it was standing on the seventeeth floor. I ran down the stairs, and in my mind—perhaps even aloud—I cursed the day I was born. As I ran, I heard the service elevator descending. I reached the lobby, and two moving men had the exit blocked with a sofa. Someone on the seventeenth floor was moving out. The lobby was filled with furniture, flower urns, stacks of books. I asked the men to let me pass, but they pretended not to hear. Well, I thought, this visit will be the death of me. Then I remembered that on the sixth floor lived a typesetter from the newspaper of which I was a staff member. If anyone in the family was home, he would help me call an ambulance and phone the office about a duplicate key. I started to run up the stairs to the sixth floor. My heart pounded and I broke out in a sweat. I rang the doorbell of the typesetter's apartment, but no one answered. I was prepared to run downstairs again when the door parted the length of the chain. I saw an eye, and a female voice asked, "What do you want?"

I began to explain to the woman what had happened.

I spoke in clipped sentences and with the frenzy of one in mortal danger. The woman's single eye bored through me. "I'm not the lady of the house. They're abroad. I'm a cousin."

"I beg you to help me. Believe me that I'm no thief or robber. Your cousin sets all my manuscripts. Maybe you've heard my name?"

I mentioned the name of the newspaper, I even cited the titles of several of my books, but she had never heard of me. After some hesitation she said, "I can't let you in. You know how it is these days. Wait here, I'll call the office on the house phone. Tell me your name again."

I repeated my name for her, gave her the number of my apartment, and thanked her profusely. She closed the door. I expected that any minute she would inform me she had called the office and help was on the way, but seven minutes went by and the door didn't open. I stood there, tense and miserable, and took a quick reckoning of man and his existence. He is completely dependent, a slave to circumstance. The slightest mishap and everything goes to pieces. There is one solution—to free oneself totally from making for oneself the Sabbath that is called life and turn back to the indifference of causality, to death, which is the substance of the universe.

Five more minutes passed and still the door didn't open. I began to skip down the stairs again, my mind churning with images of how I would punish this heartless woman if I possessed unlimited power. I reached the lobby and the sofa was standing outside. I saw Mr. Brown, the superintendent, and frantically told him my predicament. He gazed at me in astonishment. "No one called. Come. I'll give you the key."

The service elevator was free, and I rode up to the eleventh floor, opened the door, and found Elizabeth Abigail de Sollar lying on the sofa in the living room, her hair wet and disheveled, her face pale, her shoes off. I barely recognized her. She seemed to me much older— almost middle-aged. She had placed a towel under her head. She looked at me with the silent reproof of a wife whose husband has left her sick and alone and gone off somewhere for his own pleasure. I half shouted, "My dear Elizabeth, you must go home to your husband! I'm too old for such goings on."

She considered my words; then she said in a dull tone, "If you order me to go, I will go, but not back to him. I'm finished with him and with my mother, too. From now on, I am alone in the world."

"Where will you go?"

"To a hotel."

"They won't let you into a hotel without luggage. If you don't have any money, I can—"

"I have my checkbook with me, but why can't I stay here with you? I'm not altogether well, but it's nothing organic—only functional. It's *they* who made me sick. I can type. I know a little stenography, too. Oh, I forgot that you write in Yiddish. This I don't know, but I would learn it in time. My mother used to speak Yiddish with my grandmother when she didn't want me to understand what they were saying, and I picked up quite a number of words. I once bought a vegetarian cookbook, and I'd cook vegetarian meals for you."

I looked at her in silence. Yes, she was my relative— the genes of our ancestors reached out directly to both of us. The notion that it might be incest for us to be together flashed through my mind—one of those uninvited ideas that emerge, God knows from where, and shock with their ridiculous irrelevance.

"That sounds like paradise, but unfortunately it cannot be," I said.

"Why not? You probably have someone else. Yes, I understand. But is there any reason you can't have a maid? I'll be everything to you—a maid and a cook as well. Your apartment is neglected. You probably eat in cafeterias. I do nothing in my own house because I have no interest in it, but my mother made me take a course in housekeeping. I would work for you and you wouldn't have to pay me anything. My parents are both filthy rich and I'm their only daughter. I'm not interested in your money . . ."

Before I could answer her, I heard a sharp ring at the door. At the same time the telephone rang. I grabbed the receiver, told whoever was calling that there was someone at the door, and ran to open it. I saw a man who could have been no one but Oliver Leslie de Sollar—tall, lean, with a long face and neck, a ruff of faded blond hair around a bald skull, wearing a checked suit, a stiff collar, and a narrow tie with a still narrower knot of the type that reminded me of the Warsaw dandies. I nodded and returned to the telephone. I was sure that it was Elizabeth's mother calling, but a rough masculine voice spoke my name and demanded acknowledgment that it was really I. Then the caller said slowly and with the tone of an official, "My name is Howard William Moonlight and I represent Mrs. Harvey Lemkin, the mother of Mrs. Elizabeth de Sollar. I am sure that you know whom—"

I interrupted him to shout, "Mr. de Sollar is here! He'll talk to you!"

I dashed to the door, where my visitor still stood erectly, politely, waiting to be invited inside. I cried out, "Mr. de Sollar, it's not two hours since your wife came to visit me and hell is loose here! I've already received threatening calls from you, from your mother-in-law, and now from a lawyer. Your wife has managed to have an epileptic fit and only God knows what else. I'm sorry to say this, but I'm not interested in your wife, your mother-in-law, her lawyer, or in the whole crazy affair. Do me a favor and take her home. If not, I will . . ."

I was left momentarily speechless. I was about to say that I would call the police, but the words didn't come out. I glanced at the telephone and saw to my amazement that Elizabeth was mumbling into the mouthpiece with her eyes fixed on me and my visitor. He said in a thin voice that didn't match his stature, "I'm afraid there's been some misunderstanding. I'm not the person who called you. My name is Dr. Jeffrey Lifshitz. I'm an assistant professor of literature at the University of Califor-

nia and a great admirer of your writing. I have a friend
in this building who also happens to be a devoted reader
of yours, and when I visited him today we got to talking
about you and he told me that you are his neighbor. I
wanted to phone you, but I couldn't find your name in the
directory and I thought I'd ring your doorbell. Forgive
me for disturbing you."

"You haven't disturbed me. I'm pleased to have you as
a reader, but there has been a considerable commotion
going on in my house. Will you be staying in the city
for long?"

"I'll be here the whole week."

"Would it be convenient for you to come to see me
tomorrow?"

"Certainly."

"Let us say tomorrow at 11 A.M.?"

"It will be a pleasure and an honor. Again, excuse me
for dropping in on you in such a—"

I assured Professor Lifshitz that I would be happy to
meet with him, and he left.

Elizabeth had put down the receiver. She stood by the
telephone as if waiting for me to come to her. I stopped a
few paces away and said, "I'm sorry. You're a great
woman, I understand your plight, but I can't get into a
battle with your husband, your mother, and now with a
lawyer, too. What did he want? Why did he call?"

"Oh, they're all mad. But I heard what you told your
guest you mistook for my husband, and I swear I'll
trouble you no more. What happened today proves to
me that only one way remains for me to set myself free.
I just want to point out that your diagnosis was incorrect.
I'm not an epileptic."

"Then what is it?"

"The doctors themselves don't know. A kind of hyper-
sensitivity that I inherited from who knows where,
maybe from our common ancestor. What was his book?"

"The Revealer of Profundities."

"What kind of profundities did he reveal?"

"That no love of any kind is lost," I said, although I had never read a word by this ancestor of mine.

"Does he say where all the loves, all the dreams, all the desires go?"

"They're somewhere."

"Where? In the profundities?"

"In a celestial archive."

"Even heaven would be too small for such an archive. I will go. Oh, it's ringing again! Please don't answer! Don't answer!"

I picked up the receiver, but there was no one on the line. I hung up and Elizabeth said, "That's Leslie. That's one of his antics. What did the Revealer of Profundities say about madness? I must go! If I don't lose my mind, you'll hear from me. Maybe today, from the hotel."

Elizabeth de Sollar never called or wrote me again. She left behind and never claimed her ornate umbrella and her grandfather's book, *The Outcry of Mordechai,* which was supposed to be the only existing copy, so precious to her, and this has remained a mystery to me. But another mystery connected with her visit was soon unraveled. I met my neighbor the typesetter and told him about his cousin who promised to call the office and never showed herself again.

He smiled, shook his head, and said, "You knocked on the wrong door. I live on the fifth floor, not on the sixth."

Translated by Joseph Singer

Sabbath in Portugal

When one of the editors in my American publishing house heard that I would stop in Lisbon on my way to France, she said to me, "I will give you the telephone number of Miguel de Albeira. If you need something he will be glad to help you." He was said to have something to do with a publishing house or printing business. But it never occurred to me that I might need help. I had everything necessary for a trip: passport, traveler's checks, a hotel reservation. Nevertheless, the editor wrote the name and number in my address book, which was already crammed with many which I could no longer identify.

On a Tuesday evening in early June my ship docked in Lisbon and a taxi took me to the Apollo Hotel. The lobby was filled with compatriots from New York and Brooklyn. Their wives, with dyed hair and heavily made-up faces, smoked cigarettes, dealt cards, laughed and chattered all at once. Their daughters in miniskirts formed their own circles. The men were studying the financial pages of the *International Herald Tribune*. Yes, these are my people, I said to myself. If the Messiah is to come, he will have to come to them because there are no others.

A small elevator brought me up to my top-floor room, which was large, sparsely furnished, dimly lit, with a stone floor and an archaic bed with a high, ornately carved headboard. I opened the window and saw tiled roofs and a red moon. How strange—a rooster was crowing close by. I hadn't heard a rooster's crow in God knows how long. His cock-a-doodle-do reminded me that I was again in Europe, where the old and the new coexist. At the open window I was refreshed by a breeze whose aroma I had forgotten in my years in America. It had the freshness of the fields. It smelled of Warsaw, Bilgoray, and of something indefinable. The stillness seemed to emit a ringing sound, but it was hard to say whether it came from outside or from my own ears. I imagined that I heard the croaking of frogs and the chirping of crickets.

I wanted to read but there was not enough light for that. I bathed in a tub which was long and deep. I dried myself with a towel as large as a sheet. Even though the sign above the entrance claimed that the hotel was first-class, it did not provide its guests with soap. I extinguished the lamp and lay down on the bed. The pillow was high and overstuffed. Over the open window hovered the same stars which I had abandoned thirty-five years ago when I arrived in New York. I thought about the countless guests who had lived in this old hotel before me, the men and women who slept in this broad bed, many of them probably dead now. Who knows, perhaps their spirits or remnants of their being were lingering in this room. In the bathroom the pipes gurgled. The huge clothes closet cracked. A single mosquito buzzed and refused to stop until it could extract a droplet of my blood. I lay awake ready for the visitation of a dead lover.

About two o'clock I fell asleep and I was awakened in the morning by the crowing of the same rooster (I remembered his timbre) and shouting from a street market. Most probably they were selling vegetables, chickens, fruit. I recognized the cries: this was the way they had haggled and fought at Yanash's bazaar and in the Halles on Mirowski Place. I thought that I smelled horse dung, new potatoes, unripe apples.

I was supposed to remain in the hotel until Sunday, but I now learned that my travel agent in New York had reserved the room for two days only. Many Americans were arriving. The room clerk informed me that I would have to move before noon on Friday.

I asked him to find me another hotel room, but he insisted that as far as he knew all the hotels of Lisbon were filled. He had already tried to find rooms for other guests without success. The lobby was cluttered with luggage and buzzed with Americans, Italians, Germans, each group clamoring in its own language. I could not get a table in the restaurant. No one needed me or my traveler's checks. The clerks looked at me with cold indifference; for all they cared, I could sleep in the street.

Now I remembered that my editor had put a name in my notebook. I searched for it for a good half hour but could not find it. Had it flown off the page by magic, or had my editor not actually written it down after all? Then I discovered it in the margin of the very first page. I went up to my room, lifted the receiver, and waited long minutes until the telephone operator answered. I got a connection, but it was the wrong number. Someone scolded me in Portuguese and I apologized in English. After a few wrong connections I finally got the right number. A woman tried hard to spell out something to me in Portuguese. Then in broken English she gave me a number where I might be able to find Senhor Miguel de Albeira. Again I got the wrong party. I felt rage against a Europe which neither kept the old ways nor understood the new. My American patriotism was aroused and I swore I would spend every penny I made within the

United States of America. Meanwhile, I had to get in touch with Miguel de Albeira. I prayed to God for success; as always when I am in trouble, I vowed I would give money to my favorite charities.

I got the number. Senhor de Albeira spoke an English which I could barely understand. He told me that my editor had written him, and he agreed to come over right away. I was overcome with gratitude to Providence, to my editor, and to the Portuguese Miguel de Albeira, who in the middle of the day was setting aside his business to come to see me only because he had received a letter of recommendation. This was possible only in Europe. No American, including myself, would do anything like that.

I did not have to wait long. There was a knock at the door. The man who entered seemed to be in his early forties, of slight build, lean, dark, with a high forehead and sunken cheeks. For a while I saw nothing characteristic about him. He could have been a Spaniard, an Italian, a Frenchman, or a Greek. He had crooked teeth requiring dental care. He wore a gray everyday suit and a tie one can see in the shop windows of a dozen cities. He offered me his hand in the European way with a minimum of pressure. When he heard about my hotel room he said, "Don't worry. There are plenty of empty rooms in Lisbon. If it's worse than I think, I'll take you to my home. Let's just go and have lunch together."

"I invite you to lunch."

"You invite me? In Lisbon I'm the host. You will invite me in New York."

In front of the hotel we got into one of those small and shabby autos which provide transportation for most Europeans. On the back seat, between cardboard boxes and fading newspapers, there was a can of paint. I sat next to my host and Senhor Miguel de Albeira showed skill in maneuvering his little car in disorderly traffic aggravated by the absence of signal lights on the narrow and hilly streets, among houses which might have been built before the earthquake of 1755. Other cars refused to make way for us. Pedestrians were in no hurry to get

out of our path. Here and there a cat or a dog was having its siesta on the road. Senhor de Albeira seldom blew
the horn, never expressed anger. As he drove he asked
me about my trip and plans, when and why I became a
vegetarian, and if I ate eggs or milk. He pointed out
monuments, old buildings, and churches of the Alfama
quarter. We drove into an alley hardly wide enough for
a single car. Disheveled women and old men sat before
open doors; neglected children played in the gutters.
Pigeons pecked at a dirty bread crust.

Senhor de Albeira pulled into a courtyard. I followed
him into what seemed to be a third-rate lunchroom, but
we walked on into a large dining room with a skylight
and tables set with elegance. Shelves were lined with
straw-covered wine flasks in grotesque shapes. Senhor
de Albeira showed a concern for my diet which I felt
was exaggerated. Did I like cheese, mushrooms, cauliflower, tomatoes, and what kind of a salad, and what
wine, white or red? I kept insisting that he not make a
fuss about me or my food. In New York I sit on a high
stool and eat my lunch in ten minutes. But Senhor de
Albeira persisted. He had ordered a banquet, and when
I tried to pay I learned that it had already been taken
care of.

Friday at eleven in the morning Senhor de Albeira
came in his little car to my hotel, helped me load my
luggage, and took me to a smaller hotel whose windows
faced a park. My room had a balcony and cost me less
than half of the one I had at the Apollo. I lay awake a
good part of the night trying to figure out why a stranger
in Lisbon was showing so much kindness to a Yiddish
writer from New York.

2

No, Senhor de Albeira could gain nothing from my
visit to Lisbon. It is true that he was connected with a
publishing company, but my works in the Portuguese

language were to appear in Rio de Janeiro and not in
Lisbon. My editor had met him accidentally and had no
business with him. From asking questions and from
what I could understand of his conversation, I decided
he was far from rich. He had two jobs, publishing not
being sufficient to provide his livelihood. He lived in an
old house, had three children, and his wife taught in a
high school. He had read a book of mine in an English
translation but this could not be the reason for his
generosity. He remarked that he often dealt with authors
and did not have a particularly high opinion of them.

On Saturday I intended to take a guided tour by bus.
But Senhor de Albeira insisted on being my guide. He
came to my hotel in the morning and drove me around
for many hours. He showed me ruined castles, ancient
churches, parks with old trees. He recited the names of
exotic flowers and birds. He displayed erudition in discussing the history of Portugal and Spain. From time to
time he asked me questions: What is the difference between Yiddish and Hebrew? Why hadn't I settled in
Israel? He seemed to be intrigued by my Jewishness.
Did I belong to a synagogue? Was my vegetarianism
connected with religion? It was not easy to define my
Jewishness for Senhor de Albeira. The moment I answered one of his questions he came out with another.
To have conversation with him was difficult because I
hardly understood his English, despite his rich vocabulary. He had told me in advance I would have dinner at
his home and in that way become acquainted with his
family. When I wanted to stop to buy a present for
them, Senhor de Albeira made it difficult. In Sintra I
managed to buy two bronze roosters despite his protests
and with those gifts we arrived at his home at seven.

We climbed narrow winding steps in a building which
might once have been a palace but was crumbling now.
A heavy sculptured door opened to reveal an olive-
skinned woman dressed in black whose hair was swept
in a knot. She must have been a beauty in her youth, but
only traces of it remained. Her hands were worn from

housework, she was without makeup, and she smelled of garlic and onions. Her dress fell far below the knees, and had long sleeves and a high collar. When I offered the gift, she flushed as women did when I was still a boy. Her black eyes expressed an embarrassment and a modesty which I did not know still existed. She resembled my first love, Esther, whom I had never dared to kiss, and who had been shot by the Nazis in 1943.

Senhor de Albeira introduced me to the rest of his family, a girl of eighteen, a boy a year younger, and another boy of thirteen, all of them olive-skinned and with dark eyes. After a while a blond girl entered the living room. Senhor de Albeira told me that she was not his daughter. Each year his wife took into the house a poor girl from the provinces who came to Lisbon to study, as in my time they took in poor boys who came to study in the yeshiva. God in heaven, time had truly stopped in this place. The youngsters kept unbelievably quiet and showed the kind of respect to adults with which I myself had been brought up. Senhor de Albeira seemed to be the absolute ruler in this household. The children ran to execute his slightest command. The daughter brought me a copper basin so I could wash my hands.

The Albeiras had prepared a vegetarian meal for me. They had apparently gotten the idea that my vegetarianism had something to do with the dietary laws of my religion. On the table I saw a loaf of braided bread, a carafe of wine, and a goblet of the kind my father used for a blessing. The Sabbath I had desecrated for years had caught up with me in a Gentile home in Lisbon.

During the time we spent at the table, the children never spoke. They sat straight and silent, and though they understood no English they listened with reverence to our talk. I remembered my mother's admonition: Children should be silent when the elders speak. The girls helped Senhora de Albeira serve. Miguel de Albeira continued to query me about my Jewishness. In what way is the Ashkenazi different from the Sephardi? Are

Jews excommunicated if they return to Germany? Are
there Israeli Christians? I had the notion that Senhor de
Albeira was attempting to atone for the wrongs of the
Inquisition, the sins of Torquemada, and the zealots of
Portugal through me. He translated my replies into Por-
tuguese for his wife. I began to feel uncomfortable, as if
I were exploiting or cheating these gentle people by pre-
tending I was a pious Jew. Suddenly Senhor de Albeira
put his fist on the table and announced solemnly: "I am
Jew."

"Oh."

"Please wait moment."

He got up and left the room. After a while he returned
with a miniature cabinet made of dark wood, an antique
with two doors in relief. He opened them and removed a
book with wooden covers which he placed before me. It
was a Hebrew manuscript written in Rashi characters.
He said, "One of my ancestors wrote this. Six hundred
years ago."

The company became even quieter than before. I began to turn the pages carefully and, though they were
faded, I could still make out the text. After a while
Senhor de Albeira brought me a magnifying glass. It was
a book of *responsa*. I read about a deserted wife whose
husband was found in a river with his nose eaten away
and about a man who schemed to marry a servant girl
with a small coin, but before he managed to recite, "Be
thou sanctified to me according to the laws of Moses and
Israel," she threw the coin away defiantly. Each word,
each sentence in that old parchment was familiar to me
with all its implications. I've studied the same laws in
other volumes. Here and there I even noticed an error
made by the unknown scribe.

The family watched me and waited for my verdict as
if I had been reading hieroglyphs or clay tablets. Senhor
de Albeira asked, "Do you understand this?"

"I'm afraid I understand nothing else."

"Written by one of my forefathers. What does it say?"

I tried to explain it to him. He listened, nodded,

explained my words to his family. Long after its disappearance Senhor de Albeira was carrying on the tradition of Marranos, those Spanish and Portuguese Jews who had accepted Christianity nominally while practicing Judaism clandestinely. He had a personal association with the Jewish God. Now he had invited a Jew to his home who still knew the holy tongue and could decipher the writings of his ancestors. He had prepared a Sabbath repast for him. I knew that in former times to keep such a book in the house was highly dangerous; a single line in Hebrew found in the house of a man would have led him to the stake. Nevertheless, this token of the past had been preserved for centuries.

"We are not pure Jews. We come from generations of Catholics. But the Jewish spark remains in us. When I married I told my wife about my origins, and when the children grew up I revealed the genealogy to them. My daughter wants to visit Israel. I myself would like to settle there, but what would I do? I'm too old to enter—how do you call it—a kibbutz. But my daughter could marry a Jew."

"The Jews in Israel are not all religious."

"Why not? Well, I understand."

"Modern men are skeptical."

"Of course. But I wouldn't give away this book for anything. How is it that so many nations vanished and Jews still lived to return to their land? Doesn't it prove the Bible is true?"

"For me, yes."

"The War of the Six Days was a miracle, absolutely a miracle. My company printed a book about it and it sold well. We have a few Jews in Lisbon, refugees from Hitler and others. A delegate from Israel was here."

An old clock with a huge pendulum struck nine. The girls got up and quietly cleared the dishes from the table. One boy offered me his hand and then left. Senhor de Albeira replaced the old book in the cabinet. It was becoming dark, but they had not turned on the electric light. I realized that it was because of me. The man and his wife had probably read somewhere that one shouldn't kindle a light on the Sabbath until three stars appear. The room became full of shadows. The yearning of old Sabbath dusks overcame me and I was reminded of my mother's prayer, *"God of Abraham."*

We remained silent for a long while. In the half light the woman became younger and more like Esther. Her black eyes stared straight into mine, inquiringly and with perplexity, as if she, too, had recognized in me someone from the past. My God, it was Esther, the same figure, hair, forehead, nose, throat. I was seized by trembling. My old love awakened. Esther had returned! Only now did I grasp why I had decided to stop in Portugal, and why Senhor de Albeira had accepted me with such fervor. Through this couple Esther had arranged a rendezvous with me.

I sat there awe-stricken, with the humility of those on whom Providence bestows special favors. I could barely restrain myself from running to her, falling to my knees, covering her with kisses. It occurred to me that I had scarcely heard the sound of her voice. In that moment she spoke and it was Esther's voice. She asked me a question in Portuguese, but it had the tone and tremor of Esther's Yiddish. I thought I understood her words even before they were translated for me.

"Do you believe in the resurrection of the dead?"

I heard myself reply, "They never died."

Translated by the author and Herbert R. Lottman

The Yearning Heifer

In those days I could find great bargains in the small advertisements in my Yiddish press newspaper. I was in need of them because I earned less than twelve dollars a week—my royalties for a weekly column of "facts" gleaned from magazines. For example: a turtle can live five hundred years; a Harvard professor published a dictionary of the language spoken by chimpanzees; Columbus was not trying to discover a route to the Indies but to find the Ten Lost Tribes of Israel.

It was during the summer of 1938. I lived in a furnished room on the fourth floor of a walk-up building. My window faced a blank wall. This particular advertisement read: "A room on a farm with food, ten dollars weekly." After having broken with my girl friend Dosha "forever," I had no reason to spend the summer in New York. I packed a large valise with my meager belongings, many pencils as well as the books and magazines from which I extracted my information, and took the Catskill Mountain bus to Mountaindale. From there I was supposed to phone the farm. My valise would not close and I had bound it together with many shoelaces which I had purchased from blind beggars. I took the 8 A.M. bus and arrived in the village at three o'clock in the afternoon. In the local stationery store I tried to make the phone call but could not get connected and lost three dimes. The first time I got the wrong number; the second time the phone began to whistle and kept on whistling for minutes. The third time I may have gotten the right number but no one answered. The dimes did not come back. I decided to take a taxi.

When I showed the driver the address, he knitted his brows and shook his head. After a while he said, "I think I know where it is." And he immediately began to drive with angry speed over the narrow road full of ditches and holes. According to the advertisement, the farm was situated five miles from the village, but he kept on driving for half an hour and it became clear to me that he was lost. There was no one to ask. I had never imagined that New York State had such uninhabited areas. Here and there we passed a burned-down house, a silo which appeared unused for many years. A hotel with boarded windows emerged from nowhere and vanished like a phantom. The grass and brambles grew wild. Bevies of crows flew around croaking. The taxi meter ticked loudly and with feverish rapidity. Every few seconds I touched the trouser pocket where I kept my money. I wanted to tell the driver that I could not afford to drive around without an aim over heather and through deserts, but I knew that he would scold me. He might even drop me off in the middle of the wilderness. He kept on grumbling and every few minutes I heard him say, "Sonofabitch."

When, after long twisting and turning, the taxi did arrive at the correct address, I knew that I had made a bad mistake. There was no sign of a farm, just an old ruined wooden house. I paid four dollars and seventy cents for the trip and I tipped him thirty cents. The driver cast a murderous look at me. I barely had time to remove my valise before he started up and shot away with suicidal speed. No one came out to meet me. I heard a cow bellowing. As a rule, a cow bellows a few times and then becomes silent, but this cow bellowed without ceasing and in the tone of a creature which has fallen into an insufferable trap. I opened a door into a room with an iron stove, an unmade bed with dirty linen, a torn sofa. Against a peeling wall stood sacks of hay and feed. On the table were a few reddish eggs with hen's dirt still stuck to them. From another room came a dark-skinned girl with a long nose, a fleshy mouth, and angry black eyes beneath thick brows. A faint black fuzz grew on her upper lip. Her hair was cut short. If she hadn't been wearing a shabby skirt, I would have taken her for a man.

"What do you want?" she asked me in a harsh voice.

I showed her the advertisement. She gave a single glance at the newspaper and said, "My father is crazy. We don't have any rooms and board, and not for this price either."

"What is the price?"

"We don't need any boarders. There is no one to cook for them."

"Why does the cow keep on screaming?" I asked.

The girl appraised me from head to foot. "That is none of your business."

A woman entered who could have been fifty-five, sixty, or sixty-five years old. She was small, broad, one shoulder higher than the other, with a huge bosom which reached to her belly. She wore tattered men's slippers, her head was wrapped in a kerchief. Below her uneven skirt I could see legs with varicose veins. Even though it was a hot summer day she had a torn sweater on. Her slanted eyes were those of a Tartar. She gazed at me with sly satisfaction as if my coming there was the result of a practical joke. "From the paper, huh, aren't you?"

"Yes."

"Tell my husband to make a fool of himself instead of others. We don't need boarders. We need them like a hole in the head."

"I told him the same thing," the girl added.

"I am sorry but I got here with a taxi and it has gone back to the village. Perhaps I could stay for one night?"

"One night, huh? We have for you neither a bed nor linen. Nothing," the woman said. "If you like, I will call you another taxi. My husband is not in his right mind and he does everything for spite. He dragged us out here. He wanted to be a farmer. There is no store or hotel here for miles and I don't have the strength to cook for you. We ourselves eat out of tin cans."

The cow did not stop bellowing, and although the girl had just given me a nasty answer, I could not restrain myself and I asked, "What's the matter with the cow?"

The woman winked at the girl. "She needs a bull."

At that moment the farmer came in, as small and broad-boned as his wife, in patched overalls, a jacket which reminded me of Poland, and a cap pushed back on his head. His sunburned cheeks sprouted white stubble. His nose was veined. He had a loose double chin. He brought in with him the smells of cow dung, fresh milk from the udder, and newly dug earth. In one hand he held a spade and, in the other, a stick. His eyes under bushy brows were yellow. When he saw me he asked, "From the paper, huh?"

"Yes."

"Why didn't you call? I would have come with my horse and buggy to meet you."

"Sam, don't make a fool of the young man," his wife interrupted. "There's no linen for him, no one to cook for him, and what are ten dollars a week? It would cost us more."

"This leave to me," the farmer answered. "I have advertised, not you, and I am responsible. Young man"—he raised his voice—"I am the boss, not they. It's my house, my ground. Everything you see here belongs to me. You should have written a card first or phoned, but since you are here, you are a welcome guest."

"I am sorry, but your wife and your daughter—"

The farmer didn't let me finish. "What they say is not worth more than the dirt under my nails [he showed me a hand with muddy fingers]. I will clean up your room. I will make your bed, cook your food, and provide you with everything. If you receive mail I will bring it to you from the village. I go there every second or third day."

"Meanwhile, perhaps I can sleep here tonight? I'm tired from the trip and—"

"Feel at home. They have nothing to say." The farmer pointed at his family. I had already realized that I had fallen into a quarrelsome house and I did not intend to be the victim. The farmer continued, "Come, I will show you your room."

"Sam, the young man won't stay here," his wife said.

"He will stay here, eat here, and be satisfied," the farmer replied, "and if you don't like it, go back to Orchard Street together with your daughter. Parasites, pigs, *paskudas!*"

The farmer put the spade and the stick into a corner, grabbed my valise, and went outside. My room had a separate entrance with its own flight of stairs. I saw a huge field overgrown with weeds. Near the house was a well and an outhouse like in a Polish shtetl. A bedraggled horse was nibbling on some grass. Farther away there was a stable, and from it came the plaintive cry of the animal, which had not stopped in all this time. I said to the farmer, "If your cow is in heat, why doesn't she get what she needs?"

"Who told you that she's in heat? It is a heifer and I just bought her. She was taken from a stable where there were thirty other cows and she misses them. She most probably has a mother or a sister there."

"I've never seen an animal that yearns so much for her kin," I said.

"There are all kinds of animals, but she will quiet down. She's not going to yell forever."

2

The steps leading into my room squeaked. One held on to a thick rope instead of a banister. The room smelled of rotting wood and bedbug spray. A stained,

lumpy mattress with the filling sticking out of the holes
was on the bed. It wasn't especially hot outside but inside the room the heat immediately began to hammer at
my head and I became wet with perspiration. Well, one
night here will not kill me, I comforted myself. The
farmer set my valise down and went to bring linen. He
brought a pillow in a torn pillowcase, a coarse sheet with
rusty spots, and a cotton-filled blanket without a cover.
He said to me, "It's warm now, but the moment the sun
sets, it will be deliciously cool. Later on you will have to
cover yourself."

"It will be all right."

"Are you from New York?" he asked me.

"Yes, New York."

"I can tell from your accent that you were born in
Poland. What part do you come from?"

I mentioned the name of my village and Sam told me
he came from a neighboring village. He said, "I'm not
really a farmer. This is our second summer here in the
country. Since I came from Poland I was a presser in
New York. I pulled and pushed the heavy iron so long
that I got a rupture. I always longed for fresh air and,
how do you call it—Mother Earth—fresh vegetables, a
fresh egg, green grass. I began to look for something in
the newspapers and here I found a wild bargain. I
bought it from the same man who sold me the heifer. He
lives about three miles from here. A fine man, even
though he's a Gentile. His name is Parker, John Parker.
He gave me a mortgage and made everything easy for
me, but the house is old and the earth is full of rocks. He
did not, God forbid, fool me. He told me everything
beforehand. To clean up the stones would take twenty
years. And I'm not a young man any more. I'm already
over seventy."

"You don't look it," I complimented him.

"It's the good air, the work. I worked hard in New
York, but only here I started to work for real. There we
have a union, it should live long, and it did not allow the
bosses to make us slaves like the Jews in Egypt. When I
arrived in America, the sweatshops were still in exis-

tence, but later on things got easier. I worked my eight hours and took the subway home. Here I toil eighteen hours a day and, believe me, if I did not get the pension from the union I could not make ends meet. But it's all right. What do we need here? We have our own tomatoes, radishes, cucumbers. We have a cow, a horse, a few chickens. The air itself makes you healthy. But how is it written in Rashi? Jacob wanted to enjoy peace but the misfortune with Joseph would not allow it. Yes, I studied once; until I was seventeen I sat in the study house and learned. Why do I tell you this? My wife, Bessie, hates the country. She misses the bargains on Orchard Street and her cronies with whom she could babble and play cards. She's waging war on me. And what a war! She went on strike. She doesn't cook, she doesn't bake, she doesn't clean the house. She refuses to budge and I do everything—milk the cow, dig in the garden, clean the outhouse. I should not tell you, but she refuses to be a wife. She wants me to move back to New York. But what will I do in New York? We have given up the rent-controlled apartment and gotten rid of the furniture. Here we have something like a home—"

"How about your daughter?"

"My Sylvia takes after her mother. She's already over thirty and she should have gotten married, but she never wanted to become anything. We tried to send her to college and she refused to study. She took all kinds of jobs but she never stuck with them. She has quite a good head, but no *sitzfleisch*. She tires of everything. She went out with all kinds of men and it always ended in nothing. The moment she meets one, she immediately begins to find fault with him. One is this way, the other one is that way. For the past eight months she's been with us on the farm, and if you think she helps me much, you are mistaken. She plays cards with her mother. That's all she does. You will not believe me, but my wife still has not unpacked her things. She has, God only knows, how many dresses and skirts, and everything is packed away like after a fire. My daughter, too, has a lot of rags but hers are also in her trunk. All this is to spite me. So I decided, Let some people move in here and I will have someone to talk to. We have two other rooms to rent. I'm not trying to get rich by offering a room and three meals a day for ten dollars weekly. I won't become a Rockefeller. What is your business? Are you a teacher or something?"

After some hesitation I decided to tell him the truth, that I write for a Yiddish newspaper as a free-lancer. The man's eyes immediately lit up.

"What is your name? What do you write there?"

"A Bundle of Facts."

The farmer spread out his arms and stamped his feet. "You are the writer of *A Bundle of Facts?*"

"It's me."

"My God, I read you every week! I go to the village Friday especially to get the paper, and you won't believe me, but I read *A Bundle of Facts* before I even read the news. The news is all bad. Hitler this, Hitler that. He should burn like a fire, the bum, the no-good. What does he want from the Jews? Is it their fault that Germany lost the war? From just reading about it one could get a heart attack. But your facts are knowledge, science. Is it true that a fly has thousands of eyes?"

"Yes, it's true."

"How can it be? Why does a fly need so many eyes?"

"It seems that to nature everything comes easy."

"If you want to see the beauty of nature, stay here. Wait a minute. I must go and tell my wife who we have here."

"What for? I'm not going to stay here anyhow."

"What are you saying? Why not? They are bitter women, but when they hear who you are, they will be overjoyed. My wife reads you too. She tears the paper out of my hand because she wants to read *A Bundle of Facts* first. My daughter also knows Yiddish. She spoke Yiddish before she knew a word of English. With us she speaks mostly Yiddish because—"

The farmer dashed out. His heavy shoes pounded on

the steps. The heifer kept howling. There was frenzy in
her voice, an almost-human rebellion. I sat down on the
mattress and dropped my head. Lately I had been com-
mitting one folly after another. I had quarreled with
Dosha over a foolishness. I had already spent money to
get here and tomorrow I would have to take a taxi and a
bus to get back to New York. I had begun to write a
novel but I got bogged down and I couldn't even decipher my own scribbling. As I sat here, the heat roasted
my body. If only there were a shade to cover the window! The heifer's lamenting drove me mad. I heard in it
the despair of everything that lives. All of creation was
protesting through her. A wild idea ran through my
mind: Perhaps during the night I should go out and kill
the heifer and then myself. A murder followed by a
suicide like this would be something new in the history
of humanity.

I heard heavy steps on the staircase. The farmer had
brought his wife over. Then began the apologies and the
strange exaggerations of simple people when they encounter their beloved writer. Bessie exclaimed, "Sam, I
must kiss him."

And before I managed to say a word, the woman
caught my face in her rough hands, which smelled of
onion, garlic, and sweat.

The farmer was saying good-naturedly, "A stranger
she kisses and me she lets fast."

"You are crazy and he's a scientist, greater than a
professor."

It took but a minute and the daughter came up. She
stood in the open door and looked on half mockingly at
the way her parents fussed over me. After a while she
said, "If I have insulted you, excuse me. My father
brought us here to the wasteland. We have no car and
his horse is half dead. Suddenly a man with a valise
drops from the sky and wants to know why the heifer is
yelling. Really funny."

Sam clasped his hands together with the look of a man
about to announce something which will astound every-

one. His eyes filled with laughter. "If you have so much pity on animals, I am going to give back the heifer. We can do without her. Let her go back to her mother, for whom she pines."

Bessie tilted her head to one side. "John Parker won't give you back the money."

"If he won't return the whole amount, he will return ten dollars less. It's a healthy heifer."

"I will make up the difference," I said, astonished at my own words.

"What? We will not go to court," the farmer said. "I want this man in my house all summer. He won't have to pay me. For me it will be an honor and a joy."

"Really, the man is crazy. We needed the heifer like a hole in the head."

I could see that husband and wife were making peace because of me.

"If you really want to do it, why wait?" I asked. "The animal may die from yearning and then—"

"He's right," the farmer called. "I'm going to take the heifer back right now. This very minute."

Everyone became silent. As if the heifer knew that her fate was being decided this minute, she let out a howl which made me shudder. This wasn't a yearning heifer but a dybbuk.

3

The moment Sam entered the stable the heifer became quiet. It was a black heifer with large ears and huge black eyes that expressed a wisdom which only animals possess. There was no sign that she had just gone through so many hours of agony. Sam tied a rope around her neck and she followed him willingly. I followed behind with Bessie near me. The daughter stood in front of the house and said, "Really, I wouldn't believe it if I hadn't seen it with my own eyes."

We walked along and the heifer did not utter a sound.

She seemed to know the way back because she tried to run and Sam had to restrain her. Meanwhile, husband and wife argued before me the way couples used to argue when they came to my father's court for a Din Torah. Bessie was saying, "The ruin stood empty for years and nobody even looked at it. I don't think someone would have taken it for nothing. Suddenly my husband appears and gets the bargain. How does the saying go? 'When a fool comes to the market, the merchants are happy.'"

"What did you have on Orchard Street? The air stank. As soon as daylight began, the crash and noise started. Our apartment was broken into. Here you don't have to lock the door. We can leave for days and weeks and no one will steal anything."

"What thief would come to such a desert?" Bessie asked. "And what could he take? American thieves are choosy. They want either money or diamonds."

"Believe me, Bessie, here you will live twenty years longer."

"Who wants to live so long? When a day is over, I thank God."

After about an hour and a half I saw John Parker's farm—the house, the granary. The heifer again tried to run and Sam had to hold her back with all his strength. John Parker was cutting grass with a crooked scythe. He was tall, blond, lean, Anglo-Saxon. He raised his eyes, amazed, but with the quiet of a person who is not easily astounded. I even imagined I saw him smiling. We had approached the pasture where the other cows were grazing and the heifer became wild and tore herself out of Sam's hands. She began to run and jump with the rope still around her neck, and a few cows slowly raised their heads and looked at her, while the others continued to rip the grass as if nothing had happened. In less than a minute the heifer, too, began to graze. I had expected, after this terrible longing, a dramatic encounter between the heifer and her mother: much nuzzling, fondling, or whatever cows do to show affection to a daughter who was lost. But it seemed that cattle didn't greet one another that way. Sam began to explain to John Parker what had happened and Bessie too chimed in. Sam was saying, "This young man is a writer. I read his articles every week and he is going to be our guest. Like all writers, he has a soft heart. He could not stand the heifer's suffering. My wife and I cherish every line he writes. When he said that the heifer might disturb his thinking, I made up my mind, come what may. So I brought the heifer back. I am ready to lose as much as you will say—"

"You will lose nothing, it's a good heifer," John Parker said. "What do you write?" he asked me.

"Oh, facts in a Yiddish newspaper. I am trying to write a novel too," I boasted.

He remarked, "Once I was a member of a book club, but they sent me too many books and I had no time to read. A farm keeps you busy, but I still get *The Saturday Evening Post*. I have piles of them."

"I know. Benjamin Franklin was one of the founders." I tried to show erudition about American literature.

"Come into the house. We'll have a drink."

The farmer's family came out. His wife, a darkish woman with short black hair, looked Italian to me. She had a bumpy nose and sharp black eyes. She was dressed city-fashion. The boy was blond like his father, the girl Mediterranean-looking like her mother. Another man appeared. He seemed to be a hired hand. Two dogs dashed out of somewhere and, after barking for a few seconds, began to wag their tails and to rub up against my legs. Sam and Bessie again tried to explain the reason for their visit, and the farmer's wife scrutinized me half wondering and half with irony. She asked us in, and soon a bottle of whiskey was opened and we clinked glasses. Mrs. Parker was saying, "When I came here from New York I missed the city so much that I almost died, but I'm not a heifer and nobody cared about my feelings. I was so lonesome that I tried to write, even though I'm not a writer. I still have a few composition books lying around and I myself don't remember what I put down in them."

The woman looked at me hesitatingly and shyly. I

knew exactly what she wanted and I asked, "May I look at them?"

"What for? I have no literary talent. It is kind of a diary. Notes about my experiences."

"If you have no objections, I would like to read them, not here, but back at Sam's farm."

The woman's eyes brightened. "Why should I object? But please don't laugh at me when you read the out-pourings of my emotions."

She went to look for her manuscript and John Parker opened a chest drawer and counted out the money for the heifer. The men haggled. Sam offered to take a few dollars less than what he had paid. John Parker wouldn't hear of it. I again proposed to make good the difference, but both men looked at me reproachfully and told me to mind my own business. After a while Mrs. Parker brought me a bundle of composition books in an old manila envelope that smelled of moth balls. We said goodbye and I took their phone number. When we got back, the sun had already set and the stars shone in the sky. It was a long time since I had seen such a starry sky. It hovered low, frightening and yet solemnly festive. It reminded me of Rosh Hashanah. I went up to my room. I could not believe it but Sylvia had changed my linen: a whiter sheet, a spotless blanket, and a cleaner pillow-case. She had even hung up a small picture with a wind-mill.

That evening I ate supper with the family. Bessie and Sylvia asked me many questions and I told them about Dosha and our recent quarrel. Both wanted to know the reason for the quarrel, and when I told them they both laughed.

"Because of foolishness like this, a love should not be broken," Bessie said.

"I'm afraid it's too late."

"Call her this very moment," Bessie commanded.

I gave Sylvia the number. She turned the crank on the wall phone. Then she screamed into the phone as if the woman at the phone company were deaf. Perhaps she was. After a while Sylvia said, "Your Dosha is on the telephone," and she winked.

I told Dosha what I had done and the story about the heifer. She said, "I am the heifer."

"What do you mean?"

"I called you all the time."

"Dosha, you can come up here. There is another room in the house. These are kind people and I already feel at home here."

"Huh? Give me the address and phone number. Perhaps this coming week."

About ten o'clock Sam and Bessie went to sleep. They bid me good night with the gay anticipation of a young couple. Sylvia proposed that we go for a walk.

There was no moon, but the summer night was bright. Fireflies lit up in the thickets. Frogs croaked, crickets chirped. The night rained meteors. I could make out the whitish luminous band which was the Milky Way. The sky, like the earth, could not rest. It yearned with a cosmic yearning for something which would take myriads of light-years to achieve. Even though Sylvia had just helped me make peace with Dosha, she took my hand. The night light made her face feminine and her black eyes emitted golden sparks. We stopped in the middle of the dirt road and kissed with fervor, as if we had been waiting for each other God knows how long. Her wide mouth bit into mine like the muzzle of a beast. The heat from her body baked my skin, not unlike the glowing roof a few hours earlier. I heard a blaring sound, mysterious and other-worldly, as though a heavenly heifer in a faraway constellation had awakened and begun a wailing not to be stilled until all life in the universe shall be redeemed.

Translated by the author and Ruth Schachner Finkel

The Witch

"In a culture of pure egotism, how can you call anyone an egotist?" Mark Meitels half thought, half mumbled. But Lena's self-love virtually bedazzled one. Even her own mother spoke of it. All of Mark's friends maintained that Lena was capable of loving only herself. A doctor had once labeled her a narcissist.

Yes, he, Mark Meitels, had made a fatal mistake. But at least he didn't have to fear that Lena would fall in love with someone else.

Now Lena had just finished breakfast. The maid, Stasia, had made up the bedroom, and Lena lay down on the sofa in the living room—a small woman with black hair worn in a high pompadour, black eyes, and high cheekbones. At thirty-seven she still looked like a girl, exactly as she had when he first met her.

Lena refused to have children. She told Mark on frequent occasions that she hadn't the slightest urge to get pregnant and go into labor just so that another brat could wander in the world. It never occurred to her to take a job and help Mark earn a living. Even in bed, she constantly worried him not to disarrange her hairdo, not to wrinkle or tear her silk nightgown. He kissed her tiny mouth but she rarely kissed back.

Now, in her flowered kimono and slippers with pompons, she looked Japanese. Everything about her had remained petite, smooth, and delicate. She reminded Mark of the china dolls sometimes seen in antique-store windows.

"Lena, I'm going."

"Eh? Well, all right."

He bent down to kiss her forehead. Although it was still early in the day, her lips were already heavily rouged. Her fingernails were long, pointed, freshly manicured. She had eaten her breakfast exactly as the doctor had prescribed it for her—an egg, a single slice of bread, and a cup of black coffee. Lena weighed herself several times daily, and if she had gained a quarter of a pound, she promptly took measures to lose it again. She passed the day reading fashion magazines, visiting dressmakers, milliners, and Stanislaw the hairdresser. Occasionally she strolled down Marshalkowska Street window-shopping. She was always on the lookout for bargains and coveted all kinds of trinkets—Mark never understood why—an ivory-inlaid music box that played "Good Morning!", countless strings of imitation pearls in all shades and colors, exotic earrings, bracelets, and chains that could be worn only to a masquerade.

Mark Meitels had long faced the realization that Lena was still a child but without any childish joy—a pampered, angry little girl, ready to pout if something interfered with her whims. "An error, a fatal error," Mark Meitels grunted to himself for the hundredth time. But to divorce such a creature would be impossible. She would get sick and her mother would raise hell. One way or another, he had grown accustomed to her caprices. The apartment was always spotless. Stasia feared Lena and gave in to all her wishes. The floor always

gleamed and every stick of furniture was dusted and
polished daily. Without lifting a finger herself, Lena ran
an exacting household. Fortunately, Stasia was a healthy
wench and good-natured besides. She labored from six-
thirty in the morning until late into the night and took
off only a few hours every other Sunday to go to church
or possibly to meet some boy friend.

Mark Meitels was a tall man in his early forties, a
teacher of mathematics and physics at a private girls'
Gymnasium. He couldn't have existed if he didn't hold
down a second job—writing textbooks that were used in
the Polish schools and received laudatory reviews in peda-
gogic journals. Mark Meitels had been an officer in
Pilsudski's Legion and had won a medal for heroism in
the 1920 Polish-Bolshevik war. He was one of those rare
individuals who excel at whatever they undertake. He
knew languages, played the piano, rode horseback, and
had the reputation of being one of the best teachers in
Warsaw. His pupils were infatuated with him, but he
avoided all indiscretions. Something of the military
lingered in his erect carriage and his entire conduct. He
spoke sparingly and to the point. He was courteous toward
the school authorities and the students. His chief virtue lay
in the fact that he could explain an algebraic formula or
geometric theorem to girls who had no aptitude for
mathematics. He received frequent offers from other
Gymnasium principals but he stayed at the school where
he had begun his teaching career.

Now, before leaving the house, Mark Meitels checked
himself in the hall mirror. The overcoat hung smoothly
on his erect figure, the tie was straight, the derby fit
perfectly. Mark Meitels had a long face and nose, full
lips, a narrow chin, and big black eyes beneath dark
brows. His gaze expressed a sense of discipline and the
gravity of one who knows exactly how to behave, and
who possessed sufficient inner strength to remain consistent. His friends, male and female, all of whom were in
the teaching profession, spoke of him with admiration.
Mark Meitels practiced what he preached, kept his temper,
avoided all intrigue and lander. After a drink at a

party he might become somewhat ironical, but even then
he behaved with dignity.

But his failure in marriage was indisputable. True, his
mother-in-law was rich and in due course he would in-
herit her wealth, but for now she was in vigorous health,
and stingy besides. The situation in Poland in the early
1930's was such that you couldn't plan too far ahead.

Mark Meitels could easily have had affairs on the side,
but as far as anyone could tell, he remained faithful to his
wife. It was apparent to everyone that Lena could offer
him neither spiritual nor physical satisfaction. In a
moment of weakness he had even confided this to an
intimate, and the "secret" soon spread. To dissipate his
energies, Mark Meitels took long walks. In the summers
he swam in the Vistula, and before retiring for the night
he lifted weights and gave himself cold rubs. This led to
quarrels with Lena, who complained that he wet the
bathroom floor and messed up the study.

Actually, Lena wasn't merely his direct opposite but a
deadly opponent. If he praised a book, she immediately
found fault with it. If a play pleased him, she forced him
to leave the theater before the second act. Lena hated
mathematics, physics, and everything connected with
science. She read the popular novels of Dekobra and
Marguerite. She liked sentimental dramas and tragedies.
In her thin little voice she sang the hits from the musical
Qui pro Quo and other revues. She often ordered Stasia
to prepare dishes that Mark couldn't stand—bouillons to be
sipped out of tiny cups, cakes soggy with cream, too-sweet
cocoa. Mark was always hungry after dinner. On his long
evening walks across the Praga Bridge as far as Pel-
cowizna or past Mokotów on the way to Wilanów, he
would buy a loaf of pumpernickel or a bag of apples.

Lena's self-love was especially evident in the bedroom.
She forbade him to come near her for days preceding and
following her period. She didn't like conversation in bed
and clamped his mouth shut when he said something she
considered unaesthetic. Before going to sleep she spent an
hour in front of her mirror conducting various experi-
ments with her hair and anointing, smearing, and per-

fuming herself. She often said that sexual intercourse was dirty and brutal. She urged him to get it over with quickly, and complained that he was hurting her. If it was true that marriages are made in heaven, Mark often mused, then someone had either erred grievously or played a foul joke on them

2

Mark Meitels always managed to leave the house on time so that he could walk to the Gymnasium. He didn't like the crowded streetcars and wanted to stretch his legs a bit before commencing the lessons.

How odd! He had been born and raised in Warsaw but the city often appeared alien to him. He had little contact with Poles. Although Jews had lived in Poland for eight hundred years, a chasm existed between the two peoples that time couldn't eradicate. However, the Jews were as remote to Mark as the Poles—not only the pious ones with their long gaberdines and small hats, but the modern ones as well. Mark Meitels's father, an assimilated Jew, an architect, a liberal and an atheist, hadn't given his only son any religious training whatsoever. From childhood on, Mark had heard all kinds of mocking remarks about the Hasidim and their rabbis, their filth and fanaticism, but he had never really found out what it was they espoused. After the First World War Jewish nationalism had flourished. The Balfour declaration had been issued and many Chalutzim had sailed off to Palestine. At the Gymnasium where he taught, the curriculum had been enlarged to include more Hebrew studies, but he had never been drawn either to religion or to Palestine, a half-desolate wasteland in Asia Minor. He felt an even stronger aversion against the Jewish Communists and their demonstrations.

His father wouldn't have had any objections had his son converted, but Mark had no interest in Jesus. The assimilated Jews of Warsaw called themselves Poles of

Mosaic Faith, but Mark had no faith in anything
except scientifically established facts.

Many of his former comrades in the Legion had been
issued high military ranks and given important posts in the
ministry following Pilsudski's uprising in 1926. Mark
Meitels had grown estranged from them and didn't attend
their reunions. There was too much brandishing of swords
there, and many of them had become anti-Semites. The
newspaper, even the semiofficial *Gazeta Polska,* needled
the Jewish minority. In Germany the Nazi Party kept
gaining new adherents. In Soviet Russia they arrested
Trotskyites and sent millions of peasants, so-called kulaks,
to Siberia.

Striding along Marshalkowska Street, Mark Meitels felt
as if he were a stranger. But where would he feel at home?

Passing Grzybow Place was a source of fresh irritation
each day. In the midst of a European capital the Jews
had established a ghetto. Women in wigs and bonnets
sold rotten fruit, chick-peas with beans, and potato cakes
covered with rags. They hawked their wares in a gibberish
and a whining chant. Men with black or red beards,
stooped shoulders, and heavy boots engaged in surrepti-
tious business. Not infrequently funerals passed by—a
black, shiny hearse, a horse draped in black with holes
cut out for the eyes, the mourners lamenting in shrill
voices. Even in Baghdad you couldn't see such sights,
Mark Meitels thought.

In the midst of the whole turmoil, a running and a
chasing ensued. Ragged youths with caps pulled down
over their eyes had scrounged up a red flag somewhere
and were shouting, "Long live the Soviet Union! Down
with Fascism! All power to the workers and peasants!
. . ." They were pursued by policemen waving guns and
rubber truncheons.

Even the Gymnasium wasn't the same as before. The
old teachers had retired or been dismissed. Others had
died. The new teachers were mostly Jewish nationalists.
Teaching most of the girls logarithms and trigonometry
served no purpose: their minds weren't on mathematics,

nor would they ever find much use for it. They all
yearned for one thing—to get the diploma so that they
could marry well and have children. Most of them had
voluptuously ripened and their limbs showed an un-
abashed urge to mate and multiply.

One girl in particular made Mark Meitels feel that all
his effort was for naught. She called herself Bella, but her
birth certificate read Beile Tzypa Zylberstein. Mark
taught from the fifth grade up, and he had the chance to
become thoroughly acquainted with his pupils. Bella came
from a poor home. Her father was a clerk in some store on
Gnoyna Street that sold oil and green soap. He had a
half dozen other children at home. The Gymnasium had
reduced her tuition to a minimum, but the father couldn't
even pay those few zlotys. If she had at least been
capable! But Bella received the worst marks. She had
gone on to the eighth grade, but Mark Meitels knew that
she still didn't grasp the most rudimentary rules of
arithmetic. Actually, she failed in every subject. She had
spent two years each in the sixth and seventh grades and
it was obvious to everyone that she would never graduate.

The principal had called in Bella's parents and had
advised that they enroll her in a vocational school, but
they were determined that their oldest daughter should
get a diploma, enter the university, and become a doctor
or, at the very least, a dentist.

On top of all this, Bella was ugly—the homeliest girl
in the school. Her head was too big for her body, her
low brow seemed sunken, her eyes were black and bulging
—calf's eyes—her nose curved; her bosom was large,
her hips wide, and her legs bowed. Her mother took care
that the girl should be decently dressed but whatever
Bella wore looked ridiculous. The other girls called her
the Freak.

Mark Meitels realized that it was his duty to explain
the principles of mathematics to Bella again and again.
He began with axioms: Ten groschen added to ten
groschen made twenty groschen. If equal numbers were
added to each unit of ten groschen, the results would
remain equal. If equal numbers were subtracted, they

would still remain equal . . . But even though by definition axioms are self-evident truths, Bella still couldn't grasp them. She opened her thick lips, exposing a mouthful of uneven teeth, and smiled in guilty fear, with the submissiveness of an animal trying to grasp human concepts.

But in one area at least Bella was overendowed—that of emotions. She sat on her bench and didn't turn her big black eyes away from Mark. They exuded a love and a reverence like that seen occasionally in a dog's eyes. She followed Meitels with her gaze and her lips repeated every word he uttered. When Mark called her name, she paled and trembled. On the rare occasions he called her to the blackboard, she approached with quaking step and Mark was afraid that she would faint. The piece of chalk fell from her fingers, and the class jeered.

One time Mark Meitels asked her to stay after the others had gone. He tried to give her individual instruction. He sat her down on the bench and began from the beginning. How had primitive man discovered numbers? By ticking off the fingers of his hands . . . Mark took Bella's wrist. Her hand was damp and it shook. Her bosom heaved. She stared at him in fear and in a rapture that astounded him. What can it be she sees in me? he wondered.

He put the tip of his index finger to her pulse. It beat as quickly and strong as in a high fever. Mark asked, "What is it, Bella, are you ill?"

She tore her hand from his and broke out in childish weeping. Within a second her face grew contorted and wet like that of a small girl who has just suffered an unbearable blow.

3

Lena frequently doctored herself. She was forever taking medicines. When she said that she wasn't feeling well, Mark didn't take it too seriously, but soon he noticed that her face was assuming a yellow tinge. It soon turned out that she suffered from a grave illness, cancer of the spleen. The doctors didn't tell Lena this, but apparently she gathered that her chances were slim. A team of consulting specialists decided that she should enter the hospital—she couldn't get the help she needed at home—but Lena refused to consider even a private clinic. Her mother came and tried to persuade her to take the doctors' advice, but Lena stuck to her decision and the mother hired a private nurse to care for her at home.

Three women—her mother, Stasia, and the nurse— watched over Lena. A doctor came each day, but she didn't improve. The doctor told Mark the truth—the cancer had spread to the other organs and there was no chance whatsoever.

Mark looked on with amazement as the once-spoiled Lena, who made a fuss when a fingernail broke or a filling fell out of her tooth, now accepted her fate with silence and resignation. She lay in bed in a silk robe, all powdered, rouged, perfumed, coiffed, and manicured, and read the same fashion magazines as before. Her mother brought her the latest Polish and French novels and illustrated magazines both Polish and foreign.

Lena had few girl friends, two or three former school-mates from the Gymnasium, one of them a cousin, and she wrote a will designating who would get what after her death—the fur coat, the dresses, the jewelry, and the rest of the trinkets.

Only now did Mark Meitels realize that Lena's egotism was actually the instinct of one with insufficient powers who didn't want to dissipate them too soon. One night when they were alone he knelt at her bedside and apologized for his sharp words and reproaches, for the misunderstandings that had evolved in their relationship. Lena stroked his hair (which was already thinning in the middle, the beginning of a bald spot) and said, "You were good to me. It's not your fault. Next time find yourself someone healthier."

"No, Lena, I don't want anyone else."

"Why not? You always yearned for a child, but I didn't want to leave any orphans."

"Does that mean she knew she wouldn't live long?" Mark asked himself later. "Did she live with the knowledge that she would die young?" But how was this possible? Had the doctors told her? Was there something in a person that foresaw the future?

It was all a puzzle—his falling in love with Lena, the alienation that had evolved later between them, the years that had passed without any real intimacy, and the present finale. He might have fallen in love with Lena anew, but she was apparently no longer receptive to sentiment. She grew more rigid, more taciturn, completely absorbed in herself. She demanded he sleep on the sofa in the living room. She grew more preoccupied with the illustrated magazines, the shallow stories about royal courts, American millionaires, and Hollywood film stars. Did this really interest her or was it all merely to forget? Mark Meitels realized that the estrangement between him and Lena would never be eased. It became ever more obvious to him that she wished to avoid him. She never addressed him first, and when he spoke to her, she replied curtly and in such a way that it left nothing more to be said. She didn't even look up from the magazine. She probably felt some resentment against him, but was determined to take it with her to the grave.

The doctor told Mark frankly that all that could be done for her was to keep her drugged to ease her pain until she died.

After a while Lena gave up reading almost entirely. When Mark opened the door to the bedroom he often found her asleep. Other times she lay there with her eyes open, deep in thoughts to which no healthy person could be privy. Gradually she grew indifferent to her appearance, stopped using cosmetics, and no longer spoke on the telephone to her mother.

Lena now seemed to have but one wish—to be left alone. But the visitors kept coming. The girl friends she had named in her will brought flowers, all kinds of delicacies that Lena wouldn't taste, and magazines that no longer interested her. The doctor mouthed the same banalities calculated to encourage the patient: "She drank the soup? Good, fine. She took her pill? Wonderful!" He ordered the window to be opened to let in fresh air. When the nurse announced that she had bathed the patient with cologne, he exclaimed, "Excellent!" If Mark Meitels was home when the doctor came, he would advise him as he was leaving, "Don't neglect your own health. You don't look too well yourself." He told Mark to take vitamins, which were then still something of a novelty in Poland.

During the whole crisis Mark had to continue teaching at the Gymnasium and to finish a textbook on geometry that was scheduled to go to press at a specific date.

The winter passed and spring had come. The girls in the eighth grade now behaved as if the school were some kind of joke. They stopped treating Mark like the teacher, didn't rise when he entered the classroom, and addressed him smilingly, insinuatingly, ironically. They dressed in a provocative way that was forbidden to students. Although they were preparing for their final examinations and spent nights poring over textbooks, they looked on the subjects as if they were merely husks to be cracked and discarded. The core of it all was to find the proper husband, to marry, and to bear children. Their mothers waited impatiently for the satisfaction grandchildren would bring. The fathers yearned to be free of the burden of raising daughters. It seemed to Mark that he had been deceiving these girls all the while and that they had finally uncovered his deception—shapely legs and a chiseled nose were more important than all the Euclidian theorems. The only worth of a diploma was that it might help secure a more favorable match.

The girls looked at Bella just as Lena's friends looked at Lena—as a hopeless case. Bella hadn't the slightest chance of getting her diploma. It was actually a bad mark against the Gymnasium that it had allowed this girl to get as far as the eighth grade. The principal was determined to keep her from taking the final examinations. There were a few other girls in the eighth grade who had received poor marks, but these came from affluent families and were pretty besides. One of them was even engaged, and her fiancé waited outside for her every afternoon.

Mark Meitels avoided looking at Bella. There was no way he could help her. She sat there on the bench and gaped at him, half laughing, half pleadingly, with veneration in her eyes. She had apparently persuaded herself that he could swing things in her favor. But she was wrong. When examination time came around, he would have no choice but to vote against her.

4

Lena's final weeks continued to be a gradual decline. The doctors kept her drugged all the while, but she suffered pain nevertheless. Her face had changed almost beyond recognition. It became brown-yellow, congealed, similar to the faces one sees in a wax museum. They prepared pullets for her but she didn't touch them. She was fed medicines, which frequently dribbled out of her mouth. Even when she did say something, her voice was too weak to hear.

Lena waited for death, but death was apparently in no hurry to take her. Her heart went on beating, even if weakly and with hesitation. The other organs still went on functioning too, one way or another.

Lena's mother had never maintained friendly relations with Mark. She felt that her daughter could have done better than to marry a teacher. Since Lena's sickness, the mother had stopped speaking to him altogether. She glared at him and hinted that he was responsible for her daughter's death. He didn't even have enough money for the doctors, medicines, and nurses, and she had to cover all these expenses.

Shortly before the final examinations Lena died. She

asked the nurse to turn her toward the wall. The nurse went into the kitchen to boil some water, and when she came back, Lena was gone. Mark didn't take part in the examinations. After the funeral someone from the Gymnasium called to say that Bella hadn't been allowed to take the tests, and of those who had, two had failed to graduate.

The mother-in-law proposed to Mark that he observe the seven days of mourning at her house, but Mark told her that he didn't believe in such rituals. He even declined to say Kaddish over Lena's grave. Why participate in rites in which he didn't believe? What sense did it make to pray to a God who was eternally silent, whose goals could never be established, nor even his existence? If Mark had ever acknowledged that a person possessed a soul, Lena's illness convinced him that this was sheer absurdity. Lena's body disintegrated along with her so-called spirit. During her entire illness, she didn't utter a word to indicate that she was passing over into some other sphere. Well, and what would Lena's soul do even if it did survive? Again read fashion magazines? Dawdle along Marshalkowska Street window-shopping? On the other hand, if Lena's soul became different from what it had been here on earth, it would no longer be Lena's soul! . . . Mark Meitels had heard a lot about the Polish medium Kluski, at whose séances the dead allegedly left their palm imprints in a basin of paraffin. He read the essays of the Polish occultist Professor Ochorowicz, as well as those of Conan Doyle, Barrett, Sir Oliver Lodge, and Flammarion. He had had moments when he thought, Maybe yes? After all, what do we know about nature and her secrets? But Lena's sickness had erased all his illusions. Nothing remained after her death but a deep emptiness and the feeling that all was vanity. There wasn't, nor could there be, any basic difference between Lena and the pullets which had been prepared for her and which, the following day, were thrown into the garbage.

Mark Meitels had received a number of condolence

letters, telegrams, and even a few bouquets of flowers, but
hardly anyone came to pay a consolation call. The teachers
had all dispersed for the summer and Stasia the maid
had gone back to her parents' village. He hadn't a close
friend in Warsaw. Out of habit he took long walks during
the day and spent the evenings at home alone. He was in
no hurry to turn on the lights, and sat in the dark. In his
childhood he had been afraid of the dead. A funeral
would cast a pall over him. But what did he have to fear
from Lena now? Mentally he called to her: "Lena, if you
exist, give me some sign . . ."

At the same time he knew that no sign would be
forthcoming.

Strange, but for all his sorrow over Lena's senseless
life and premature death, Mark's mind kept turning to
Bella. This puzzled him. What reason did he have to
think about some homely girl who was a dimwit besides?
But the moment he stopped sulking about Lena and her
fate, his thoughts inevitably turned to Bella. What was she
doing? How had she taken her failure? Did she know that
he had lost his wife? The other pupils—the pretty, able,
and popular ones—were almost forgotten by him, but
Bella's face hovered before his eyes. In the dark he saw
her as if she were present—the narrow forehead, the
humped nose, the thick lips, the great bulging eyes. In his
fantasy he stripped her naked. How loathsome she must
be with her huge breasts, jutting hips, and bowed legs!

This girl bore a streak of madness within her. Within
her there laughed and cried out generations of primitive
women who lived in caves and struggled against wild
animals, lice, hunger, and men—throwbacks to the apes.

For all his preoccupation, Mark had to smile as he
recalled how he had tried to teach her mathematics.
Intellectually she was thousands of years behind Euclid,
but her parents wanted her to become a scholar, no less.
What would the parents of such a girl look like?
She had to carry someone's genes within her. A strange
urge began to take form within Mark Meitels—to seek
out Bella. He didn't have her address and such paupers

would have no telephone. Her address was surely kept
somewhere at the Gymnasium, but it was closed during
the vacation. Mark was well aware how pointless all this
was. A mourner didn't go to comfort others. And what
could he say to her? Her kind was best left to their own
devices. Nature, which watched over everything from a
bacterium and a bedbug to a whale, would somehow
provide for Bella or bring about her perdition, which
from a higher standpoint was a kind of provision, too.

Mark told himself that he must put an end to such idle
thoughts. Normally he had means of disciplining his mind,
but Bella's image wouldn't let itself be shunted aside. Am
I going crazy or what? Mark wondered.

One evening he suddenly reminded himself that her
father worked in an oil and soap store on Gnoyna Street.
Gnoyna was a short street. How many such shops could
it contain? However, it was too late by now—all the
stores would be closed. Tomorrow . . .

Mark began to pace through the dark rooms filled
with a restlessness that baffled him. He was consumed by
curiosity about that repulsive girl, along with something
akin to passion. "Is this possible? Am I in love with her?
It can't be otherwise but that I've lost my senses . . ."
He listened in astonishment to the chaos raging within his
own brain. For reasons that defied explanation, this Bella
obsessed him more and more. He suffered from what
might be called an *idée fixe*. At times he had the strange
feeling that Bella was calling to him, shouting his name.
He saw her with striking clarity, all the curves of her
face, the whole deformity of her body. The urge to find
her and speak to her grew stronger from minute to
minute . . . "I'll walk over to Gnoyna," he decided.
"Sometimes they stay open late there . . . Someone
might give me the information I need."

Mark rushed to go out. He had the feeling that if he
ran he would get there before it was too late. At the
same time the sober spirit within him asked, "What's
happened to you? Where are you running to? What kind
of madness are you heading for?" He slammed the front

door, ready to skip down the stairs, when he heard the
sharp, insistent ringing of the telephone inside the apartment. "It's she! I've summoned her up with my mind!"
he cried to himself.

He grabbed the key to unlock the door again and
fumbled momentarily in the keyhole. In the hallway he
bumped against a chair and hurt his knee. The phone
didn't stop ringing the whole time. When he finally reached
the instrument, it became silent. Mark seized the receiver
and exclaimed, "Hello? Who is it? Answer! . . ."

He felt a wave of heat and in a flash his body became
wet with perspiration. He put down the receiver with a
crash and said aloud, "It's she, the beast! . . ."

He was seized by rage and shame. He was no longer
Mark Meitels but some superstitious dupe driven by a
compulsion or, as it might be described in Jewish terms,
possessed by a dybbuk.

5

Mark again prepared to leave, this time no longer with
the intention of going to Gnoyna Street but to some
restaurant for dinner. True, he had lost his appetite, but it
made no sense to neglect himself completely. "First thing
tomorrow I'll go away some place," he decided. "To
Zakopane, or maybe to the seashore . . ." He was half-
way to the door when the telephone rang again. He ran
up to the instrument in the dark and in a muffled breath
exclaimed, "Hello?"

There was a stammering at the other end. Yes, it was
Bella. He caught scattered words that lacked cohesion.
She was making an effort not to choke on her words.
Mark listened in amazement. Would anyone believe this?
he wondered. There is such a thing as telepathy. Aloud he
asked, "Is this Bella Zylberstein?"

"Teacher recognizes my voice?"

"Yes, Bella, I recognize your voice."

She paused a moment.

"I'm calling because I heard of your tragedy," she

went on haltingly. "I'm very sorry . . . The whole class sympathized . . . I myself suffered a misfortune, but compared to yours—" She grew silent.

Mark asked, "Where are you?"

"Eh? On Prosta Street . . . That's where we live."

"You have a phone at home?"

"No, I'm speaking from a delicatessen store."

"Maybe you'd like to come over to my place?"

An oppressive silence ensued; then she said with a flutter in her voice, "If that is Teacher's wish . . . It would be a great honor for me . . . Teacher could never know how much—"

And she did not finish the sentence.

"Come over and don't call me Teacher any more."

"What shall I call you?"

"Whatever you want. It can be simply Mark."

"Oh, Teacher is joking. I felt so sorry . . . I suffered terribly for you . . . The idea that—"

Mark gave her precise instructions on how to get to his house. She thanked him again and again. She kept repeating how she had suffered in his behalf. "Terribly, terribly. Simply day and night . . ."

After a while Mark hung up the receiver.

"Well, what kind of madness is this?" he asked himself. "Is it telepathy, hypnotism? It certainly was no coincidence. I must be careful with this girl," he warned himself. "Her kind go off their head immediately." He switched on the light. "She'll probably be hungry and I'll have to offer her something." He went into the kitchen and began to rummage about in the pantry. He seldom ate at home since Lena's death, and all he could find now was a stale loaf of bread and several cans of sardines. "I'll take her down some place," he decided. But where? One of his acquaintances was liable to drop in and spot him. He was ashamed to be seen with a girl so soon after Lena's death—especially one so ugly. There was an unwritten law at the Gymnasium that teachers must never fraternize with a student. "I'll bring up some rolls and sausage," he finally decided.

He went downstairs, bought sausage, rolls, and fruit.

He hurried lest Bella come too early (assuming she took a taxi) and found no one at home. What if Lena's soul is here and sees what I'm doing? it occurred to him. If there can be such a thing as telepathy, why can't souls linger on after death? . . . No, it has to be that from all my troubles I've simply lost my reason.

He waited a long time, but no one came. Earlier he had lit all the lights in the living room, then put them out again, leaving only a small lamp burning. He sat down on the sofa and cocked his ears for any sound at the front door. She might have gotten lost. She was hopelessly ineffectual in every respect . . .

The doorbell resounded in a long, piercing ring. Mark ran to open it and found Bella in a black dress and a straw hat. She carried a bouquet of flowers. She seemed older. She was perspiring and out of breath.

He said, "Oh, flowers! For me?"

"Yes, for you . . . you shouldn't know of any more grief," she said, translating the Yiddish expression into Polish.

Mark took her wrist and led her into the living room. He put the flowers in a pot and ran water into it. Where did she get money for flowers? he wondered. Probably spent her last groschen . . . I'll be nice to her, but I dare not give her even the slightest hope! he warned himself.

Bella took off her hat and it struck Mark for the first time that she had pretty hair. It was chestnut-colored, thick, and exuded a natural gleam. She sat on a chair and looked down at her feet in the black shoes and stockings. She seemed ashamed of her clumsy appearance —the overblown bosom, the wide hips, the hawk nose, the popping eyes. No, those aren't calf eyes, Mark decided. They're reflecting fear and a love as old as the female species itself.

She kept both her hands on her purse—hands too big for a schoolgirl. Mark noticed that they were stained with ink, as if she had just come from the Gymnasium. She said, "We heard about everything that happened and the whole class was beside itself . . . The others couldn't go to the funeral because it was during examination time, but I wasn't allowed to take them . . . But surely Teacher didn't notice me?"

"Eh? No. Unfortunately I didn't."

"Yes, I was there."

"What are you doing now?"

"Oh, what can I do? Everyone in the house is disappointed in me. Bitterly so. Wasted all that money on me for nothing, and all the rest. After all, the diploma isn't everything. I did learn something—literature, history, a little drawing. I'll never be any good at mathematics. It's a lost cause."

"You can be a good person without mathematics."

"Maybe. I'm looking for some kind of work, but everyone in the house says that without a diploma you can't get a job. There was an ad for a girl to work in the chocolate store and I went there. They said it was already filled. They didn't ask about any diploma."

"Our grandmothers had no diplomas either, but they were pretty good women."

"Of course. My mother can't read the Yiddish paper, yet they wanted to make a doctor out of me. I don't have the knack for it."

"What would you like to do—marry and have children?"

Bella's eyes filled momentarily with laughter. "Yes, that, but who would have me? I love children. I love them terribly. It wouldn't have to be my own children. I would take a widower with children and I would raise them as if they were my own. Even better—"

"Why not have your own children?"

"Oh, I'm only saying that. Naturally that would be better, but—"

It became quiet. A clock tolled in the other room.

"Maybe I could do something for Teacher?" Bella asked. "I can sweep, dust, wash—everything. But nothing for pay, God forbid!"

"Why would you work for me for nothing?" Mark asked.

Bella thought it over a moment and a smile showed on

her lips. Her eyes looked at him—black and burning. "Oh, I would do anything for Teacher. As they say in Yiddish, Wash the feet and drink the water . . ."

8

Mark came up and put his hands on her shoulders. His knees pressed against hers. He asked, "Is what you just said the truth?"

"Yes, the truth."

"Do you love me that much?"

"More than anything in the world."

"More than your parents?"

"Much more."

"Why?"

"Oh, I don't know. Because Teacher is wise and I'm a dumb cow. When Teacher smiles, it's so interesting, and when he is stern, he draws up his brows and everything is somehow so—" She didn't finish. Heat emanated from her, the warmth one feels occasionally standing next to a horse.

Mark asked, "Can I do with you what I want?"

"Anything."

"Slit your throat?" he asked, astounded at his own words.

Bella trembled. "Yes! The blood would gush and I'd kiss the blade . . ."

He was overcome by a lust such as he hadn't felt in years, perhaps never. "Don't do anything stupid!" an inner voice warned. "Send her straight home!" Aloud he said, "Good, I'm going for the knife."

"Yes."

He went into the kitchen, opened a pantry drawer in the dark, and took a knife out from among the utensils. He realized full well that it was all a game, yet he was possessed by a sense of grave earnestness. He came back with the knife. Bella sat in the chair, her face pale, her eyes full of expectation. A pagan ecstasy exuded from her, an eagerness that frightened him.

He said, "Bella, you'll soon be dead. Say what you have to say."

"I love you."

"Are you ready to die?"

"Yes, ready."

He put the blade to her throat. "Shall I slash?"

"Yes."

Mark put the knife down deliberately on the dresser. He recalled the story from the Bible in which God ordered Abraham to slay his son Isaac and the Angel cried out: "Lay not thy hand upon the lad . . ." It was all like a repetition of something that had happened before.

"How long has this love of yours lasted?" he asked in the grave tone of a doctor treating a dangerously ill patient. He sensed the rattling of his own teeth.

"From the day I first saw you."

"The whole time?"

"Day and night."

He stood still and listened to his own breathing. His nose snorted of its own volition. He said, "You knew, after all, that I had a wife."

Bella didn't answer for a long time. "Yes, I knew, but I put a curse on her. That's why she died."

"What are you, a witch?"

"Yes, a witch."

At that moment it struck Mark that Bella looked just like the pictures and carvings of witches in ancient volumes. All she lacked were the elflocks and the wrinkles. Well, those witches hadn't been born old, either. They had probably started practicing sorcery in their youth. Mark told himself that this was all superstition, but Lena's death *had* been a mystery. Even the doctors had said that her illness had been puzzling, flaring up as suddenly as it did. Lena had observed all the rules of hygiene. She ate no fat foods, she didn't smoke, or drink alcohol. The cancer had spread incredibly fast. Mark reminded himself now of what Lena had said: "Someone has cursed me. They envied my good fortune . . ."

The ecstasy dimmed in Bella's eyes and she looked at him gravely, with preoccupation and anxiety.

He said, "I don't belicve in such junk. It's all nonsense. But since you do believe it, from your standpoint you murdered a person."

"True. God will punish me for it."

"Did you think that I would marry you?"

"I didn't know myself."

"How did you put a curse on her?"

"Oh, I wished for her death. I woke up in the middle of the night and prayed for her to die."

"You didn't even know her."

"I did know her. I've already been here many times before. Not in the house, but outside. I waited till she looked out the window. One time I rang the door and asked her if she needed a maid. She said, 'I wouldn't take in anyone from the street,' and she slammed the door in my face."

"Wasn't what you did crazy?"

"Yes, crazy."

Mark glanced toward the dresser, where he had put down the knife. "You deserve to die, but I'm no murderer. In that respect I'm still a Jew. But I'll never have anything to do with you. Go and never come back. You can put a curse on me, too."

"No, I'll bless you to my dying breath."

Bella made a gesture as if to rise, but she remained seated.

Mark said, "That means all you babbled about sympathy was nothing but lies. You were glad she died."

"No. I didn't know I possessed such powers. When I heard the news I became flabbergasted and—"

"You're a stupid ass, that's what you are," Mark said, not certain where his tongue would lead him. "Had you put your mind to your studies instead, you might have gotten your diploma. What will become of you now? You see me today for the last time. I loved Lena dearly, and from now on I'll hate you as I would a spider."

Bella's face drained of color. "And I will go on loving you till I'm in my grave."

"It's all idiocy, hysteria."

"No."

"Did you try calling me earlier this evening?" Mark asked. "I had started out and the phone rang. By the time I got to it, it was too late. Was that you?"

"Yes."

"Why this evening of all times?"

"Oh, I had to."

"It's all self-delusion. You're still stuck back somewhere in the Middle Ages. I'm beginning to understand why they burned witches. Those like you deserve to die. You actually look like a witch," he said, regretting his own words.

"Yes, I know."

"Well, I don't mean that for real. Are you ready to become my lover?" he asked, bewildered at his own words. "I mean a mistress, not a wife. I'd be ashamed to be seen with you in the street. I'm completely frank with you."

Something like anger and mockery flashed in Bella's eyes. "You can do what you want with me."

"When?"

"Now . . ."

7

At three o'clock in the morning Bella began to get dressed. A red lamp gleamed in the bedroom. Mark was too tired to help her. He lay in bed with one eye closed and watched her struggling to fit her bosom into the dress. At twenty, her pendulous breasts dangled. Her stomach was wide and bloated. Black hair sprouted on her belly. The hips bulged at either side like two basins. Her hair fell over her short brow and crooked nose. The protruding eyes looked out, frightened, like hunted animals from between bushes.

A witch, a witch! Mark said to himself. He wouldn't have believed that this young girl, and a virgin besides, could fall into such a frenzy. She had clawed at his flesh, bitten his shoulders, spoke strange words, and cried in such a wild voice that he was afraid it might rouse his neighbors. He had sworn to marry her. "How could this happen? Have I lost my mind? Can there really be such a thing as black magic?" Mark heard Bella say, "Mother will kick up such a fuss! They might have called the police by now. No doubt of it. If only the janitor will open the gate for me!"

"Do you have any change?"

"Eh? No, I spent it on the taxi."

"There is change in my pants pocket."

"Where are your pants? There they are, on the floor . . ."

She picked up his pants and went through the pockets. Mark looked on agape. She was acting like a wife already. "Well, I'm finished," he decided.

Bella took out a few coins and laid the trousers carefully out on the dresser. She ambled around on her hairy legs. How can such large feet fit into women's shoes? Mark wondered. He heard Bella ask, "What shall I tell Mama and Papa? They'll make a frightful scandal!"

"Tell them whatever you want."

"If you have any regrets, I can go straight to the Vistula and put an end to it," Bella said.

"I have no regrets."

"Life to me isn't worth two groschen. I can go where your wife is. She'll take revenge upon me in any case."

"The dead can't take revenge," Mark said in a dull voice.

"They can, they can. She came to me in a dream. She held a dagger and a kerchief full of blood. She screamed at me and spat—"

Mark didn't answer. He had had other women in his life but none who had exhausted him like this girl. She was undoubtedly impregnated, too. He had forgotten to take precautions. Well, this is suicide, he thought. Everything within him filled with a sense of wonder. How had it all come about? What had happened to his reason? All Warsaw would ridicule him. He wouldn't be able to stay on at the Gymnasium. The pupils would laugh in his face.

Bella said, "Well, I'll be going. At least take me to the door."

He got out of bed and shuffled after her. How odd she looked in the black dress and straw hat with the tousled hair dangling from underneath! He took her hand, which was damp and hot. She stood so close to him that she pressed him with her bosom. She said, "If only I didn't have to go home. They will make me miserable. Do you really love me? I beg you, don't deceive me. If it was nothing more than a lark to you, say so."

"What for? So that you can run to the Vistula?"

"That means that it was all a big lie!"

"Bella, I can't marry you."

It grew quiet. In the dimness of the early morning he could see only her eyes. They reflected something mad and savage. He was afraid she would spring at him like some animal and he was too weak now to defend himself.

She said, "Well, all right. It's all over. Good night."

"Where are you going?"

"What's that to you? But don't think badly of me. The way I love you, no one will ever love you again."

"Bella, I beg you, don't do anything foolish!"

"Death isn't foolishness."

"Bella, stay here!" he cried. It was no longer he, Mark Meitels speaking, but some force that had the final say. He went on: "We can't stay here in Warsaw, but there's a big world out there. We'll go to Kraków, or maybe even abroad. I heard one can still get a visa to Cuba or Honduras. What does it matter so long as we are together."

"I'm ready to follow you to the end of the world."

They stood in the dark, brooding. Bella's breath came heavy and hot. He was overcome with a fresh passion.

"Come back!"

"Wait. Mama has a weak heart. She's liable to die from worry."

"She won't die. And if she does, too bad!"

"You sweet murderer of mine!"

"You really are a witch, aren't you?"

"Yes, but don't tell anybody."

"How do you do it?"

"Oh, I pray to God, or maybe it's to the devil. I don't know myself who I pray to. I lie in bed and it just comes out of me. You can't untangle yourself from me and that's the truth. We're like two dogs locked together . . ."

"Come back!"

"If you want us to run away from Warsaw, let's do it right now," she said.

"This minute?"

"Today."

"I have furniture. Books."

"Leave everything behind. Mama and Papa will die of worry, but since I've already murdered one person, what difference does it make?"

"They don't have to die. We'll telegraph them from the road."

"Well, all right. From that first day in the fifth grade, when you came in to give the math lesson, I started wanting you, and a minute hasn't gone by that I haven't thought of you. Where is Honduras, in Africa?"

"You've studied geography, you should know."

"I don't remember a thing. For the whole four years I studied only you, nothing else."

"Come!"

He took her around and they stumbled back to the bedroom, past the living room. The sun had risen and it cast a red glow through the windows. Bella's face seemed to be bathed in blood. Clusters of fire ignited within her eyes. He stood by her, half naked, and they stared into a mirror.

He said, "If there is such a thing as black magic, maybe there is a God, too."

He couldn't wait to get to the bedroom and pushed her down onto the rug—a witch drenched in blood and semen, a monster that the rising sun transformed into a beauty.

Translated by Joseph Singer

Sam Palka and
David Vishkover

Sam Palka sat on the sofa—stocky, a tuft of white hair on each side of his bald head, his face red, with bushy brows and bloodshot eyes that changed from pale blue to green to yellow. A cigar stuck out between his lips. His belly protruded like that of a woman in late pregnancy. He wore a navy-blue jacket, green pants, brown shoes, a shirt with purple stripes, and a silk tie on which was painted the head of a lion. Sam Palka himself looked to me like a lion which by some magic had turned into a rich man in New York, a Maecenas to Yiddish writers, a supporter of the Yiddish theater, president of an old-age home in the Bronx, the treasurer of a society that supported orphans in Israel.

Talking to me, Sam Palka shouted as though I were deaf. He lifted a thick manuscript from the coffee table and yelled, "Over a thousand pages, huh! And this is not one-hundredth part of what I could have written. But fix it up the way it is."

"I will do what I can."

"Money doesn't matter. Even if I should live a thousand years, I have enough. I will pay you three thousand dollars for the editing, and when the book comes out and they write about it in the papers I will give you—what do they call it?—a bonus. But make it tasty. I can't read the books writers bring me—three or four lines of a novel and you have to fight to stay awake. In my day a book grabbed you. You began to read a novel and couldn't put it down, because you wanted to know what happened. Dieneson, Spector, Seifert! And there were thoughts that took you who knows where. They contained history, too. Samson and Delilah, Jephthah's daughter, Bar Kolchba. They hit the spot. Today you read half a book and you still don't know what it's about. These scribblers write of love, but they know as much of love as I know of what's going on on the moon. How should they know? They sit all day long and half the night in the Café Royal and argue about how great they are. They have sour milk and ink in their veins, not blood. I haven't forgotten Yiddish. The man I dictated this book to tried to correct me all the time; he didn't like my Polish Yiddish. But he didn't bother me. I would dictate an episode and he would ask, 'How can that be? It's not realistic.' He came from Ishishok, some godforsaken village, and to him whatever he hadn't experienced didn't exist—a bookworm, an idiot.

"Now, I want you to know that even though I dictated over one thousand pages I had to leave out the main thing. I could not describe it because the heroine is alive and she reads. She does one thing in her life—she reads. She has heard of all today's writers. Wherever a new book can be found, she gets it and reads it from cover to cover. My life wouldn't be worth living if I were to publish the truth and she should learn about it. What I am going to tell you can be written only after my death. But who is there to do it? You are still a young man, you know your way around, and when I kick the bucket I want you to add this story to the book. Without it the whole thing isn't worth a damn. I will provide for your additional work in my will.

"Where should I begin? I was born in a pious home. My parents were old-fashioned Jews, but even when I was still a cheder boy I heard about love. Does one have to look far for it? It's right in the Torah. Jacob loved Rachel, and when Laban, the cheat, substituted Leah in the dark night Jacob labored another seven years. Well, and what about King David and King Solomon with the Queen of Sheba and all that stuff? Book peddlers used to come to our village and they brought storybooks—two pennies to buy a book, one penny to borrow it. I was a poor boy, but whenever I could get hold of a penny I spent it on reading. When I came to America and I earned three dollars a week, I spent my last cent on books or on tickets for the Yiddish theater. In those times actors were still actors and not sticks of wood. When they appeared on stage the boards burned under their feet. I saw all of them! Adler, Mme. Liptzin, Schildkraut, Kessler, Tomashevsky—every one of them. Well, and the playwrights of those times—Goldfaden, Jacob Gordin, Lateiner! Each word had to do with love, and you could have kissed each one. When you read my book you will see that I had no luck in my marriage. I fell for a rotten woman—a bitter piece, a bitch. How she ruined my days and how she set my children against me is all there. As long as I was young and poor I worked in a sweatshop, and then I took to peddling. I had no time for love. I lived in a dark alcove and I couldn't afford to buy clothes. We worked then fourteen hours a day, and when it was busy even eighteen. When it became slack we had barely a crust to eat. If your stomach is empty you forget about love.

"I built my first bungalow quite a number of years after I married, and I soon became so successful it was as though Elijah had blessed me. One day I had nothing and the next money poured in from all sides. But I still worked hard, perhaps even harder than ever. No matter how successful

a man is, he can slip in no time from the top of the heap
to the very bottom. You have to be on the watch every
minute. As long as I had a job or carried a pack on my
shoulders and peddled, at least I rested on the Sabbath.
With prosperity, my Sabbaths too were gone. My wife got
wind that I had a spare dollar and began to tear pieces off
me. We moved from the Lower East Side and took an
apartment uptown. The children came one after the other
and there were doctors, private schools, and the devil
knows what else. My wife—Bessie was her name—
bedecked herself with so much jewelry you could hardly
see her. She came from petty and mean people, and when
these get the smell of money they lose their heads. I was
in my late thirties, and I still had not tasted real love. If I
had ever loved my wife it was only from Monday to Tuesday. We quarreled constantly, and she threatened me with
jail and judges. She kept reminding me that in America a
lady is something so special you have to bow to her as
though she were an idol. She carried on until I couldn't
look at her any more. When I heard her voice I felt like
vomiting. She indulged in all sorts of trickery, but she still
expected me to be a husband to her. Impossible! We no
longer shared a bedroom. By this time I had an office, and
secretly I got a little apartment in one of my buildings. I'm
sorry to admit it, but if you hate a wife you're bound to
care less for the children. After Bessie, that fishwife, realized we would never be close again, she began to look for
others. She did it so crudely men were afraid to start anything with her. She snatched at their sleeves like Potiphar's
wife. I know what you want to ask me—why I didn't get a
divorce. First of all, in those times to get a divorce you
had to jump through hoops, knocking on the doors of the
courts and so on. Today you fly to Reno and in six weeks
you are as free as a bird. Secondly, she would have set a
bunch of shysters on me and they would have fleeced me
of my last penny. Besides, one gets a divorce when one is
in love with someone else. If no one is waiting for you,
why look for more headaches? I had partners in the business, and even though they had good wives they kept com-

pany with loose women. Today these women have become
fancy call girls, but a whore is a whore. They all did it—
the manufacturers, the jobbers, anyone who could pay. For
them it was a game. But if these prostitutes were all you
had, you realized your misfortune. It happened more than
once that I just looked at one of these sluts and lost my
appetite. I would give her a few dollars and run away like
a yeshiva boy. I would go to a movie and for hours watch
the gangsters shooting one another. So the years passed,
and I thought that I would never learn what love was. Do
you want to hear more?"

"Yes, of course."

"This alone would make a book. When you write it, you
will know how to embellish it."

"Why embellish? As you tell it it is good enough."

"Well, writers like to embellish.

"When I was about forty-two or forty-three I was really
rich. Once the money starts to flow, you can't stop it. I
bought houses and lots and made huge profits. I bought
stocks and they rose overnight. Taxes were nothing in
those days. I owned a limousine and wrote checks for all
kinds of charities. Now women swarmed around me like
bees around honey. I got more love in a week than I could
make use of in a year. But I am not a man who fools himself. I knew what they wanted was my money, not me. As
they kissed me and tried to make me believe I was the
great lover, they talked about what they would get out of
it: trips to Florida, to Europe; mink coats; diamonds. It
was all bluff. You lie in bed with them and they don't let
you forget that what you really are is a sugar daddy. I
wished I could meet a woman who did not know about my
money or an heiress so rich that in comparison I would
seem poor. But where and when? I began to think that
true love was not for me. How do they say it in Poland?
Sausage is not for dogs.

"Suddenly a miracle happened. I acquired an old house
on Blake Avenue in Brownsville. Today Brownsville is
full of Negroes and Puerto Ricans; then it was the land of

Israel. You couldn't find a Gentile to save your life. I wanted to put up a new building, but first I had to get rid of the tenants. Often these things went easily, but this time some of them balked. I didn't believe in going to court; I preferred to settle with them myself. I had a free Sunday and decided to go and see what could be done. My car happened to be in the garage, so I took the subway. After all, I wasn't born a Rockefeller.

"At the house I knocked on a door, but in Brownsville they didn't know the meaning of that. I pushed the latch, the door opened, and I saw a room that looked exactly like one in the old country. If I hadn't known that I was in Brownsville, I would have thought that I was in Konskowola: whitewashed walls, a board floor, a broken-down sofa with the stuffing sticking out. Even the smells were from Konskowola—fried onions, chicory, moldy bread. On the sofa sat a girl as beautiful as Queen Esther. One difference. Esther was supposed to be greenish and this girl was white, with blue eyes and golden hair—a beauty. She was dressed like a greenhorn who had just arrived: a long skirt and shoes with buttons. And what was she doing? Reading a storybook: *Sheindele with the Blue Lips*. I had read it years before on the other side. I thought I was dreaming and I pinched myself, but it was no dream.

"I wanted to tell her that I was the landlord and had come to make her move out. But some power stopped me. I began to play a role as if I were an actor in the theater. She asked me who I was and I said I was a salesman of sewing machines. I could get one for her cheap. She said, 'What do I need a sewing machine for? When I want to sew something, I use my own ten fingers.' She spoke a familiar Yiddish.

"I could sit with you until tomorrow and not tell half of it, but I will make it short. She had been in this country only two years. Her father had been a Talmud teacher in Poland. He was brought to this land of gold by an uncle. Three days after the father and daughter left Ellis Island, the uncle died. Her father became a beadle for some little

rabbi here. I asked her how old she was and she said
twenty-six. 'How does it happen,' I asked her, 'that such a
beautiful girl is unmarried?' She answered, 'They offered
me many matches but I refused to marry through a matchmaker. I have to be in love.' What she said was not silly;
she was like a child and her talk was also like that of a
little girl. She was not retarded—just naïve. She had lived
for twenty-four years in a tiny village in the hinterland—
Wysoka. Her mother died when she was still young. Each
word she uttered was the pure truth. She could as much
lie as I could be the wife of a rabbi. I asked her name and
she said, 'Channah Basha.' Why drag it out? I fell in love
with her—head over heels. I couldn't tear myself from her.
I was afraid she would make me go, but she asked, 'Aren't
you hungry?' 'Yes, I am hungry,' I said and I thought, For
you! She said, 'I cooked burned-flour grits and I have a
full pot of it.' I hadn't heard the words 'burned-flour grits'
for goodness knows how long and, believe me, no aria sung
by an opera singer could have sounded sweeter.

"Soon we were seated at a broken-down table, eating
the burned-flour grits like an old couple. I told her that I
too read storybooks. I could see that she had a whole pile
of them, all brought over from the old country: *The Story
of the Three Brothers, The Tale of Two Butchers, The
Adventures of the Pious Reb Zadock and the Twelve
Robbers*. She asked me, 'Do you earn a living by selling
sewing machines?' I said, 'I manage to scratch together a
few dollars.' She asked, 'Do you have a wife and children?'
I told her about my wife and poured out my bitter heart
to her. Channah Basha listened and she grew pale. 'Why
do you hold on to such a shrew?' I said, 'Here in America
when you divorce a wife you have to pay alimony. If not
you go to jail. The alimony amounts to more than a man
earns. This is the justice in the land of Columbus.' She
said, 'God waits long but He punishes severely. She will
soon come to a bad end.' She cursed my wife. She said,
'How do you live if she takes away your last bite?' I said,
'I still have enough for a piece of bread.' She said, 'Come
to me. I often cook more than I need for my father and

myself. I am always alone because my father comes home late, and with you it will be cozy.' It was the first time that someone showed compassion for me and wanted to give instead of take. We ate the grits with fresh bread from the bakery and we washed it down with watery tea while we babbled about the Three Brothers, of whom the first took upon himself the good deed of ransoming innocent prisoners, the second of helping poor orphans to marry, and the third of honoring the Sabbath. Then I told her a story about a young man who found a golden hair and traveled all over the world in search of the woman from whose head it had fallen. He found her on the island of Madagascar and she was the queen herself. Channah Basha listened eagerly to every word.

"Why go on? There grew up a great love between us. I saw to it that the house remained untouched. I visited her each week, and some weeks I took the Canarsie line to Brownsville two or three times. Whenever I went there, I wore a shabby suit and an old hat. I brought her presents of the kind that a sewing-machine salesman might bring: a pound of farmer cheese, a basket of fruit, a box of tea. The neighbors knew me and they wanted to buy sewing machines on the installment plan. I soon realized that if I sold them such bargains all of Brownsville would run after me, and I told Channah Basha that I had changed to the insurance business. I have forgotten the main thing: I called myself by another name—David Vishkover. It wasn't invented; I had a cousin of that name.

"For some time I managed to avoid her father, the beadle. As for Channah Basha, she fell in love with me with such passion that no words can describe it. One day I was a stranger and four weeks later her whole life hung on me. She knitted sweaters for me and cooked for me every dish I like. Whenever I tried to give her a few dollars she gave the money back and I had to beg her to accept it. I was a virtual millionaire, but on Blake Avenue I became a poor insurance agent, a starving schlemiel whose wife bled him of his last penny. I know what you want to ask; yes, Channah Basha and I became like husband and

wife. She was a pure virgin. How a girl like that could be
talked into an affair is a story in itself. I know a little
Jewish law, and I persuaded her that according to the
Torah a man is permitted to have two wives. As far as she
was concerned, since she was unmarried she was not com-
mitting adultery. If I had told her to stand on her head,
she would have done that too.

"As long as Channah Basha's father did not learn what
was going on, everything went smoothly. We lived like two
pigeons. But how long can such an affair remain a secret?
When he found out that a married man was visiting his
daughter and she had accepted him like a bridegroom, all
hell broke loose. I assured him that the moment my vixen
of a wife divorced me I would stand under the wedding
canopy with his daughter.

"Just as Channah Basha was beautiful, her father was
ugly, sick, a broken shard. He warned me that I would be
excommunicated. As time went on he grew more violent;
he even hinted that he might have me thrown into prison.
I was frightened, all right. One shouldn't say it, but luck
was on my side. He became mortally sick. He had bad
kidneys and God knows what else. I sent him to doctors,
took him to the hospital, paid for nurses, and I pretended
that he was getting all this care for nothing. He lingered
a few months and then he died. I erected a tombstone for
him that cost fifteen hundred dollars and I made his daughter believe that it came from the *landsleit* of Wysoka. One
lie leads to another. How is it written in the Talmud?"

"One sin drags another after it," I said.

"Right.

"After her father's death, Channah Basha became even
more childish than before. She mourned him as I never
saw a daughter mourn her father. She hired a man to recite
the Kaddish for him. She lighted candles in the synagogue.
Every second week she visited his grave. I told her that
my business was going well and I tried to give her more
money. But no matter how little it was, she insisted it was
too much. All she needed, she said, was a loaf of bread, a

few potatoes, and once in a while a pound of tripe. Years
passed and she still wore her same shabby dresses from
the old country. I wanted to give her an apartment on
Ocean Avenue and furnish it. She refused to move. She
kept on dusting and polishing her old junk. She read the
Yiddish papers, and once she found my picture there. I
had become the president of an old-age home and it was
written up. She said, 'See here, that Sam Palka looks just
like you. Is he a relative or something?' I said, 'I wish he
was a relative. In my family we are all paupers.' If I had
told her then that I was Sam Palka, our love would have
been finished. She needed a poor man to look after, not a
rich one to pamper her. Every time I left her to go home
she offered me a bag of food so that I wouldn't starve on
my wife's rations. Funny, isn't it?

"The years passed and I scarcely knew where they went.
One day I had dark hair and it seemed overnight that I
turned gray. Channah Basha too was no longer a spring
chicken. But her thoughts stayed those of a child. The
house on Blake Avenue became so ramshackle I worried
that the walls might cave in. I had to bribe the inspectors
not to condemn it. The storybooks that Channah Basha
brought from Wysoka had finally fallen apart, and she
now read the books of the Yiddish writers in America.
There was no lack of that merchandise in my house! Every
time I went to Brownsville I brought her a stack, and she
admired them all no matter how bad they were. She loved
everyone except my wife. On her she poured sulphur and
fire. She never tired of hearing about the troubles Bessie
made for me, and I had plenty to tell. She had gotten herself a gigolo, a faker, and she traveled all over Europe
with him. My children gave me no joy, either. My son
didn't even graduate from high school. I have three
daughters and none of them married happily. Their mother
planted hatred of me in them. I was good for only one
thing—to write checks. Still, I had a great happiness:
Channah Basha. She was always the same. In all those
years she learned only a few words of English. Most of
the Jewish tenants had moved out of the house and Puerto

Ricans had moved in. Only two old women—widows—stayed, and Channah Basha watched over them. One had cataracts and later became blind. The other one had dropsy. Channah Basha took care of them like the best nurse.

"Would you believe it? In all this time Channah Basha never visited Manhattan. The subway terrified her with its din and noise. There was a Yiddish theater on Hopkinson Avenue, and once in a while I took her there. Sometimes they showed a Yiddish movie. There were moments when I thought I ought to put an end to this false game I was playing. Why shouldn't she enjoy my riches? In the summer I wanted to rent a cottage in the Catskills for her. I offered her a trip with me to California. But she wouldn't hear of it. Air conditioning did not exist then, and I wanted to buy her a fan. She refused it. She had a deathly fear of machines. She wouldn't allow me to install a telephone. The one thing she accepted was a radio; it took her a long time to learn how to turn on the Yiddish stations. This is Channah Basha—so will she be until her last day.

"My dear friend, I promised to make it short and I will keep my word. Bessie died. She had a quarrel with her gigolo—the pimp—and she went alone to Hong Kong. What she was looking for there I will never know. One day she collapsed in a restaurant and died. It was 1937. In all the years I had been coming to Channah Basha, we promised ourselves that if something happened to Bessie we would get married. But somehow I postponed telling her. There could be no thought of living with Channah Basha in the ruins of Blake Avenue. It was just as impossible to take her to my ten-room apartment on Park Avenue. My neighbors were all snooty rich. I had a Negro maid and an Irish housekeeper. I went to parties and I gave parties. No one spoke a word of Yiddish in my crowd. How could I bring Channah Basha into this Gentile-like world? With whom would she be able to talk? Besides, to find out that I had been lying to her all these years might be a shock that would tear our love apart

like a spider web. I began to plan to go with her to
Palestine, maybe to settle somewhere in Jerusalem or at
Rachel's grave, but Hitler was already baring his teeth.
At a time like that it was good to be in America, not
wandering around in faraway countries.

"I put things off from day to day, from month to month.
Why deny it—I wasn't completely faithful to her during all
those years. As long as I didn't have true love I spat on
frivolous women, but now that I had a true love it suited
me to play around with others too. When women know
that a man is alone they offer themselves by the dozen. I
became a real Don Juan. I frequented nightclubs and
restaurants where you meet the big shots. My name was
even mentioned in the gossip columns. But these phony
loves were enjoyable only because in Brownsville on Blake
Avenue a real love waited. Who said it? One ounce of
truth has more weight than ten tons of lies. I figured one
way, then another, and meanwhile the war broke out.
There was no place for us to flee to any more—unless,
perhaps, Mexico or South America. But what would we
two do there?

"My dear man, nothing has changed up to today, except
that I have become an old man and Channah Basha is in
her fifties. But you should see her; her hair is still gold
and her face is that of a young girl. It is said that this
comes from a pure conscience. Now that there was war
and she heard how the Jews were tortured in Europe, she
began to cry; she went on crying for years. She fasted and
recited prayers, like the God-fearing matrons in my
village. Some organization advertised that they mailed
packages to Russia, and every cent that I gave her Channah Basha sent there. She was so upset that she forgot I
was a poor insurance agent and she took large sums of
money from me I was supposed to have been saving for
my old age. If she hadn't been Channah Basha she would
have recognized that something was wrong. But suspicion
was not in her nature. She hardly knew the value of money
—especially when it was in checks. I knew that the
shrewd people in charge of those packages swindled her

right and left, but I also knew that if even one dollar out of a hundred served its purpose the deed was good. Besides, if I had told Channah Basha that people with beards and sidelocks stole money from refugees, she could have suffered a heart attack. Finally, I gave her so much that I had to tell her I was connected with a relief organization and they provided me with funds. She questioned nothing. Later, when Palestine became a Jewish state and the troubles with the Arabs began, she again tried to help. Believe it or not, I am still getting money from all those nonexistent committees."

Sam Palka winked and laughed. He puffed once on his extinguished cigar and threw it in the ashtray. He lit another and said, "You may call me a charlatan, but I have never been able to tell her the truth. She loved David Vishkover, the poor man, the victim of a false wife, not Sam Palka, the landlord, the millionaire, the woman chaser, the gambler. Everything had to stay the same. I still visit her on Blake Avenue. It has become almost completely black. It makes no difference to Channah Basha. 'Here I have lived,' she says, 'and here I want to die.' I come to her in the morning, spend the day with her—we take a walk and go to bed right after supper. I'm known there. The blacks and the Puerto Ricans say, 'Hi, Mr. Vishkover.' We still eat burned-flour grits, noodles with beans, kasha with milk, and we talk about the old country as though we had stepped off the ship just yesterday. It's no longer a game. To her, Bessie is still alive, making me miserable. She thinks that I sustain myself on a small annuity from the insurance company and my Social Security. The buttons keep falling off the jacket and pants I wear, and Channah Basha continues to sew on others. She begs me to bring her my shirts; she wants to wash them. She darns my socks. A pair of my pajamas that are twenty years old hang in her bathroom. Every time I come, I have to report about Bessie. Is she still so wicked? Haven't the years softened her? I tell her that age doesn't change character—once bad, always bad. Channah Basha asked me to buy a plot in the cemetery of the

Wysoka *landsleit* so that when we die we can lie side by
side. I did so, even though another plot waits for me next
to Bessie's grave. I will have to die twice. When I die,
Channah Basha is going to be surprised by my legacy to
her. I have made her the beneficiary of an insurance policy
for fifty thousand dollars. The house on Blake Avenue
will also be hers. But what will she do with it? There
comes a day when money is useless. We are both on diets.
She now cooks with vegetable oil instead of butter. I am
afraid to eat a piece of babka—cholesterol.

"One day I was sitting with Channah Basha and we
were talking about olden days—how they used to bake
matzo, send gifts on Purim, decorate the windowpanes for
Shevuot—and suddenly she asked, 'What is the matter
with your wife? Will her end never come?' I answered,
'Weeds are hardy.' Channah Basha said, 'I would still like
to be your wife before God and the people, even if only
for one year.'

"When I heard these words I was beside myself. I
wanted to cry out, 'Channah Basha, my darling, no one
stands in our way any more. Come with me to City Hall
and we will get the license.' But this meant killing David
Vishkover. Don't laugh—he is a real person to me. I have
lived with him so long that he is closer to me than Sam
Palka. Who is Sam Palka? An old lecher who has made a
fortune and doesn't know what to do with it. David Vishkover is a man like my father, peace be with him. Well—
and what would happen to Channah Basha if she should
hear the truth? Instead of becoming Sam Palka's wife, she
would become David Vishkover's widow."

Translated by the author and Dorothea Straus

A Tutor in the Village

At the end of 1922, or perhaps it was at the beginning of 1923, I was offered a teaching job in the village of Kocica. I had left home and become "enlightened." I had taken off my Jewish cap and my gaberdine and put on a Polish cap and a short jacket. Nevertheless, my new employer, Naphtalie Tereshpoler, hired me to teach his children—first, because he had known my grandfather, the rabbi of Bilgoray, and, second, because he wanted his boys and girls to learn not only the Torah but a little Polish and arithmetic as well. He promised me a room, food, and a small salary in marks. The zloty wasn't yet established as a currency.

I was living with some distant relatives in Bilgoray. One winter morning Naphtalie stopped his sleigh in front of the house. I had packed all my belongings into one valise —a few shirts, underwear, socks, a Polish grammar, an eighty-year-old algebra text, and Spinoza's *Ethics* translated into German. Naphtalie had his own Jewish library.

It had snowed for days, and frost had set in the night before. As we drove along, the sky was clear and blue. The sun hung low, a summery gold, familiar—a lamp that seemed to light up only our region: Bilgoray, Janów, Zamość, Tomaszów. It drew sparks from the bluish pillows of snow. I felt that its warmth would soon make the sap flow in the trees and burst open the kernels in the planted fields. From time to time a warm breeze brought the fragrance of the surrounding pinewoods. Crows aired their wings, cawing. We passed a number of hamlets. The thatched roofs were covered with white; ice spears hung from the eaves; smoke curled from the chimneys. The landscape reminded me of a tapestry I had seen in the hut of a *gazda* in the Tatra Mountains. The mare's brown hide turned gray, as if old age had suddenly overtaken her. The bell on her neck tingled constantly, telling of a rest not of this world. The sleigh glided in an easy zigzag. From time to time Naphtalie turned his face to make sure that I hadn't dozed off and fallen from my seat. He had broad shoulders, a long black beard, large black eyes under bushy brows. He wore a fur hat and a sheepskin. Even though he waved his whip and spoke to the horse in the coachman's argot, one could hear gentleness in his voice. Naphtalie Tereshpoler was known as a man of learning and charity, eager for good deeds. He gave lavishly to buy books for the study house and to the community in Bilgoray for the poor; he provided wheat for the Passover matzos. Each Purim he sent generous gifts to my grandfather, Rabbi Jacob Mordecai, and, after my grandfather died, to my Uncle Joseph.

In an hour, the sleigh reached Kocica, a large village a few kilometers long. The soil here was black and rich, as in the Ukraine. From the surrounding hills, water flowed even in years of drought, and the harvest was always abundant. Wheat, rye, barley, buckwheat, and hops grew here. The village had a brewery and a water-mill. Naphtalie's house was bigger than the others and had a shingled roof. His wife and five children came out to meet me. On the way Naphtalie had told me a little about his family. His

oldest daughter, Devoraleh, was already engaged to the
owner of the mill in Kocica, but she had never learned to
write. His boys, Leibel and Bentze, had neglected their
studies. I saw heads of black hair, a black wig, black eyes.
Naphtalie made his boys shake hands with me. The mother
and the girls bade me welcome. I entered a huge kitchen
which smelled of groats, borscht, mushrooms, kindling
wood, and smoke. On the table lay an enormous loaf of
black bread. The kitchen had three windows facing south
and two west. Shafts of sun quivered on the floor and the
whitewashed walls. After a while I went up narrow steps
to the garret, where I was to lodge. A fire burned in a
small tin stove. On the bed was a pillow with a fresh-
washed covering.

I lay down on the bed and fell asleep. When I opened
my eyes, the sun was setting among the naked trees. I took
out the *Ethics* and the algebra. I had supplied myself with
what Spinoza called "adequate ideas"—according to him,
the highest state of enjoyment, the perfect expression of an
active mind.

Naphtalie's house had four or five rooms, but the family
seemed to prefer the kitchen. There the kerosene lamp was
lit. Naphtalie, the boys, and I recited our evening prayers
at the eastern wall. Then our supper was served—rye
dumplings with milk and chicory coffee without sugar.
Naphtalie's wife, Beile Tsivya, came from Greater Poland,
and she spoke with the dialect of that area. She had a
broad face, wide shoulders, an overflowing bosom, unusually thick arms. She had borne eleven children, of whom
six had died. In addition to the household, Beile Tsivya
managed the tavern and the store. She also milked the
cows.

Devoraleh was three weeks older than I. She had just
turned eighteen. She was small, slender, with a narrow
face, delicate features. Only her hands were too large, and
red from work. She wore her hair in a bun. She did a large
share of the household chores and made clothes for the
family. Her sister Etke, fourteen, had gone to a Polish
school in a nearby village for some years. Etke was taller

than Devoraleh and had two long braids. The youngest, Rachele, was still a little girl. She did not yet know her alphabet. The two boys—Leibel, twelve, and Bentze, eleven—were short, dark, with thick lips, high cheekbones, broad noses, short foreheads. They looked like twins. The moment I saw them, I knew they had no desire to study. There was a peasant stubbornness about them. Their father confided to me that they had grown up wild and spent their time with peasant youths. They had a pigeon coop. They had already begun to do business—bought hides of calves, as well as pigs' bristles, from the peasants and sold them to a peddler. Their father said to me, "I don't need their business, I want them to be Jews."

While we ate, peasants began to arrive. One came to see about buying a calf from Naphtalie, another to arrange to go with a sleigh at four o'clock in the morning to bring wood for the house. A peasant girl with green eyes and sparse white teeth came to return a cup of flour that she had borrowed the day before. Devoraleh told me that she actually had come to get a glimpse of me, the new teacher. Between visits, Naphtalie explained how difficult it was to live among the peasants. Weeks passed without his being able to pray with a quorum. Agitators from the Rozwoj movement instigated the peasants to stop buying in his store. They had opened a Polish store in the village and put up a sign, BUY FROM YOUR OWN. During the Polish-Bolshevik war, windowpanes were broken in his house and his store had been set on fire. Just the same, here he was making a living, and what would he do in Bilgoray or in Lublin? "Jews are in exile everywhere," Naphtalie said.

"But here one is not sure of one's life," Beile Tsivya complained.

"And where is one sure?"

I was to begin my tutoring the next morning, but the long winter night had only just begun. My vest watch showed twenty minutes to six. The night seemed to creep more slowly here than in Bilgoray. I went out and stood before the door to breathe some fresh air and to view the village at night. Here and there I saw the trembling glimmer of a wick in an oil lamp, but in most of the huts there was no light. It seemed that the peasants were already sleeping, or they hadn't lit their lamps. Kerosene was a luxury in the villages and was used only on festive occasions. The full moon rested on the village with radiance. The stars seemed closer and larger than in town. I felt far from Bilgoray now, and even farther from Warsaw, where I grew up and for which I constantly yearned. I reminded myself that for the Substance with the infinite attributes of whom I read in the *Ethics,* Kocica was not a forsaken hamlet but an integral part of being. I had to seek comfort in eternity, in Spinoza's *"amor Dei intellectualis,"* because in the world of the *modi,* in the caldron of cause and effect, purpose and achievement, everything went against me. My attempts to write had failed. I had tried writing in Hebrew, but the results were artificial. I turned to Yiddish, and still my inhibitions didn't leave me; they hung on my pen like imps. In love, I had fallen into the pettiness of the emotions, the affects, which according to Spinoza are never good. My coming to Kocica was an attempt to abandon the daily drudgeries, the joys and catastrophes of fools, and to consider everything *sub specie aeternitatis.*

The door opened and Devoraleh came out. She asked, "Why do you stand outside? Aren't you cold?"

"No, thank you."

"Would you like to see our store and the tavern?"

What can I learn from a store and a tavern? the Spinozaist in me thought. But I said, "Yes, thank you."

I walked with Devoraleh, and the snow crunched under our feet. Devoraleh had covered her head with a shawl. She was no longer a stranger to me. I was her teacher and she my pupil. I resolved to teach her to read and to write Yiddish and Polish, and perhaps a little philosophy: had not young idealists in Russia abandoned palaces and gone to teach the people? We came to a low building, and there were the store and the tavern. The store was lit by a hanging kerosene lamp, its tin shade adorned with paper fringes. On the shelves was a conglomeration of merchandise—dry goods and iron pots, cork innersoles for shoes and rolls of chicory, pretzels strung on a string and mousetraps. Behind the counter sat Beile Tsivya, knitting a stocking with four needles. From time to time she used one of the needles to scratch under her wig. A peasant in a sheepskin and shoes made of rags and tree bark was bending over a barrel of herring with his hand in the brine.

Beile Tsivya smiled. "You brought me a customer?"

"Can I buy ink and paper?" I asked.

"Ink? Who needs ink here? Still, we have a few bottles and some composition books. Once in a blue moon somebody may ask for it."

I bought ink and half a dozen composition books. I would have plenty of time to write here. All I needed was inspiration. While I stood there, Beile Tsivya spoke to me about my grandfather—may he intercede for all of us—about my grandmother, and some cousins who had died in the cholera epidemic during the war. How strange, but Beile Tsivya remembered my mother's wedding; she had been a girl of five at the time.

After a while Devoraleh took me to the tavern. Two tables and benches ran the length of the room. Near the wall stood a keg of beer with a brass spout. Behind the counter, under the shelves of vodka bottles, sat Etke, reading a Polish textbook. She half smiled, half winked at Devoraleh and me and continued to read. The room was dimly lit and cold. At one of the tables, a peasant snored as he slept. Two peasants were talking over empty vodka glasses. They looked at us with anger and began to talk about how the Jews were invading the villages. Again and again I heard the word *"zydy."*

Devoraleh said to me, "Don't be afraid. It's just silly talk." She called over to the men, "If you don't keep your mouths shut, I'll throw you out right away."

"Look at her, a real *panienka!*" one of them called back. He laughed and belched.

Devoraleh said to me, "Beasts, that's what they are. In

the summer they work a little, but in the winter all they
do is lie on the stove and scratch themselves, or they come
here to get drunk. No wonder they envy the Jew."

"After eight hundred years, we're still strangers," I said
to Devoraleh and to myself.

"Is it our fault? They want to kill us. The boys who
came back from the war carry guns. They shoot them
every night just to frighten the old people."

What do you say to that, Jean Jacques Rousseau? I
thought. And how about you, Spinoza? Was it really necessary for Divine Thought to scheme all this?

After we left the tavern, Devoraleh said, "In town,
somehow one is still a human being. Here everything is
rough and mean. Father says we must thank God every
day for our lives. Is it true that you're a writer?"

"I want to write."

"What—books?"

"Yes, books."

"You must have a lot of education. I wasn't taught.
Etke went to the Polish school, but I had to take care of
the children. I had a teacher, but he was no good. He
stole from our chests. My father sent him back to town
in the middle of the year."

"I hear that you're already engaged."

Devoraleh stopped walking. "Yes, to Zelig, from the
water mill."

"What kind of man is your betrothed?"

"Oh, he's a nice boy. He's taken over the business from
his father. I've known him since we were babies—we used
to play at the sluice. He will visit us tomorrow. He knows
Polish, but he wants to learn some Hebrew from you.
Father says it's not fit that he and I study together. What's
wrong with it? Papa's so old-fashioned!"

We returned to Reb Naphtalie's house. Before we went
in I asked, after some hesitation, "Where is the outhouse?"

Devoraleh didn't answer immediately. "There is no outhouse. You go behind the bushes. There's only one outhouse in the village—at the priest's."

"Well, thank you."

Devoraleh entered the house quickly. I remained standing outside. I will leave the place first thing tomorrow, I decided. I dragged myself in back of the house, sinking deep into the snow. I was barely eighteen years old, but already I could find no place for myself in the world. My father had left Warsaw and became a rabbi in a tiny village in Galicia. The Jews there were all Hasidim of the rabbi of Belz. I could not go home to my parents with my shorn sidelocks, modern clothes, my worldly books and manuscripts—I would cause my father to lose his job. In Warsaw I had no one. In Bilgoray I supported myself by giving Hebrew lessons, but these had diminished from week to week. I suffered from bashfulness, fixed ideas. My lust for women disturbed my sleep at night. My brain ground like a millstone. In my imagination I carried on long discussions with writers, philosophers, with God Himself. Somewhere I had read an essay about von Hartmann, and I considered him the only consistent thinker. I agreed with him that there was no hope for humanity. There was only one way out for the whole species—to commit suicide. But to this von Hartmann, like Schopenhauer, said no.

I never knew that a night could be so long. My watch showed fifteen minutes to eight, but everyone in Naphtalie's household was already sleeping. Up in my garret room I sat down to write a play, trying to imitate Ibsen's *When We Dead Awaken*. After I spoiled three pages of a composition book, I tore them up and threw them into the tin stove, where the last coals were dying. Then I solved an algebraic problem for which it was necessary to apply a second-degree equation, but I had no desire to try another one. I had just read Kant's *Prolegomena*. If quantity is nothing more than a category of pure reason and has nothing to do with the thing in itself, it doesn't really pay to indulge in mathematics. I read a few theorems in the *Ethics* and I was suddenly angry with Spinoza and with my enthusiasm for him. To prove the existence of God by definition was too easy to convince anybody. Well, and what kind of God is He if He doesn't know of justice, mercy, doesn't punish crimes and reward good deeds? I was in need of a personal God to whom I could speak and from whom I could expect an answer. I had to come to grips with everything this very night.

I lay down on the bed and fell asleep. Immediately I was assailed by dreams. They followed one after another, unusually vivid and clear. I wrangled with someone, a female. In a strange way, my powers entered her and hers became mine. We poured fluid from one body into the other as if our bodies were vessels. Then we entered a little cell, but we were not alone. A man accompanied us, loudly singing a rhymed song. I wanted him to leave us alone, but his chanting said this could not be. Each verse was an aphorism, a revelation. "If I could only write this down!" I said to myself in the dream. I started and awoke. The kerosene lamp had gone out; my room was bathed in moonlight. I truly felt the earth cruising around the sun, running a sure course through the Milky Way for some divine purpose. "Don't be in despair," I said to myself. "God cannot be so mute, so deaf and amoral as the materialists profess." I stood at the window and raised my eyes to the stars. "I see you. Perhaps you see me too? I am of the same substance as you." I heard a shot, and all the village dogs began to bark lamentingly. I looked at my watch—a quarter past three. Could I have slept so long? It was as cold in the room as it was outside.

I put on my jacket and cap and went down the steps. In the kitchen, a candle was burning. Reb Naphtalie sat at the table in a cotton robe with a skullcap on his head, murmuring into a volume of the Mishnah. He was so engrossed that he didn't hear my steps. Everything in me became tense, and I felt both sorrow and joy. The world is asleep, but a Jew sits in this distant hamlet studying the Torah in the middle of the night. Here was eternity. Such Jews came to Poland hundreds of years ago, banished by the Teutons, the Celts, or whatever their names. They left graves all along the roads. They carried into the lands of the pagans bags with dry bread and books written on parchment and scrolls. Nothing has changed. They're the same Jews, and the books are the same.

Reb Naphtalie slowly turned his head toward me. "Have you wakened already?"

"The night is as long as the exile," I said.

"It will soon be day," Naphtalie answered. And I knew what he really meant: The redemption is near.

The next day I got acquainted with Zelig, Devoraleh's fiancé. He was a small fellow, young, with red cheeks and a shock of hair that seemed gray from the flour that had fallen on it. His shoes, his jacket, and his pants were also covered with flour. He smoked a cigarette from the corner of his mouth and let out rings of smoke. He spoke to me in a friendly and confidential manner. He had no use for Hebrew, but he wanted to study it because his dead father would have liked him to. The newspaper he read was in Polish. All his customers were Gentiles. He told me about the mill. He had just bought new machinery in Warsaw and was planning to build a sawmill; the water stream was strong and there were forests in the vicinity. Devoraleh happened to be busy in the store, and Zelig took me for a walk to the mill. I said I had decided to leave the village and return to Bilgoray, and he asked, "Why leave? I will recommend a shiksa to you."

He told me many things. The peasants were becoming enlightened. The young generation wanted leather boots, not makeshift shoes of rags and bark. They wanted shingled roofs, not thatch. The girls wanted to dress in the city style. Witos, the leader of the peasant party in the Sejm, sent speakers to Kocica, who lectured to the peasants on their needs. The Communists, too, had their agitators. Boys from Bilgoray, Zamość, Janów came and incited the villagers to rebellion. One of the agitators had been arrested and was waiting in the Janów prison. The trial would take place soon.

In front of the mill stood carts, sleighs—peasants waited for their turn to have their grain milled. Zelig and I stopped on the bridge and watched the water turning the wheel, whose spokes were glittering with ice. From here, one could see the chimney of the brewery. Zelig said to me, "If you yearn for Bilgoray, you can visit as often as you like. I go there every week. My future father-in-law also drives there frequently. He takes his wife to the ritual bath. He waits in a sleigh in front of the bathhouse. It is quite a task in the winter, but what won't a Jew do to please God?"

"You don't believe in such things, huh?"

"Nonsense. She could wash herself at home."

That day I began to tutor. Leibel and Bentze didn't want to study. They weren't interested at all in the story in Genesis of how Jacob left Beersheba and went to Haran. Their attention was all for the windows and the cooing of their pigeons. The boys had pockets full of nails and screws. They were building a sled. Devoraleh took to lessons fervently, but I realized at once how difficult it was for her to learn. She was slow to comprehend. She made many blotches. I wondered if she needed glasses. Rachele was the only one who showed promise. As to Etke, she could read and write a little Yiddish but had no desire to continue her studies. That fourteen-year-old girl said quite openly that the Jews should assimilate.

The following day Zelig took me to a young peasant woman—Mania, a widow. She lived not far from the brewery in a broken-down hut with a dirt floor. She had two black braids and a face as pockmarked as a potato grater. Zelig admitted to me that he slept with her—of course, only until he could be married to Devoraleh. Inside the hut one wall was hung with holy pictures. Mania sat barefoot on a stool, braiding a rope of straw. She smiled shyly, winked, and said about me, "He looks like a fifteen-year-old boy."

"He is our teacher."

"I let him come Saturday night."

I didn't stay in the village that long. Thursday, toward evening, Naphtalie drove his wife to the ritual bath in Bilgoray. That day I gave up tutoring and went with him. Besides his wife and myself, the sleigh carried a huge sack

of buckwheat. A heavy snow had obliterated the road.
Naphtalie wore a hood over his head; Beile Tsivya was
wrapped in a sheepskin and a Turkish shawl. I sat near
her on the back seat. She took up three-quarters of the
space. It was impossible to move away from her. She was
silent and bashful, and I imagine that I felt the heat that
emanated from her body. The sky hung low, laden with a
blizzard. The falling snow was as dry as salt, and it
whipped my face. We all kept silent. The wind howled
and whistled. The mare stopped from time to time. Once
in a while she turned her head backward with the kind of
curiosity animals sometimes display about human behavior. The horse seemed to wonder what sense it made to
roam in this kind of weather.

Night fell suddenly. One moment it was still day, and
then it became dark. The cold penetrated my coat. Beile
Tsivya purred like a cat. The horse maintained a slow
pace. Naphtalie was hunched over as if he had fallen
asleep. When we entered Bilgoray, I hardly recognized
the town—it was as if I had returned after years of absence. Snow had enveloped the entire settlement and only
outlines remained. Hills seemed to have formed where
before there were none. All the shutters were closed. I was
returning to a house where I was not wanted. I got off the
sleigh, took my valise, and said in a voice that sounded
changed even to me, "Please, Reb Naphtalie, forgive me.
I'm sorry."

I expected the sleigh to move on immediately in the
direction of the bathhouse, since we had been delayed in
the storm, but it remained standing. Naphtalie said to me,
"If you want, you can come back to us."

And I understood the real meaning of his words: The
gates of repentance are always open.

Translated by the author and Rosanna Gerber Cohen

The New Year Party

A woman called me on the telephone. She said, "I'm sure you don't know who I am, but from reading your books I've known you for at least twenty years. Also, we met once. My name is Pearl Leipziger."

"I know you quite well," I said. "I've read your poems. We met at Boris Lemkin's apartment on Park Avenue."

"Well, so you do remember. This is what I'm calling about. A few Yiddish women writers and some lovers of Yiddish literature have decided to celebrate New Year's. Boris Lemkin will be coming. As a matter of fact, it was his idea. We all thought it would be good if you could come. There will be several women, and two men besides you: Boris Lemkin and Harry, his shadow. I know that you're a well-known writer while we are just a bunch of old beginners—practically amateurs—but we love literature and we're your faithful readers. Believe me, you'll be in the midst of true admirers."

"Pearl Leipziger, I shall be honored to come to your

party. What's the address and what time should I be
there?"

"Oh, this will be a treat. After all, New Year's Eve is
something of a holiday even for us. Come whenever you
like—the earlier the better. Wait, I have an idea—why not
come for supper? Boris will join us, and Harry and the
others can come later. I know what you want to tell me
—that you're a vegetarian. You can depend on me. I will
prepare for you a soup like the soups your mother used
to make."

"How do you know about my mother's soups?"

"From your stories, of course."

Pearl Leipziger gave me her address in the East Bronx,
along with the exact instructions of how to get there by
subway. She thanked me again and again. I knew that
Pearl was past fifty, but her voice sounded young and
strong.

On the day of New Year's Eve, a heavy snow fell. The
streets were white, and toward evening the sky turned
violet. New York reminded me of Warsaw. All that was
lacking was the horse-drawn sleighs. Walking in the snow,
I imagined that I heard their bells jingling. I bought a
bottle of champagne and I managed to catch a taxi to the
Bronx—no small accomplishment on New Year's Eve. It
was still early but already children were blowing their
horns to usher in the New Year. The taxi drove through a
Jewish neighborhood, and here and there I saw a Christ-
mas tree strung with little lights and tinsel. Some of the
stores were closed. In others, late shoppers were buying
food and liquor. Riding along, I reproached myself for
avoiding other writers and for staying away from their
meetings and parties. The trouble was that the moment I
met them they would give me the latest gossip of what this
one had said of me and what another had written. Leftist
writers scolded me for failing to promote world revolution.
The Zionists reproached me for not dramatizing the struggle of the Jewish state and the heroism of its pioneers.

Boris Lemkin was a rich real-estate man who, in a small
way, patronized Yiddish writers and artists. Authors sent

him their books and he mailed them checks. He bought
paintings. He lived on Park Avenue with Harry, an old
friend from Rumania. Boris used to call him "my dictator."
Actually, Harry, or Herschel, was Boris's butler and cook.
Boris Lemkin was known as a gourmet and a ladies' man.
For years he had been separated from his wife. Someone
told me that he owned a huge collection of pornographic
photographs and films.

At a quarter past six my taxi stopped in front of the
building where Pearl lived, and I took the elevator to the
fourth floor. She was waiting for me at the open door of
her apartment. She was short, with a high bosom, broad
hips, a round forehead, a hooked nose, and large black
eyes, from which shone the Polish-Jewish joy of life that
no troubles seem able to mar. She wore a sequined evening dress and gold kid shoes. Her hair was freshly dyed
black and swept up. Her fingernails were lacquered with
crimson polish. A gold Star of David hung around her
neck, long earrings dangled from her earlobes, and a diamond sparkled from one of her fingers—surely all gifts
from Boris Lemkin. She had probably had a few drinks
already, because although she hardly knew me she kissed
me. Even as I stepped over the threshold, I smelled the
aroma of my mother's soup: the barley, the lentils, the
dried mushrooms, the fried onions. The living room was
cluttered with bric-a-brac. On the walls hung paintings
which I guessed were done by Boris Lemkin's protégés.

"Where is Boris?" I asked.

"Late as always," Pearl said, "but he phoned to say that
he would be here soon. Let's have a drink while we wait.
What would you like? I have almost anything you can
name. I baked the anise cookies that you love—don't ask
me how I know."

As we drank sherry and ate anise cookies, Pearl said,
"You have many enemies but also many friends. I am one
of your true advocates. I don't let anyone slander you in
front of me. And what don't they say! That you're a snob,
a cynic, a misanthrope, a recluse. But I, Pearl Leipziger,
defend you like a lioness. Some kibitzer went so far as to

hint that I must be your mistress! I tell them all the same
thing: I have only to open one of their books to begin to
yawn, but when—"

The telephone rang and Pearl snatched up the receiver.
She said, "Yes, he's here. He came right on time. He
brought me champagne like a real cavalier. Boris? No,
not yet. He's probably busy with one of his yentas. My
literary stock must have fallen, but I remind myself that
before God we are all equal. To Him a fly is no less important than Shakespeare. Don't be late. What? You don't
have to bring anything. I've bought so much cake that it
will last until Passover."

It was twenty past seven and Boris had still not arrived.
In one hour Pearl and I had become so intimate that she
entrusted me with all of her secrets. She was saying, "I
come from a pious home. If anyone had told me that I
wouldn't marry according to the Law of Moses and Israel
I would have thought it a bad joke. But America shattered
us. My father was compelled to work on the Sabbath and
this was a terrible blow to him and my mother. Actually,
it killed them. I began to attend leftist meetings where
they preached atheism and free love. At one of them I met
Boris. He swore to me that the minute he was divorced
from his shrew we would stand under the wedding canopy.
I swallowed everything. He's such an ingenious liar it took
me years to catch on to what he was. Even today he won't
admit that he has other women, and this makes me sick.
Why does a man of seventy need so many affairs? He's
like those Romans with their vomitoriums, getting rid of
one repast in order to partake of another. He's crazy too.
How crazy he is you will never know, but when it comes
to making money he's smarter than all of us. Four weeks
before the Crash in 1929 he sold all his stocks and was
left with a half-million dollars in cash. In those days, with
that much cash you could have bought half of America.
He doesn't know himself how rich he is now. But just the
same every penny he gives me he doles out. When he goes
on a binge he'll squander thousands, and suddenly he's

stingy about a nickel. There's someone at the door—it's him at last."

Pearl ran to let him in. I soon heard Boris Lemkin's voice. He didn't speak—he bellowed. He sounded as if he were drunk. Boris Lemkin was short, as round as a barrel, with a red face, white hair, and white bushy eyebrows from under which a pair of beady eyes peered out. He wore a tuxedo, a pink ruffled shirt, and patent-leather shoes. A cigar was stuck between his thick lips. He extended a hand to me that had rings on three fingers, and shouted, *"Shalom aleichem!* I read every word you write. Please don't seduce my Pearl. She's all I have. What would I be without her? Less than nothing. Pearl darling, give me something to drink, my throat is dry."

"You'll drink later. Now we'll go to eat."

"Eat? Who invented that? Not on New Year's Eve."

"You'll eat whether you like it or not."

"Well, if she insists on eating, one eats. Do you see my belly? It could eat its way through a grocery store and a butcher shop and still not be full. I've donated my body for dissection after my death. The doctors will discover wonders of medical knowledge there."

We went to the kitchen. Though Boris maintained that he wasn't hungry, he gulped down two bowlfuls of soup. He slurped and sighed, and Pearl said, "Still a pig."

"I had a clever mother," Boris said, "and she used to say, 'Berele, take it all in while you can. You can't eat in the grave.' In Bessarabia we had a dish called *karnatzlech,* and there's only one man in America who knows how to make them and that's Harry. He's no good for anything else, that eunuch. You can give him a five-dollar bill and make him believe it's one hundred dollars, but when it comes to cooking, the chef of the Waldorf Astoria can't hold a candle to him. Then he has an instinct that God gives only to idiots. When Harry tells me to buy a stock I don't waste a second; I call my broker and tell him to buy. And when Harry says sell, I sell. He knows absolutely nothing about stocks—General Motors he calls General Mothers. How can you explain this?"

"There's no explanation for anything," I said.

"My own words. There is a God, no doubt about it, but since He's chosen to be silent for the last four thousand years and doesn't want to say a word even to Rabbi Stephen Wise, then we owe Him nothing. We must do what is written in the Haggadah: 'Eat, drink, and enjoy yourself.' "

About nine o'clock the women writers began to arrive. One of them, Mira Royskez, a woman of eighty, I remembered from Warsaw. Her face had innumerable wrinkles, but her eyes were as lively and clear as those of a young girl. Mira Royskez had published a book titled *Man Is Good*. She had brought Pearl a schmalz cake that she had baked herself.

Matilda Feingevirtz—short, broad, with a huge bust and the face of a Polish peasant—wrote love poems. Her contribution was a bottle of syrup to pour on Hanukkah latkes.

Berta Kosatzky, her disheveled hair dyed carrot color, was known as a writer of pulp novels for the Yiddish press. Her heroines were all country girls who were seduced by big-town charlatans, then driven into prostitution, and then to suicide. Before she came, Pearl Leipziger had sworn to me that Berta was still a virgin. Berta Kosatzky brought a babka, and the moment Boris Lemkin saw it he grabbed it and ate half of it, hollering that only saints in Paradise were served such delicacies.

The most diminutive of the group was Comrade Tsloveh, a midget of a woman who was supposed to have played a giant part in the Revolution of 1905. Her husband, Feivel Blecher, was hanged for an assassination attempt on a police commissioner in Warsaw. Tsloveh herself had been an expert at making bombs. Her gift to Pearl was a pair of woolen stockings—the kind that schoolgirls used to wear in Warsaw fifty years ago.

Harry came last. He brought Pearl a magnum of champagne, which Boris had told him to buy for the party. Harry was tall, lean, with a long, freckled face and yellow hair that hadn't a strand of gray. He looked like an

Irishman. He wore a derby, a bow tie, and a summer coat.
The moment Harry entered, Boris cried, "Where's the
duck?"

"I couldn't get any duck."

"There's not a duck left in the whole of New York?"
Boris shouted. "Was there a duck epidemic? Were all
ducks deported back to Europe?"

"Boris, I couldn't find a single duck."

"Well, we'll have to do without duck. I got up this morning with a craving for roast duck. For every duck that
could be bought tonight in New York I would like to have
a million dollars tax-free."

"What would you do with so much money?" I asked.

"I would buy up all the ducks in the whole of America."

Even though Pearl lived on a side street, from time to
time one could hear the sound of party horns. Matilda
Feingevirtz turned on the radio and the broadcaster announced that approximately one hundred thousand people
had gathered at Times Square to celebrate the New Year.
He also predicted the number of traffic accidents that
would occur over the holiday. Boris Lemkin had already
begun to kiss Pearl and the other women. He was pouring
himself one drink after another, and as his face became
redder his hair seemed to become whiter. He laughed,
clapped his hands, and tried to force Comrade Tsloveh,
the bombmaker, to dance with him. He lifted Pearl off
the floor, and she complained that he was tearing her
garters.

All the while Harry sat on the sofa quietly and soberly,
with the seriousness of a valet looking after his master. I
asked him how long he had known Boris and he said, "We
went to cheder together."

"He looks twenty years older than you."

"In my family we don't turn gray."

The telephone rang and Pearl went to answer it. She
began to speak in a singsong voice in the Warsaw manner:
"Who? What? *Nu,* are you teasing or what? Huh? I'm not
a prophet." Suddenly she became tense. "Well, I'm lis-

tening," she murmured. Boris had gone to the bathroom. The women exchanged glances of curiosity. Pearl remained silent but her face acted out astonishment, anger, disgust, though from time to time her eyes filled with laughter. Before Pearl began to write, she had done some acting on the Yiddish stage. At last she spoke again. "What is he—a half-year-old infant who's been kidnapped by gypsies? A man of seventy should know what he wants. I seduced him? Forgive me, but when he started playing around with you I was still in my cradle."

Boris came back to the living room. "Why is it so quiet in here? Are you all reciting the Silent Benedictions?"

Pearl covered the mouthpiece of the telephone with the palm of her hand. "Boris, it's for you."

"For me? Who is it?"

"Your great-grandmother has risen from the grave. Go pick up the extension in the bedroom."

Boris looked at Harry questioningly. He walked unsteadily toward the bedroom. At the door he threw Pearl a glance that seemed to ask, "Do you intend to listen in?" Pearl sat in the corner of the sofa, the receiver pressed to her ear. We could hear muffled shouts. Harry knitted his yellow eyebrows. Some of the women writers shook their heads and others tsk-tsked. I went to look at the paintings that hung in the open-arched foyer adjoining the living room: Jews praying at the Wailing Wall, Hasidim dancing, scholars studying the Talmud, and a bride being led to the wedding canopy. I removed a book from the bookcase and read a scene in one of Berta Kosatzky's novels about a man who entered a brothel and there recognized his former fiancée. By the time I put it back, Boris had returned from the bedroom. "I don't need spies and I owe nothing to anyone!" he was yelling. "Go to hell, all of you. Parasites, schlemiels, leeches!"

"The bubble has burst." Pearl Leipziger spoke triumphantly. She tried to light a cigarette, but the lighter did not work.

"What bubble? Who has burst? As of this minute the comedy is over. I don't need a bunch of old harridans who

drain me dry and keep on demanding more. I never promised to be faithful to any of you or all the other garbage.
Phooey!"

"The truth hurts, huh?"

"The truth is you're as much a writer as I am a Turk!"
Boris bellowed. "Every time you write something, I have
to bribe the publisher to print it. And that goes for the
lot of you." Boris pointed at the other women. "I tried to
read your poetry. *Hertz-schmertz! Liebe-schmiebe!* Eight-
year-old schoolchildren can do better. Who needs your
writing? The only thing it's good for is to wrap herring
in."

"May God shame you the way you are shaming me!"
Pearl cried out.

"There is no God. Harry, come."

Harry did not stir. "Boris, you are drunk. Go to the
bathroom and wash your face. Maybe you have Alka-
Seltzer?" he asked Pearl.

"I'm drunk, huh? Everyone throws the truth in my face,
but the one time I speak the truth you call me a drunk. I
don't need to wash my face and I don't need Alka-Seltzer.
I told you to bring me a duck, but you were too lazy to
look for one. You're like all of them—a *schnorrer,* a beggar, a bum. Listen to me!" Boris howled. "If I don't get a
roast duck tonight, you're fired and you can go to hell.
Tomorrow morning I'll throw out your junk and you'll
not show your face in my house again. Is that clear?"

"Clear enough."

"Will you get me a duck now or not?"

"Not tonight."

"Tonight or never. I'm going. You can stay here."

Boris started toward the foyer. Suddenly he saw me
and took a step backward. He looked at me with bewilderment. "I didn't mean you—not you. Where did you
disappear? I thought you'd left already."

"I was looking at the paintings," I answered.

"What paintings? Imitations, smudges. Those Hasidim
have been dancing for a hundred years. So-called artists
smear mud on canvas and want me to pay them for it.

Pearl has saved a nest egg from my money—the reason she's so high and mighty. Up to two years ago I worked sixteen hours a day. I work ten hours every day now. That ignoramus Harry thinks I can't do without him. I need him like a hole in the head. He can't so much as write his name. He couldn't even become a citizen. He drives the car with my license, and I have to sit in front because he can't read the signs. I'm leaving the whole rotten bunch and going to Europe or to Palestine! Where's my coat?"

Boris ran to the door but Pearl blocked his way. She spread out her hands with the red fingernails and cried, "Boris, you can't drive the car in the state you're in! You'll kill yourself and ten others. The radio said—"

"It's myself I'll kill, not you. Where's my coat?"

"Harry, don't let him go. Harry," Pearl whined.

Harry approached slowly. "Boris, you're making an ass of yourself."

"Shut up! You can play the gentleman for them, but I know what you are. Your father was a coachman's helper and your mother . . . You yourself ran away to America because you stole a horse. Is that true or not?"

"True or not, I've served you for forty years. I could have made a fortune, but I never got a penny from you. As Jacob said to Laban, 'I have taken from you neither an ox nor a donkey.' "

"That's what Moses said to the Jews, not Jacob to Laban."

"Let it be Moses. If you want to kill yourself, open the window and jump like those suckers in the time of the Crash. Why ruin the Cadillac?"

"Idiot, it's my Cadillac—not yours," Boris said, and laughed so hard that the women came running. He bent over, about to collapse from the weight of his laughter. With one hand Harry grabbed Boris's shoulder and with the other he slapped him on the nape. Mira Royskez hurried to the kitchen and brought a glass of water. Boris straightened. "Water you give me? Vodka is what I need —not water." He embraced Harry and kissed him. "Don't leave me, pal, brother, heir. I've willed you everything—

my whole fortune. All the others are enemies—my wife, my children, my girl friends. What do I want from life? A little friendship and a piece of duck." Boris grimaced, his eyes filled with tears. He coughed, wheezed, and began to cry as violently as he had laughed a moment before. "Harry, save me!"

"Drunk as Lot!" Pearl Leipziger called.

"Come, lie down," Harry said. He took Boris's arm and he half led, half dragged him into the bedroom. Boris fell on Pearl Leipziger's bed, snored once, and slept immediately. Pearl's face, which in the beginning of the evening seemed young and lively, had become pale, wrinkled, and wilted. Her eyes expressed a strange mixture of sorrow and anger. "What will you do with so much money, Harry?" she asked. "Be as foolish as he was?"

Harry smiled. "You don't have to worry. He'll outlive us all."

The four women writers had apartments in the East Bronx, and Harry drove them home. I sat beside him up front. So much snow had fallen that Harry had difficulty driving on the side streets where they lived. Like an old-country coachman, he carried every one of them over the mounds of snow and set them down on their stoops. All this time Harry was silent. But when he drove out to Seaman Avenue he said, "Well, so we have a New Year."

"I hear that you are a specialist in preparing *karnatzlech*," I said, just to say something.

Harry immediately became talkative. "There's no trick to it. If the meat is good and you know what ingredients to use, they have to come out right. In your country, Poland, the Jews went to their rabbis. In Lithuania they studied in yeshivas, but in Bessarabia we ate *mameliga* and *karnatzlech* and we drank wine. There it was Purim all year round. Boris called me ignoramus. I am not an ignoramus. I went to cheder and on Friday I knew the chapter of the Pentateuch better than he. But here in America he studied a little English and I had no patience for it. I know Yiddish better than he. And for what did I

need to become a citizen? Here no one asks for a passport.
He went into business and I worked in shops. Over a few
years we didn't meet at all. By the time I came to him he
had a wife—Henrietta is her name, a harpy, a bitch.
'Where did you get a Xanthippe like this?' I asked him.
'Herschel,' he said, 'I was blind. Help me, because if you
don't she will drive me into my grave.' They weren't separated yet. He had an office and I moved into it. He had
developed stomach ulcers from Henrietta's cooking—she
overseasoned everything. Who knows, perhaps she wanted
to poison him. There was a gas range in the office and I
became his cook. He has a license, but he can't drive a car.
When he drives he has accidents, so I became his chauffeur. I know how to read signs; I have never needed him to
read them for me. When I drive on a road once, I can
recognize it in the middle of the night. We became like
brothers—even closer. He let Henrietta torture him for
another couple of years, and altogether she bore him two
daughters and one son. None of them is any good. His
older daughter has been divorced five times. The other is
a vicious spinster. The son became a lawyer for gangsters.
Before the thugs go out on a job, they come to him and he
teaches them how to outsmart the law. Boris said that I
stole a horse. I didn't steal it. It was my father's horse.
What was I saying? That Henrietta never gave him a divorce. Why should she divorce him when she could have
everything she wanted? Today it's easier to get rid of a bad
wife. In those times every yenta in America was considered
a lady and could send her husband up before the judge.
Boris is crazy about women, but they don't attract me.
Most females are gold diggers. All they want is your
money. I don't like their slyness, but Boris enjoys being
taken in. He falls for writers, painters, actresses, and the
like. When they go after him with their smooth talk from
the books, he loses his mind. After he got his separation
from Henrietta, Boris moved into an apartment on Park
Avenue, and I left the office and joined him. Many a time
he would come home and cry out, 'Harry, I can't take it
any more—they're as false as the pagan gods!' 'Get rid of

them,' I would say. He would fall on his knees and swear
by his father's soul that he would send them away to hell,
but the next day he'd be back with one or another.

" 'Eunuch,' he calls me. I'm not a eunuch. I'm a normal man. Women have loved me for myself, not for my
checks. Where would I get checks? Boris is mad about
money. But to me friendship is dearer than millions. I
work for him for nothing, just like that slave in the Bible.
All I needed was for him to take me to the doorpost and
pierce my ear. I never had anything from him except the
piece of bread I ate and the bed I slept in. There was one
girl I liked and it might have worked out for us, but
when Boris heard of it he made such a ruckus you'd have
thought I was going to kill him. 'How can you do that to
me!' he cried. He promised to make me a partner in the
business—anything. He bothered me about it until I got
cold feet. I have no feeling for books, but I always liked
the theater. I took her to the Yiddish theater. I saw them
all—Adler, Tomashevsky, Kessler. She and I used to
share our thoughts, as they say, but I let Boris tear us
apart. I have a weak character. He is as strong as I am
weak. He can make you do anything he wants. He could
make wives leave their husbands. He dragged women
from good homes into affairs with him. This Pearl
Leipziger is nothing more than a fifth wheel to the
wagon. Some of his girl friends got old and died. Others
are sick. One of them he put into an institution. He
boasts about his stomach. The truth is, his ulcers never
healed. Then he has high blood pressure. Another person would have died long ago, but he's decided to live
for one hundred years, and when he makes up his mind
about something it has to come true. There was an
actress by the name of Rosalia Carp, a beautiful woman,
a real prima donna. She had a voice that you could hear
half the length of Second Avenue. When she stepped out
on the stage and played Cleopatra, all the men fell in
love with her. In those days Boris used to tell me everything. He never kept a secret from me. One night he
came home from the theater and said, 'Harry, I've fallen

in love with Rosalia Carp.' *'Mazeltov,'* I said. 'That's all you need.' 'What's the matter?' he asked. 'She's made for men, not for the angel Gabriel.' In those years, when Boris fell for a woman he kept on sending her gifts— huge bouquets of flowers, boxes of chocolates, even furs. Of course I was the go-between, and I couldn't tell you how many times Rosalia Carp insulted me. She even threatened to call the super. Once she said to me, 'What does he want from me? I don't care for him.' Then she smiled and said, 'If I were on an island with both of you, guess who I would choose.' That time she spoke sweetly to me and used all her female tricks. Any other person in my place would have known what to do. But it isn't in my nature to be false."

"What happened—Boris got her?" I asked.

"What a question! And two years later he threw her away. This is Boris Lemkin."

The car had stopped at my building on Central Park West. I wanted to get out but Harry said, "Wait another minute."

A predawn stillness hovered over New York. The traffic lights changed, but not a single car passed by. Harry sat sunk in thought. He seemed to have grasped the riddle of his own being and was trying to solve it. Then he said to me and to himself, "Where can I get a duck in the middle of this night? Nowhere."

Almost three years passed. One afternoon, when I was sitting in my office reading proofs, I saw Harry. His hair had turned platinum white, but he still looked young. He said, "I bet you don't recognize me, but—"

"I remember you very well, Harry."

"I expect you know that Boris has been dead for more than a year."

"Yes, I know. Sit down. How are you?"

"Oh, fine. All right."

"I even know that Boris didn't leave you a penny," I said, regretting my words at once.

Harry smiled bashfully. "He left nothing to anyone—

not to Pearl or any of the others. All those years he
talked about a will, but he never wrote one. A good half
of his fortune was taken by Uncle Sam and the rest by
his wife, that bitch, and his children. The son, the shy-
ster, came running the morning after his father's death
and threw me out of the apartment. He even tried to
grab some of my belongings. But it didn't kill me; I earn
my bread."

"What do you do?"

"Oh, I've become a waiter. Not in New York. Here
the union wouldn't take me, but I got a job in a hotel in
the Catskills. In the winter I go to Miami Beach and I
am a cook there in a kosher hotel. My *karnatzlech* are
famous. Why did I need his money?"

For a while we were both silent. Then Harry said,
"You must be wondering why I came to you."

"No, I'm not wondering at all. I'm glad to see you."

"This is the thing. Boris still has no headstone. A few
times I called his son to remind him about it, and he kept
on promising—later, tomorrow, next week he would
order one. But it was to put me off. I have saved a little
money and I decided to order a headstone for Boris myself. After all, we were like brothers. Once a teacher
came to our town and he said that what has already happened even God cannot change. Is that true?"

"I believe so."

"After there was a Hitler, how could God have turned
back time and made him not to be? Boris and I were
brought up together. He wasn't a bad man—only superstitious and selfish. He didn't write a will because he
was afraid that this would make him die sooner. We
were together for over forty years, and I don't want his
name to be forgotten. I've come to New York today to
take care of this. I went to a headstone engraver and I
asked him to engrave an inscription in Yiddish. I don't
know much Hebrew and neither did Boris. I wanted him
to engrave, 'Dear Boris, be healthy and happy wherever
you are,' but the engraver said that one cannot say 'Be
healthy' of a dead man. We began to argue and I told

him about you—that I knew you and that we once had spent a New Year's Eve together. He told me to come to you and that if you said it's all right he would engrave what I wanted. That's why I am here."

"I'm afraid that the engraver is right," I said. "You can say 'Be happy' to the dead if you believe in the hereafter, but health is a property of the body. How can you wish health to a body which has decayed?"

"You mean one cannot write what I want?"

"Harry, it doesn't make sense."

"But 'healthy' doesn't mean just healthy. It used to be said, 'In a healthy body there is a healthy soul.' "

How strange—Harry began to debate with me about the usage of words. From his examples, I realized for the first time that in Yiddish one often uses the same word for "sound," "sane," and "healthy"—*gesunt.* I proposed to Harry that instead of "healthy" he inscribe "content," but Harry said, "I lay awake many nights thinking. These words came into my mind and I would like the inscription to be like that. Is it written in the Torah that such words are forbidden?"

"No, there is no law in the Torah about such things, but if someone passes by and reads it, he may smile."

"Let him smile. I don't care. Boris didn't care when people made fun of him."

"So you want me to call up the engraver and tell him that I agree?"

"If you don't mind."

Harry gave me the engraver's number. Even though I had a telephone on my desk, I went to another room to make the call. The engraver tried to prove to me that wishing health to a corpse was a kind of sacrilege, but I offered a quotation from the Talmud to refute this. I felt like a lawyer who defends a case against his own convictions. After a while the engraver said, "If this is your verdict, I will do as you say."

"Yes, I'll take it upon myself."

I walked back toward my office, and through the open door I saw Harry sitting engrossed in his thoughts, look-

ing at the Williamsburg Bridge, which was visible from
my window, and at the streets of the East Side, the ma-
jority of whose tenements had been torn down and re-
built or were in the process of being reconstructed. I
myself barely recognized the neighborhood. A golden
dust fell over the wrecked buildings, the ditches, the
bulldozers, the cranes, the heaps of cement and sand.
I stood gazing at Harry's profile. How had he become
what he was? How did this illiterate man reach a spiritual height that is rare even among thinkers, philosophers, poets? That New Year's Eve when I had come
home from Pearl Leipziger's party at four o'clock in the
morning, I felt that the hours I had spent there had been
wasted. Now, almost three years later, I learned a lesson
I would never forget. When I told Harry that the inscription would read as he wanted it to, his face lit up.
"Thank you, thank you. You did me a great favor."

"You are one of the noblest men I have ever met," I
said.

"What have I done? We were friends."

"I didn't know that such friendship existed."

Harry looked at me questioningly. He rose, extended
his hand, and murmured, "Only God knows the whole
truth."

Translated by the author and Rosanna Gerber Cohen

A Tale of Two Sisters

Leon, or Haim Leib, Bardeles poured cream into his coffee. He put in a lot of sugar, tasted it, grimaced, added more cream, and took a bite of the macaroon the waiter had brought him.

He said, "I like my coffee sweet, not bitter. In Rio de Janeiro they drink tiny little cups of coffee that's as bitter as gall. They serve it here, too—espresso—but I like a glass of coffee like you used to get in Warsaw. When I sit here with you, I forget that I'm in Buenos Aires. It seems to me we're in Lurs's in Warsaw. What do you say to the weather, eh? It took me a long time to get used to Sukkoth falling in the spring and Passover in the fall. I can't even begin to tell you the confusion this topsy-turvy calendar brings out in our people. Hanukkah comes during a heat wave and you can melt. On Shevuot, it's cold. Well, at least the spring smells are the same— the lilac has the same aroma that used to waft in from the Praga Woods and the Saxony Gardens. I recognize the smells, but I cannot identify them. The Gentile writers list every flower and plant, but how many names are there for flowers in Yiddish? I know only two kinds of flowers—roses and lilies. When I go to a florist's once in a while to buy someone a bouquet. I always rely on the clerk. Drink your coffee!"

"Tell the story," I said.

"Eh? Can it be told? Where shall I begin? I promised to tell you everything, the whole truth, but can you tell the truth? Wait, I'll have a cigarette first. Actually, one of your American cigarettes."

Leon Bardeles took out one of the packs of cigarettes I had brought him from New York. I had known him over thirty years. I had once even written an introduction for a book of his poems. He was fifty-three or fifty-four and had survived the Hitler hell and the Stalin terror, but he still looked young for his age. He had a head of black curly hair, big black eyes, a thick lower lip, and a neck and shoulders that exuded masculine strength. He still wore a shirt with a *Slowacki* collar, just as in Warsaw. He blew smoke rings and gazed at me with narrowed eyes, like an artist at a model.

He said, "I'll begin in the middle. I beg you: Don't ask me for any dates, because when it comes to that I'm completely disoriented. It must have been 1946, or maybe it was still the end of '45. I had left Stalin's Russia and gone back to Poland. In Russia I was supposed to go into the Polish Army, but I wormed my way out of it. I went through Warsaw and saw the ruins of the ghetto. You wouldn't believe this, but I actually went looking for the house where I had lived in 1939—maybe I'd find some of my manuscripts among the bricks. The chances of recognizing the house on Nowolipki Street and finding a manuscript after all the bombardments and fires were less than zero, but I recognized the ruins of the house and found a printed book of mine, actually the one with your introduction. Only the last page was missing. I was amazed, but not terribly so. So many incredible things have occurred in my life that I have become completely blasé. If I came home and found my dead mother tonight, I wouldn't blink an eye. I'd say, 'Momma, how are you?'

"From Warsaw I stumbled on to Lublin and from there to Stettin. Most of the cities lay in ruins and we slept in stables, barracks, and in the street, too. They berate me here in Buenos Aires why I don't write about my experiences. First of all, I'm not a prose writer. Secondly, everything has grown jumbled in my mind, particularly the dates and names of towns, and I'm sure that I'd brew up such a stew of errors that they'd call me a liar and a fabricator. Some refugees were half-mad. One woman had lost a child and she looked for it in ditches, in haystacks, in the most unlikely places. In Warsaw a deserter from the Red Army took it into his head that there were treasures buried beneath the rubble. He stood in the bitter frost and dug with a spade among the bricks. Dictatorships, wars, and cruelty drive whole countries to madness. My theory is that the human species was crazy from the very first and that civilization and culture are only enhancing man's insanity. Well, but you want the facts.

"The facts, to make it brief, were these: In Stettin I met a woman who literally bewitched me on the spot. You know that I've had a good many women in my life. In Russia there was a lack of everything except so-called love. The way I am, no danger, crisis, hunger, or even sickness can rob me of that which is now called a libido, or whatever names the professors dream up for it. It was as far from the romantic love of our youth as we're now from Jupiter. All of a sudden, I'm standing in front of a woman and gaping as if I'd never seen a female before. Describe her? I'm not good at description. She had long black hair and skin white as marble. You must forgive me all these banalities. Eyes she had that were dark and strangely frightened. Fear was nothing unusual in those days. You risked your life every second. Russia wouldn't let us out and we were supposed to enter Palestine illegally, since England wouldn't let us in. False papers were arranged for us, but it was easy to tell that they weren't in order. Well, but those eyes reflected another kind of fear. It was somehow as if this girl had been dropped on earth from another planet and didn't know where she was. Maybe that's what the fallen angels looked like. But those were men. She wore cracked shoes and a magnificent nightgown that she mistook for a dress. The Joint Distribution Committee had sent underwear and clothes to Europe that rich American ladies had donated to the refugees, and she had received this costly nightgown. Besides fear, her face expressed a rare kind of gentility. All this somehow didn't jibe with reality. Such delicate creatures usually didn't survive the war. They dropped like flies. Those who made it were the strong, the resolute, and often those who walked over the corpses of others. For all my womanizing, I am somewhat bashful. I'm never the one to make the first move. But I virtually couldn't tear myself away. I mustered my courage and asked her if I could help her. I spoke to her in Polish. At first she was silent and I suspected that she was mute. She looked at me with the kind of helplessness often seen in a child. Then she replied in Polish, 'Thank you. You cannot help me.'

"Ordinarily, when someone gives me this kind of rebuff, I walk away, but this time something held me back. It turned out that she came from a Hasidic home and was the daughter of a Warsaw landlord, a follower of the Alexander rabbi. Deborah, or Dora, was one of those Hasidic girls who are raised in an almost assimilated atmosphere. She attended a private girls' Gymnasium and studied piano and dancing. At the same time, a rabbi's wife came to her house to tutor her in prayers and Jewish law. Before the war, she had two older brothers, the elder of whom already had a wife in Bedzin, while the younger studied in a yeshiva. She also had an older sister. The war made a quick mess of the family. The father was killed by a German bomb, the older brother in Bedzin was shot by the Nazis, the younger brother was drafted into the Polish Army and killed somewhere, the mother died of starvation and kidney disease in the Warsaw ghetto, and the sister, Ytta, disappeared and Dora didn't know where she was. Dora had a French teacher on the Aryan side, a spinster named Elzbieta Dolanska, and she saved Dora. How she did this would take too long to tell. Dora spent two years in a cellar and the teacher fed her with her last savings. A saint of a woman, but she perished during the Polish uprising. That's how the Almighty rewards the good Gentiles.

"I didn't get all this out of her at once but gradually, literally drawing out word after word. I said to her, 'In Palestine you'll get back on your feet. You'll be among friends.'

" 'I can't go to Palestine,' she said.

" 'Why not? Where, then?'

" 'I must go to Kuibyshev.'

"I couldn't believe my own ears. Imagine, a trip in those days from Stettin back to the Bolsheviks—and to Kuibyshev. The road was rife with danger.

" 'What business have you in Kuibyshev?' I asked her and she told me a story that, if I hadn't confirmed it myself later, I would have called the ravings of a sick mind. Her sister, Ytta, had jumped from the train taking her to the concentration camp and made her way through the fields and forests to Russia. There she lived with a Jewish engineer who had attained a high rank in the Red Army. This officer was later killed in the war and Ytta lost her mind. She was confined in an insane asylum in that area. Through wild chance, actually a miracle, Dora found out that her sister was still alive. I asked her, 'How can you help your sister when she is insane? There she at least gets medical care. What can you do for a deranged woman without money, an apartment, or a groschen to your name? You'll both die.'

"And she said, 'You are perfectly right, but she is the only one left of my family and I can't leave her to waste her years away in a Soviet asylum. It's possible that she'll get well when she sees me.'

"It's usually not my way to mix into other people's

business. The war taught me that you can't help anybody. In essence, we were all walking on graves. When
you spend years in camps and prisons and stare death in
the face ten times a day, you lose all compassion. But
when I heard what this girl proposed to do, I was filled
with a kind of pity that I had never felt before. I tried to
talk her out of it time and again. I offered a thousand
arguments.

"She said, 'I know that you are right, but I must go
back.'

" 'How will you get there?' I asked her, and she said,
'I'm ready to go even on foot.'

"I said, 'I'm afraid you're no less crazy than your
sister.'

"And she replied, 'I fear that you're right.'

"After all his wanderings and tribulations, the person
sitting here next to you gave up the chance to go to
Israel, which was to me at that time the most beautiful
dream, and I went off with a strange girl to Kuibyshev.
It was actually an act of suicide. One thing I found out
then was that pity is a form of love and, actually, its
highest expression. I won't describe the trip to you—it
was not a trip but an odyssey. I can only tell you that the
Reds detained us twice along the way and it failed by a
whisker that we didn't both end up in prison or in a slave
camp. Dora behaved in a strangely heroic fashion during
the trip, but I sensed that this was more resignation than
bravery. I forgot to tell you—she was a virgin and
underneath all that despair lay a passionate woman. I
was used to women loving me, but this was different
from anything I had ever known. She clung to me in a
mixture of love and desperation that frightened me. She
had an education and in the cellar where she had hidden
for two years she had read a whole library in Polish,
French, and German, but she lacked all experience.
Every little thing frightened her. In her hiding place she
had read many Christian books as well as the works of
Madame Blavatsky, and occult and theosophic writings
that had been left to Miss Dolanska by an aunt. Dora

babbled on about Jesus and ghosts, but I had no patience for such things, even though I myself had become a mystic, or at least a fatalist, during the Holocaust. Oddly enough, she combined all this with the Jewishness of her home.

"There was no particular hardship in crossing the border into Russia, but the trains were jammed. In the middle of everything, the locomotive was uncoupled, hooked on to some other wagons, and we were left standing there for days on end. In the cars, the passengers fought constantly. A brawl would erupt and everyone would be shoved out of the wagons. Corpses lay scattered along the tracks. The cold inside the cars was frightful. Some people even rode on flatcars while the snow fell on them. In the closed cars you had to carry a chamber pot or a bottle in which to relieve yourself. A peasant sat on the roof of a car, and when the train entered a tunnel, he lost his head. And that's how we got to Kuibyshev. All the way there, I couldn't stop wondering at myself over what I had done. This thing with Dora was no simple affair. I had actually bound myself up with her for life. To abandon someone like that would have been like leaving a child alone in a forest. Even before we got there, we got into all kinds of conflicts, all of which had to do with the fact that Dora was afraid to leave me alone for even a minute. When the train stopped at a station and I tried to get some food or hot water, she didn't let me get off. She was always suspicious that I was trying to desert her. She would seize my sleeve and try to drag me back. The passengers, especially the Russians, had something to laugh at. A streak of insanity seemed to run through this family; it manifested itself in fear, suspicion, and a kind of mysticism that stemmed from the time when man still lived in caves. How this primitive heritage reached all the way to an affluent Hasidic family in Warsaw is a riddle. This whole adventure that I went through remains an enigma to me to this day.

"We got to Kuibyshev and it seemed all in vain.

There was no sister and no insane asylum. That is to say, there was an asylum, but not for strangers. The Nazis destroyed hospitals, clinics, and asylums as they retreated. They shot or poisoned the patients. The Nazi murderers hadn't reached Kuibyshev, but the hospital was jammed with the heavily wounded. Who in those days worried about the insane? Well, but a woman had told Dora all the details. The Jewish officer's name was Lipman, the woman was Lipman's relative, and there was no reason for her to lie. Can you imagine the disappointment? We had endured the whole trek with all its miseries for nothing. But wait, we did find Ytta, not in an insane asylum, but in a village living with an old Jew, a shoemaker. The woman hadn't invented things. Ytta had suffered from depression and had been treated for it at some institution and after a while they had discharged her. I never learned all the facts, but even those that she told me I later forgot. The whole Holocaust is tied up with amnesia.

"The shoemaker was a Polish Jew, actually from one of your towns, Bilgoray or Janów, an old man nearly eighty but still active. Don't ask me how he got to Kuibyshev or why Ytta moved in with him. He lived in some dump, but he could patch boots and shoes and there is need for this everywhere. He sat there with his long white beard, surrounded by old shoes in a shack that was more like a chicken coop, and as he hammered tacks or drew the thread, he mumbled a verse of the Psalms. By a clay stove stood a red-haired woman—barefoot, ragged, disheveled, and half naked—cooking barley. Dora recognized her sister at once, but the other didn't know Dora. When Ytta finally realized that this was her sister, she didn't cry but started to bay like a dog. The shoemaker began to rock to and fro on his stool.

"There was supposed to be a communal farm, a kolkhoz, somewhere nearby, but all I could see was an old-fashioned Russian village with wooden huts, a little church, deep snow, and sleighs harnessed to dogs and

skinny nags, just the way I used to see them in pictures
in a Russian-language textbook. Who knows, I thought,
maybe the whole Revolution had been only a dream.
Maybe Nicholas still sat on the throne. During the war
and afterward, I saw many reunions of people with their
loved ones, but these two played out a shattering sisterly
drama. They kissed, licked, howled. The old man mumbled through his toothless mouth, 'A pity, a pity . . .'
Then he turned back to his shoes. He seemed to be deaf.

"There was nothing to pack. All that Ytta had were a
pair of shoes with thick soles and heels and a sheepskin
without sleeves. The old man took a black loaf of bread
out of somewhere and Ytta tucked it away in her sack.
She kissed the old man's hands, his brow and beard and
commenced to bark anew, as if possessed by the spirit of
a dog. This Ytta was taller than Dora. Her eyes were
green and as fearsome as a beast's. Her hair was of an
unusual shade of red. To describe to you how we made
our way from Kuibyshev to Moscow and from there
back to Poland again, I'd have to sit here with you till tomorrow. We dragged along and smuggled our way
through, facing arrest, separation, or death at any moment. But summer had come, and after lengthy travails,
we finally got to Germany, and from there to Paris. I
make it sound so simple. Actually, we only got to France
by the end of 1946, or maybe it was already 1947. One
of the social workers on the Joint Distribution Committee was a friend of mine, a young man from Warsaw
who went to America in 1932. He knew English and
other languages as well. You can't imagine the power
Americans wielded in those days. I could easily have ob-
tained a visa to America through him, but Dora took it
into her head that I had a sweetheart there. In Paris, the
Joint—actually, that same young man—got us a small
apartment, which was no easy task. We received a
monthly stipend from this same organization.

"I know what you're about to ask me—have a little
patience. Yes, I lived with them both. I married Dora
officially in Germany—she wanted to stand under a can-

opy and she did—but, in actuality, I had two wives, two
sisters, just like the patriarch Jacob. All I lacked was a
Bilhah and a Zilpah. What would stop the likes of me?
Not the Jewish and certainly not the Gentile laws. In the
war, the whole human culture crumbled like a ruin. In
the camps—not only in Germany but in Russia and
later in the DP camps where the refugees lived for
years—all shame vanished. I knew of one case where a
woman had her husband on one side and her lover on
the other and all three of them lived together. I've witnessed so many wild things that to me they've become
normal. A Schicklgruber or a Dzhugashvili comes along
and moves the clock back ten thousand years. Not completely, mind you. There were also instances of rare
piety and of self-sacrifice for a minor law in the
Shulchan Aruch, or even for some custom. This itself
may be a bit of wildness, too.

"I didn't want all this. It's one thing to have an adventure—it's quite another to make a permanent institution
out of it. But it was out of my hands. From the moment
the two sisters met, I was no longer a free man. They
enslaved me with their love for me, their love toward
each other, and their jealousy. One minute they would
be kissing and crying from great devotion and suddenly
they would begin to slug away, pull hair, and curse each
other with words you wouldn't hear in the underworld. I
had never before seen such hysteria or heard such
screams. Every few days one of the sisters, or sometimes
both, tried to commit suicide. One moment it would be
quiet. The three of us might be sitting eating or discussing a book or picture—all of a sudden a horrible shriek
and both sisters would be rolling on the floor, tearing
pieces from each other. I'd run up, trying to separate
them, but I'd catch a slam in the face or a bite and the
blood would be dripping from me. Why they were fight-
ing I would never know. Fortunately, we lived on the
upper story, a garret, and we had no neighbors on our
floor. One of the sisters would run to the window and
try to throw herself out, while the other seized a knife

and went for her own throat. I'd grab one by the leg and
take the knife away from the other. They'd howl at me
and at each other. I'd try to find out what caused the
outburst, but I learned in time that they didn't know the
reason themselves. At the same time, I want you to know
that both of them were intelligent in their own fashion.
Dora had excellent taste in literature. She'd offer an
opinion about a book and it was accurate to the dot.
Ytta was musically inclined. She could sing whole sym-
phonies. When they had the energy, they displayed great
capability. They had picked up a sewing machine somewhere and from scraps and pieces they sewed dresses of
which the most elegant ladies would be proud. One thing
both sisters shared, a complete lack of common sense.
Actually, they shared many traits. At times it even
seemed to me that they were two bodies with one soul. If
there had been a tape recorder to take down the things
they said, particularly at night, it would make Dostoev-
sky seem trite. Complaints against God poured out of
them, along with laments for the Holocaust that no pen
could transcribe. What a person really is comes out only
at night, in the dark. I know now that both of them
were born crazy, not the victims of any circumstances.
The circumstances, naturally, made everything worse. I
myself became a psychopath living with them. Insanity
is no less contagious than typhus.

"Besides squabbling, brawling, telling endless stories
of the camps and of their home in Warsaw, and chatter-
ing about clothes, fashions, and what not, the sisters had
one favorite topic: my treachery. They forged an indict-
ment against me that made the Moscow trials seem like
pure logic by comparison. Even as they sat on the sofa,
kissed me, waged a playful competition over me, and indulged in a game that was both childish and animalistic
and therefore indefinable, they kept abusing me. It
boiled down to the fact that I had only one urge—to be-
tray them and carry on with other women. Each time the
concierge called me to the telephone, they ran to listen
in. When I received a letter, they promptly opened it. No

dictator could have enforced such a strict censorship as
these sisters did over me. They left no doubt that the
mailman, the concierge, the Joint Committee, and I
were all part of a conspiracy against them, although
what kind of conspiracy this was and what was its purpose was something even their twisted minds couldn't
establish. Lombroso contended that genius is insanity.
He forgot to say that insanity is genius. Their helplessness was genius too. I sometimes had the feeling that
getting through the war had drained them of that specific power for survival that every human and animal
possesses. The fact that Ytta hadn't been able to find
another job in Russia besides that of a maid and mistress
to that old shoemaker only accented her lack of initiative. They often toyed with the notion of becoming
maids in Paris, governesses, or something in that vein,
but it was clear both to me and to them that they
couldn't hold any kind of job for more than a few hours.
They were also the laziest creatures I had ever met,
although from time to time they were seized by a burst
of effort and energy that was as exaggerated as their
usual laziness. Two women should have been able to
keep house, but our apartment was always a mess. They
would prepare a meal and argue as to who should wash
the dishes until it came time to cook again. Sometimes
days and even weeks went by and we ate only dry food.
The bedding was often dirty, and we had cockroaches
and other vermin. The sisters weren't physically dirty.
They boiled pots of water at night and turned the apartment into a bathhouse. The water dripped down below,
and the downstairs tenant, an old French cavalier,
banged on our door and threatened us with the police.
Paris was starving, but in my house food was thrown out
in the garbage. The apartment was piled with rags. They
hardly ever wore the dresses that they sewed or received
from the Joint Committee, but they went around half
naked and barefoot.

"As alike as the sisters were, so were they also different. Ytta possessed a brutality that was completely
foreign to a girl from a Hasidic home. Many of her

stories dealt with beatings and I knew that bloodshed and violence of any kind roused her sexually. She told me that, while she was still a girl in her father's house, she once sharpened a knife and slaughtered three ducks that her mother kept in a shed. Her father beat her for this severely and Dora used to throw this up to her when they quarreled. Ytta was unusually strong, but each time she tried to do something, she managed to hurt herself. She walked around covered with bandages and plasters. She often hinted that she would take revenge on me, even though I had rescued her from slavery and want. I suspected that somewhere inside her she would have been glad to remain with the old shoemaker; maybe because this would have allowed her to forget her family and especially Dora, with whom she maintained a love-hate relationship. This hostility used to come out in every quarrel. Dora was the one who screamed, wept, and scolded, while Ytta resorted to blows. I was often afraid that she might kill Dora in a rage.

"Dora was better educated, more refined, and possessed of a sick imagination. She slept fitfully and kept telling me her dreams, which were sexual, diabolical, tangled. She awoke quoting verses from the Bible. She tried to write poems in Polish and in Yiddish. She had formulated a sort of personal mythology. I often said that she was possessed by the dybbuk of a follower of Sabbatai Zevi or Jacob Frank.

"I had always felt a curiosity about the institution of polygamy. Could jealousy be rooted out? Could you share someone you loved? In a sense, the three of us were taking part in an experiment whose results we all awaited. The longer the situation lasted, the more obvious it became to us all that things couldn't remain the way they were. Something had to happen and we knew that it would be evil, a catastrophe. Each day posed a new crisis, each night carried the threat of some scandal or impotence. Although our neighbors on the lower floors had their own troubles and were accustomed to wild doings from the time of the German Occupation, they began to look at us suspiciously, to nose around,

and to shake their heads in disapproval. As sinful as was
our behavior, our religious upbringing soon began to
make demands on our Jewishness. Dora made the bene-
diction over the Sabbath candles every Friday and then
sat around smoking cigarettes. She had formulated her
own version of the Shulchan Aruch in which pork was
forbidden but horsemeat was kosher, in which there was
no God but you had to fast on Yom Kippur and eat
matzo on Passover. Ytta had become an atheist in
Russia, or so she said, but every night before going to
sleep she mumbled a nightly prayer or some incantation.
When I gave her a coin, she spat on it to ward off the
evil eye. She would get up in the morning and announce,
'Today will be an unlucky day . . . something bad is
going to happen . . .' Inevitably, what happened was
that she hurt herself, or broke a dish, or a stocking tore
on her.

"Dora kept the funds in our household. I always gave
her more than she needed, since I received stipends from
a few institutions and later money from relatives in
America as well. After a while I noticed that she had ac-
cumulated a nest egg. Her sister apparently knew of this
and received her share of the loot. I often heard them
whispering and arguing about money.

"I forgot the main thing—children. Both sisters
wanted a child by me and many arguments erupted because of this. But I was dead set against it. We were
living on charity. Each time the conversation came
around to children, I came up with the same answer:
'For what? So the next Hitler would have someone to
burn?' I don't have a child to this day. As far as I'm concerned, I want to put an end to the human tragedy. I sus-
pect that neither Dora nor Ytta was even capable of
bearing children. Such females are like mules. I'll never
understand how a Hasidic Jew came to have two such
daughters. We carry stray genes going back to the time
of Genghis Khan, or the devil knows when.

"The calamity that we anticipated came in a quiet
fashion. The arguments gradually subsided to be replaced by a depression that consumed the three of us. It

began with Dora's getting sick. Exactly what was wrong
with her, I never found out. She lost weight and coughed
a lot. I suspected consumption and took her to a doctor,
but he found no evidence of illness. He prescribed vitamins and iron, which didn't help. Dora became frigid,
too. She no longer wanted to join in our nightly games
and idle chatter. She even got herself a cot and set it up
in the kitchen. Without Dora, Ytta soon lost interest in
our sex triangle. She had never been the one to take the
initiative; in fact, she did only what Dora told her. Ytta
was a big eater and a heavy sleeper. She snored and
snorted in her sleep. A situation soon developed in
which, instead of having two women, I had none. Not
only were we silent at night but during the day too; we
became steeped in moroseness. Before, I used to get
weary from all the babbling, endless wrangling, and ex-
travagant praises the sisters heaped on me, but now I
longed for those days. I talked the situation over with the
sisters and we decided to put an end to the alienation
that lay between us, but such things can't be changed
with decisions. I often had the feeling that some invisible
being lurked among us, a phantom who sealed our lips
and burdened our spirits. Each time I started to say
something, the words stuck in my throat. When I did say
it, the words that came out required no answer. I looked
on with amazement as the two chatterbox sisters became
close-mouthed. All the speech seemed to have been
drained from them. I became as taciturn as they. Before,
I could babble on for hours without any thought or re-
flection, but suddenly I became diplomatic and careful
to weigh every word, afraid that no matter what I said
would cause a commotion. I used to laugh when I read
your stories about dybbuks, but I now actually felt myself possessed. When I wanted to pay Dora a compliment, it came out an insult. Oddly enough, the three of
us couldn't stop yawning. We sat there, yawned, and
looked at one another with moist eyes in astonishment,
partners in a tragedy we could neither understand nor
control.

"I became impotent too. I lost the urge for the two

sisters. I lay in bed nights, and instead of lust, I felt
something that can only be called anti-lust. I often had
the uncomfortable feeling that my skin was icy cold and
my body was shrinking. Although the sisters didn't mention my impotence, I knew that they were lying in bed
with their ears cocked, listening to the strange process
taking place within my organs—the ebbing of the blood
and the cramping and shrinking of the limbs that seemed
to degenerate to the verge of withering. I often imagined
that in the dark I saw the silhouette of a figure that was
as flimsy and transparent as a spider web—tall, thin,
long-haired—a shadowy skeleton with holes instead of
eyes, a monster with a crooked mouth that laughed
soundlessly. I assured myself that it was nerves. What
else could it be? I didn't believe in ghosts then and I
don't to this day. I became convinced of one thing one
night—thoughts and emotions can literally materialize
and become entities of some substance. Even now, as I
think about it, ants crawl up and down my spine. I've
never spoken about this to anyone—you're the first
and, I assure you, the last person to ever hear this.

"It was a spring night in 1948. A spring night in Paris
can sometimes be bitter cold. We went to sleep separately—I on the cot, Dora on the sofa, and Ytta in bed.
We put out the lights and lay down. I don't remember
such a cold night even in the camps. We covered ourselves with all the blankets and rags we had in the house,
but we still couldn't get warm. I put the sleeves of a
sweater over my feet and threw my winter coat over the
blanket. Ytta and Dora burrowed into their covers. We
did all this without speaking and this silence lent our
frantic efforts a brooding oppressiveness that defies description. I remember precisely lying there in bed and
thinking that the punishment would come that night. At
the same time, I silently prayed to God that it shouldn't.
I lay there for a while half frozen—not only from the
cold but from the tension too. I searched in the dark for
the *shed* (as I called the creature of spider webs and
shadows), but I saw nothing. At the same time, I knew
that he was there, hovering in some corner or possibly

even behind the bedboard. I said to myself, 'Don't be an idiot, there are no such things as ghosts. If Hitler could slaughter six million Jews and America sends billions of dollars to rebuild Germany, there are no other forces except the material. Ghosts wouldn't permit such an injustice . . .'

"I had to urinate and the toilet was out in the corridor. Usually I can hold myself in, if need be, but this time the urge was too insistent. I got up from the cot and went creeping toward the kitchen door, which led to the outside. I had taken only two steps when someone stopped me. Brother, I know all the answers and all the psychological flimflam, but this thing before me was a person and he blocked my path. I was too frightened to cry out. It's not in me to scream. I'm sure that I wouldn't scream even if it were killing me. Well, and who was there to help me, even if I did? The two half-mad sisters? I tried to push him aside and I touched something that might have been rubber, dough, or some sort of foam. There are fears from which you can't run away. A furious wrangling erupted between us. I pushed him back and he yielded a bit, yet offered resistance. I remember now that I was less afraid of the evil spirit than of the outcry the sisters might raise. I can't tell you how long this struggle lasted—a minute or perhaps only a few seconds. I thought I would pass out on the spot, but I stood there and stubbornly and silently wrestled with a phantom, or whatever it was. Instead of feeling cold, I became hot. Within a second, I was drenched as if standing under a shower. Why the sisters didn't scream is something I'll never understand. That they were awake I am sure. They were apparently terrified of their own fear. Suddenly I caught a blow. The Evil One vanished and I sensed that my organ was no longer there, either. Had he castrated me? My pajama bottoms had fallen. I felt around for my penis. No, he hadn't torn it out but had jammed it so deep into me that it had formed a negative indentation rather than a positive. Don't look at me that way! I'm not crazy now and I wasn't crazy then. During this whole nightmare, I knew that it was nerves—nervousness that had assumed substance. Einstein contends that mass is energy. I say that mass is compressed emotion. Neuroses materialize and take on concrete form. Feelings put on bodies or are themselves bodies. Those are your dybbuks, the sprites, the hobgoblins.

"I walked out into the corridor on wobbly knees and found the toilet, but I literally had nothing to urinate with. I read somewhere that in the Arab lands such things happen to men, especially to those who keep harems. Strange, but during the whole excitement I remained calm. Tragedy sometimes brings a kind of brooding resignation that comes from no one knows where.

"I turned back to the apartment, but neither of the sisters made a rustle. They lay there quiet, tense, barely breathing. Had they cast a spell over me? Were they themselves bewitched? I began to dress slowly. I put on my drawers, my pants, my jacket, and my summer coat. I packed some shirts, socks, and manuscripts in the dark. I gave the two sisters enough time to ask me what I was doing and where I was going, but they didn't utter a peep. I took my satchel and left in the middle of the night. Those are the bare facts."

"Where did you go?"

"What's the difference? I went to a cheap hotel and took a room. Gradually everything began to return to normal and I was able to function again. I somehow managed to overcome the nightmarish night and the next morning I caught a plane to London. I had an old friend there, a journalist on the local Yiddish newspaper, who had invited me to come a few times. The editorial office consisted of a single room and the whole paper went under soon afterward, but in the meantime I got some work and lodgings. From there, I left for Buenos Aires in 1950. Here I met Lena, my present wife."

"What became of the two sisters?"

"Do *you* know? That's as much as I know."

"Didn't you ever hear from them?"

"Never."

"Did you look for them?"

"Such things you try to forget. I hypnotized myself into thinking that the whole thing had been only a dream, but it really happened. It's as real as the fact that I'm sitting here with you right now."

"How do you explain it?" I asked.

"I don't."

"Maybe they were dead when you left."

"No, they were awake and listening. You can differentiate between the living and the dead."

"Aren't you curious to know what happened to them?"

"And if I am curious, what of it? They're probably alive. The witches are somewhere—maybe they've married. I was in Paris three years ago, but the house where we lived no longer exists. They put up a garage there."

We sat there silently; then I said, "If mass consisted of emotion, every stone in the street would be a skein of misery."

"Maybe they are. Of one thing I'm sure—everything lives, everything suffers, struggles, desires. There is no such thing as death."

"If that's true, then Hitler and Stalin didn't kill anyone," I said.

"You have no right to kill an illusion, either. Drink your coffee."

For a long while neither of us spoke; then I asked half in jest, "What can you learn from this story?"

Haim Leib smiled. "If Nietzsche's crazy theory about the exhaustion of all atomic combinations and the eternal return is true, and if there'll be another Hitler, another Stalin, and another Holocaust, and if in a trillion years you'll meet a female in Stettin—don't go with her to look for her sister."

"According to this theory, I will have no choice but to go and to experience everything that you did," I said.

"In that case, you'll know how I felt."

Translated by Joseph Singer

A Pair

Among those who ran away from Hitler and managed to reach America was the poet Getzele Tertziver—a tiny, dark-complexioned man with a small head, shoulder-length hair, and on his chin a wisp of a beard. He had a crooked nose, widely spaced teeth as black as lead, and large, black, wandering eyes—the right one looked up, the left one down. Years after pelerines went out of fashion, Getzele's apparel was a pelerine hanging to his ankles, a flowing tie, and a black, wide-brimmed hat. He smoked a long pipe. The humorists in the Warsaw Yiddish press often printed jokes about his wild appearance and his poems, which not even the critics who believed in modernism could understand. Getzele Tertziver had published one book—a mixture of poems, aphorisms, and vignettes titled *The World History of My Future*. It was said that only one typesetter in Warsaw could decipher his handwriting.

Getzele Tertziver, like his grandfather the Tertziver

Rabbi Alterel, slept in the daytime and stayed awake at
night. Even though the Tertziver Hasidim considered
him a nonbeliever who shamed his pious ancestors in
paradise, they surreptitiously sustained him. Old Hasidim who remembered Rabbi Alterel when he was young
swore that Getzele resembled him like two drops of
water—the same face, the same way of walking, the
same mannerisms. True, Rabbi Alterel ascended in his
saintliness toward the mansions of heaven while Getzele
had fallen into apostasy. Still, they would not allow the
rabbi's grandson to starve.

How strange that wild-eyed Getzele, who could not
make himself understood either in his writing or in his
speech, which he spewed forth quickly and in a Hasidic
singsong, had married three times, each time a beauty.
When the writers in the Yiddish Writers' Club in Warsaw tired of discussing literature and reviling one another, it was enough to mention the name Getzele
Tertziver to revive the conversation. Everyone asked
the same question: What had those rich girls, beautiful
and educated, seen in Getzele?

I was a beginner then and did not dare speak up in
front of well-recognized writers, but I knew Getzele
Tertziver when he wore sidelocks, a gaberdine, rabbinical breeches and stockings. For a time he was a friend of
my older brother, Joshua. It happened this way: Rabbi
Alterel had only one son, Jonah Jerucham—a silent,
melancholy recluse. Jonah Jerucham married the
Rimpiner rabbi's daughter, Ittah Shevach. But ten years
later she ran away from him. She took their child,
Getzele, with her to Rimpin. After some time, Jonah
Jerucham left his father's court and drifted around Warsaw, avoiding the Tertziver Hasidim. Some said that he
was starving, others believed that he had fallen into the
net of the Christian missionaries. When it became clear
that with Rabbi Alterel's demise Jonah Jerucham would
have no following, the Tertziver Hasidim began to praise
Getzele; they maintained that he was growing up a God-
fearing man, a great Talmudic scholar, and that he

would be worthy to sit in his grandfather's chair. His mother, however, used him as a pawn: if the Tertziver Hasidim wanted access to Getzele, they would have to make Jonah Jerucham give her a divorce. Some rich Tertziver Chasidim tried to persuade Jonah Jerucham to divorce his wife, but he vacillated. One day he promised, the next day he changed his mind. He would disappear for months, and no one knew what had happened to him. Finally, in 1909, Jonah Jerucham divorced Ittah Shevach. Within four weeks he was found dead in a basement room occupied by paupers. He left a sack of manuscripts, which the Tertziver Hasidim burned.

After Jonah Jerucham's death, Ittah Shevach married a rich wine merchant in Warsaw. She took Getzele, who was now sixteen, with her. Rabbi Alterel had become senile in his old age, and his demise was expected any day. Getzele was about to take over the court, but he started to show deviant traits. He quarreled with his mother and stepfather. He stopped going to the study house of the Tertziver Hasidim, began to read worldly books, and became a frequent visitor to the house of the heretic writer Peretz. A few times he visited our house, since my brother Joshua, too, had left the path of righteousness. Getzele expressed himself so vehemently and conducted himself so wildly that even my father, accustomed as he was to Hasidic fervor, was baffled. Getzele ran from wall to wall like a caged animal. My mother offered him a glass of tea, which he immediately dropped. My sister Hinda asked him why he didn't go to visit his sick grandfather. Getzele cupped his ear as if he were deaf, looked at her with astonishment, and recited a Hasidic obscurantism which meant: Ask me no questions, I'll tell you no lies. He snatched my father's pen, dipped it in ink, and seemed to be writing in the air. Then he put it back into the inkwell upside down. He ran to the open window, leaned out so far that my mother wrung her hands, afraid that he would fall from our third-floor apartment to the stone pavement below. When he had left, my mother said, "I don't envy the girl

who'll get *him*." To which my sister replied, "A crazy
creature, but he has charm."

Rabbi Alterel died in 1915, by which time the Germans and the Austrians had occupied Poland. Getzele
had already discarded his Hasidic attire, he wrote
worldly poems and was carrying on a love affair with the
daughter of a Warsaw builder. Without the knowledge of
my parents, I went to Hazamir Hall, where my brother
Joshua was then the secretary, organizing lectures and
concerts, and where Getzele was to read his poem "The
Queen of Unrest." He ran onto the stage, read from bits
of paper in a shrill voice. He stumbled against the po-
dium; he waved his fist, chortled, laughed, and cried. He
finished the first part of his long poem with a strophe
that I still remember:

> Queen mean,
> Strike with a cane,
> Swallow the ocean,
> Eat hurricane.

The audience clapped their hands, cried "Bravo," and
would not stop applauding. My brother, who was sitting
next to me, whispered, "The power of insanity has no
limit."

After the war Getzele's popularity abated. Communism
came into fashion, and Getzele was against Communism.
The Poale Zion tried to involve him in their movement,
but Getzele did not believe in Zionism. His third wife
divorced him, and for the next years Getzele's romantic
adventures ceased. His room was a garret. He became a
mystic and made his living from begging. Every fall, the
Yiddish Writers' Club organized an evening benefit for
him. Getzele always read poems that were supposed to
reveal the secret of creation. The audience laughed. Once,
someone threw a rotten potato at him. Like his father,
Jonah Jerucham, Getzele would disappear for months.
People began to say that he had died, then he would

emerge again. They asked him where he'd been and he answered, "Who knows?"

In 1934 Getzele vanished for a longer time than usual. The date was approaching for his evening benefit, and he was not to be found. The secretary of the Writers' Club went to look for him in his garret; it was occupied by another tenant. Suddenly it became known that Getzele was in Paris. How he got the fare and managed to acquire a visa remained a riddle. Warsaw painters who went to Paris to familiarize themselves with the new trends in art and Yiddish actors who went on tour to Paris brought news of Getzele. He was to be seen late at night in the cafés. He read his poems on the streets in the Jewish section of Paris, Belleville, and collected donations. He was having an affair with a half-crazed woman painter, and he himself had begun to paint—the kind of painting for which no training is necessary. I had emigrated to America and was working for a Yiddish newspaper. The Second World War had begun. I had almost forgotten about Getzele.

Then, in 1944, as I sat in the editorial room writing an article, I saw Getzele. He stood at my table, ragged, with a disheveled beard, his long, matted side hair hanging down to his shoulders, and he asked me in a nasal voice, "For whom are you scribbling—for Hitler?"

"Getzele!" I exclaimed.

"You considered me dead, ha? I have risen from the grave."

It was the same Getzele, although there were now streaks of gray in his hair. He wore the same kind of black hat he had worn in Warsaw, and instead of a pelerine a broad caftan with gilded buttons that might have once been a military coat or the uniform of a letter carrier. In one hand he held a briefcase, in the other a satchel bound with string. He smiled, showing a single crooked tooth. When the writers saw him, they all put down their pens and came over to my desk. The chief editor also came out of his room. Seldom did anyone in these years manage to get to America from Europe. But

Getzele had run away from the Nazis to Morocco, had
lived for some time in Palestine, got to Argentina, and
had entered the United States through Cuba—at least,
this was his story. His speech was disjointed; he swallowed
words and mixed up dates. The Litvaks could not understand his gibberish at all. He made jokes that had to do
with the Warsaw Writers' Club and the Tertziver
Hasidim, and he used idioms recently coined by Polish
refugees. He mentioned names I had long forgotten. He
coughed, giggled, and suddenly became angry. Then he
said, "Why don't you publish some of my poems? Here
they are."

He opened his briefcase and pulled out dirty pieces of
paper, scribbled and scrawled, with ink spots and
erasures. On the margins he had doodled snakes, thorns,
and horned fishes. The writers tried to read his poems.
Some smiled, others shrugged. The chief editor adjusted
his spectacles, read a few lines, and asked, "What is
this—Turkish?"

"If you don't understand poetry, organize an evening
for me."

"We don't organize evenings."

"What do you do? You're all going to be wiped out.
Even the stain of a dog's urine won't be left. It is the
twilight of all values. You sit here in your American
offices and invent lies while there the War of Gog and
Magog is raging. The House of Edom is burning red. A
black plague on all of you! Where is the toilet?"

I showed Getzele the way to the bathroom. He went in
and stayed for a long time. He was shaky when he came
out. "It's worse here than there," he said. "Let's go and
eat something."

I put aside my article and went with him to the
cafeteria. He asked for dry bread with onion and black
coffee. Into the coffee he poured salt. He told me that on
the freighter from Egypt to Buenos Aires he became
seasick and while passing the equator he experienced a
revelation: The whole history of the world, all the seven
wisdoms are hidden in the first chapter of Genesis, which

is based on mystic numerical values and acrostic patterns —*gematria* and *notarikon*. Everything is foretold there: Napoleon's wars, the First World War, the Second, Hitler, Stalin, Mussolini, Roosevelt. The secret of redemption is also there, less obscure than in the Book of Daniel. Every word has to be read backward. One has to watch the small numbers and the big numbers—*mispar koton* and *mispår godol*—and especially the cryptic musical symbols. Getzele was saying, "Who was Adam? Who was Eve? What did the Serpent want? Why did Cain kill Abel? You'll find the answers to the smallest detail. Once you've got the key to the code, your entire being lights up. I am not alone here. I came with a woman. She is the one who saved me. Don't ask any questions. Jewish but assimilated. A Polish poetess. One of the greatest— perhaps the greatest of all times—but unknown. The esoteric well of instinct. A first vessel, not a second vessel. How do you go from here to Third Avenue?"

"To what street?"

"Huh? She has a relative there. An old deaf woman. Malicious, too. She is not in her right mind. Where do you find the Joint Distribution Committee? They helped me. I was sinking into the depths, toward the abyss. I began to think, Who knows? Since the messengers of evil were granted powers, perhaps they are the men of destiny—I mean both sons of Amalek, Stalin and Hitler. The first is primeval Satan, the second is the scum of Asmodeus, therefore father of all defilement. In Cuba I met someone who escaped from both the Nazis and the Red ones. He is a genius of an escaper but a perverted writer. He told me many things.

"What the Nazis are everybody knows. But Russia is still a puzzle. For a moment, they raise you up to the very skies, and then they throw you, as the Talmud says, from a high roof into a deep ditch. One day they want to know your biography down to the smallest particular, and the next day they spit on you and throw you into jail to die.

"As to Morocco, they haven't eaten yet from the tree of knowledge. Not everyone. In all this debasement you find a spark of the Godhead. Palestine is a chapter in itself. They try to force the End of Days. To make it short, I surrendered. Since there has to be slime, perhaps the deeper the better. Then the revelation came. Be so good, hand me the pepper."

"Pepper in the coffee?"

"What is America? I cannot grasp it. Is it the principle of *Nogah*—where the divine and demonic rule together? Karola is her name. Karola Lipinska Kohen. She read you in the camp near Munich. You find there everything— the whole truth."

"In Munich?"

"In the Book of Genesis."

Many weeks passed. I had said I would telephone Getzele, but I kept on postponing the call. When I did get round to it, I had lost his telephone number and address. One evening, as I sat reading a newspaper, some-one knocked at my door. I asked who it was and heard a muttering sound. I opened the door and saw a woman with red unruly hair and a pointed face sprinkled with freckles. She was wearing a long coat girded with a mannish belt. It was snowing outside, and she had on boots of a kind I had not seen in America. On her shoulders she wore a huge canvas bag. Her entire appearance was outlandish and somewhat crazed. She looked me over and cried, "This is him! Exactly as I imagined but a little different. Actually, completely different!"

"May I ask who you are?"

"Karola Lipinska Kohen, Getzele Tertziver's shadow, victim, and alter ego."

I asked her to come in. The moment she closed the door, she cried, "I have to kiss you!"

She embraced me with her wet hands. From her sleeves, melted snow ran onto my neck. She screamed, "I know you! I know you! You are my brother, whether you want it or not. All this time I hoped that you would visit us as you promised. But since you are a liar, a bluffer, and an

American all-right-nik, I came to you. Try to throw me out. I won't go."

"God forbid! You are a welcome guest."

"Why am I welcome? If I were twenty years older and had a hunchback, you would most probably not let me in. I know you men. You are all egotists, whether you are murderers or have God-given talents. I am hungry and without a groschen. If you won't give me something to eat and a glass of tea, I will die in your house and you'll have to pay for the burial."

"Take off your coat. I will give you something to eat."

"Let me look at you again. From your writings I knew already that we both belonged to the red-haired race. But where is your hair? I thought you would be taller. Where are the wild women you describe in your stories? I imagined that when I opened the door I would see an orgy. I want you to know from the very beginning that between Getzele and me everything is finished. Dead and buried! Don't be afraid. I'm not going to throw myself at you. Hitler and Stalin have taught me to bend my pride, but I have not yet reached the stage where I will force myself on any man. Oy, see what I've done to your rug!"

A pool had formed from the snow on her coat and boots. She removed them and remained standing in her stocking feet, in a red dress. I noticed now that she had green eyes, a turned-up nose, high cheekbones, a long neck. She was not young—she could have been forty or even more. She called, "Give me a cigarette! I am dying for a smoke. To me a cigarette is more important than bread. In prison I gave away my last bit of food for some crushed leaves and sawdust. I have a notion that you don't smoke and don't drink."

"No, but I keep cigarettes and liquor in the house."

"For whom? For others? Oh, you disappoint me. It's fortunate that Verlaine and Novalis are dead. If they were alive, they might disappoint me, too. I'm afraid you're a philistine."

I gave her a cigarette and put a bottle of cognac on the table. I brought from the kitchen bread, dates, cheese, and the remainder of a cake. Karola Lipinska Kohen was eating, smoking, and pouring herself one glass of cognac after another. She called out, "What? You're a vegetarian, too? All I need to hear is that you are also a eunuch. Getzele has completely lost his mind. Absolutely. He has relatives here, but he found in the Book of Genesis that he is not allowed to meet them. There was a notice in your Yiddish paper about him, and a whole bunch of Tertziver Hasidim sought him out. Woe is me, what kind of Hasidim they were! No gaberdines and clean-shaven. They could barely speak Yiddish. Earlier, we lived with an aunt of mine—deaf, crazy, and a miser. Now he has got himself into a furnished room infested with mice and cockroaches. One of these so-called Hasidim—Sam Parsover, a man in the liquor business, a swindler—has a wife, a real monster. A vulgar piece, perhaps sixty years old, her hair dyed a disgusting yellow, wrinkled like a witch and rouged like a whore. She attached herself to Getzele like a leech. Her husband must have other women, and he is happy to be rid of her. She has a business of her own—how do you call it, real estate. To make it short, Getzele has convinced her that she is a heroine of the Pentateuch. If I didn't know that he's a psychopath, I would swear he's the worst charlatan I ever met. L'chayim." Karola Lipinska Kohen poured a whole glass of cognac down her throat. She grimaced and shook her head.

I asked, "Can you tell me what all these women see in him? Or is this a secret from the Book of Genesis?"

Karola Lipinska Kohen's face started to break into a smile. Then she became serious. "What others see in him, ask them. I can only speak for myself."

"Well, what about you?"

"Shall I be frank with you?"

"Yes, frank."

"You will most likely not believe me. People believe all kinds of lies, but when they are told the truth they spit on you. Getzele Tertziver is the strongest man I've ever met—and believe me, I know men—let alone that he's

romantic and terribly interesting. I know what you're
thinking. He's small, and you probably consider him ugly.
Someone once asked me how I could love such a freak.
This freak becomes a giant when he makes love. It is my
deepest conviction that he is the strongest lover in our
spiritually castrated generation."

"In that case, perhaps the Book of Genesis does contain
everything he says!"

"No, this is an *idée fixe*. I forgot the main thing. He is
a great poet. Not with his pen. He speaks his poems the
way the poets did in prehistoric times, before man could
write. Sometimes when he falls into despair and begins to
speak, all the spheres cry with him. When he becomes
ecstatic, he exudes a joy out of this world. The Bible says
that the morning stars sing together. But the stars of night
sing separately. I want you to know that I am a poet
myself—according to my own estimation, the greatest in
our miserable time. I write in Polish, this is my misfortune. My poems lie dead in Poland, together with the
Jews. There was one great poet besides me in Poland, and
as far as I know he is not among the living any more. I
myself have stopped writing. I lie in bed at night and
speak my poems to the ceiling."

"Here in America you can begin to write again. They
are hungry for a true talent. They will even translate
what you write."

"No. I have gotten out of the habit of writing. One day
a Hitler comes and burns books. The next day it's a Stalin
who demands that all poets exalt his murders. New tyrants
will emerge and they will destroy the literature of the
world. Since sex is only for two—and sometimes even
for one—why must poetry be for many? I am my own
bard. Sometimes when I used to lie with Getzele in bed,
we held a poetic duet. Well, but two can also be too many.
L'chayim."

A few months passed. Karola Lipinska Kohen had
promised to call me, but I didn't hear from her. There
was no lack of eccentrics without her. I attracted them:

the graphomaniacs, the spiritualists, the astrologers, all types of repentants, those who believed in fasting, half-baked Buddhists, all sorts of do-gooders, and even a few unrecognized inventors—especially those who never gave up hope of producing perpetual motion. At three o'clock one morning the ringing of the telephone awoke me. It was Karola Lipinska Kohen. She said, "Forgive me for disturbing you in the middle of the night. Getzele is dead." And I heard a yowl—it was difficult to know whether she was crying or laughing.

"What was the matter?"

"What was not the matter? The man committed suicide, but slowly. In the last weeks we were together again. He died in my arms. I am calling because the Tertziver Hasidim have kidnapped his body. They persecuted him when he was alive, and now he has suddenly become one of their own. Getzele's will was to be cremated, but they plan to bury him near some American rabbi. I let the police know, but it seems they have been bribed. If you do not help me immediately, Getzele will be buried against his wish. This is the worst kind of vandalism. The Yiddish press should make an outcry."

It took a while before I shook off my sleep. I said, "The Yiddish press is not the American press. By the time I write something and the editor reads it and the typesetter sets it in type, a week may pass—even two. They don't know about hurrying. Better get a lawyer."

"Where can I get a lawyer in the middle of the night? They went to the hospital and took him away. If you won't help me, I'll hang myself."

We spoke for half an hour. Karola Lipinska Kohen promised to telephone me the next morning, but she did not. In the afternoon a call came for me in the office. A deep masculine voice in Polish-Yiddish, flavored with all the characteristic drawn-out intonations of my own region, said, "My name is Sam Parsover. I have sad tidings for you. Reb Getzele Tertziver is demised. We Tertziver Hasidim had many complaints against him, but he was a great man with a high soul. We tried to help him with all

our power, but when a man fasts constantly, how can he
live? He expired like a saint. His funeral will be tomorrow, and we want you to say a few words at his bier.
After all, you were his friend. He spoke about you many
times to me and to my wife."

"I was told that Getzele's wish was to be cremated."

"Who told you that—the crazy woman? Don't believe a
word of hers. She tortured Getzele and took away his last
penny. He wept before me and implored me to save him
from her hands. She has converted to Christianity. How
such a tender person as Getzele could have relations with
an abomination like that is beyond me. Come and do the
last honors to Reb Getzele. He left my wife a com-
mentary on the Book of Genesis, and we want to publish
it with an introduction by you. The service will begin
at . . ."

Sam Parsover gave me the time of the service, the
address of the chapel, and information about how to go
by subway. I still expected to hear from Karola Lipinska
Kohen, but I heard nothing. The next day, I went to the
chapel and was confronted by a crowd of American
Hasidim—some in skullcaps, others in hats; some with
goatees, others without beards. There were many women
in wigs. They waited for me and my eulogy. In the
chapel, electric tapers threw a flickering light. The coffin
had been placed near the pulpit. A rabbi with a pitch-
black beard delivered a sermon. Then Sam Parsover
spoke. He was short, broad-shouldered, with a protruding
paunch and a thin beard that seemed to be glued to his
round chin. With my eyes I searched the audience for
Karola Lipinska Kohen, but I did not see her. After I
spoke a few words and the cantor recited "God Full of
Mercy," there were sounds of a commotion. A woman in
black, with a veil over her face, tried to force her way to
the pulpit. It was Karola Lipinska Kohen. She screamed,
"Hypocrites! Thieves! Gangsters! Police! Police!"

She wanted to read a poem of Getzele's. Two young
Hasidim held her by the wrists, a third covered her

mouth with his hand. The crowd scolded, cursing. An old man wailed, "Woe, sacrilege to the deceased!"

I did not intend to go the cemetery, but two Hasidim pushed me into a limousine that seemed to have been reserved for non-Hasidim, because inside sat a portly young man, clean-shaven, without a hat, wearing a light suit and a red tie. His black hair glistened with pomade. His dark eyes smiled at me knowingly and sweetly. He said, "May I introduce myself? Dr. Max Baskind. Getzele Tertziver was my patient. Unfortunately, by the time he came to me it was too late to save him." Dr. Baskind extended a puffy hand, with a signet ring on his pinky.

We spoke and I mentioned Karola Lipinska Kohen. Dr. Baskind knew her. "A sick person, a pathological liar. I am not a psychiatrist, but one doesn't need to be a psychiatrist to know she is paranoid. My father is one of the Tertziver Hasidim, and I know all about it. The old Tertziver rabbi himself was not normal. A deranged dynasty. I was told that he ate on Tishah-b'Ab and fasted on Purim. He struck his beadle with his long pipe."

"What kind of woman is Sam Parsover's wife?" I asked.

"Oh, I'm their doctor, too. They are filthy rich. He made a fortune in the liquor business. They support all sorts of rabbis, here and in Jerusalem. They eat too much, and both of them are diabetic. Once, they invited me for the Sabbath and they gave me such portions that an elephant might have overeaten. The schmalz was running from everything: from the onions, the Sabbath stew, the pudding—not one kind of pudding but three. And at the end I was treated to schmalz cake. She suffers from the gallbladder in addition."

"Is it true that Mrs. Parsover had an affair with Getzele?"

"An affair? What kind of an affair? Getzele expressed his wild thoughts to her and this fascinated her. She used to bring him to me for an examination. He tried to give me lessons in medicine."

"Was he really such a sexual giant?"

Dr. Baskind smiled and showed a mouth of teeth as

small as a child's. He asked, "From what? From fasting? A doctor should be discreet, but what difference does it make now? Getzele suffered from impotence for many years. He admitted it himself."

The cortege stopped to let a long line of the cars of an Italian wedding pass by. Each car was hung with ribbons of many colors. Horns tooted, tin dishes clanged, the wedding guests shrieked. Dr. Baskind turned the signet ring on his pinky and examined its seal.

He said, "It seems there is no remedy for this, even in the Book of Genesis."

Translated by the author and Blanche and Joseph Nevel

The Fatalist

     Nicknames given in small towns are the homely,
familiar ones: Haim Bellybutton, Yekel Cake, Sarah
Gossip, Gittel Duck, and similar names. But in the Polish
town to which I came as a teacher in my young days I
heard of someone called Benjamin Fatalist. I promptly
became curious. How did they come to the word "fatalist"
in a small town? And what did that person do to earn it?
The secretary of the Young Zionist organization where I
taught Hebrew told me about it.

    The man in question wasn't a native here. He stemmed
from somewhere in Courland. He had come to town in
1916 and posted notices that he was a teacher of German.
It was during the Austrian occupation, and everyone
wanted to learn German. German is spoken in Courland
and he, Benjamin Schwartz—that was his real name—
got many students of both sexes. Just as the secretary was
talking, he pointed to the window and exclaimed, "There
he goes now!"

I looked through the window and saw a short man, dark, in a derby and with a curled mustache that was already long out of style. He was carrying a briefcase. After the Austrians left, the secretary continued, no one wanted to study German any more and the Poles gave Benjamin Schwartz a job in the archives. If someone needed a birth certificate, they came to him. He had a fancy handwriting. He had learned Polish, and he also became a kind of hedge lawyer.

The secretary said, "He came here as if dropping from heaven. At that time, he was a bachelor of some twenty-odd. The young people had a club, and when an educated person came to our town this was cause for a regular celebration. He was invited to our club and a box evening was arranged in his honor. Questions were placed in a box, and he was supposed to draw them out and answer them. A girl asked whether he believed in Special Providence, and, instead of replying in a few words, he spoke for a whole hour. He said that he didn't believe in God, but that all things were determined, every trifle. If one ate an onion for supper, it was because one *had* to eat an onion. It had been so preordained a billion years ago. If you walked in the street and tripped over a pebble, it was fated that you should fall. He described himself as a fatalist. It had been destined that he come to our town, though it appeared accidental.

"He spoke too long; nevertheless a discussion followed. 'Is there no such thing as chance?' someone asked, and he replied, 'No such thing as chance.' 'If that is so,' another asked, 'what's the point of working, of studying? Why learn a trade or bring up children? Well, and why contribute to Zionism and agitate for a Jewish homeland?'

" 'The way it is written in the books of fate, that's how it has to be,' Benjamin Schwartz replied. 'If it was destined that someone open a store and go bankrupt, he has to do this. All the efforts man made were fate, too, because free choice is nothing but an illusion.' The debate lasted well into the night and from that time on, he was called the Fatalist. A new word was added to the town's vocabulary.

Everyone here knows what a fatalist is, even the beadle of the synagogue and the poorhouse attendant.

"We assumed that after that evening the crowd would get tired of these discussions and turn back to the real problems of our time. Benjamin himself said that this wasn't a thing that could be decided by logic. Either one believed in it or not. But somehow all our youth became preoccupied with the question. We would call a meeting about certificates to Palestine or about education, but instead of sticking to these subjects, they would discuss fatalism. At that time our library acquired a copy of Lermontov's *A Hero of Our Time,* translated into Yiddish, which describes a fatalist, Pechorin. Everyone read this novel, and there were those among us who wanted to test their luck. We already knew about Russian roulette and some of us might have tried it if a revolver were available. But none of us had one.

"Now listen to this. There was a girl among us, Heyele Minz, a pretty girl, smart, active in our movement, a daughter of a wealthy man. Her father had the biggest dry-goods store in town, and all the young fellows were crazy about her. But Heyele was choosy. She found something wrong in everybody. She had a sharp tongue, what the Germans call *schlagfertig.* If you said something to her she came right back at you with a sharp and cutting retort. When she wanted to she could ridicule a person in a clever, half-joking way. The Fatalist fell in love with her soon after he arrived. He wasn't at all bashful. One evening he came up to her and said, 'Heyele, it's fated that you marry me, and since that is so, why delay the inevitable?'

"He said this aloud so that everyone would hear, and it created an uproar. Heyele answered, 'It's fated that I should tell you that you're an idiot and that you've got lots of nerve besides, and therefore I'm saying it. You'll have to forgive me, it was all preordained in the celestial books a billion years ago.'

"Not long afterward, Heyele became engaged to a young man from Hrubieszów, the chairman of the Poale

Zion there. The wedding was postponed for a year because the fiancé had an older sister who was engaged and who had to be married first. The boys chided the Fatalist, and he said, 'If Heyele is to be mine, she will be mine,' and Heyele replied, 'I am to be Ozer Rubinstein's, not yours. That's what fate wanted.'

"One winter evening the discussion flared up again about fate, and Heyele spoke up, 'Mr. Schwartz, or Mr. Fatalist, if you really believe in what you say, and you are even ready to play Russian roulette if you had a revolver, I have a game for you that's even more dangerous.'

"I want to mention here that at that time the railroad didn't reach to our town yet. It passed two miles away, and it never stopped there at all. It was the train from Warsaw to Lvov. Heyele proposed to the Fatalist that he lie down on the rails a few moments before the train passed over them. She argued, 'If it's fated that you live, you will live and have nothing to fear. However, if you don't believe in fatalism, then . . .'

"We all burst out laughing. Everyone was sure that the Fatalist would come up with some pretext to get out of it. Lying down on the tracks meant certain death. But the Fatalist said, 'This, like Russian roulette, is a game, and a game requires another participant who must risk something, too.' He went on: 'I'll lie down on the tracks as you propose, but you must make a sacred vow that if I should live, you'll break your engagement to Ozer Rubinstein and marry me.'

"A deadly silence fell over the hall. Heyele grew pale, and she said, 'Good, I accept your conditions.' 'Give me your sacred vow on it,' the Fatalist said, and Heyele gave him her hand and said, 'I have no mother, she died of the cholera. But I swear on her soul that if you will keep your word, I will keep mine. If not, then let my honor be stained forever.' She turned to us and went on, 'You are all witnesses. If I should break my word, you can all spit in my face.'

"I'll make it short. Everything was settled that evening.

The train would pass our town around two in the afternoon. At one-thirty our whole group would meet by the tracks and the Fatalist would demonstrate whether he was a real fatalist or just a braggart. We all promised to keep the matter secret because if the older people had found out about it there would have been a terrible fuss.

"I didn't sleep a wink that night, and as far as I know, none of the others did either. Most of us were convinced that at the last minute the Fatalist would have second thoughts and back out. Some also suggested that when the train came into sight or the rails started to hum, we should drag the Fatalist away by force. Well, but all this posed a gruesome danger. Even now as I speak of it a shudder runs through me.

"The next day we all got up early. I was so scared that I couldn't swallow any food at breakfast. The whole thing might not have happened if we hadn't read Lermontov's book. Not all of us went; there were only six boys and four girls, including Heyele Minz. It was freezing cold outside. The Fatalist, I remember, wore a light jacket and a cap. We met on the Zamość road, on the outskirts of town. I asked him, 'Schwartz, how did you sleep last night?' and he answered, 'Like any other night.' You actually couldn't tell what he was feeling, but Heyele was as white as if she had just gotten over the typhoid. I went up to her and said, 'Heyele, do you know that you're sending a person to his death?' And she said, 'I'm not sending him. He has plenty of time to change his mind.'

"I'll never forget that day as long as I live. None of us will ever forget it. We walked along and the snow kept falling on us the whole time. We came to the tracks. I thought that on account of the snow the train might possibly not be running, but apparently someone had cleared the rails. We had arrived a good hour too early, and, believe me, this was the longest hour I ever spent. Around fifteen minutes before the train was due to come by, Heyele said, 'Schwartz, I've thought it all over and I don't want you to lose your life because of me. Do me a favor and let's forget the whole thing.' The Fatalist looked at her and asked, 'So you've changed your mind? You want that fellow from Hrubieszów at any price, huh?' She said, 'No, it's not the fellow from Hrubieszów, it's your life. I hear that you have a mother and I don't want her to lose a son on account of me.' Heyele could barely utter these words. She spoke and she trembled. The Fatalist said, 'If you will keep your promise, I'm ready to keep mine, but under one condition: stand a little farther away. If you try to force me back at the last minute, the game is over.' Then he cried out, 'Let everyone move twenty paces back!' He seemed to hypnotize us with his words, and we began to back up. He cried out again, 'If someone tries to pull me away, I'll grab him by his coat and he will share my fate.' We realized how dangerous this could be. It happens more than once that when you try to save someone from drowning, both are dragged down, and drown.

"As we moved back, the rails began to vibrate and hum and we heard the whistle of the locomotive. We began to yell as one, 'Schwartz, don't do it! Schwartz, have pity!' But even as we yelled, he stretched out across the tracks. There was then just one line of track. One girl fainted. We were sure that in a second we would see a person cut in half. I can't tell you what I went through in those few seconds. My blood literally began to seethe from excitement. At that moment a loud screech was heard and a thud, and the train came to a halt no more than a yard away from the Fatalist. I saw in a mist how the engineer and fireman jumped down from the locomotive. They yelled at him and dragged him away. Many passengers disembarked. Some of us ran away out of fear of being arrested. It was a real commotion. I myself stayed where I was and watched everything. Heyele ran up to me, put her arms around me, and started to cry. It was more than a cry, it was like the howling of a beast— Give me a cigarette. I can't talk about it. It chokes me. Excuse me . . ."

I gave the secretary a cigarette and watched how it

shook between his fingers. He drew in the smoke and said, "That is actually the whole story."

"She married him?" I asked.

"They have four children."

"I guess the engineer managed to halt the train in time," I remarked.

"Yes, but the wheels were only one yard away from him."

"Did this convince you about fatalism?" I asked.

"No. I wouldn't make such a bet even if you offered me all the fortunes in the world."

"Is he still a fatalist?"

"He still is."

"Would he do it again?' I asked.

The secretary smiled. "Not for Heyele."

Translated by Joseph Singer

Two Markets

I never learned his name. On Krochmalna Street they called him the hunchback. As a schoolboy it didn't occur to me that he might have another name. Nor did I know if he had a wife or children. He was small, dark, and his head sat on his shoulders as if he had no neck. He had a high forehead, a sparse black beard, a beaklike nose, and the round yellow eyes of an owl. He dealt in rotten fruits at the gate of Yanash's Bazaar. Why rotten? Because fruits that hadn't yet begun to rot were expensive. The ladies whose maids followed them with baskets bought their fruit in stores where apples and oranges were wrapped in tissue paper; where strawberries, gooseberries, and currants lay in little wooden baskets, and the cherries were all the same size, the same color, and without stems, ready to be tasted. The owners of these stores did not pull at their customers' sleeves. They sat outside their stores, their broad behinds on narrow benches, huge purses hanging at their loins. They con-

versed with one another without any sign of being com-
petitors. I often saw them nibble on their own goodies.

These merchants paid rent and were issued licenses by
the municipality. Some of them were wholesalers. They
rose early in the morning when the carts arrived from the
orchards. It was said that they all belonged to a "syndi-
cate" of strong men who never allowed outsiders in.
When a strange hustler tried to break in, they poured
kerosene on his fruit, and if he couldn't take a hint, he
would be stabbed and found dead on a heap of garbage.

While the business of unspoiled fruit went along in a
relaxed fashion without too much hustle and bustle, the
trade of spoiled fruit was one big adventure. First the
merchandise had to be got cheap from the wholesalers.
Then it had to be sold the same day. Also, there was
always trouble with the police. Even if one policeman
was bribed, the others remained a threat. They would
sneak over and, with the points of their boots, kick the
merchandise into the gutter.

Fruit dealers of this kind would hawk their bargains
from early in the morning until late in the evening. They
had special praise for their leftovers. Squashed grapes
they called wine; softened oranges—gold; blemished
tomatoes—blood; wrinkled plums—sugar. The customers
had to be overwhelmed by praise, frightened by curses,
reassured by vows: "If I am lying I should get a black
verdict from heaven," "I shouldn't live to lead my
daughter under her wedding canopy," "My children should
become orphans," "Grass should grow on my grave." It
was accepted as fact in the market that those who hollered
the loudest sold their fruit the quickest and for the highest
price. Toward evening one had to get rid of the rot for
practically nothing. Each day was a never-ending struggle
with the bargain-hunting pickers and the greedy tasters.
One had to have determination, strength, a voice that
didn't get hoarse, and the ambition to wrangle for one's
groschen of profit until the end. It happened more than
once that such a merchant passed out while haggling.

How strange that some became wealthy and even grew rich.

The hunchback was one of them. Shouting was not in his power because hunchbacks have weak lungs. For swearing and cursing, women are more adept. The hunchback sang the good qualities of his merchandise with all kinds of melodies, some gay, some sad, some with the festive chant of holiday rejoicing, and some with the mournful tune of the prayer for the dead. He often joked about his goods. He was an expert in making rhymes like a wedding jester. If he was in the mood, he mocked his customers and rebuked them, all the while grimacing like a clown. If a healthy man, not a cripple, had dared to treat the matrons of Krochmalna Street this way, he would never have been able to show his face in Yanash's Bazaar again. But no one was willing to deal harshly with this unfortunate character. Even the policemen did not attempt to overturn his merchandise. All they would do was lightly kick his basket and say, "Selling here is forbidden."

"Forbidden, forshmidden, as long as one is permitted to starve and spit out one's soul three times a day, one can still go on living. I will go home and eat the whole garbage myself. Hurrah, long live the czar! To me the law is dear, have no fear, may all the Ivans kiss my rear."

The moment the policeman turned, the hunchback again started to heap praise on his merchandise, ascribing all sorts of healing powers to it—healthy for the stomach, good for the liver, a prevention against miscarriage, scabs and rashes, itching and heartburn, dysentery and constipation. The women laughed and bought. They cried from too much laughter. Girls fell into each other's arms: "Mother dear, he's funny."

They touched his hunched back for good luck.

Toward evening, when the other sellers were still screaming and swearing, the hunchback would go home with empty baskets and with a purse full of groschens, kopecks, five-kopeck pieces, and guldens. Sometimes he would stop over in the Radzymin prayer house, where my

father and I were praying. He placed his baskets on a
bench, tied a string around his waist instead of a sash,
wet the tips of his fingers on a moist windowpane, and
began to recite, "Happy are they who dwell in Thy
house." It was fun to watch this scoffer bend before the
Lord and beat his breast in repentance for his sins. I
liked to touch his scales, with their rusted chains. Once,
before Passover he came to my father's court to sell his
unleavened bread just like any other Jew. In the house of
a rabbi he had to behave. My father asked him to touch
his handkerchief as a token that he would sell his sour-
dough bread and non-Passover dishes to our Gentile
janitor during the eight days of Passover. I remember
that my father asked him if he had any alcoholic
beverages in his house—vodka, arrack, perhaps beer—
and the hunchback smiled and replied wryly, "You can
always find some of them in my place."

Another time he came to our house for a wedding. He
was one of the guests. He had changed from his patched
jacket and his dirty pants into a knee-length robe, a black
cap, a stiff collar and dickey, and patent-leather shoes.
He even wore shiny cuff links. A watch chain dangled
from his vest. In his holiday clothes his hunched back
seemed more prominent. He tasted a piece of the honey
cake, washed it down with liquor, extended a hand too
large for his small figure to the bridegroom, and said, "I
guess we will soon meet at a circumcision." And he winked
knowingly and made faces. Even I, a young boy of eleven,
could not fail to notice that the bride's belly was high and
pointed. The hunchback came over to my father and
said, "Rabbi, don't draw out the ceremony, the bride may
soon have to go to the hospital."

2

Many years passed, how many I am ashamed to tell. I
was walking with my Hebrew translator, Meirav Bashan,
in Tel Aviv, where Ben Yehudah and Allenby Streets

meet. Pointing to the large square, I asked, "In what way
is this the land of Israel? If it were not for the Hebrew
signs it could just as well be Brooklyn—the same buses,
the same noise, the same stench of gasoline, the same
movie houses. Modern civilization wipes out all individuality. I foresee that if life is discovered on the planet Mars,
we will soon have—"

I barely had time to describe what we will have there
when I looked to the right and saw Krochmalna Street.
It happened with the suddenness of a dream or a mirage:
a narrow street full of stands with fruit and vegetables,
tables with shirts, underwear, shoes, remnants of all sorts.
The crowd did not walk but pushed itself forward. I
heard the same voices, smelled the same odors, and
sensed some other sameness that my memory had retained
but for which I could find no words. For a moment I
imagined that the hustlers were shouting out their merchandise in Warsaw Yiddish, but I soon realized that it was
Hebrew. "What is this?" I asked, and my translator
answered, "Shook Ha-Carmel."

I was trying to make my way through the mob when a
second miracle occurred. I saw the hunchback. He was so
like the one in Warsaw that for an instant I thought it
was he. But only for an instant. Was it his son? His
grandson? Is a hunched back hereditary? Was the hunchback of Krochmalna Street resurrected? I stood on the
narrow pavement and gaped. This hunchback's strawberries were not really rotten, but in the glare of the
burning noon sun they appeared soggy and dyed. The
hunchback cried out his merchandise in a mocking singsong, pointing with an index finger, his yellow eyes full of
laughter. The women and girls who surrounded his stand
laughed with him and shook their heads with both ap-
proval and reproach. As I stood and observed him, I saw a
bunch of young men in caps with shiny visors and emblems
that reminded me of the Warsaw police. They wore their
shirts over their pants. They jostled and pushed one
another like playful schoolboys. They made their way
through the crowd, approached the hunchback's stand,

and without a word started to remove his boxes of strawberries. They did not seem to be regular policemen but
overseers of the market. The hunchback began to scream
frantically and to gesticulate wildly. He even tried to grab
a box of strawberries from one policeman's hands, but
another policeman lightly pushed him away. Near me
stood a man whose face somehow told me that he spoke
Yiddish. I asked him, "What do they want?" And he
replied, "They think he takes up too much space. They
want to squeeze in another merchant. May the devil tear
out their guts."

At that moment a man as swarthy as a gypsy emerged
in a red beanie and a yellow shirt. While the hunchback
was screaming, jumping, and convulsing, the man whispered something into his ear. For a moment the hunchback became quiet, listened, and nodded with businesslike
awareness. Then he continued to protest the injustice done
to him, but in a milder tone and with a different expression. He seemed both to scold and to beg for mercy.
I thought that he was throwing in words that were either
a warning or an offering. The officers exchanged glances
and shrugged their shoulders. They seemed to console
each other without words. Then the swarthy man, the
advice-giver, once more whispered into the hunchback's
ear, and now he rebuked his tormentors in a businesslike
style. Some kind of game I could not fathom was going
on here. A crowd of curious onlookers pressed against me,
and they all appeared to be on the side of the hunchback.
Everything happened quickly, and because I could not
hear the words I felt as if I were looking at a silent film
where the actors just move their lips and gesture. Events
passed without apparent connection. One moment the
officers were removing the boxes, and then they were
putting them back. The whole scene didn't last more than a
few minutes. The hunchback wiped his face with his sleeve,
and although he breathed heavily, there was triumph in
his gaze. Did his shouting cancel the verdict? Had he
promised something to the officers? And what had happened to his advice-giver? One moment he emerged and

the next moment he vanished. If a scene like this was shown in a theater, I said to myself, the critics would call it melodrama. But the truth is not ashamed of appearing contrived. I worked my way to the stand. I wanted to buy a kilo of strawberries, for my sake as well as the hunchback's, and in the confusion I forgot that in Hebrew they are called *tut-sadeh.* I tried to speak Yiddish to him and immediately realized that he was a Sephardi, one of the African Jews. All I could say was *kilo echad,* one kilo.

Before I could get the words out of my mouth, he hastily scooped up the strawberries from the very bottom, where the small and soft ones are hidden. He weighed them with such rapidity that there was no way of seeing the correct weight. I gave him a bank note and in a split second I got the change—liras, half liras, quarter liras, and cog-wheeled aluminum piasters. Such speed I have never witnessed, even in New York. The plastic bag jumped into my hand as if by magic.

Only now it occurred to me that I had lost my translator. I had forgotten about her and she had disappeared. I went to look for her and I was jostled, squeezed, and deafened by the noisy blare and clang of the multitude. Here they didn't sell gadgets for tourists like on Ben Yehudah Street, but the products of God's earth—onions and garlic, cauliflower and mushrooms, bananas and apricots, nectarines and St. John's bread, oranges and avocados. In the midst of the hustling, beggars stretched out their hands for alms. A blind man was howling lamentations, lifting an accusing hand to heaven, threatening those high up with consequences that even the Throne of Glory could not withstand. A Yemenite with the white beard of a prophet, in a garment of black and white stripes like a prayer shawl, menacingly shook a charity box with an inscription I could not make out. In other streets it was siesta time, but here in the Carmel market the battle raged on.

I heard a familiar knocking and raised my eyes. On a crooked balcony with half its plaster missing, a matron

was beating her featherbed with a stick and with the
same vengeance as they did on Krochmalna Street. Disheveled women and half-naked children stared out from
windows with cracked shutters, their eyes black with fore-
boding. Emaciated pigeons perched on broken-off ledges
—descendants of the doves sacrificed in the Temple. They
gazed over the flat roofs far out to a space that might
never have been revealed to man, awaiting a pigeon
Messiah. Or were they creatures, cave-dwelling cabalists
created from the Book of Creation? I found myself both
in old Warsaw and in Eretz Yisrael, the land that God
had promised to Abraham, Isaac, and Jacob, but He had
never really kept His word. A khamsin wind blew from
the Sinai desert, salted by vapors from the Dead Sea.
Suddenly I saw my translator. Apparently she had forgotten that she was a modern writer, a disciple of Kafka,
a commentator of Joyce, and that she was writing a book
about Agnon. She stood at a stand, rummaging through a
heap of female underclothing, absorbed in the ancient
feminine lust for bargains. She lifted up a yellow slip and
tossed it back immediately. She dug out a red brassiere,
hesitated for a while, and let it go. She picked up a pair of
black velvet panties with golden stars and silver dots,
studied them, patted them, and measured them against
her thighs. I approached her, put my hand on her shoulder,
and said, "Take them, Meirav. These panties were worn
by the Queen of Sheba when King Solomon solved all
her riddles and she showed him all her treasures."

Translated by the author and Hannah Koevary

The Gravedigger

"One can get used to everything," my Aunt Yentel said. And as she uttered those words I knew she was ready to tell a story. She wiped her upper lip, stroked the ribbons and beads on her bonnet, and squinted her right eye. The left one stared at me, at the roof across from the bench where she was sitting, and at the chimney perching in Sabbath idleness. The two women who came to converse with my aunt after the Sabbath meal, Beila Riva and Breina Gitel, nodded their heads. I was sitting on half of a stool. On the other half rested the cat that had never yet missed one of my aunt's stories. The cat's eyes became like two green slits. She had eaten the leftovers of our midday repast and was all wrapped up in Sabbath peace.

"It's no wonder people get used to good things," my aunt said. "Make a chimneysweep a king, and it will be beneath him to eat with a general. But one can also get accustomed to bad things. In our town, Turbin, there was a

man called Mendel Gravedigger. I see him before my
eyes, tall, straight, broad-shouldered, with a black beard
—a handsome man. He was somewhat versed in the holy
books. Why did he choose such work? He could have
been a community elder. Here in Bilgorary the gravedigger is also the caretaker of the poorhouse, the overseer
of the ritual bath, and what not—but Mendel did nothing
else. The community gave him a hut near the cemetery
and there he lived. His wife, Pesha, was always sick, spat
blood. But sick as she was, she bore her husband five
daughters, one more beautiful than the other. They all
took after their father. How much money does a gravedigger make? He would have starved except for them—
Pesha knitted skirts and jackets and the girls went into
service when they were only nine years old. The hut had
about half an acre of land and the family cultivated
vegetables—potatoes, beets, carrots, turnips. They also
kept chickens and geese. What kind of a life was this? I
visited them once. The window looked out on the graves.
Near the hut was a shack where the corpses were cleansed
called the 'cooling shack.' How one can look at death all
the time is beyond me. When I used to go there in the
months of Nisan and Elul to prostrate myself and pray
at the graves, I could not touch food for the whole day.
Pesha sewed shrouds. She belonged to the women's burial
society. I was told that once, during an epidemic, the
cooling shack was full of corpses and there wasn't room
for any more. So Mendel took the corpses into his house.
The girls were familiar with death. They were gay
wenches, noisy and laughing. They would do anything
for their parents. Such devoted children were rare even for
those times.

"Since Pesha knitted and also mended table linen and
turned over dresses, she used to visit our house once in a
while to do some work for us. Just as Mendel was large,
he could hardly enter a door, Pesha was tiny and shrunken.
She suffered from consumption. She used to say, 'God in
heaven, for myself I don't care any more. But I want my
children to live among people, not in a desert.' Her

prayers were heard. All the girls left for America. The
oldest daughter married a tailor who refused to serve the
czar. She sent for her sister, who in turn sent for the next
one. Every time a daughter left, Pesha cried as at a
funeral. The house became empty. From America they
immediately began to send money. They had married good
providers and never forgot their parents. Every month the
letter carrier brought their letters with money orders.
Mendel became prosperous. People said to him, 'Why do
you need the cemetery now?' You know how busybodies
mind everyone's business. There was a poor man in town
who was a charge of the community and the elders
wanted to give him Mendel's job. His name was Pinie—
Pinie, the son of Deborah Keila. But Mendel was in no
hurry to resign. Pesha gave all kinds of excuses to her
cronies. Naturally it wasn't gay to live on the outskirts of
town far from the stores and the synagogue, but the air
was pure. It was quiet. She liked the garden, her own
vegetables, the birds. The women asked, 'Aren't you
afraid at night?' She replied, 'What is there to be afraid
of? We will all be there. Corpses don't walk around. I
wish they would. I could tell all my troubles to my
mother.' In a small town there are no secrets. When the
letter carrier took a drink, he told everything. Mendel
became rich. An American dollar is two rubles, and the
daughters continued to send money. One of them married
a rich boy in New York. Her name was Dobella and she
was beautiful as a queen. He fell in love with her and
granted her every wish. Mendel was now lending money,
not for interest, just for the good deed. He contributed to
the poorhouse, the study house, all kinds of charities.
Wandering beggars learned of his generosity and they
came to him from all sides. None left with empty hands.

"The townspeople kept on asking, 'Since God raised
you up, why be a gravedigger?' Meanwhile, Pesha got
sick and died. She spat out her last piece of lung. God
protect us. Mendel buried her himself. After the seven
days of mourning the community did not allow him to
stay alone. They were afraid he might lose his mind.

Mendel tried to resist but Rabbi Chazkele sent for him
and he said, 'Mendel, enough!' When Rabbi Chazkele
uttered a word he was not contradicted. Mendel moved
out. Pinie had a wife and children and they moved in.
Anything is better than starving.

"How long can a man stay single, especially when he is
stuffed with money? The matchmakers swarmed around
him like locusts. They proposed widows, divorcées, even
girls to him. Mendel lived as a boarder with a shoemaker
on Bridge Street but he was persuaded to buy a house in
the market. If you have a house, then you certainly need
a wife. He finally married a twenty-six-year-old spinster,
Zissel, an orphan. Her father had been a scribe. That
Zissel was even smaller than Pesha. She was a maid at the
rabbi's. The rabbi's wife used to complain that Zissel
couldn't even boil an egg. They called her Zissel the
lazybones. Why did Mendel marry Zissel when he could
have gotten a pretty woman, a homemaker? There are
no answers to such questions. He rejected all the matches,
but when Zissel was proposed to him he consented. People
scoffed. The ruffians who sat in the taverns and gossiped
said that Zissel and Pesha were as alike as two drops of
water. You never know what a man thinks. The truth is
it was ordained in heaven that Zissel should better herself. She didn't have a penny but Mendel generously
gave her a trousseau, wedding gifts. Since she was a
virgin, they placed the canopy in the synagogue yard.
People went to that wedding without being asked. Zissel
was dressed in silk and velvet, but she looked as though
she had just been dragged out from behind the stove. I
myself went to that wedding and I danced a scissors
dance with the girls. Soon after the wedding Mendel
engaged a servant for her. Taking care of a house requires
strength and also deftness, but Zissel had none. The
rabbi's wife thanked God to be rid of her. The day after
the wedding Zissel put on a shabby dress, a pair of torn
shoes, and she shuffled from room to room. The servant
didn't even ask her what to cook. To all the questions
Zissel had one answer, 'What do I care?' It was all the

same to her. She lay on her bed and dozed. It was expected that she would have children. She wasn't good
even for that. She miscarried once, then her womb closed
forever."

"Such schlemiels you find in every town," Beila Riva
remarked.

"My mother used to say that the worst cur gets the
fattest bone," Breina Gitel agreed.

2

"Wait, don't interrupt," Aunt Yentel said. "Yes, she got
married. That's all she needed. She was lazy before too,
but now that she was her own boss she became a clod of
clay. She slept by day, she slept by night, she was even
too lazy to eat. When she was spoken to she didn't know
what it was all about. 'Huh, what, who, where,' she
mumbled as in a dream. When Mendel's children in
America heard that their father had replaced their mother
with Zissel they stopped sending money. But he had
enough. After some time the servant left and no one
missed her. Zissel lay around as though paralyzed, and if
Mendel did not bring her food she didn't eat. Mendel,
himself, was satisfied with a loaf of bread and an onion.
It is not the custom to visit the grave of a relative before
a year has passed, but he went to the cemetery every day.
He ordered a bench to be made by the side of Pesha's
grave and there he sat and recited psalms.

"That Pinie was not really a gravedigger, he could not
hold a spade in his hand, and Mendel helped him. Pinie's
wife did not know how to keep a garden and Mendel became the gardener. He plowed, he sowed, he weeded. He
also slept at Pinie's and came home only for the Sabbath.
People asked him, 'What's the sense of it, Mendel?' He
replied, 'I feel more at home there.' What did the poor
man have in his real home? Zissel could not even prepare
a Sabbath pudding, and if she did, it came out either raw
or burned. There was certainly no one to talk to. If she

answered at all it was one word out of ten. She didn't go
to the ritual bath either. She did not need a man and it
seemed he did not need a wife. And if he did, what kind
of a wife was Zissel? She wasn't a female but a heap of
garbage, God forgive my language. He even began to eat at
Pinie's. At night they put a straw pallet on the floor for
him and this was his bed. Mendel was the gravedigger,
not Pinie, who just got paid. Mendel did the work of the
burial society, too. He went to those about to die and put a
feather to their nostrils. He also cleansed the bodies. He
was the watchman, the pallbearer, whoever was needed.
There was a custom that on the Day of the Rejoicing of
the Law the warden of the burial society gave a banquet.
Since Mendel did so much all year round, they wanted to
honor him. Those people could drink! A whole barrel of
aqua vitae was set out for them. The women roasted
geese, ducks, chickens and cooked caldrons of cabbage
with cream of tartar. And they baked strudels, cakes,
royal biscuits, and whatever one could desire. The members wanted to put a pumpkin with candles on Mendel's
head and to lift him up and dance with him as a sign of
recognition. But he left it all and ran to a corpse. Those
who died on the eighth day of Sukkoth are buried on the
Day of the Rejoicing of the Law. This is according to the
Talmud.

"That summer, two years before the market burned
down, we had an epidemic. God protect us, what went on!
Half the town died in seven weeks' time. Grass grew on
the streets. Today you spoke with a person and he was
fresh and healthy, the next day he was gone. Dr. Obolowski forbade the eating of raw fruit and the drinking of
unboiled water. This did not stop the dying. When someone got the cramps there was one remedy, to rub his legs
and belly with vodka. But who should do the rubbing?
The moment one touched a sick person one got the
cramps oneself. After a while Dr. Obolowski refused to
visit the sick; not that it helped him, he died too, and his
wife soon after. The druggist closed the drugstore. He
went up to an attic room and no one was permitted to

enter except the cook, who brought him his food. He did not save himself. On the other hand, there were those daredevils who drank water from the well and ate unripe apples and nothing happened to them. Still, people were careful. My dear friends, only then did the town learn to appreciate Mendel. He went from house to house and massaged the sick. When someone died Mendel carried him to the cemetery. Half the burial society had departed for the other world, the rest hid like mice. Mendel became everything, the doctor, the gravedigger. Pinie and his family found refuge in some hamlet.

"The market was empty. One looked out the window and didn't see a living soul. Even the dogs who hung around the butcher shops had succumbed or run away. But Mendel walked around with a jug of spirits and, wherever he was needed, he was there. He stopped sleeping altogether. His hands were like iron, and when he rubbed someone, the alcohol went into the flesh. He had saved God knows how many people, and the others he buried. He went into the dry-goods stores and helped himself to linen for shrouds. When the cholera began his beard was still black mixed with gray; when it ended he was as white as an old man. I forgot to mention that Zissel died too. Since she was dead when alive, what difference did it make? Mendel buried her—not next to Pesha but near her father. The plague began on the seventeenth day of the month of Tammuz, a fast day, and when it stopped it was already the middle of Elul.

"When Turbin came to itself, they wanted to pay homage to Mendel, but he refused. They asked him, 'What do you want?' And he said, 'I want to be Mendel the gravedigger again.' The community elders could not believe their own ears. 'What is the purpose of it?' they asked. And he said, 'There I lived and there I want to die.' Pinie was not alive any more. He had gotten the cramps at the peasant's house, so Mendel moved back. They tried to find him a new wife, because how can a man live alone, especially near a cemetery? But he said, 'Twice is enough.' The rabbi admonished him that it was

not the right way to behave. Mendel was by nature a
silent person; he listened and nodded.

"When the daughters in America got the news that their
stepmother was no more, they again began to shower him
with money. Every few days the letter carrier appeared
with a registered letter. Mendel said to him, 'I don't need
so much money.' And the Gentile answered, 'If you don't
need it, you can give it to me. But before this you have to
take it and sign a paper.' He gave so much to charity that
he had no like in the whole of Poland. People moved into
his house in town and he asked no rent. They tried to
match him with the most beautiful girls but he shrugged
his shoulders. It became the custom that on Saturdays in
the summer when the common people went for a walk to
the forest, they stopped at Mendel's cemetery hut. A few
logs lay in front of the hut and the tailor's apprentices sat
there with the seamstresses and Mendel brought them refreshments. He had already been named Mendel Corpse.

"What does a nickname matter? He lived into his
eighties. Once in the winter I passed his hut in a sleigh.
It had snowed for three days and three nights. The cemetery was buried in snow. Beech trees are white even in
summer but on this day they looked like corpses in
shrouds. I saw Mendel digging himself out of a mountain
of snow. The sleigh had stopped, and my first husband,
he should intercede for all of us, asked him, 'Reb Mendel,
do you want some help?' 'None at all,' he said. 'Do you
have enough to eat?' and he answered, 'I roast potatoes for
myself.' 'Aren't you lonely?' my husband asked, and Mendel said, 'Why should I be lonely?'

"I wasn't in Turbin any more when Mendel died. I was
told that he dug his own grave next to Pesha's. He had
become sick, and during his sickness he went out to dig
his grave."

"Is such a thing permitted?" Beila Riva asked.

Aunt Yentel pondered for a while. "Most probably it is
permitted. He was a pious man."

"What is the meaning of all this?"

"I ask you."

"It is written that if one remembers the day of death one eschews sin," Breina Gitel remarked.

"It is one thing to remember, and another to spend one's life among corpses. Even the greatest saint would not do this."

"It must have been a kind of madness," Beila Riva spoke.

"It was certainly something. A person takes a notion into his head and it gets stuck there. Near Kocica, there was a squire, Count Chwalski, and he did not sleep in bed but in a coffin."

"Why in a coffin?"

"Since the coffin is the end, one should get accustomed to it, he said. He had neither wife nor children. Crazy Chwalski, he was called."

"Did he die there?" Breina Gitel asked.

"He was burned to cinders. His castle was all wood and one night it lit up like a lantern."

It became quiet. The cat had fallen asleep. Aunt Yentel glanced at me. "Do you like stories?"

"Yes, Aunt, very much."

"What is the good of stories? You better go and study the Ethics of the Fathers."

"Later."

"I am going to lie down myself. Wait, I have a cookie and Sabbath fruit for you."

Translated by the author and Dorothea Straus

The Sorcerer

"There are such things as sorcerers, yes, there are," Aunt Yentel said. "I know of one myself, but it's not a story for the Sabbath."

"Why not?" Aunt Rachel asked. "You are allowed to talk about magic on the Sabbath."

"Oh really? Well, when I was a child, the Crazy Squire —that's what they used to call him—was already an old man. He lived a long time, nearly a hundred years, or maybe the whole hundred. He spent twelve of them in the Janów prison. He died when I was a girl, seventy years ago, and I saw him a few times: a short man, broad, with white hair down to the shoulders. You couldn't see his eyes, they were like a hedgehog's. He had bristly eyebrows like two brushes and whiskers like a tomcat's. He had grown deaf in his old age and they said that he was senile. His name was Count Stefan Leszczynski and it was rumored that he was descended from Polish kings. He wore clothes from the reign of King Sobieski in the summer and

in the winter a fur hat and a fur-lined coat trimmed with
foxtails.

"He spoke in a gasping voice and no one understood a
word he said. While he was in prison there was an insur-
rection in Poland. Part of his estate had been confiscated
even earlier when the czar freed the serfs. The rest was
squandered away by his bailiffs. He was left with the ruins
that were called the castle or the court. The evil spirits
cavorted there even during the day. They celebrated wed-
dings and circumcisions. Some of these demons were Jewish. The shutters were always closed. People said that the
squire had stopped eating altogether. He had a farmhand
who was even older than himself. He could brew aquavit
out of barley and this is what the squire drank from a jug
through a straw. He was left with a few acres of land and
he leased them to a peasant, a former serf of his.

"I don't know if he was still a sorcerer during my time.
You have to have strength to conjure up the powers of the
night. It was on account of this sorcery that he landed in
jail. My grandfather Lemel was his Court Jew. He remembered the squire when he still had black hair and had
fooled around with all the village girls. Before the peasants
were freed, a squire could do whatever he wanted with his
serfs. He went into a peasant's hut, saw that he had a pretty
wife, and said, 'Stach, your woman appeals to me. Let her
come to me, but in a clean shirt, no lice.'

"At night the husband brought the wife and waited outside. If he refused, he'd be lashed.

"What did he need with peasant wenches when his own
wife was a beauty? She came, they said, from the highest
nobility, but her father had lost his fortune and she was
orphaned at an early age. The life she led with this
Leszczynski, I wouldn't wish on my enemies. The local
gentry avoided him like a leper. He messed around with
the creatures of darkness. There is a hill near the castle
and the squire had a cave dug there where he dabbled in
black magic. After he was imprisoned, the sons-in-law had
the cave filled in. It was said that they found the bones of
dead people there, braids, elflocks, and devil's dung.

"What did he get out of this sorcery? Every sorcerer has his kind of madness. There were those who tried to make gold from lead, others took revenge on enemies. Stefan Leszczynski had confided to my grandfather that he would create a female who would possess all the virtues. God save us from what he considered virtues! The countess was ailing and she apparently wouldn't let him near her any more. Who would give herself to such a beast? He had grown bored with the peasant women. He talked to no one, but he did confide in my grandfather. That was the way the squires used to feel: that all Jews were rascals except for their Court Jew.

"When Leszczynski needed money, my grandfather sold a piece of the forest for him, some land, or cattle. He had pawned some of the countess's jewelry. Stefan Leszczynski always carried a riding crop, and when the countess said something that annoyed him, he whipped her in front of everybody. He beat his daughters, too. He liked my grandfather, but more than once sicced the dogs on him. Anyhow, he lusted for a woman such as didn't exist in the world, and he found a book that showed how such a woman could be brought into being. The squire said that he would build her piecemeal—first the legs, then the torso, then the head. I shudder when I speak about it. These females are half human, half spirit. Our holy books speak of them, too. I read it myself somewhere."

"In *The Righteous Measure*," Aunt Rachel said. "About the goldsmith."

"Eh? You remember. My memory is a little foggy. He warned my grandfather to keep the secret, or else he would cut him to pieces and douse the wounds in vinegar. Grandfather told no one, not even Grandmother. Only after Leszczynski had been put in chains and the abomination became common knowledge did Grandfather tell Grandmother.

"Grandmother told my mother, and after I was married, my mother felt that she could now discuss it with me.

"Such things aren't done in a hurry. The squire had to fast, light black candles, burn spices, and utter incantations. Time and time again he sent Grandfather to Lublin for cloves, incense, bird feathers, and all kinds of rare herbs. You aren't allowed to help such people, but if Grandfather had refused, the count would have punished him severely.

"The night came that the woman was complete. He wanted to show her to Grandfather, but at this point Grandfather put his foot down. 'I'm a Jew,' he said, 'and our law forbids this.'

"The squire said to Grandfather, 'The Bible praises the beauty of Bathsheba, Abigail, and Queen Esther, but my woman is more beautiful than all of them. You can't look at her face, for it will blind your eyes. When she speaks, your blood starts to seethe as in a kettle. She is wiser than the Queen of Sheba.'

"He wanted Grandfather to bring him tapestries for the walls and rugs for the floor of the cave. Talk started in town that the squire had brought in a mistress from somewhere. She was never seen during the day, but at night she seemed to float by—with her face veiled. Now she was here, now she dissolved.

"Once when my mother, may she rest in peace, went out late at night to empty the slops, she saw Squire Leszczynski ride by on a black horse with some kind of female monster riding beside him. The horses were galloping, but you couldn't hear any hoofbeats. Mother came back as white as chalk. She told Grandfather what she had seen and he said, 'Hush, not a word.' The following day he sent for the scribe and had him examine the mezuzah.

"I think the squire's daughters were no longer living at the castle by that time. Their mother had sent them to an aunt's so that they wouldn't be witness to the goings on. The countess was already accustomed to her misery. Many nights he didn't come home to sleep at all but gamboled with the she-demon in the cave. The peasants began to gossip that the squire was bathing with her in the river in the dead of winter. At times, lecherous laughter was heard from the cave. It was the squire chortling at her obsceni-

ties. He said to Grandfather, 'One night with her is better
than all the pleasures in the world.'

"Grandfather reminded him that there was a God and
that one was punished for one's iniquities, but the squire
replied, 'We'll all roast in hell together,' and he howled
like a madman.

"He thought that things would go smoothly for him,
but no good can come of such idolatry. Give me a drink
of water. When I talk about it, my throat goes dry.

"Yes, people like this think that they will live forever.
He didn't go to church on Sundays. It's their custom that
before Easter the priest comes to consecrate the bread,
but Leszczynski wouldn't let the priest into the house and
the woman cursed him with foul oaths. At one time they
burned sorcerers at the stake. It was this way among Jews,
too. I read that one sage hanged eighty witches.

"To make a long story short, the count did whatever
he wanted. All of a sudden the countess became sick; her
face turned yellow as if from jaundice. She stopped eating. A doctor came from Zamość, but what do doctors
know? The daughters came home to see her. Talk started
that the squire had poisoned her. But he didn't have to
poison her—a broken heart is the worst kind of poison.

"The countess owned jewelry. So that her husband
shouldn't steal it, she had hidden it somewhere where no
one could find it. When she saw that her time was drawing
close, she called in her daughters and revealed the hiding
place to them. 'I inherited it from my grandmother,' she
said, 'and I don't want him to grab it.' The daughters
searched, but they found nothing. Their father had used
black magic to grab the jewelry. When the countess found
out, she went into her death throes. The sons-in-law came
to the squire to demand an accounting and he took a pistol
to them. He wanted the countess buried on the grounds
without a ceremony, but the daughters wouldn't stand for
this. They held a funeral and the squire didn't walk behind the hearse. If he had, the mob would have stoned
him.

"After their mother's death, the daughters left and they never came back again.

"My grandfather tried to make peace between the father and children. A Court Jew used to be like one of the family. The girls knew my grandfather. He used to carry them in his arms when they were little. He would bring them candy and cookies. But they said, 'He is not our father and we are not his children.'

"Now that the countess was dead, the estate began to fall to pieces. The walls were crumbling, the floors rotting, the granaries teemed with rats and mice. Even the trees looked sick; they were covered with spider webs that hung from the branches like ropes. One steward died, a second left. The peasants stopped working and no one said anything to them. At this estate it had been arranged that some of the peasants were given a piece of their own land. They would work two days a week for themselves, and four days for the squire. With no one watching over them, Leszczyn-ski's peasants did as they pleased. The squire called in my grandfather and said, 'Lemel, you take a lease.' He signed a paper and Grandfather took over the estate. If not for him, everything would have fallen apart years sooner."

2

"Where is it written, 'A thief ends up on the gallows'?
"For a year or two the squire was left alone. What did he need with a wife if he could mate with the evil spirit? He was drinking heavily, too. Once in a while a leaseholder has to ask the owner about this and that. He can't take everything upon himself. Grandfather had to come to the squire to sign a deed, but there was no one to talk to. If the squire had been drinking, he would lie down to sleep and no one would be able to rouse him. What Jew would dare wake a squire? He would snore there like a slaughtered ox. He didn't even take off his coat and boots. The peasants said that he no longer went to the she-demon in

the cave, but she came to his bed at night. In the winter
the tracks of goose feet could be seen in the snow.

"The chambermaid complained that the sheets stank of
sulfur. This Lilith attracted foxes and martens to the region
and the peasants swore that owls and bats came flying in
at night and befouled the grain. Grandfather already
yearned to be rid of the whole business, but since there
was no one with whom to speak, how could he come to
any agreement?

"In the midst of all this, the rumor spread that the
squire had acquired a gypsy mistress. Gypsies used to come
every year to us. They may still do so to this day. They
always came right after Passover in wagons, and set up
camp in a clearing near the forest. The men had black
beards like Jews. They polished copper pans, sharpened
knives, and traded in horses. The women read cards. Our
old rabbi forbade any contact with them, but people
wanted to know what their end would be. With all due
respect to her, my own aunt, may she intercede for me in
heaven, called in one of them and asked her to read her
fortune. She guessed it to the smallest detail. She told my
aunt, 'Seven good years are left you, exactly to the day.'
And that's how it happened. She lived another seven years
with my uncle. And they lived like a pair of turtledoves.
One day after Passover, my uncle came from the house
of worship and said, 'Hayale, I feel a pressure in the pit
of my stomach. Bring me a glass of water.' She went to
the barrel to draw the water and heard a thud. He had
fallen down dead.

"Yes, gypsies. Who are they, eh? Someone said that they
are Jews who have been cursed. Perhaps descendants of
the Lost Tribes. I don't believe it. Anyway, that time they
brought along a woman the likes of which the world has
never seen. I saw her once and I grew bedazzled. A pair
of eyes like burning coals. I'm not a man, but she seared
me with a glance. How she ended up with the squire no
one knows till this day. It is possible that her father sold
her, or maybe it was her husband. Gypsies steal children

and it's possible they had kidnapped her somewhere. She wasn't dark, only tanned from the sun.

"When my grandmother heard about this gypsy, she said, 'Two cats in a single sack. There'll be a war between them and it will end in a turmoil.'

"It seems Leszczynski fell so in love with the gypsy that he neglected the she-demon. By that time, my grandfather no longer held the lease on the estate. He had also stopped being the Court Jew. He had opened a store and made his living from it. He had married off his children and had been left with only Grandmother. How long could he stay with a mad sorcerer?

"They said that the gypsy tried to run away and the squire chained her to the bed. It seemed he also flogged her, because one could hear her wailing at night like a she-wolf. Whoever is raised among the gypsies can never settle down, not even in a king's palace. They're drawn to the fields, the forests, the free air. What they do in winter I don't know. They say that when a child is born among them they douse it in a bucket of cold water. If it dies, it dies. If it lives, it can go around naked in frosts.

"Once after Sukkoth, when Grandmother was sitting in the store saying her prayers—it happened that there were no customers there—a Gentile came in, not a peasant, but a city man. He said, 'Lemlicha'—that's what they called her—'our squire Leszczynski has killed the gypsy.' Grandmother began to tremble. 'How do you know?' she asked, and the man said, 'A peasant was walking by at night—he probably was out to steal a chicken or some eggs—and he saw the squire burying the gypsy in a grave.' Grandmother didn't believe it, but it was true. Such things don't remain a secret. It traveled from mouth to ear until it reached the authorities. Two investigators came from Janów to question the squire. He flatly denied it. What gypsy? 'There was a gypsy here,' he said, 'but I sent her away.' But someone had informed on the squire and the men went to a spot among the trees where the earth had been freshly disturbed. They ordered the peasants to dig, and right near the surface they found the body, naked, not even in a shroud. They took her out and her throat was blue. The officials asked, 'How do you explain this?' And the squire said, 'I don't know. Probably one of the peasants did it.'

"They shackled him in chains and took him to Janów. The wagon rode past the marketplace and a big commotion ensued. The squire was sitting on a pile of hay bound like a calf for the slaughter, but he hadn't lost his tongue and he cried, 'Hey, you Jews, your God is taking revenge on me.'

"My grandfather had found out about it and he came running up. 'Illustrious squire, what's going on here?' he asked. And the squire said, 'I didn't do it. She did it, the she-demon. Come to Janów and bear witness for me. You know the truth. Only you can save me!' Grandfather went to Janów and told the whole story, but the authorities didn't believe him. It wouldn't have taken much more for Grandfather to be arrested, too. There was one investigator there who didn't believe in black magic. He taunted Grandfather: 'If you knew that he was living with a she-devil, why did you keep your mouth shut? Besides, there are no such things as devils or hobgoblins, it's all nonsense.'

"Still, he came with a whole retinue and examined the cave. They found the skeleton of a baby there and all kinds of herbs and charms, but no she-demon.

"Grandfather Lemel was able to talk Russian and he managed to convince them to let him see the squire in his cell. The squire said, 'I didn't lie to you. As soon as I brought the gypsy into the house, they began to fight like cat and dog. I had already grown tired of the other one. These creatures are wind and foam, not flesh and blood. Their whole power is in their tongues. The other, the gypsy, had a body that was like fire. I realized that the first one had no substance, and I tried to get rid of her, but she wouldn't let herself be driven away. I lay with the gypsy and the she-demon placed herself between us and wouldn't let us copulate. There was a struggle between them, all in the dark; then it grew quiet. I touched the gypsy and she was cold. I realized that the she-demon had strangled her and I buried her in the woods.'

"Grandfather repeated all this to the officials and they wrote it down in the books. When it came time for the trial, they called on Grandfather and he repeated the same story. But the judge demanded, 'Were you present at all this?'

"He sentenced the squire to twelve years. He said to him, 'It's a miracle that your life is being spared. A hundred years ago you would have been burned at the stake.'

"As long as Grandfather lived, he sent the squire vodka and tobacco to the jail. The daughters and sons-in-law wanted nothing to do with him.

"Listen to this now! Since this Leszczynski was a count after all, he was given preferential treatment in prison and a cell all to himself. The *nachalnik* used to invite him to his house for lunch or dinner. The *nachalnik* had a wife and children and Leszczynski used to tell them stories. When he wanted, he could be kind. He became like one of the family. The children called him Grandpa and it went so far that his cell door was left unlocked. We found out about this from a man who knew my mother. Since Leszczynski had grown close to them, the *nachalnik* and his wife asked him about the gypsy and why he had killed her, and he stuck to his story that the she-demon had done it. They didn't believe him. All the thieves and murderers claim to be innocent. There were some other prisoners there who had been sentenced to life, and they had been there so many years that the officials no longer worried about them escaping; they acted as servants to the *nachalnik,* chopped firewood, helped in the kitchen, and worked in the garden.

"I once saw the Janów prison. It wasn't easy to escape from there. It had an iron gate as black as pitch, and high walls all around. There were guards, too. One night one of those lifers passed Leszczynski's cell and heard talk inside. A man spoke and a woman answered. They laughed and frolicked. The prisoner became petrified. He knew that there was only one woman in the building—the *nachalnik*'s wife. They didn't keep a maid since the prisoners did all the work, even the cooking and washing. The prisoner figured that, if he told the *nachalnik* that he was being betrayed, he would have his sentence reduced.

"The next day he went to the *nachalnik* and quietly told him what he had heard. This could have caused a great misfortune, because when a Russian becomes jealous, he goes right for a weapon. But it just so happened that the *nachalnik*'s wife had gone to Lublin to shop for clothes and she couldn't be suspected.

"Why belabor the point? It was no one else but the she-demon. It seemed that she was still alive and Leszczynski had summoned her again with black magic. The *nachalnik* later wrote to the governor about it, but they only laughed at him."

"If he was such a great sorcerer," Aunt Rachel asked, "why didn't he run away from prison?"

"I don't know. He didn't lack for anything there. Maybe he got accustomed to it like a bird gets used to its cage. It seems that the goldsmith in *The Righteous Measure* had five children with the she-demon and he was a father to them."

"Yes, true."

"I still remember a little. It is said in the Holy Book: 'If people could only see how many devils and imps hover about them, they would all perish from fright.' "

Translated by Joseph Singer

Moishele

Dusk was gathering at the close of the bleak winter afternoon. All day the snow had been falling in thick flakes and the balconies opposite were piled high with drifts. Smoke from the chimneys, too dense to rise, curled around the rooftops like sooty draperies. The day hung in the balance, as though hesitating: could something yet be accomplished before nightfall, or was it too late? All at once, as though a switch had been turned, the light went out. Darkness fell, and the day was beyond repair.

Shadows lengthened along the tile stove with its gilded top, along the paintings which lined the walls, along the piano, the armchairs, the carpets. The pendulum of the mantel clock, a legacy from Reb Tzodek Walden, moved slowly and as though about to stop. In a huge overstuffed armchair, his short arms propped up on ivory armrests, his tiny feet in their plush slippers resting on a footstool, sat Moishele Walden, looking across the room at his wife, Esther, who lay stretched out on the sofa.

Moishele was a tiny man with a triangular face, a thin nose, and a pointed chin. The fringes of hair surrounding his bald spot were long and straight, like a child's that has just come from its bath. Though he wore no beard and had adopted (since his father's death) the modern mode of dress, he still tugged at his chin occasionally. Every so often his fingers strayed to his temples, seeking the sidelocks that were no longer there.

The twilight hour had plunged Moishele into melancholy. It called up memories of the evening prayer which Jews intone at dusk, and of the Woman's Prayer his mother recited at the close of the Sabbath: "God of Abraham, Isaac, and Jacob . . ." Yes, he was grown up now and even had a wife, yet Moishele still thought of himself as an orphaned child. A part of him had never ceased to mourn his parents and to recite the Kaddish. He remembered the graves at the Gesia Cemetery and imagined how they would look piled with snow up to the very tombstones. And what were his mother and father doing beneath the ground? Could they know anything? Did they ever think of him? Were they, perhaps, cold? Moishele knotted the sash of his silk dressing gown a little tighter and raised the collar. He was susceptible to colds.

As the room darkened, Moishele's eyes appeared to grow larger and more luminous. He stared at Esther with a child's wonder—he seemed to see in her something which could not really be there. In the shadows her narrow face glowed white, as though lighted from within. A light from the sunset beyond the clouds played about her hair. Esther yawned and nodded, pondering her fate. Her dressing gown had slipped open, revealing the dazzling whiteness of her skin. Just as Moishele lived in perpetual fear of colds, so was she fond of going about half naked, even in winter.

Cover yourself, the flu is going around, Moishele was about to tell her, but he stopped himself. What was the use? She would only do the opposite. Since her quarrel with

Kuva she had withdrawn entirely into herself. She was
constantly busy with her own thoughts, which he dared
not interrupt. In vain he had tried to reason with her, but
she always cut him off—"Leave me alone!" Won't she
ever get tired of brooding? Moishele asked himself. We'll
both go crazy, God forbid!

Esther's break with Kuva, the painter, was not Moishele's doing. He had no say in the matter. Though he had
been rich when he married her, and the son of a good
family, and she quite penniless and an orphan, she dom-
inated him from the very beginning. He yielded to all of
her whims. She dragged him with her on endless trips
abroad, frittered away thousands on absurd trinkets, extended invitations far and wide to people he detested. To
please his wife, Moishele had squandered his inheritance.
Now all they had left was the apartment house in which
they lived.

As for Esther's liaison with the painter, they had been
at each other from the moment of their first meeting, and
their bickering had never let up. At first their quarrels
were playful—mere lovers' spats—but they soon grew
more and more bitter. She would embrace him at one moment and, at the very next, fling insults at him. She would
telephone him to come to her and, when he arrived, lock
herself in her room, leaving him to pass the time with
Moishele. Their latest squabble had been over a trifle.

Yet it was clear that Esther could not do without him.
She wandered about the house aimlessly. The lights in her
bedroom burned all night as she lay in bed reading. Then
she would sleep until late in the afternoon as though
drugged. She scarcely ate at all. Daily she grew thinner.
Moishele had urged her countless times to swallow her
pride and ask Kuva back, but she would not hear of it.
"Ask him back? Not on his life! I'll see him rot first—the
fraud!" "Stubborn, stubborn," Moishele would mutter.

But where would it all end? Only when Esther was con-
tented could Moishele attend to his affairs—talk on the
telephone to Lazar, his accountant, write a letter, read
the financial page of the *Kurier Warshawski*. When she

was depressed, he became helpless. He lost his appetite, could not sleep. A painful rash developed on his skin, which he could not keep from scratching. There was a persistent gnawing at the pit of his stomach, and he could barely hold back the tears.

Ai, Moishele mused. She has me wrapped around her little finger. She's made a doormat of me. But what can I do? She can't be blamed for it—it's her nature. She has to be in love with someone. It's like a disease. He glanced toward the French windows and saw that it was evening. The street lamps in their pale-blue globes had already been lighted. It had stopped snowing, but now and then a single flake fluttered downward, past the windows. The city shimmered in a strange light, silvery white and violet, as it is said to be in those northern lands where night goes on for months. An unearthly, almost audible stillness had descended. Could it be Hanukkah already? Moishele wondered. To please Esther, he had cultivated an interest in antiques, become a patron of the arts, and he owned a fine collection of Hanukkah lamps. But they were never used, for Moishele had long since discarded his religion and become a free-thinker.

"Cover yourself, Esther!" Moishele said finally. "It's chilly in here."

"I'm not cold."

"Esther, this must come to a stop!" He was astonished at his own boldness.

"Are you starting that again?"

"I won't beat around the bush. This makes no sense at all. If you can't fight your feelings, you must give in to them."

Esther sighed impatiently. "What do you want me to do? Throw myself at his feet?"

"Nothing of the kind. Just call him up. It's a sin to be so proud. He must be suffering just as much. It's some sort of crazy whim you both have!"

Moishele's voice rose. That Esther had not cut him off instantly gave him courage. She drew her robe more tightly about her. The sofa creaked in the silence. Esther groaned. For a moment Moishele thought she might scream, or even throw one of her slippers at him, but the moment passed and she continued tossing about on the sofa, like an insomniac seeking sleep. To Moishele, intent upon the squeaking of each separate coil of the bedsprings, it seemed as though the sofa had in some mysterious way become imbued with Esther's restlessness.

"I *won't* call him!" she said, but her tone lacked conviction.

"Then *I'll* call him!"

"What? You can do what you want—but not from my house!" Esther spoke warningly. "If you want to be a jellyfish, I can't stop you. Go ahead, do it! Crawl, creep, like a bedbug . . ."

The final insult seemed torn from Esther's throat against her will. She became rigid. Moishele was stung by the pain known only to those who sacrifice themselves in vain. Of all the insults she had ever hurled at him, this was the cruelest.

Oy, how low I have sunk, he thought pityingly. If my mother, may she rest in peace, had heard that! He was listening to his own humiliation. "Well—I will put a stop to it," he said aloud, not knowing exactly what he had in mind, divorce or suicide.

Moishele knew the bitter truth—he, too, wanted Kuva back! He had grown accustomed to his jokes, to his irony, to his witty barbs at the expense of other painters, sculptors, critics. Kuva, the incorrigible, mimicked everyone— the Yiddish literati, the Hebrew teachers, the idealists who frequented the vegetarian restaurant, the society women who commissioned portraits or marble busts from him. With a few words, Kuva could create a caricature. He tore everyone to shreds, yet his presence never failed to put Moishele into a good humor. Kuva demanded cognac, and after a while Moishele would drink along with him. Kuva would embrace Esther in Moishele's presence, and in spite of his jealousy Moishele would be overcome with an exhilaration which he could not understand. Kuva had told him often enough that he was a masochist, yet Moi-

shele realized this was not the explanation. It was simply
that he loved Esther far more than he loved himself. When
she was happy, so was he. When she suffered, he suffered
twice as much—ten times as much. Because of her beauty
he had lost himself in her completely, but even more com-
pelling than her beauty was her restlessness. A tapeworm
seemed to gnaw at her vitals. Every few weeks she would
attempt to do away with herself—to take poison or hang
herself, to turn on the gas or throw herself out of the
window.

No outsider would ever know the torments she suffered.
Born into an impoverished family, she had been orphaned
early and reared by a vicious aunt. She had even been
raped as a small child. How can a stranger, seeing such a
beautiful woman, exquisitely dressed, with the face of an
angel, guess what she goes through?

Moishele got up. "I'm going out."

"Where are you going?"

"It's no concern of yours."

Esther was silent. Moishele went to his room to dress.

Moishele put on his fur-lined overcoat, a pair of over-
shoes that looked like a woman's boots, and a plush cap
with earflaps. His small hands were gloved. He stepped
down the corridor to a paneled elevator. Only he, the landlord, had the key to it. Inside, he pressed a button and the
little cage descended slowly. He still took a boyish delight
in this downward journey. Emerging from the house, he
glanced around, taking in the square courtyard, the five-
story building with its lighted windows, the locked privy
—it all belonged to him! He owned it outright. Moishele
often pondered the fact that by law the boundaries of his
property extended all the way up to the sky and down to
the very bowels of the earth. If he, Moishele, wanted
to, and could get the necessary funds, there was nothing to
prevent him from building a skyscraper fifty stories high
on his property—just like in America. With the right tools
he could if he chose dig a hole on his property that would
reach down to the very abyss. Moishele knew that these

were only idle fantasies, but he could not resist them. He
was as fond of such speculation as a schoolboy.

Moishele passed the gate and came out onto the street.
The frosty air seized him by the nose, plucked at him,
nipped into him. He felt drunk; his eyes swam with tears.
The street was one of the finest in Warsaw, but the snow
lent it an aspect of supernatural beauty. The glassy
branches of the trees sparkled in the moonlight like great
crystal chandeliers. Precious stones were scattered about
in the snow, reflecting all the colors of the rainbow. The
street lamps wore little caps of snow and trailed an aura
of mist beneath them. Moishele breathed deeply. A schoolboy prankishness took hold of him. He had an impulse to
shout and then wait for an answering echo. He left the
pavement for a little while and slid about on the ice in the
gutter like a child. Then he continued his walk. Well, he
consoled himself, things could certainly be better, but on
the whole life was good. In spite of everything, Esther
belonged to him. At night, it was his room to which she
finally came. When she needed money, she had to ask him
for it. Moishele patted the pocket where his leather purse
lay; he felt for his vest pocket and the gold watch with its
seventeen jewels and three lids. His face was cold, but
through his limbs coursed the warmth that comes from
good food, fine clothing, a substantial income.

Let Esther play around, he thought. We're not getting
any younger. Sooner or later she's bound to get tired of it.
Nearby was a café with a public telephone, but Moishele
changed his mind about going in. It wouldn't do to talk
Yiddish in a roomful of Poles. On the other hand, he could
hardly—even if his grammar had been up to it—talk to
Kuva in Polish. Moishele bent down and scooped up a
handful of snow. He looked up at the sky. Yes, there were
the stars. A solar system was up there, made up of planets,
and some of the planets were even bigger than the earth.
There was even the likelihood—so the scientists said—
that these planets were inhabited by human beings. Well,
if that were the case, who up there in those lofty heights,
millions and millions of miles away, was the least bit con-

cerned if someone called Esther was making a fool of herself over a painter called Kuva—was even, so it was said,
having an affair with him? Compared to the cosmos, we
are all flies.

Moishele did not know how it happened, but his feet
had carried him straight to Kuva's studio. He found himself standing in the courtyard looking upward past the
blazing windows to Kuva's skylight. A faint light could be
seen, almost hidden by the snow. So he *is* at home, Moishele thought. I'll just drop in and have a few words with
him.

The house had no elevator and Moishele climbed the
four flights of stairs. He paused before Kuva's door to
stamp his boots and shake the snow from his coat. Let
him be alone, Moishele prayed. He screwed up his courage
and pressed his finger to the doorbell. At once he heard
footsteps. The door opened and there stood Kuva—tall,
dark-eyed, with a lean face, a narrow nose, and a long
chin, his hair black and wavy as a gypsy's. In one hand
he held a palette and a brush. He wore a white smock,
spattered like a butcher's apron. Moishele thought for a
moment that Kuva might slam the door in his face, but
then the painter smiled, showing wrinkles around the
mouth, and crooked teeth. "Well, look who's here! Come
in!"

"I was just passing by," Moishele mumbled as he
entered the studio. Thank God, there are no visitors, he
thought. Kuva was a sculptor as well as a painter. Electric
lamps, like spotlights, blazed everywhere. In their harsh
light stood groups of female figures—some draped with
sacks, others quite naked. Each time Moishele came to
Kuva's studio, he felt as though he had stumbled into
some ancient temple. Kuva moved among his statues like
the high priest of an idolatrous cult. The studio was chilly
and reeked of paint and turpentine; Moishele had an urge
to sneeze.

"I was just passing by," he repeated, "when I saw your
lights on. After all, we are old friends . . ." The words
stuck in his throat. Kuva nodded knowingly, as though he

had foreseen this turn of events. The smile that played about his lips had bitterness in it—a bitterness which Moishele would never understand.

"And how is Esther?"

"Thank you—not too well," said Moishele, unsure of how to go on. "Everything would be all right if not for—after all, you become attached to people—friendship is no trifling matter. How does it go? Blood is thicker than water. Suddenly something goes wrong and it's all over. What's the point? After all, we're civilized people. She's eating her heart out. She lies around on the sofa all day, pining away. She's even stopped eating. I'm afraid she'll get sick, God forbid, and what good would that do? What if she *did* speak hastily? She meant no harm. May her wishes for you come true. And as for her loyalty to you, why even when she's upset she won't hear a single word against you—especially not against your talent . . ."

Once more a lump formed in Moishele's throat.

Kuva shrugged one shoulder. "Did she send you here?"

"What's the difference? Did I have to be sent? I wasn't born yesterday. I understand such things. It's a matter of feeling. The more you fight it, the worse it gets. It hurts, and you let it out on others. It's all psychological." Moishele came to the end of his speech and broke out in a sweat.

"Well—so?"

"Come see us. She'll be delighted—she'll be so surprised. She'll come back to life. What's the whole fuss about? A mere trifle. Even a husband and wife disagree occasionally, but do they rush off to the divorce court? We're modern people, after all—"

"Very well. I'll be over sometime."

"Why not come now? She hasn't had a bite to eat all day, not since this morning. If you come, everything will get brighter. I'll tell you the truth. It's not easy for me to say, but when she's in this state you can't talk to her at all. She's proud, but inside she suffers. Sensitive, overly sensitive. She's truly sorry, but her pride won't let her admit it, so she suffers all the more. It's getting late, you've had enough creating for one day. You need some rest, some diversion. It'll even do your work good."

"You could convince a stone." Kuva nodded as if to an invisible third person. Then he disappeared into a back room.

Moishele waited, overcome with shame, among the statues. It was as though these objects of clay had senses, were able to perceive his disgrace. If only she doesn't throw him out, he prayed. You never can tell with these creatures.

Kuva returned. He had taken off his smock and put on a jacket with a fur collar and a broad-brimmed hat. He wore high boots. He looked both like an aristocrat and a tough from the streets. "Well, let's go," he growled, turning off the lights. Moishele stumbled and nearly fell over the threshold. Kuva let Moishele precede him, then hung a padlock on his door. They walked down the stairs together, but Kuva was silent. Once outside, he strode so quickly on his long legs that Moishele had to run to keep up with him. Suddenly Kuva stopped.

"In view of the situation, it might be better if we were left alone."

Moishele flushed to his ears. "For what reason? I won't disturb you."

"I think we should be left alone," Kuva repeated. He spoke to Moishele with an adult's brutality to a child. Moishele was dumbfounded.

"Where can I go now? It's freezing out."

"Go to the opera. There's still time."

"Alone—to the opera?"

"Why not? Or sit in a café and read the papers."

"I promise I won't be in your way," Moishele pleaded.

"Come back later. Leave us alone for at least two hours. There are certain—misunderstandings—that we can clear up only by ourselves," argued Kuva to Moishele and the empty streets.

"If that's the way it must be."

"Don't hold it against me, but it must." Kuva avoided Moishele's eyes and pursed his lips as though to whistle.

His face became suddenly yellow and like that of some clay images in his studio. He grumbled.

"Tell Esther I'll be home at eleven," Moishele muttered. "Adieu."

They parted, going off in opposite directions. Moishele walked with tiny steps, listening to the sound of his own shoes crunching in the snow. Who knows what will come of this, he mused, she may even hold it against me. The opera? No! A café? In cafés you run into people you know. They start asking questions, probing this . . . that . . . Moishele needed to be alone. He walked as far as Marshalkowski Street, then turned and headed in the direction of the Vienna railway station. I haven't been to a train station in a long time, he thought, as though excusing himself. A stillness had overwhelmed him, and a childlike surrender. Kuva takes me for a fool, he thought. He'll make a laughingstock of me. He'll tell it all over town. Artists can't keep secrets. And for what reason does he have to be alone with her? It's clear, only too clear. What do they call it—a cuckold?

Moishele caught sight of the station clock. Its face shone through the snow festively. He made for the entrance with the sensation of a moth being drawn to a flame. He half walked, half slid. He felt weightless. The street pitched forward suddenly at an angle, and he ran headlong downhill. For a moment the cold took his breath away, and he said to himself, Could you explain such a thing to anybody at all? No, not even to a psychologist . . .

Translated by Marion Magid

Three Encounters

I left home at seventeen. I told my parents the truth: I didn't believe in the Gemara or that every law in the Shulchan Aruch had been given to Moses on Mount Sinai; I didn't wish to become a rabbi; I didn't want a marriage arranged by a matchmaker; I was no longer willing to wear a long gaberdine or grow earlocks. I went to Warsaw, where my parents had once lived, to seek an academic education and a profession. My older brother, Joshua, lived in Warsaw and had become a writer, but he wasn't able to help me. At twenty I came back home with congested lungs, a chronic cough, no formal education, no profession, and no way that I could see of supporting myself in the city. During the time I was away, my father had been appointed rabbi of Old-Stikov in Eastern Galicia—a village of a few dozen crooked shacks, with straw-covered roofs, built around a swamp. At least, in the fall of 1924 that's how Old-Stikov appeared to me. It had rained all October, and those shacks lay reflected in the swamp as if

it were a lake. Ruthenian peasants, stooped Jews in gaberdines, women and girls wearing shawls over their heads
and men's boots waded in the mud. Clouds of mist swirled
in the air. Crows soared overhead, cawing. The sky hung
low, leaden, heavy with storms. The smoke from chimneys
didn't rise but drifted downward toward the soaked earth.

The community had assigned Father a semi-ruin of a
house. In the three years I was away, his beard, red when
I left, had become streaked with strands of white. Mother
had discarded her wig for a kerchief. She had lost her
teeth and her sunken cheeks made her nose hooked, her
chin receded. Only her eyes remained youthful and sharp.

Father warned me, "This is a pious community. If you
don't conduct yourself as you should, they'll drive us out
of here with sticks."

"Father, I'm giving in. My only hope is that the army
won't take me."

"When do you have to report for conscription?"

"In a year."

"We'll arrange a match for you. God willing, your
father-in-law will ransom you. Put aside your foolishness
and study the Yoreh Deah."

I went to the study house but no one was studying there.
The congregation, mostly artisans and dairymen, came to
pray early in the morning and returned for the evening
services; in between times, the place was deserted. I found
an old volume on the cabala there. I had brought along
from Warsaw an algebra book and a Polish translation of
Baudelaire's poems.

Abraham Getzel the matchmaker came to look me over
—a little man with a white beard ranging nearly to his
loins. He was also the village beadle, the cantor, and the
Talmud teacher. He measured me up and down and sighed.
"These are different times," he complained. "Girls want a
husband who's a provider."

"I can't blame them."

"The Torah has lost its value in our generation. But
don't you worry, I'll find you a bride."

He proposed a widow who was six or seven years older than I and had two children. Her father, Berish Belzer, managed a brewery owned by an Austrian baron. (Before the war, Galicia had been ruled by Emperor Franz Josef.) When the weather cleared somewhat during the day, one could see the brewery chimney. Black smoke sat on it like a hat.

Berish Belzer came to the study house to have a chat with me. He had a short beard the color of beer. He wore a fox coat and a derby. A watch on a silver chain dangled from his silk vest. After we had talked for a few minutes, he said, "I see you're no businessman."

"I'm afraid you're right."

"Then what are you?"

And the match was off.

All of a sudden the mail brought news from Warsaw. My brother had become co-editor of a literary weekly and I was offered the job of being its proofreader. He said that I could publish my stories there if they proved good enough. The moment I read the letter my health improved. From then on I didn't cough once during the night. I regained my appetite. I ate so much that my mother grew alarmed. Enclosed with the letter was the first issue of the magazine. It discussed a new novel by Thomas Mann, *The Magic Mountain,* and it contained poems in free verse, illustrated with Cubistic drawings. It reviewed a book of poetry entitled *A Boot in the Lapel.* Its articles spoke of the collapse of the old world and the emergence of a new man and a new spirit that would reappraise all values. It printed a chapter of Oswald Spengler's *The Decline of the West,* as well as translations of poems by Alexander Blok, Mayakovsky, and Esenin. New writers had appeared in America during the war years, and their work was beginning to be published in Poland. No, I could not while away my days in Old-Stikov! I waited only for the train fare to be sent me from Warsaw.

Now that I was about to return to modern culture, I began to observe what was happening in Old-Stikov. I

listened to the women who came to consult Father on
ritual matters and to gossip with Mother. We had a
neighbor, Lazar the shoemaker, and his wife brought us
the good tidings that their only daughter, Rivkele, was
marrying her father's apprentice. Soon afterward Rivkele
herself came to invite us to the engagement party. I looked
at her with amazement. She reminded me of a Warsaw
girl. She was tall, slim, with unusually white skin, black
hair, dark-blue eyes, a long neck. Her upper lip drew back
slightly to reveal white teeth without a blemish. There was
a watch on her wrist and earrings dangled from the small
lobes of her ears. She wore a fancy shawl with fringe and
boots with high heels. She glanced at me shyly and said,
"You are invited!"

We both blushed.

The next day I went with my parents to the party. Lazar
the shoemaker's house had a bedroom and a big room
where the family cooked, ate, and worked. Scattered on
the floor around the worktable were shoes, boots, heels.
Rivkele's fiancé, Yantche, was short, broad, and dark, with
two gold front teeth. The nail of his right index finger was
deformed. For the party he had put on a paper collar
and dickey. He passed cigarettes to the male guests. I
heard him say, "Marry and die are two things you must
do."

Warsaw was in no rush to send me train fare. Snow had
fallen and a frost gripped Old-Stikov. Father had gone to
the house of prayer to study and warm himself at the stove.
Mother went to pay a call on a woman who had slipped on
the ice near the well and broken a leg. I sat alone at home,
going over my manuscripts. Although it was daytime, a
cricket chirped, telling of a story as old as time. It stopped,
listening to its own silence, then commenced again. The
upper panes of the window were covered with frost flowers,
but through the lower panes I could see a water carrier
with icicles in his beard carrying two pails of water on a
wooden yoke. A peasant in sheepskin hat, his feet
wrapped in rags, followed a sledge loaded with logs and

pulled by an emaciated horse. I could hear the tinkling of the bell on its neck.

The door opened and Rivkele entered. "Your mother isn't here?" she asked me.

"She went to pay a sick call on somebody."

"I borrowed a glass of salt from her yesterday and I'm giving it back." She put a glass of salt on the table, then looked at me with a bashful smile.

"I didn't get the chance to wish you good luck at the engagement party, so I'm doing it now," I said.

"Thank you kindly. God willing, the same to you." After a pause, she added, "When it's your turn."

We talked, and I told her that I was going back to Warsaw. This was supposed to remain a secret, but I boasted to her that I was a writer and had just been made a staff member on a periodical. I showed her the magazine, and she gazed at me in astonishment. "You must have some brain!"

"To write, what you need most is an eye."

"What do you write—your thoughts?"

"I tell stories. They call it literature."

"Oh yes, things happen in the big cities," Rivkele said, nodding. "Here time stands still. There used to be a fellow here who read novels, but the Hasidim broke in on him and tore them all to shreds. He ran away to Brody."

She sat down on the edge of the bench and glanced toward the door, ready to spring up the moment anyone might come in. She said, "In other towns they put on plays, hold meetings, and what not, but here everyone is old-fashioned. They eat and they sleep, and that's how the years go by."

I realized that I was doing wrong to say this, but I said it anyway: "Why didn't you arrange to marry someone from a city?"

Rivkele thought it over. "Do they care around here what a girl wants? They marry you off and that's that."

"So it wasn't a love match?"

"Love? In Old-Stikov? They don't know the meaning of the word."

I am not an agitator by nature, and I had no reason to praise the Enlightenment that had disenchanted me, but somehow, as if against my will, I began to tell Rivkele that we lived in the twentieth century, not in the Middle Ages; that the world had awakened and that villages like Old-Stikov weren't merely physical quagmires but spiritual ones as well. I told her about Warsaw, Zionism, Socialism, Yiddish literature, and the Writers' Club, where my brother was a member and to which I held a guest pass. I showed her pictures in the magazine of Einstein, Chagall, the dancer Nijinsky, and of my brother.

Rivkele clapped her hands. "Oy, he resembles you like two drops of water!"

I told Rivkele that she was the prettiest girl I had ever met. What would become of her here in Old-Stikov? She would soon begin bearing children. She would go around like the rest of the women in coarse boots and a dirty kerchief over a shaved head and take old age upon herself. The men here all visited the Belzer rabbi's court and he was said to perform miracles, but I heard that every few months epidemics raged in town. The people lived in filth, knew nothing about hygiene, science, or art. This was no town—I spoke dramatically—but a graveyard.

Rivkele's blue eyes with the long eyelashes gazed at me with the indulgence of a relative. "Everything you say is the pure truth."

"Escape from this mudhole!" I cried out like a seducer in a trashy novel. "You are young and a beauty, and I can see that you're clever, too. You don't have to let your years waste away in such a forsaken place. In Warsaw you could get a job. You could go out with whoever you please and in the evenings take courses in Yiddish, Hebrew, Polish—whatever you wish. I'll be there, too, and if you want we'll meet. I'll take you to the Writers' Club, and when the writers get a glimpse of you they'll go crazy. You might even become an actress. The actresses who play the romantic parts in the Yiddish theater are old and ugly. Directors are desperate to find young, pretty girls.

I'll get a room and we'll read books together. We'll go to the movies, to the opera, to the library. When I become famous, we'll travel to Paris, London, Berlin, New York. There they're building houses sixty stories high; trains race above the streets and under the ground; film stars earn a thousand dollars a week. We can go to California, where it's always summer. Oranges are as cheap as potatoes . . ."

I had the odd feeling that this wasn't I talking but the dybbuk of some old enlightened propagandist speaking through my mouth.

Rivkele threw frightened glances toward the door. "The way you talk! Suppose someone hears—"

"Let them hear. I'm not afraid of anybody."

"My father—"

"If your father loved you he should have found you a better husband than Yantche. The fathers here are selling their daughters like the wild Asiatics. They're all steeped in fanaticism, superstition, darkness."

Rivkele stood up. "Where would I spend the first night? Such a fuss would break out that my mother couldn't endure it. The outcry would be worse than if I converted." The words stuck in Rivkele's mouth; her throat moved as if she were choking on something she couldn't swallow. "It's easy for a man to talk," she mumbled. "A girl is like a—the slightest thing and she is ruined."

"That's the way it used to be, but a new woman is emerging. Even here in Poland women already have the right to vote. Girls in Warsaw study medicine, languages, philosophy. A woman lawyer comes to the Writers' Club. She has written a book."

"A woman lawyer—how is this possible? Someone's coming." Rivkele opened the door. My mother was standing at the threshold. It wasn't snowing, but her dark kerchief had turned hoary with frost.

"Rebbitsin, I brought over the glass of salt."

"What was the hurry? Well, thank you."

"If you borrow, you have to pay back."

"What's a glass of salt?"

Rivkele left. Mother looked at me suspiciously. "Did you talk to her?"

"Talk? No."

"As long as you're here, you must behave decently."

2

Two years passed. The magazine of which my brother was editor and I the proofreader had failed, but in the meantime I managed to publish a dozen stories and no longer needed a guest pass to the Writers' Club, because I had become a member. I supported myself by translating books from German, Polish, and Hebrew into Yiddish. I had presented myself before a military board, which had deferred me for a year, but now I had to go before another. Although I often criticized Hasidic conscripts for maiming themselves in order to avoid being accepted for service, I fasted to lose weight. I had heard horrible stories about the barracks: young soldiers were ordered to fall in muck, to leap over ditches; they were wakened in the middle of the night and forced to march for miles; corporals and sergeants beat the soldiers and played malicious tricks on them. It would be better to sit in jail than to fall into the hands of such hooligans. I was ready to go into hiding —even to kill myself. Pilsudski had ordered the military doctors to take only strong young men into the army, and I did everything I could to make myself weak. Besides fasting, I went without sleep; I smoked steadily, lighting one cigarette from the butt of the last; I drank vinegar and herring brine. A publisher had commissioned me to do a translation of Stefan Zweig's biography of Romain Rolland, and I spent half my nights working on it. I rented a room from an old physician, a onetime friend of Dr. Zamenhof, the creator of Esperanto. The street was named after him.

That night I had worked until three o'clock. Then I lay down on the bed in my clothes. Every time I fell asleep I woke up with a start. My dreams had become strangely vivid. Voices spoke to me from all sides, bells rang, choirs sang. When I opened my eyes I could still hear their reverberations. My heart palpitated, my hair pricked my skull like wires. My hypochondria had returned. My lungs felt compressed and about to collapse. The day was rainy. Whenever I looked out the window I saw a Catholic funeral cortege on its way to Powązek Cemetery. When I finally sat down to work on the translation, Yadzia, the maid, knocked on my door and announced that a young woman was asking for me.

My caller turned out to be Rivkele. I didn't recognize her immediately. She was smartly dressed in a coat with a fur collar, and a modish hat. She carried a purse and an umbrella. Her hair was cut *à la garçon,* and her dress was stylishly short; it came just to her knees. I felt so addled I forgot to be surprised. Rivkele told me what had happened to her. An American had come on a visit to Old-Stikov. He was a former tailor who said he had become a ladies'-clothing manufacturer in New York. He was a distant relative of her father's. He assured the family that he had divorced his wife in America and began to court Rivkele. She broke her engagement to Yantche. The visitor from America bought her a diamond ring, went with her to Lemberg, took her to the Yiddish theater, to the Polish theater, to restaurants, and generally behaved like a prospective bridegroom. Together they visited Kraków and Zakopane. Her parents demanded that he marry her, but he came up with all kinds of excuses. He had divorced his wife according to Jewish law, he said, but he still needed a civil decree. On the road, Rivkele began to live with him. Rivkele talked and cried. He had seduced and deceived her. He owned no factory; he worked for someone else. He had not divorced his wife. He was the father of five children. All this came out when his wife suddenly arrived in Old-Stikov and made a scandal. She had family in Jaroslaw and Przemyśl—butchers, draymen, tough fellows. They warned Morris—that was his name—that they would break his neck. They turned him in to the police.

They threatened to report him to the American consul. The result was that he went back to his wife and they sailed together to America.

Rivkele's face was drenched with tears. She trembled, convulsed by hiccuplike sobs. Soon the truth came out. He had made her pregnant; she was in her fifth month. Rivkele moaned. "Nothing is left me but to hang myself!"

"Do your parents know that—"

"No, they don't know. They'd die of shame."

This was another Rivkele. She bent down to take a draw on my cigarette. She had to go to the bathroom, and I took her through the living room. The doctor's wife—a small, thin woman with a pointed face, many warts, and popping eyes that were yellow as if from jaundice—glared at her. Rivkele lingered in the bathroom for such a long time that I feared she had taken poison.

"Who is that creature?" the doctor's wife demanded. "I don't like the looks of her. This is a respectable house."

"Madam, you have no reason to be suspicious."

"I wasn't born yesterday. Be so good as to find lodgings somewhere else."

After a while Rivkele came back to my room. She had washed her face and powdered it. She had put on lipstick.

"You are responsible for my misfortune," she said.

"*I* am?"

"If it weren't for you, I wouldn't have let myself go with him. Your words stuck in my mind. You spoke in such a way that I wanted to leave home right then and there. When he came, I was—as they say—already ripe."

I had the urge to scold her and tell her to be on her way, but she started to cry again. Then she began to sing a tune as old as the female sex: "Where do I go now and what do I do? He has slaughtered me without a knife . . ."

"Did he leave you some money at least?" I asked.

"There is a little left."

"Maybe something can still be done."

"Too late."

We sat without speaking, and the lessons of the moral

primers came back to me. No word goes astray. Evil words
lead to iniquitous deeds. Utterings of slander, mockery,
and profanity turn into demons, hobgoblins, imps. They
stand as accusers before God, and when the transgressor
dies they run after his hearse and accompany him to the
grave.

As if Rivkele guessed my thoughts, she said, "You made
me see America like a picture. I dreamed of it at night.
You made me hate my home—Yantche, too. You promised to write me, but I didn't get a single letter from you.
When Morris arrived from America, I clutched at him as
if I were drowning."

"Rivkele, I have to report for conscription. I'm liable
to be sent to the barracks tomorrow."

"Let's go away somewhere together."

"Where? America has closed its gates. All the roads
are sealed."

3

Nine years went by. It was my third year in New York.
From time to time, I published a sketch in a Yiddish newspaper. I lived in a furnished room not far from Union
Square. My room was dark. I had to climb four stories to
get to it, and it stank of disinfectant. The linoleum on the
floor was torn, and cockroaches crawled from beneath it.
When I turned on the naked bulb that hung from the ceiling, I saw a crooked bridge table, an overstuffed chair
with torn upholstery, and a sink with a faucet that dripped
rusty water. The window faced a wall. When I felt like
writing—which was seldom—I went to the Public Library
at Forty-second Street and Fifth Avenue. Here in my
room, I only lay on the sagging bed and fantasized about
fame, riches, and women who threw themselves at me. I
had had an affair, but it ended, and I had been alone for
months. I kept my ears cocked to hear if I was being
summoned to the pay phone below. The walls of the house
were so thin that I could hear every rustle—not only on

my floor but on the lower floors as well. A group of boys and girls who called themselves a "stock company" had moved in. They were getting ready to put on a play somewhere. In the meantime, they ran up and down the stairs, shrieking and laughing. The woman who changed my bedding told me that they practiced free love and smoked marijuana. Across from me lived a girl who had come to New York from the Middle West to become an actress, and for whole days and half the nights she sang wailing melodies that someone told me were called the "blues." One evening, I heard her sing over and over again in a mournful chant:

> He won't come back,
> Won't come back,
> Won't come back,
> Never, never, never, never.
> Won't come back!

I heard footsteps and my name being called. I sat up so hastily that I nearly broke the bed. The door opened and by the dim light of the hall I saw the figure of a woman. I didn't put on my light because I was ashamed of the condition of my room. The paint on the walls was peeling. Old newspapers lay scattered around, together with books I had picked up along Fourth Avenue for a nickel each, and dirty laundry.

"May I ask who you are looking for?" I said.

"It's you. I recognize your voice. I'm Rivkele—Lazar the shoemaker's daughter from Old-Stikov."

"Rivkele!"

"Why don't you put on the light?"

"The light is broken," I said, baffled by my own lie. The blues singer across the way became quiet. This was the first time that I had ever had a visitor here. For some reason her door stood always ajar, as if deep inside her she still hoped that he who wouldn't come back would one day come back after all.

Rivkele mumbled, "Do you at least have a match? I don't want to fall."

It struck me that she spoke Yiddish in an accent that wasn't exactly American but no longer sounded the way they had spoken back home. I got off the bed carefully, led her over to the easy chair, and helped her sit down. At the same time I snatched one of my socks from the back of the chair and flung it aside. It fell into the sink. I said, "So you're in America!"

"Didn't you know? Didn't they write you that—"

"I asked about you time and again in my letters home, but they never answered."

She was silent for a time. "I didn't know that you were here. I only found out about it a week ago. No, it's two weeks. What a time I had finding you! You write under another name. Why, of all things?"

"Didn't they tell you from home that I'm here?" I asked in return.

Rivkele didn't reply, as if she were thinking the question over. Then she said, "I see you know nothing. I'm no longer Jewish. Because of this, my parents have disowned me as a daughter. Father sat shiva for me."

"Converted?"

"Yes, converted." Rivkele made a sound that was something like laughter.

I pulled the string and lit the naked bulb that was half covered with paint. I didn't know myself why I did this. My curiosity to see Rivkele in the role of a Gentile must have outweighed any shame I felt about my poverty. Or maybe in that fraction of a second I decided her disgrace was worse than mine. Rivkele blinked her eyes, and I saw a face that wasn't hers and that I would never have recognized on the street. It seemed to me broad, pasty, and middle-aged. But this unfamiliarity lasted only an instant. Soon I realized that she hadn't really changed since the last time I had seen her in Warsaw. Why, then, had she seemed so different at first glance? I wondered.

Apparently Rivkele went through the same sensations, because after a while she said, "Yes, it's you."

We sat there, observing each other. She wore a green coat and a hat to match. Her eyelids were painted blue and her cheeks were heavily rouged. She had gained weight. She said, "I have a neighbor who reads the Yiddish paper. I had told her a lot about you, but since you sign your stories by another name, how could she know? One day she came in and showed me an account of Old-Stikov. I knew at once that it was you. I called the editorial office, but they didn't know your address. How could that be?"

"Oh, I'm here on a tourist visa and it's expired."

"Aren't you allowed to live in America?"

"I must first go to Canada or to Cuba. Only from the American consul in a foreign country can I get a permanent visa to return."

"Then why don't you go?"

"I can't go on a Polish passport. It's all tied up with lawyers and expenses."

"God in heaven!"

"What happened to you?" I asked. "Did you have a child?"

Rivkele placed a finger with a red, pointed nail to her lips. "Hush! I had nothing. You know nothing!"

"Where is it?"

"In Warsaw. In a foundling home."

"A boy?"

"A girl."

"Who brought you to America?"

"Not Morris—somebody else. It didn't work out. We split up and I went to Chicago, and there I met Mario . . ." Rivkele began to speak in a mixture of Yiddish and English. She had married Mario in Chicago and adopted the Catholic faith. Mario's father owned a bar that was patronized by the Mafia. Once, in a quarrel, Mario stabbed a man and he was serving his second year in prison. Rivkele—her name was now Anna Marie—was working as a waitress in an Italian restaurant in New York. Mario had at least a year and a half left to serve. She had a small apartment on Ninth Avenue. Her husband's friends came by, wanting to sleep with her. One

had threatened her with a gun. The owner of the restaurant
was a man past his sixties. He was good to her, took her
to the theater, the movies, and to nightclubs, but he had
an evil wife and three daughters, each one more malicious
than the next. They were Rivkele's mortal enemies.

"Are you living with him?"

"He is like a father to me." Rivkele changed her tone.
"But I never forgot you! Hardly a day goes by that I don't
think of you. Why this is I don't understand. When I heard
that you were in America and read that article about Old-
Stikov, I became terribly excited. I called the paper maybe
twenty times. Someone told me that you sneak into the
pressroom at night and leave your articles there. So I went
there late one night after work, hoping to find you. The
elevator man told me that you had a box on the ninth floor
where I could leave a letter for you. I went up and all the
lights were on, but no one was there. Near the wall a
machine was writing by itself. It frightened me. It reminded me of what they recite on Rosh Hashanah—"

"The Heavenly Book that reads itself and everyone in-
scribes his own sins in it."

"Yes, right. I couldn't locate your box. Why are you
hiding from the newspapermen? They wouldn't denounce
you."

"Oh, the editor adds all kinds of drivel to my pieces.
He spoils my style. For the few dollars he pays me, he
makes me look like a hack."

"That article about Old-Stikov was good. I read it and
cried all night."

"Do you miss home?"

"Everything together. I've fallen into a trap. Why do
you live in such a dump?"

"I can't even afford this."

"I have some money. Since Mario is in jail, it would be
easy for me to get a divorce. We could go to Canada, to
Cuba—wherever you ought to go. I'm a citizen. We'll
marry and settle down. I'll bring my daughter over. I
didn't want any children with him, but with you . . ."

"Idle words."

"Why do you say that? We are both in trouble. I got myself into a mess and was feeling hopeless. But when I read what you wrote everything came back to me. I want to be a Jewish daughter again."

"Not through me."

"You are responsible for what has happened to me!"

We grew silent, and the girl across the way who had stopped singing and seemed to be listening to her own perplexity, like the cricket in Old-Stikov, resumed her mournful song:

> He won't come back,
> Won't come back,
> Won't come back,
> Never, never, never, never.
> Won't come back . . .

Translated by Joseph Singer

The Adventure

For years I did business with him and he never had a good word for me. A state of friendly hostility existed between us. Morris Shapiro was the owner of the well-known printing shop Kadimah, and I, David Greidinger, was the unknown editor of a budding magazine, *Sproutings*. Morris Shapiro disliked both our pretentious writings and the new Yiddish orthography. Besides, we always owed him money. Often the young writers revised their stories and essays when the typed pages were already going to press. Morris Shapiro used to tell them, "The stuff reads better with the errors than without them."

Before the war, Morris Shapiro's printing shop was one of the largest in Warsaw, with fifteen linotypes and two printing presses. After the war the competition became intense. The Printers' Union demanded higher wages. Morris Shapiro constantly threatened that he would sell out or give everything away to the scrap dealer. The modern Hebrew was as obnoxious to him as the newfangled

Yiddish. He ridiculed the so-called futuristic poetry, which had neither rhyme nor rhythm. He often spoke nostalgically of Peretz, Frishman, Spector, and the other classic writers whose works he printed.

Although there were constant rumors about his being on the verge of bankruptcy, he still conducted himself as if he were a rich man. He never touched the typed pages and never came near the machines, where he might soil his hands. He sat in his office behind a fancy mahogany desk and a manservant brought him tea, cookies, an orange. Morris Shapiro was short, broadly built, with a gray mustache and a shock of white hair that used to be pitch black but never lost its youthful luster. On the bridge of his wide nose he wore a gold-rimmed pince-nez which was attached to his lapel by a black ribbon. His shirt was invariably spotless and there were golden cuff links in his shirtsleeves. Even the abacus on which he made his calculations was an expensive one, with wires that shone like silver and with discs of ivory. His dark eyes behind the thick lenses expressed stern dignity. When the telephone rang, Morris Shapiro did not answer immediately. He finished reading the paragraph of his newspaper, or slowly chewed and swallowed the bite in his mouth. Only then would he lift up the receiver and say, *"Nu"* . . .

I had heard that Morris Shapiro had a wife and that some misfortune had befallen his son. I knew nothing else about his family nor did it concern me. All I wanted from him was the correction of typographical errors and the lines to be in proper order. Printers always considered young writers half-idiots, and writers never took printers seriously.

I did not really know how the change came about, but Morris Shapiro began to treat me more kindly. It seemed to me a sign that my literary stock had risen. Once in a while he threw in a word of praise for my writing. He offered me a glass of tea or a cookie. Formerly he never asked me to sit down when I entered his office. Now he would point to a chair. It pleased me, but not excessively.

I had no desire to engage in conversations with him and to listen to his opinions. Without his angry looks and his caustic comments, Morris Shapiro appeared less interesting. He used to criticize severely all the allusions to sex in my stories; now he began to point out how true they were. It became clear that his whole attitude toward me had changed. But why? Had he read a laudatory review somewhere about me? Did one of the older writers praise me? It was not worth pondering about. I had come to the conclusion long ago that it made no sense to look for consistency in people. Things soon came to such a pass that Morris Shapiro wanted to converse with me for more time than I was inclined to offer him. Often I had to interrupt him and excuse myself. Then he would frown and ask, "What is your rush? Your little scribblers will wait for you."

One day Morris Shapiro invited me to his home for supper. I was amazed; I did not have the slightest desire to spend an evening with him. But I could not refuse. I was sure I would find a bunch of printers, paper dealers, bookbinders, and fat women in his house. I had to brace myself with patience. That evening I shaved carefully, put on my best suit, and bought some flowers. Then I took a droshky to his house. It was an ordeal for me, but I hoped that the magazine might benefit from it, although I knew quite well that he would not print for us without charge. I walked up the marble steps, pressed the bell on the right-hand side of the carved door, where the brass tab with the engraved name of the tenant sparkled. I soon heard steps. I expected to hear the noise of guests and to see many overcoats and hats on the clothes rack in the foyer. But the apartment was quiet. The door was opened by a middle-aged woman, small, girlishly slender, her hair streaked gray and brown, combed in a bun, not cropped as was then the fashion. Her dress, too, was longer than those worn by the fashionable women. A motherly kindness looked out from her dark eyes. She had a narrow nose, thin lips, and a youthful chin. She smiled at me with knowing friendliness. "Pan Greidinger, please give me your coat. My husband is a little late. He asked me to excuse him. Something went wrong with a machine."

"It's all right."

"Please, come in."

She led me into a living room furnished in middle-class style: an ottoman, upholstered chairs with fringes, a piano, a threadbare Oriental carpet, lithographs on the walls. The house smelled of naphthalene and bygone affluence. On a low table stood a bottle of cordial and a glass bowl filled with cookies. The woman poured a glass for me and one for herself and she said, "I want you to know that my husband is a great admirer of yours. He often talks about you and praises you highly. I rarely used to read Yiddish, mostly Polish and Russian. But some time ago he began to bring your magazine to me and I am now an ardent reader of yours."

"This is a pleasant surprise to me," I said. "Mr. Shapiro used to be highly critical of my work."

"True, he disliked your too daring descriptions of— what shall I call it?—private matters. Well, but times do change. In comparison with the modernists you are quite modest. Also, one cannot deny that these things are important. Besides, no one can dictate to a writer how to write. The main thing is that it is interesting and—"

The woman spoke slowly and thoughtfully. During the course of our conversation, I learned that her father was a rich man in Warsaw, one of the enlightened. She, Anna, had studied in a boarding school for *Panienkas*. She had had a son by Morris Shapiro but he had died during a flu epidemic some years ago. Mrs. Shapiro pointed to a portrait of a boy in the uniform of a Gymnasiast. Her eyes became moist and her chin trembled. She said, "Lost is lost," and she took a sip of the brandy.

It was quite difficult for me to imagine her as the wife of the severe Morris Shapiro, but on the other hand, he must have been a handsome young man. He knew Hebrew, Russian, once took part in a Zionist Congress. I was glad that I did not find a house full of guests. The cordial was sweet and strong, the cookies melted in my mouth. The woman spoke quietly, gently, with the special confidence women show to their favorite writers. She said to me, "You are still quite young. How old are you? You are only beginning to develop. You have the courage to be yourself."

"How can one not be oneself?" I asked, just to make conversation.

"Most people try to imitate someone, or to satisfy others. Take me, for example—"

And the woman tactfully hinted that she married at the wish of her parents, not of her own choice. Her real desire was to go abroad to study at a university instead of becoming a housewife. But when Grisha was born, she decided to devote herself entirely to his upbringing, both intellectually and physically. "Then came a microbe and destroyed the work of a lifetime. What is there to be done? One has to suffer and go on living."

"Yes, true."

"Why do you let me talk only about myself? Why don't you tell me something about yourself? Actually, I know quite a lot about you from your stories."

The longer the woman talked, the clearer it became to me that it was for a special purpose that they had invited me—a strange and sensational purpose. The woman confided in me, told me the most intimate facts of her marriage. They were as follows: Since their son, the relationship between her and her husband had deteriorated. To begin with, she became frigid. She could not let Morris approach her. This went on for two years. Later, when she learned that Morris had engaged in a clandestine affair with the wife of a typesetter, her sexual desire rekindled, but Morris had become impotent toward her. They spent a lot of money for doctors, spas, hydropathy. Nothing helped. The situation was now so bad that, if she did not have sexual relations, she would break down. The family doctor had advised her to find someone, but who could it be? She had no male friends whom she could proposition. Her husband's cronies were all solid citizens, married for many years, fathers of grown children, even grandfathers. Besides, she had to maintain her reputation.

She still had an old mother, uncles, aunts, a whole clan of nephews and nieces. Anna emptied her glass of cordial and spoke to me clearly: If I agreed, she would be mine —not here in Warsaw, but on a trip somewhere in Zakopane or Zoppot. In what way was she worth less than the loose females with whom, according to my writings, I caroused? She would cover all the expenses. At least I would not contract a venereal disease from her.

I sat there shocked. I said in a choked voice, "Does your husband know about this?"

"It is his idea."

I drank a whole glass of the cordial. "Why did he choose me?"

"Oh, because of your writings. We would not choose a man off the street. There must be some feeling and all the rest of it. You are so much younger than I, true. But you mentioned in one of your sketches that you like older women."

"Yes, I do."

"We had to come to a decision."

I marveled how this modest woman could speak of such matters so directly. But I had already convinced myself that the quiet and the introverted can be unbelievably daring. My knees shook.

"Your husband will undoubtedly change his mind."

"No, he understands and is tolerant. He is under the spell of the other woman, even though she is a vulgar creature. Grisha's death shattered both of us. How I remained alive after this blow is beyond me. But we changed thoroughly. Our life together does not depend on physical contact any more. We are like brother and sister."

"Aha!"

"Whatever your answer will be, I hope you won't compromise us."

"God forbid! I swear by all that is sacred to me."

"Well, it is not necessary. Ten years ago, if someone would have told me that I was capable of such talk or even of such thoughts, I would have considered him a degenerate and crazy too. But it seems that this blow has

numbed me. I feel as though I were in a trance. Just the
same, instincts awoke in me of which I was never aware.
Perhaps it is only an illusion but I'm constantly tortured.
Morris has suffered too much at my hands to be able to
approach me. It may sound strange to you, but Grisha
comes between us always to prevent any intimacy. He appears to me in his shroud and wails at me. Even though
you are a writer, you won't understand this."

"I do understand."

"How? No. I intended to go about it gradually, but I
have no more patience. I decided to speak to you openly."

"You did the right thing."

"What is your answer? You do not have to decide right
now. If you don't like me and I am not—as they say—
your type, please don't be embarrassed. You owe me nothing. I could almost be your mother."

"You are a beautiful and a noble woman."

"Neither beautiful nor noble. You speak to a person
who is spiritually crushed. When Grisha left, he took
everything, even my sense of honor."

We were silent for a while. Then I asked, "Isn't Mr.
Shapiro going to come home now?"

"No, he went to the other one. Come, let's have dinner."

At dinner I promised my hostess an answer within three
days. I thereby implied that I had actually accepted her
proposition. We would go to Zoppot, or maybe to Danzig,
where we would have complete privacy. Mrs. Shapiro had
prepared a sumptuous meal but I had no appetite. I
wanted to compliment her, embrace her, kiss her, but
some inner force withheld me. I could not even look her
straight in the face. My boyhood bashfulness had returned
and paralyzed me. Everything remained untouched: the
soup, the meat, the dessert. I was even unable to drink
my glass of tea. Mrs. Shapiro too became silent. We faced
one another across the table, mute and tense. I had the uncanny feeling that an invisible being lurked between us,
watching all our movements. Was it Grisha? My nerves,
or whatever it was, began to play tricks on me. My
intestines seemed to shrink and my stomach bulged. I

needed to urinate but I dared not ask for the bathroom. After trying to taste the piece of honeycake which Mrs. Shapiro pressed on me, I rose and said in a strangely official tone, "I will call you, I must leave."

"You are running away already? Well . . ."

The woman handed me my coat and hat. In the hallway she offered me her hand and both our palms felt wet. I hurried down the stairs. I belched and hiccuped. A sour fluid filled my mouth and I was about to throw up. I ran along the street and I imagined that the gutter rose in front of me and that any minute I would fall backward.

That night I could not sleep. Each time I dozed off, my leg twitched and the mattress under me rang as if a bell were hidden among the springs. The next day I was supposed to go to the printing shop for what was called the last revision, but I lacked the courage to meet Mr. Shapiro. I thought I would have to contact another printer for the coming issues, but this would have been a cowardly step, to say the least, toward a man who had placed such extraordinary trust in me. There was only one way out: to dispense with the magazine. It hadn't turned out as I had expected anyway. Writers of whom I had a low opinion had managed to worm their way in.

During the three days in which I was supposed to give my answer, my mood vacillated. For a while my nervousness abated and I was about to call Mrs. Shapiro and make an appointment. Then again I was seized with terror and a desire to escape and hide. At night I dreamed that a young man with a face as white as chalk scolded me and tore at my hair. I took sleeping pills but continued to awaken. Although there was no heating in my room, I perspired. My pajamas became drenched and my pillow twisted as if it had gone through a wringer. My skin pricked, and every few minutes I jumped up as if bitten by a bedbug. The third day I rose at dawn, took out the Bible from my bookcase, raised my hand, and vowed that I would never take any part in this adulterous adventure.

Thank God, the apartment in which I roomed had no telephone. There was no danger that Mr. Shapiro or his

wife might call. I had left everything at the printing shop
—typed copy, manuscripts, proofs. The young writers who
contributed to the magazine came to investigate why we
had stopped publishing. My co-editors wanted to give me
extended authority. I had made believe that I was leaving
because of a review which appeared against my wish and
which raved about a mediocre book. A meeting of all the
contributors and editors was called. I did not attend. The
last issue, which contained a sketch of mine, appeared
five weeks late. I did not read the proofs and it came out
with many mistakes and garbled lines.

I don't know to this day whether Mr. Shapiro got fully
paid for that number. Not only did I avoid his printing
shop but even the street where it was located. I joined a
new group of writers and we published a magazine which
was printed out of town. For some years I never heard the
name Morris Shapiro mentioned. The former group of
writers fell apart. Some left for the United States or
Argentina. Others got married and went into business. I
myself got a job on a newspaper.

One day, while working on my column, a colleague of
mine said, "Have you heard the latest? Mr. Shapiro, the
printer, died."

"When?"

"The city room just got the call."

Again some time passed. I had entered a trolley car that
went to Danzig station. There was one vacant seat and I
sat down near a woman. I looked up and I recognized
Mrs. Shapiro. She was still in mourning. Her hair had
turned white. I wanted to rise and get off at the next station but she had already seen me. She said, "I don't know
if you remember me, but I remember you quite well."

"Mrs. Shapiro!"

"Yes, it's me."

For a long while we were both silent. Mrs. Shapiro swallowed hard.

"Perhaps it is too late for it, but I want to thank you."

"What for?" I asked.

"Oh, I was insane at that time, simply out of my mind. It was a miracle that you were wiser and more reponsible."

"I was simply shy."

"Nothing would have come of it anyhow. I loved my husband with all my heart. It was all a result of my agony. Until my last day I will thank God that He spared me this kind of downfall. I am grateful to you, too. I guess you know, Morris is not alive any more."

"Yes, I am deeply sorry."

"I tortured him so that he too became deranged. We often spoke about you. He actually mentioned your name a few days before his death."

A conductor came in and clipped off parts of our tickets. Mrs. Shapiro looked at me sideways and nodded. I heard her murmur, "Grisha would never have allowed it."

Translated by the author

Passions

"When a man persists he can do things which one might think can never be done," Zalman the glazier said. "In our village, Radoszyce, there was a simple man, a village peddler, Leib Belkes. He used to go from village to village, selling the peasant women kerchiefs, glass beads, perfume, all kinds of gilded jewelry. And he would buy from them a measure of buckwheat, a wreath of garlic, a pot of honey, a sack of flax. He never went farther than the hamlet of Byszcz, five miles from Radoszyce. He got the merchandise from a Lublin salesman, and the same man bought his wares from him. This Leib Belkes was a common man but pious. On the Sabbath he read his wife's Yiddish Bible. He loved most to read about the land of Israel. Sometimes he would stop the cheder boys and ask, 'Which is deeper—the Jordan or the Red Sea?' 'Do apples grow in the Holy Land?' 'What language is spoken by the natives there?' The boys used to laugh at him. He looked

like someone from the Holy Land himself—black eyes, a
pitch-black beard, and his face was also swarthy.

"Once a year a messenger used to come to Radoszyce, a
Sephardic Jew. He was sent to collect the alms that were
given in the name of Rabbi Meir the Miracle Worker, that
he should intercede for them in the next world. The messenger wore a robe with black and red stripes and sandals
that looked as though they were of ancient times. His hat
was also outlandish. He smoked a water pipe. He spoke
Hebrew and also Aramaic. His Yiddish he had learned in
later years. Leib Belkes was so fascinated by him that he
went with him from house to house to open the alms boxes.
He also took him to his home, where he ate and slept.
While the messenger stayed in Radoszyce, Leib Belkes did
no work. He kept on asking questions like 'What does the
Cave of Machpelah look like?' 'Does one know where
Abraham is buried and where Sarah?' 'Is it true that
Mother Rachel rises from her grave at midnight and weeps
for her exiled children?' I was still a boy then, but I too
followed the messenger wherever he went. When could one
see such a man in our region?

"Once, after the messenger left, Leib Belkes entered a
store and asked for fifty packs of matches. The merchant
asked him, 'What do you need so many matches for? You
want to burn the village?' And Leib said, 'I want to build
the Holy Temple.' The storekeeper thought that he had
lost his mind. Just the same, he sold him all the matches
he had.

"Later, Leib went into a paint store and asked for silver
and gold paint. The storekeeper asked him, 'What do you
need these paints for? Do you intend to make counterfeit
money?' And Leib answered, 'I am going to build the
Holy Temple.' The messenger had sold Leib a map, a large
sheet of paper showing the Temple with the altar and all
the other objects of ritual. At night when Leib had time
he sat down and began to build the Temple according to
this plan. There were no children in the house. Leib Belkes
and his wife had two daughters but they had gone into
domestic service in Lublin. His wife asked him, 'Why do

you play with matches? Are you a chedcr boy again?' And
he replied, 'I am building the Temple of Jerusalem.'

"He managed to build everything according to this plan:
the Holy of Holies, the Inner Court, the Outer Court, the
Table, the Menorah, the Ark. When the people of
Radoszyce learned what he was doing, they came to look
and admire. The teachers brought their pupils. The whole
edifice stood on a table, and it couldn't be moved, because
it would have collapsed. When the rabbi had word of it,
he too came to Leib Belkes, and he brought some yeshiva
boys with him. They sat around the table and they were
dumbfounded. Leib Belkes had constructed out of matches
the Holy Temple exactly as it was described in the Talmud!

"Well, but people are envious and begrudge others their
accomplishments. His wife began to complain that she
needed the table for her dishes. There were firemen in
Radoszyce, and they were afraid that so many matches
would cause a fire and the whole town might go up in
flames. There were so many threats and complaints that
one day when Leib returned from his travels his temple
was gone. His wife swore that the firemen came and
demolished it. The firemen accused the wife.

"After his temple had been destroyed, Leib Belkes became melancholic. He still tried to do business, but he
earned less and less. He often sat at home and read
Yiddish storybooks that dealt with the land of Israel. At
the study house he bothered the scholars and yeshiva boys
by asking them questions about the coming of the Messiah.
'Will one huge cloud take all the Jews to the Holy Land,
or will a cloud descend for each town separately?' 'Will
the Resurrection of the Dead take place immediately, or
will there be a waiting period of forty years?' 'Will there
still be a need to plow the fields and to gather the fruit
from the orchards, or will manna fall from the sky?' People had something to scoff at.

"Once, late in the evening, when his wife told him to
close the shutters, he went outside and did not return.
There was an uproar in Radoszyce. Some people believed
that the demons had spirited him away. Others thought

that his wife nagged him so much that he ran away to his relatives on the other side of the Vistula. But what man would run away at night without his overcoat and without a bundle? If this had happened to a rich man, they would have sent out searchers to find him. But when a poor man disappears, there is one pauper less in town. His wife—Sprintza was her name—was deserted. She earned a little from kneading dough in wealthy houses on Thursday. She also got some support from her daughters when they married.

"Five years passed. Once on a Friday, when Sprintza was standing over the oven and cooking her Sabbath meal, the door opened, and in came a man with a gray beard, dusty and barefooted. Sprintza thought it was a beggar. Suddenly he said, 'I was in the Holy Land. Give me some prune dessert.'

"The town went wild. They all came running, and Leib was taken to the rabbi. The rabbi questioned him, and he learned that Leib had gone on foot to the Holy Land."

"On foot?" Levi Yitzchok asked.

"Yes, on foot," Zalman said.

"But everyone knows that to get to the Holy Land one must travel by ship."

Meyer Eunuch clutched his chin where a beard should have grown and said, "Perhaps he lied?"

"He brought letters from many rabbis, as well as a sack of holy earth that he dug himself at the Mount of Olives," Zalman said. "When someone died he placed a handful of it under the corpse's head. I saw it myself; it was as white as crumbled chalk."

"How long did the trip take him?" Levi Yitzchok asked.

"Two years. On the way back he went by boat. The rabbi asked him, 'How can a man do a thing like that?' And he answered, 'I yearned so much that I could not bear it any more. That night when I went out to close the shutters and I saw the moon running among the clouds I began to run after it. I kept running until I reached Warsaw. There, kind people showed me the road. I wandered over fields and forests, mountains and wasteland, until I arrived at the land of Israel.' "

"I am astonished that the beasts did not devour him," Levi Yitzchok half asked, half stated.

"It is written that the Lord preserves the simple," Meyer Eunuch said.

For a while all three were silent. Levi Yitzchok took his blue glasses off his nose and began to wipe the lenses with his sash. He suffered from trachoma. One of his eyes was milky white, and he could not see with it at all. Levi Yitzchok owned a cane that once belonged to the preacher of Kozienice. Levi Yitzchok never parted with it even on the Sabbath. He limped, and a crutch is not forbidden. For a long while he rested his chin on this cane. Then he straightened himself and said, "Stubbornness is a power. In Krasnystaw there was a tailor by the name of Jonathan. He sewed for women, not men. As a rule, a women's tailor is a frivolous person. When one sews a garment for a female, one has to take her measurements, and sometimes she may be in her unclean days. Even if she is in her clean days, it is not proper to touch a woman, especially if she is married. Well—but there must be tailors. You cannot make all garments by yourself. This Jonathan happened to be a pious man but uneducated. However, he loved Jewishness. On the Sabbath he read the Yiddish Bible with his wife, Beila Yenta. When a book salesman came to town, Jonathan bought from him all the tomes and story-books in Yiddish. There was in Krasnystaw a congregation of psalm reciters and a society of Mishnah students. Jonathan belonged to both of these groups. He listened to the lectures, but he was afraid to say anything, because whenever he uttered a word in Hebrew he mangled it and the scholars made fun of him. I see him before my eyes: tall, lean, pockmarked. Gentleness looked out from his eyes. It was said that one couldn't find a better tailor even in Lublin. When he made a dress or a cape, it fitted like a glove. He had three unmarried daughters. When I was a boy I used to see him often, because a friend of mine, Getzel, an orphan, was his apprentice. Other masters mistreated their apprentices, beat them, and did not give them enough to eat. Instead of teaching them the trade, they

sent them on errands, and ordered them to rock the babies
or to carry the slops so that they should never learn the
skill properly and have to be paid a salary. But Jonathan
taught the orphan the trade, and, from the day he learned
to make a buttonhole and to sew on a button, Jonathan
paid him four rubles a year. Getzel had studied at a
yeshiva before he became a tailor's helper, and Jonathan
used to ask him all kinds of impossible questions—like
'What was the name of the mother of Og the King of
Bashan?' 'Did Noah take flies into the Ark?' 'How many
miles between paradise and Gehenna?' He wanted to know
everything.

"Now, listen to this. Everyone knows that on the day of
the Rejoicing over the Law the honored citizens, the
learned, the affluent are called to carry the scrolls first—
before the laborers, the simple people, those of little
income. This is the way it is all over the world. But in our
town the head of the synagogue was not a native. He knew
very few people, and someone had to give him a paper
listing the order of those to be called. There was another
Jonathan in town, a scholar and a rich man, and the head
of the synagogue confused the two men and he called Jonathan the tailor first. In the study house there was murmuring and giggling. When Jonathan the tailor heard that
he had been called first, along with the rabbi and the
elders, he couldn't believe his own ears. He realized that
it was a mistake, but when a man is summoned to carry
the scroll he dare not refuse. Among the workers and the
apprentices praying at the west wall there was laughter.
They began to push Jonathan and to pinch him good-
naturedly. It was in the time before the government took
over the sale of vodka, and vodka was cheaper than
borscht. In every half-decent home, one could find a keg
of vodka, with straws for drinking, and over it hung a side
of dried mutton to munch afterward. On the day of the
Rejoicing over the Law, people allowed themselves to take
a sip before prayers, and almost everyone was tipsy.
Jonathan the tailor came over to the reading table and was
given the scroll. Everybody stared, but only one person
said anything—Reb Zekele, a usurer. He exclaimed, 'Who

calls up an ignoramus to carry the scroll first?' And he returned his own scroll to the beadle. It was beneath his dignity to carry the scroll with Jonathan the tailor.

"In the study house a commotion arose. To give back a scroll was sacrilege. The head of the synagogue was bewildered. To shame a person in the presence of a whole community is a terrible sin. No one sang and danced with the scrolls this time. The same simple people who had laughed at Jonathan and the honor given to him now cursed Reb Zekele and gnashed their teeth. When the ceremony was over, Jonathan the tailor approached Reb Zekele and said in a loud voice that all could hear, 'It is true that I am ignorant, but I swear to you that in a year from now I will be a greater scholar than you are.'

"The usurer smiled and said, 'If this happens, I will build you a house in the marketplace for nothing.' Reb Zekele the usurer dealt in lumber. He owned mortgages on half the houses in town.

"Jonathan stood for a while in perplexity. Then he said, 'If I am not a greater scholar than you are, I will sew for your wife—and for nothing—a fox-fur coat reaching to the ankles, lined in velvet and with ten tails.'

"What went on in the town that day is indescribable. In the women's section of the synagogue they heard about the bet and there was bedlam. Some women laughed, others cried. Still others quarreled and tried to snatch the bonnets off each other's head. There were many poor people in town and a few rich ones, but in those times no one skimped on a holiday. Every third citizen invited guests to his house for a drink. There was dancing in the marketplace. The women had cooked huge pots of cabbage with raisins and cream of tartar. They had baked strudels, tarts, all kinds of fruitcakes. The burial society gave a banquet and mead was poured like water. One of the elders who had special merit in the eyes of the community was honored by having a pumpkin with lighted candles placed on his head, and being carried on the shoulders of the people to the synagogue yard. Bevies of children, the holy sheep, ran after him baaing. There was in town a he-goat that was not allowed to be slaughtered because he was first-

born, and urchins put a fur hat on his horns and led him
into the ritual bath. On that particular day there was only
one topic of conversation—Jonathan the tailor's oath and
the usurer's promise. Reb Zekele the usurer could easily
afford to build a house for nothing, but how could
Jonathan become a scholar in one year? The rabbi immediately announced that such an oath was not valid. In
times of old, the rabbi said, Jonathan would have been hit
thirty-nine times with a belt for breaking the commandment 'Thou shalt not take the name of the Lord thy God
in vain.' But what could be done today? The town became
divided into two parties. The scholars maintained that
Jonathan should be fined and that he must come in his
stocking feet to the synagogue to repent in public for giving a false oath. And if he refused, he should be excommunicated and his shop should not be patronized. The
rabble threatened to burn the usurer's house and drive
him out of town with sticks. Thank God, there are no
Jewish robbers. In the evening of the holiday everybody
became sober. It began to rain, and everyone returned to
his bundle of troubles."

"Did they forget the whole thing?" Zalman the glazier
asked.

"Nothing was forgotten. Just wait," Levi Yitzchok said.

Levi Yitzchok took out his wooden snuffbox, opened
it, sniffed, and sneezed three times. His snuff was famous.
He put into it smelling salts used at the Day of Atone-
ment to revive the fasters. He wiped his red nose with his
large kerchief and said, "If Getzel the apprentice had not
been my friend I would not have known all the details. But
Getzel boarded at Jonathan's, and he told me everything.
When Jonathan came home that evening, the moment he
opened the door he exclaimed, 'Beila Yenta, your husband has died! From today on you are a widow! My
daughters, you are all orphans!' They began to cry, as on
the Ninth day of Ab, 'Husband—Father—how can you
leave us?' And Jonathan answered, 'From today until the
day of the Rejoicing over the Law next year, you have no
provider.'

"He had hidden behind his Passover dishes a nest egg

of one hundred guldens saved as a dowry for his oldest daughter, Taube. He took the money and left the house. There was in town a man called Reb Tevele Scratch-me. Scratch-me was of course a nickname. In his young years he had been a Talmud teacher. Like all teachers, he had in front of him on the table a hare's leg attached to a leather thong. Yet he did not use it to whip the children but to scratch himself. He suffered from eczema on his back. When it began to itch he handed the hare's leg to one of his pupils and ordered, "Scratch me." That is how he got his name. In his old age he gave up teaching and lived with his daughter. His son-in-law was a pauper, and Tevele Scratch-me lived in dire poverty. Jonathan the tailor went to Reb Tevele and asked him, 'Do you want to earn some money?' 'Who doesn't want money?' Tevele asked back. And Jonathan said, 'I will pay you a gulden a week if you will teach me the whole Torah!' Tevele burst out laughing. 'The whole Torah—even Moses did not know that! The Torah is like tailoring, without an end!' They spoke a long time, and finally it was decided that Tevele would teach Jonathan for a whole year and make him a greater scholar than Zekele. Jonathan calculated that if one studied seven pages of the Talmud each day of the year, all the thirty-seven tractates would be learned. It was said that Zekele had not gone through even half of this. Well —but the Talmud isn't enough. One had also to study Midrash, the Commentaries. Why draw it out? Jonathan the tailor became a yeshiva boy. He sat at a table in the study house day and night and studied with Tevele. In the middle of the week, when the women's section was empty, they carried their volumes up there in order not to be disturbed. If I tell you that they studied eighteen hours a day, this is no exaggeration. All week long Jonathan slept on a bench in the study house. He went home to sleep only on the Sabbath and holidays."

"What happened to his family?" Zalman asked.

"What happens to all families when the provider goes? They did not die of hunger. The girls all went into service. Beila Yenta was a seamstress and she accepted light work. My friend Getzel slowly became the master. Jonathan did

one thing—he studied. Such diligence the world has never
beheld! Two or three nights a week he didn't sleep at all.
The story soon spread to neighboring villages, and people
came to stare at Jonathan as though he were a miracle
worker. At the beginning, Reb Zekele laughed at the
whole business. He said, 'If this simpleton can become a
scholar, hair will grow on the palms of my hands.' Later
on, toward the end of the year, people began to speak of
the wonders of Jonathan's acquired knowledge. He recited
by heart whole sections from the Gemara. He could an-
ticipate the questions of such commentators as Rabbi Meir
of Lublin and Rabbi Shlomo Luria.

"Now Zekele the usurer grew frightened. He too began
to burn the midnight oil to overtake Jonathan. But it was
already too late. Besides, he was up to his neck in business, and he was in the middle of a lawsuit to boot. His
wife, Slikka, a greedy creature with a big mouth, was
terribly eager for Jonathan to make her a fox coat with
ten tails without cost, and for the first time in her life she
drove her husband to study. But it did not work. I will
make it short. On the eighth day of Sukkoth, the seven
elders of the town and a number of other scholars gathered
at the house of the rabbi, and they examined Zekele and
Jonathan as if they were yeshiva boys. Zekele had forgotten a lot. For years he had studied only on the Sabbath
—and there is a proverb that says, 'He who studies only
on the Sabbath is only a seventh part of a scholar.' As for
Jonathan, he remembered almost all of the Talmud by
heart. His teacher, Tevele, had remarked that in teaching
Jonathan he himself became erudite. Not only did Jonathan show knowledge but he showed astuteness as well.
The rabbi's house was jammed with people. Others had
to stand outside to hear Jonathan discuss the Law with the
rabbi. At the beginning, Zekele tried to discover flaws in
Jonathan's answers, but soon the tables were turned and
Jonathan corrected Zekele. I wasn't there, but those who
saw Zekele wrangle with Jonathan the tailor about some
difficult passage of Maimonides or about the meaning of
an obscure sentence of Rabbi Meir Schiff swore that it
was like the fight between David and Goliath. Zekele

screamed and gasped and scolded his opponent, but to no
avail. No, Jonathan the tailor did not swear falsely. The
rabbi and the seven elders unanimously gave the verdict
that Jonathan was more of a scholar than Zekele. Jonathan's wife and daughters were sitting in the kitchen, and
when they heard the verdict they fell upon each other wailing. The town seethed like a kettle. Synagogue Street was
full of tailors, shoemakers, combers of pig bristles, coach-
men, and such. It was their victory.

The next day, Jonathan was called to take the scroll
first—not by error this time. The most honored people
invited him for a drink. There was talk that now Jonathan
could become a rabbi or an assistant rabbi, or at least a
ritual slaughterer. But Jonathan let it be known that he
was returning to his scissors and iron. Zekele tried to avoid
payment by contending that he did not swear but only
promised, and a promise does not have to be kept. But
the rabbi ordered him to build a house for Jonathan, quoting from Deuteronomy: "That which is gone out of thy
lips thou shalt keep.' Zekele procrastinated as long as he
could, but after the Feast of Shevuot the house already
had a roof. Only then did Jonathan make it known that
he didn't want the house for himself but as an inn for
yeshiva boys and poor travelers. He signed a document
giving the house away to the community."

"He remained a tailor, eh?" Zalman the glazier asked.

"To the end."

"Did he marry off his daughters?"

"What else? There is no Jewish cloister."

All the time Levi Yitzchok was speaking, Meyer
Eunuch was making gestures. His yellow eyes filled with
laughter. Then he closed them, lowered his head, and
seemed as though he was dozing. Suddenly he straightened
up, clutched his beardless chin, and asked, "How did the
village peddler know the road to the Holy Land? Most
probably he asked. I guess he wandered over the Turkish
lands, Egypt, and Istanbul. How did he manage to eat?
Most probably he begged. There are Jews everywhere.
Most likely he slept in the poorhouse. In warm countries

one can even sleep in the streets. As for Jonathan the tailor, I assume that from his childhood he craved for learning, and the power of will is strong. There is a saying, 'Your will can make you a genius.' When you are idle, a year is nothing, but if you study day and night with diligence, you sop it up like a sponge. He did well not to accept the house from Reb Zekele, because it is forbidden to make a spade for digging from the Torah. As it was, he gained in addition the virtue of hospitality. Leib Belkes and Jonathan were both simple people—though not completely so. But it also happens with great men that they get an obsession in their minds. There is a saying, 'Greatness too has its share of insanity.'

"In Bechtev there was a cabalist, Rabbi Mendel. He was descended from the renowned Hodel, who used to dance in a circle with the Hasidim. She did not, God forbid, hold their bare hands directly. She kept a kerchief over each hand, and the Hasidim held on to the kerchief. Rabbi Mendel could have had a large following, but he disliked crowds and discouraged them. Even in the High Holy Days he didn't get more than a few score in his study house. His wife died young, and she didn't leave him a child to take his place after his death. Many matches were proposed, but he refused to remarry. His followers argued with him: What about the commandment 'Be fruitful and multiply'? But the rabbi answered, 'I am going to get so many whips in Gehenna that a few more won't matter. Why are they so afraid of Gehenna? Since the Almighty created it, it must be paradise in disguise.' He should forgive me, but he was a devious kind of saint—but a great spirit just the same. There was much gossip about him, but he didn't care a fig. It even happened that he uttered sharp words against the Lord of the Universe. Once when he was reciting the Psalms, he came to the passage 'He that sitteth in the heavens shall laugh.' Rabbi Mendel exclaimed, 'He shall laugh—but I am crushed!' When those who opposed him heard of this blasphemy, they almost managed to have him excommunicated.

"The disciples of the Baal Shem did not believe in fasting. Hasidism was exhilaration, not sadness. But Rabbi

Mendel indulged in fasting. He began by fasting only on
Mondays and Thursdays. Then he started to fast from one
Sabbath to the next. He also immersed himself in cold
baths. He called the body the enemy, and he would say,
'You don't have to appease an enemy. Of course, you are
not allowed to kill him, but neither are you obliged to
pamper him with marzipans.' His old Hasidic followers
died out gradually. The younger men joined the courts of
Gora and Kotzk. There remained in Rabbi Mendel's court
only twenty or thirty persistent followers, in addition to a
few hangers-on who stayed with him all year and ate from
the common pot. An old beadle, stone-deaf, cooked por-
ridge for them every day. A charitable woman went from
house to house for them and collected potatoes, groats,
flour, buckwheat, and whatever else she was offered.

"One Rosh Hashanah the rabbi had no more than
twenty people in his study house. The following Yom Kippur he had only a quorum, including himself, the beadle,
and the hangers-on. At the pulpit Rabbi Mendel recited
all the prayers—Kol Nidre, the morning prayer, the midday prayer, and the closing prayer. It was already late
when they finished the night prayer, and they blessed the
new moon. The beadle offered the fasters some stale bread
with herring and some chicken soup. None of them had
any teeth left, and their stomachs had shrunk from under-
nourishment. Rabbi Mendel was older than any of them,
but his voice remained young. His hearing, too, was good.
The rabbi sat at the head of the table and spoke: 'Those
who run after the pleasures of the world don't know what
pleasure is. For them gluttony, drinking, lechery, and
money are pleasures. There is no greater delight than the
service of Yom Kippur. The body is pure and the soul is
pure. The prayers are a joy. There is a saying that from
confessing one's sins one does not get fat. It's completely
false. When I confess my sins I become alive and vigorous.
If I could have my say in heaven, every day would be
Yom Kippur.'

"After the rabbi said these words he rose from his chair
and exclaimed, 'I have no say in heaven, but in my study
house I do. From today on for me it will be a perpetual

Yom Kippur—every day except for the Sabbath and Feast Days!' When the people of the village heard what the rabbi was about to do, there was pandemonium. The scholars and the elders came to the rabbi and asked, 'Isn't this breaking the Law?' And the rabbi replied, 'I do it for purely selfish reasons, not to please the Creator. If they punish me high up, I will accept the punishment. I also want to have some pleasure before I go!' The rabbi called out to his beadle, 'Light the candles; I am going to recite Kol Nidre.' He ran over to the pulpit and started to sing Kol Nidre. I wasn't there, but those who were present declared that such a Kol Nidre had not been heard since the world began. All of Bechtev came running. They thought that Rabbi Mendel had lost his mind. But who would dare to tear him away from the pulpit? He stood there in his white robe and prayer shawl and recited, 'It shall be forgiven' and 'Our supplications shall rise.' His voice was as strong as a lion's, and the sweetness of his singing was such that all apprehensions ceased. I will make it short. The rabbi lived two and a half years more, and those two and a half years were one long Yom Kippur."

Levi Yitzchok took off his dark glasses and asked, "What did he do about phylacteries? Didn't he put on phylacteries on weekdays?"

"He put them on," Meyer Eunuch answered, "but the liturgy was that of Yom Kippur. Toward evening he read the Book of Jonah."

"Didn't he eat a bite at night?" Zalman the glazier asked.

"He fasted six days of the week unless a holiday fell in the middle of it."

"And the hangers-on fasted with him?"

"Some left him. Others died."

"So did he pray to the bare walls?"

"There were always people who came to look and wonder."

"And the world allowed something like this?" Levi Yitzchok asked.

"Who was going to wage war against a holy man? They

dreaded his irritation," Meyer Eunuch said. "One could clearly see that heaven approved. When a man fasts so long, his voice grows weak, he doesn't have the strength to stand on his feet. But the rabbi stood for all the prayers. Those who saw him told how his face shone like the sun. He slept no longer than three hours—in his prayer shawl and robe, with his forehead leaning on the Tractite Yoma, exactly like at Yom Kippur. At midday prayer he kneeled and intoned the liturgy concerning the service in the Holy Temple of Jerusalem."

"What did he do when it actually was Yom Kippur?" Zalman the glazier asked.

"The same as any other day."

"I never heard this story," Levi Yitzchok said.

"Rabbi Mendel was a hidden saint, and of those one hears little. Even today Bechtev is a forsaken village. In those times it was far away from everything—a swamp among forests. Even in the summer it was difficult to reach it. In the winter the snow made the roads impassable. The sleighs got stuck. And there was the danger of bears and wolves."

It became quiet. Levi Yitzchok took out his snuffbox. "Nowadays something like this would not be permitted."

"Greater transgressions than that are allowed in our day," Meyer said.

"How did he die?"

"At the pulpit. He was standing up reciting, 'What can man attain when death is all he can gain?' When he came to the verse 'Only charity and prayer may mitigate death's despair,' the rabbi fell down and his soul departed. It was a kiss from heaven—a saint's death."

Zalman the glazier put some tobacco into the bowl of his pipe. "What was the sense of it?"

Meyer Eunuch pondered for a while, and then said, "Everything can become a passion, even serving God."

Translated by the author and Dorothea Straus